The Awakening of Ren Crown

Anne Zoelle

DEDICATION

To Matt, S, Mom, and Dad.

CONTENTS

	Chapter	Page
1	In the Beginning...	1
2	Daydreams and Nightmares	14
3	Finding the Rabbit Hole	38
4	Unwise Actions	51
5	Really Unwise Actions	56
6	Deadly Assailants	62
7	Conversations of the Extraordinary	65
8	Into the Rabbit Hole	79
9	Olivia Price	92
10	Culture Shock	104
11	Pain...ting...	125
12	The Cafeteria	131
13	Adventures in Campery	143
14	Plans	150
15	Ganymede Circus	161
16	On the Edge	181
17	Thieves, Pyramids, and Firesnakes	201

18	Marsgrove Redux	213
19	Preparations	217
20	Death and Consequences	225
21	The Midlands	243
22	Service with a Smile	259
23	Of Blobs and Mistakes	285
24	Living and Helping	292
25	Ambrosia for Me, Ambrosia on You	303
26	Never Normal	315
27	Reality in Death	329
28	Moving Forward	352
29	A New Beginning	372
	About the Author	379

ACKNOWLEDGMENTS

Special thanks to Martha, Maureen, Matt, Chris, Shannon, Josh, Teresa, Barbara, Poppy, Tracy, and Ny.

And to S.

Chapter One

IN THE BEGINNING...

I WOULD DO ABSOLUTELY anything for my brother.

"This is hardly a high-security lock, Ren," Christian whispered, motioning at the precise movement of my hands. "Now isn't the time to be perfect. Scrub those pins."

"Scrub these," I whispered back to my twin, my lips barely needing to move in order for him to hear me. We had perfected the art of nearly silent communication over the past seventeen years. I carefully pressed in the torque wrench and slid my lock pick across one pin at a time, feeling them, discovering their secrets, movement, and depth. A schematic of the lock drew itself in my mind, and I rotated the picture to determine which pin to move first.

Brilliant, but impatient, Christian would always be a scrub and bumper, raking a pick across the pins. Which had always worked quite well when our parents were away, and we were uncovering Christmas presents or retrieving items that had been locked up. But uncovering the secret of each lock was what I found fascinating, and doing it silently while my parents were within hearing range increased the thrill. I loved the feel of visualizing the lock, of finding the order, of fitting each pin perfectly in its slot.

I felt the tiny give as I pressed the last pin into place. "Ta-da."

"Brilliant." He flashed me a grin as I finished and soundlessly pushed open the door.

So far, so good.

No alarm on the garage. No pets. No houses nearby. Three clear exit routes through the yard. Points checked off in my mind on my "Cover for Christian" checklist. Although Christian controlled everything on the field and in his social circles, he needed me to make sure he made it out of each adventure safely.

My brother attracted attention and exuded magnetism like a planet pulling in satellites, and he would be the one to get in trouble if we were caught. I had tried to take the heat before, but people always looked amused by my attempts. Quiet, little dreamer, Florence Crown? Right.

I put my pick set in a pocket where I could easily retrieve it and dump it into a bush, in the event that an unnoticed alarm was triggered and we were grabbed by the cops. Having a pick set? Fine. Having a pick set and being caught breaking and entering? Not so fine.

Christian flashed me his widest grin, hiked his bag high onto his back, and prowled into the garage. I entered after him, as always, and quietly closed the door so we could use our flashlights.

We were on our own this time. Christian didn't want his friends to witness his idea of epic romance. After spending two hours with him this afternoon, twisting red tissue into roses, I thought that was probably wise.

I held my light steady as Christian opened the door of the cherry-red convertible, then slipped inside.

Something outside scraped across the vinyl siding on the garage, creating an eerie noise. The wind had been unusual all night. I concentrated all of my senses and took stock of our surroundings. Adrenaline was nicely buzzing through my veins, but other than the branches scraping outside, the house and garage were quiet.

Christian reappeared with a careless and easy grin on his face, sapphire-rimmed teal eyes winking. "Player?" he prodded.

I walked over, wedged the flashlight between my cheek and shoulder, and carefully unzipped my bag. "You don't want to leave it on Sleeping Beauty's pillow?"

"I'm tempted."

I could practically feel his rakish grin. I rolled my eyes, my fingers finding the wired player we had Frankensteined earlier. If he hooked it up correctly, it would start playing when the car door was opened in the morning.

He took it from me, then absently rubbed the inside of his wrist. "Think of the old man's face if he woke to hearing the music coming from his daughter's room."

"Let's not. Star quarterback or not, you are playing with fire as it is. Coach is a scary man. He probably turns into a werewolf on full moons and nights when his house gets broken into."

"Might be worth being benched, if you get to see a werewolf. Sate some of your monster-love madness." Christian smiled and whipped his hair in the familiar gesture women unrelated to me seemed to love—flicking it away from his forehead, then letting it slide down—as he began wiring the player and hooking up the trigger.

Once during middle school, I crept into his room while he slept and cut a huge patch from his bangs. The next morning, I had awakened with half my hair sawed off as well.

I touched the back of my head just to make sure my hair was still attached and hanging past my shoulders. It had taken forever to grow back and that had been a traumatic experience—short, reddish hair made my eyes look larger and my face look even younger. Looking my age was something I battled regularly as one of the shorter girls in our year. In the womb, Christian had somehow grabbed the best height gene and taken some of mine as well.

Christian examined the steering wheel where tasteful tissue flowers were now twined. He frowned. "What do they say in those romance novels and magazines you like to read? Do things need glitter to be girly and romantic? You don't like any of that kind of stuff—but you barely qualify as a girl."

"Gee, thanks." I crossed my arms. "Glitter? Seriously? I don't understand how you get dates."

"I am awesome. And there are some hot girls in your community art class who wear glittery fingernail polish. You should make friends with them—invite them over for sleepovers and nail parties."

"Great. Maybe I should transfer to a different high school too, in order to widen your selection? Would bikini models be acceptable?"

"Yes. You are the best sister ever," he said earnestly, carefully shutting the driver-side door and walking to the passenger side.

I smiled at his tone, and he winked, looking more relaxed. He absently rubbed the inside of his wrist again before entering the car from the other side.

He had been peculiarly agitated the last few weeks, and it had taken considerable effort to distract him and keep him busy. I had even dyed my hair a temporary dark brown to secure the success of this stealth mission. If all it took to get him back to his old self was a successful campaign to nab the future Homecoming Queen, I would thank her personally. It would be awkward, since we had nothing to do with each other outside of Christian, but entirely worth the weirdness.

Christian leaned over the center console to complete the last pieces of his campaign, armed the trigger on the "Franken-player," carefully shut the passenger door, and bumped my shoulder companionably with his.

I had no doubt that tomorrow morning at school he would be greeted gleefully and with an enthusiastic yes to the question taped to the dash.

We locked the garage door and crept through the shadowed yard.

Chapter One

Mission accomplished. Another operation successfully negotiated.

On the fifteen-minute walk back to our house, Christian was silent, so my mind started connecting the shadows and forming them into dark art in my mind—imaginary creatures twined up and howled as we passed.

I was a bit edgy myself. My community arts class had watched a presentation on making oil paints from scratch. There had been an itch under my skin ever since I had seen the guest artist press the spatula into the linseed and pigment. It had kept me up all last night, staring at my hand-painted celestial ceiling. I had suppressed the strange feeling, and my tiredness, in order to help Christian with the planning and execution of his task, but I couldn't remember ever feeling such a need as the one that continued to run through me—I needed to create my own paint.

After I made my first batch, I was going to paint these shadows, with their long curling fingers and slow-moving grace. Excitement built. Yes, that is what I was going to research when I got home. I could probably get Christian to help me beg Mom for the supplies.

Lightning streaked the sky, sending jagged lights through the shadows and scattering my thoughts. Odd. There was no storm forecast and heat lightning was a summer event.

I gripped my flashlight reflexively.

"I saw your mail this afternoon," Christian said casually.

My heart picked up more speed as I focused on him. "So?"

"So? They are courting you. Why didn't you say anything? Finish your application tomorrow. I bet we can get Mom to take us to the steakhouse to celebrate. Dad won't need any convincing."

"How...?" No, I knew how he knew. He had poked through my stuff, after sneaking into my room to peek at what the Harvard stationery indicated. I shook my head. "I'm not going." How could I keep an eye on him next year if he was halfway across the country, riding the football scholarship everyone knew he was going to get from State?

"What? Don't be an idiot. Of course you're going. I told you that arts and engineering exhibition was a great idea." He threw an arm around my neck and tugged my head into his space. "Once you accept their offer, I can pry you out of your art and math obsessions so you can finally relax and enjoy yourself. This is our year, Ren."

Lightning flashed again.

I punched his side, halfheartedly trying to free myself. "The year of Crown."

"We can do anything. The world is our clam shell—"

"Oyster."

"—and we are searching for the diamond—"

4

"Pearl." I tried to bump him again, but he moved his hips out of the way.

"—and the journey to find it will mature us into little mini-adults. All those teen self-help articles say so." He pulled my neck in closer.

"Christian—"

"Think outside the pyramid, dear sister. Now that you are in at Harvard, you can totally blow school."

I bent my knees, shoved my hand up against his arm vice, and twisted free. "I thought you said we were supposed to be maturing into mini-adults."

He splayed his arms wide. "Yeah, at the end of the year. This is like the opening chapter of our epic saga. We need to be frolicking in the pasture and splashing at the river's edge and playing harmless pranks." He motioned with his fingers, as if they were frolicking through tall grass.

I held up an edge of the prank bag he was carrying, in response to that remark.

He grinned and we started walking again. "I know you'll have a good time this year, if you just open up to people a little more. The guys like you, and they rag on everyone."

"The guys" being Christian's group of crazed friends. The ones who knew me as a helping hand accompanying them on missions, or the stealthy one in brutal capture-the-flag battles, or as the girl who sketched quietly at the lunch table. The girl who rarely spoke.

He frowned. "Like you as a friend, I mean. I'd have to kill them otherwise. But cultivating more girlfriends is always a good thing. For all of us."

"Very funny." Lightning lit again, but there was no accompanying thunder. Where was it coming from?

"It's all about continuing a benevolent dictatorship and having fun. And it is time for you to become a general, instead of first lieutenant."

Anxiety ran through me. I could talk to Christian easily, but with other people, words garbled strangely as they emerged from my mouth. "I don't want—"

"So, during our third week of dominion," he said, trampling over my objection, "you should be in charge of—"

Lightning seemed to light everywhere at once, and Christian suddenly stopped. He bowed forward, clutching his midsection. His bag dropped to the ground, its contents clinking.

I grabbed his arm to steady him. "What's wrong?" I demanded, all humor gone.

"Cramp."

Chapter One

A weird wave of electricity surged through my fingers where they touched him. I snatched my hand back, staring at the digits. The charged feeling dissipated within me, but increased in the air around us, swirling and darkening. I tentatively touched his arm again, and the energy shot into me once more. It was like focused euphoria.

Christian shuddered, then rolled his shoulders forward. "I feel strange." His brows drew together and he looked at his hands, extending and retracting his fingers. "But good strange. Like I've just made twelve perfect passes and could complete a hundred more."

With brows drawn together, he bent and lifted his bag. It looked like something was drawn on the inside of his right wrist. I started to ask, but spectral colors flashed out and wrapped around his duffel.

Our heads collided as we peered inside. It looked just as it had before— full of red tissue paper, green wrap, adhesives, and tools. Christian's fingers ran along the top of the bag, sparking.

His fingers, not the bag.

I stared at him, dumbfounded, moving my hand along his arm and down to his wrist. It seemed important for some reason to maintain contact. "You... You're electric."

He gave a strangled laugh, hands jamming together and pulling apart. Electricity sparked between his forefingers, then the others, forming five crackling white arcs.

"Is this real?" I reached out tentatively to touch an arc, and a sparkle fell, exploding on the ground with the report of a bottle rocket.

I let go of him in shock. The weird pressure built around us again, pushing.

"The lightning… Was it coming from you?"

There was a depression in the pavement where the spark had hit. I looked to see Christian staring wide-eyed too. "I don't know."

"You!" A man stepped out of the deep shadows cast by the trees near the end of the street.

No. I had stopped paying attention to our surroundings and now we were about to be caught far past curfew.

"Hands out, and stay right there," he growled, his voice unfamiliar, his face still too deep in the shadows.

Christian touched my arm and the grip of his fingers indicated a readiness to run. His hands still glowed an electric blue, and the strange sense of elation ran into me again at the point of contact.

I shifted my balance to an optimal flight response. If we were caught, Christian could be benched until Homecoming. No one would be pleased by that outcome.

"Hands out, and—"

Christian pushed hard on my arm. I rolled forward on the balls of my feet with the motion and we immediately tore off into the yard at our right.

"They are running!" the man shouted, as he gave pursuit.

Another man in black sprinted toward us as we reached the fenced-in backyard.

Christian swore and we veered toward a backyard play structure, frantically climbing it, then leaping over the high fence. We crashed to the grass, rolling to relieve our momentum. Blue lightning arced around us.

The man trailing us yelled and I heard him fall into the hedges. We launched forward, skirting a car parked in the driveway and sprinting through the front yard and into the street.

Another man, down the street, headed toward us.

"What the hell?" Christian asked harshly as we ran, veering again into another yard, where a fourth man appeared from the shadows. Christian ran straight at him, pushing him hard in the shoulder. The man flew back and crashed hard. Harder than it seemed he should have with a normal block, but there was no opportunity to look back or think on it further.

A man stood at the end of the next street, and we swerved to the right. We were being herded out of the neighborhood.

Lightning flashed again and a crackle of strange thunder finally accompanied it. The lightning connected with the overhead power lines around us, white, sparking lines leading toward the utility company's lot.

Christian pushed at my arm, and we ran directly toward the lot. Something whizzed through the air close to us and then clanged into the chain link fence as we scrambled up and over.

From the other side of the chain link fence, I saw a knife laying on the ground beneath where we had just been, and my heart leaped fully into my throat. A harmless prank of breaking and entering into the coach's garage deserved a punishment on par with laps around the football field, not mortal wounds.

And police didn't fling knives at fleeing suspects.

Electricity seemed to spark from the entire lot around us, the blue lines arcing from the poles and power lines toward Christian.

He pulled me behind a short, square building.

Why were we stopping? I quickly signed at him—plan? I had been in enough paintball fights at his side—staying in one position eventually meant death. But there weren't enough structures for us to move stealthily between. Why were we here? The street chase was far more in our favor.

He motioned with his glowing fingers to signal that he was going to jump the men when they came near. I signed back a quick negative with a few added expletives that we had added to the code years ago.

But there was a focused mania in his eyes. "I don't know what this is, but I can do anything right now, Ren. I can feel it."

"What?" I hissed, grabbing his arm, the terror of being discovered combining with panic at his uncharacteristic behavior. Some of the mania in his eyes immediately lessened at the skin contact, but the focus remained.

He squeezed my hand. "Run. I won't let them hurt you."

"Hands at your sides." A man stepped out of the deep shadows cast by the main tower. There was malevolence in his every movement. "Your type is so predictable, always looking for energy. Boy, put your hands against your sides now. Girl, come here. Clean and easy. There's no escape now."

The four other men appeared, surrounding our position. One of them was limping—his expression full of rage.

Christian stepped in front of me and the electric field between his fingers grew stronger.

"You don't want to do that, boy." The man lifted something dark and barreled.

I lunged at Christian's back at the same time that he half turned, grabbed me, and threw me to the side as easily as he would a child's stuffed animal. Something cracked in my right forearm as it hit the edge of the building and spun me around.

A deafening blast immediately hit the place where we had been.

As I fell back in horror, I could see Christian dodging left, then lightning lit from his fingers and three of the men went flying. The man from the shadows raised his gun toward me.

Christian's arm reached out, and a wave of something warm and protective shot from his fingers into my chest.

Then something pulsed, blinding me, filling my vision with crimson. Lights exploded and detonations rocked the universe.

Everything in my world went end over end, and my face slammed onto the concrete.

Blackness. All I saw was blackness.

Darkness blurred. Faint shapes formed. My cheek was pressed oddly to the hard ground, and dark red streams streaked away from me.

I tried to move. My cheek wouldn't lift. My neck wouldn't lift. My vision was streaked red.

I told my neck to move. My lips tried to repeat the command—soundless, something wet upon them.

On my fifth blink, my vision returned. There was a strange absence of light, only the stars and crescent moon casting any at all. Power lines and towers lay in pieces around me. No electricity arced—as if the entire supply had been used. There were six bodies lying twenty yards away. One slowly, painfully, rose—becoming a large shadow hovering above the others. The rising figure gave one of the motionless bodies a kick.

The shape and hair of the kicked body registered, and I instinctively rejected all emotion.

He was so still, splayed like a carelessly tossed doll. I had never seen Christian like that. Not even after being blindsided by a spectacular sack.

Protectiveness and primal panic surged.

I struggled to push upright, blackness completely overtaking my vision, pain radiating through my head. I closed my eyes, inhaled deeply, then forced my too-heavy head to still and my vision to clear.

My view of the obliterated lot wobbled with my success. I tried to move my left arm, but it wasn't working, so I stretched out my right and pulled myself forward. Eighteen feet away. Seventeen and a half. Seventeen. Just a little more.

Each pull scraped a layer of the void from my mind and a layer of skin from my useless left arm, and my pulling became increasingly erratic and frantic as the figure with my brother's hair didn't move. The blackening pain and the nagging thought that something else required my attention were nothing next to my need to reach him, and I curled my fingers into the grit of the concrete, pulling, trying to get to him.

Then I was splayed out on my back, looking up at the twirling night sky. Stars twinkled and whirled. A booted foot pressed heavily on my chest. I felt and heard something crack, but nothing concrete registered through the all-encompassing pain and the thwarted need to reach my brother.

I tried to separate the shadowed features and black clothing from the starry sky beyond. The man held a device over me, his boot pushed down harder, and I could feel a gurgle in my chest.

"Stupid ferals. But I've got you now." His hands moved with the device. A braided leather band dangled from his damaged fingers. Christian's band.

He pressed harder and everything started to go black.

I flung up my free arm and grabbed the end of the band. Power and pressure flooded through my hand, and the sparking seemed to travel from the leather into my bones. The release of the other end of the band sent my arm slamming to the ground, but the band stayed within my grasp, vibrating, then abruptly stilling as it calmed something deep within me. My vision continued to dim, but was now replaced by a calm blue light hovering in my mind's eye.

The shadowed man above me uttered a long stream of expletives, then stepped harder on my chest.

"Get up and get over here, you idiots," he shouted. "And either wake up

Lynch, or dispose of him."

Under the increased pressure of his boot, something else cracked in my chest.

I was...going to die.

A spark sluggishly ignited in my midsection around the steady blue light, like a wick that had been dormant too long, and the crack of another rib was echoed by a bang a few feet to my side.

"Son of a—" The foot was suddenly gone.

Flares of brown, swirling and long-tailed, flashed, then the earth trembled as a body crashed next to me, and three others fell farther away.

A long pole twirled over me and poked down toward the ground.

"Isn't hunting supposed to provide a challenge, Uncle?" The new voice was masculine and edged. Could a voice be described as chiseled? I longed to see the face attached to such a voice, but everything was going hazy again.

"You got lucky with that sudden trace that popped from nowhere," an older voice responded.

"Or maybe I'm just that good." I could almost picture the smile behind that riveting voice. I wanted to see it, but couldn't turn my head.

Not being able to move, confusion, hearing irresistible voices. Angels? Maybe I was dying.

Dying. Christian. Panic penetrated my muddiness. I tried to turn myself, to reach him, but my body was absolutely useless. Heavier now—my muscles seemingly nonexistent.

The older man sighed. "Try to stay out of the headlines this week, won't you?"

The two figures moved into view, but like images from a Kandinsky. Frenetic motion and dark colors not allowing my eye to rest.

"Wild Magic is flowing everywhere. The scavengers finished the feral off fifteen minutes ago, then drained him dry." The older voice sounded disgusted, then swore. "We have to report that they have a tool to identify and hide an Awakening."

A twinkling white light beckoned me closer, slowly strangling the rest of my senses and letting only a few words filter in.

"Scanning...difficult...heavy in the air."

"Feral...Awakening...subverts suppression field."

I couldn't cough or breathe. Christian. I pushed away from the light with difficulty. I needed to get to my brother. I tried turning again, but the only parts of me I could still feel were the two fingers clutching his band.

"The scanner stopped working."

A figure crouched next to me and touched my wrist. "The girl is fighting."

As if the touch had connected me to an external speaker source, I could hear clearly again. It was the guy with the beautiful masculine voice. Michelangelo's David would sound like this.

I tried to choke out the words for him to help Christian, but only liquid bubbled up.

I used every last resource I possessed to slowly curl my hand and touch the boy's fingers at my wrist. The pressure of his fingers increased minutely at the touch. I tried to tell him to help my brother, but I couldn't remember how to make my lips work anymore.

"I can barely tell it's human under the blood." The older man sounded extremely disinterested. "Broken nose, shattered cheekbones. Girl chose the wrong boyfriend. Poor mongrels."

"She is as human as we are, Uncle." The boy's lovely voice radiated disapproval.

The older man sighed. "The scanner is dead and soon she will be too. Let her find peace," the older voice said dismissively. "You don't waste reserves on ordinaries when you don't know who might be watching for the right opportunity to strike. If only the scanner was working."

"Maybe she isn't ordinary. I've never felt such a linger in the air."

"These scavengers are foot soldiers only—boy probably had more magic than they could deal with—bet they leaked his magic everywhere, or else we'd have found it in a container. Still...check her wrist."

I felt my wrist lifted.

"Nothing. Her skin is clear," the boy said. He carefully laid my arm back down. "But she feels..." His voice trailed off.

"Mother would heal her," the boy continued, as if to himself. "She wouldn't care that she was ordinary."

"She would care if it hurt you. You are crouching there as if that girl is the first soon-to-be dead person you've ever seen. Help me finish tying up these scumbags."

The boy stood and the heat from his hand lifted with him. Everything became cold, painful, and hazy again.

The night sky was circling. I...was at the planetarium with Christian? Any moment now there would be music and a laser show. But the manager and lighting technicians couldn't agree on something. I could hear the buzz of their furious whispers. Then someone was once again next to me, kneeling and putting a hand on my arm, and I felt some semblance of clarity, along with relief that his hand was touching me again.

A sigh issued from somewhere far to my left. "Fine. Do it, if you must. A tiny amount only. I'll transport these to Processing."

Chapter One

The hand moved to my chest. Something like strangled laughter and blood bubbled from my chest and up my throat with the thought of telling Christian that I couldn't even appreciate my first experience getting to second base.

Christian.

Heat centered in the hand pressing against my chest, and something electric and white hot shot through me.

The electricity connected and something in me—that part that felt neutralized, like a sleeping dragon—pulled greedily, demanding treasure and gold, knitting it together and throwing swashes of energy through my limbs like paint splattering a canvas. And all of a sudden, all I could see was blue. Two circles of ultramarine, the color straight from the deepest shade of The Last Judgment. Staring into those eyes, a winged henna design sketched itself slowly in my mind.

"Their police are coming." The older man's voice was flat. Sirens whined in the distance. "They will take care of her, if she lives, and—"

Her? Not them.

I flipped myself like a flopping fish, then dragged my body toward my brother's unmoving form, arm over arm. There was no pain this time, and I could use my left arm again, but it felt like I was moving through sludge. Like in a dream. A nightmare...

This had to be a nightmare.

"It—she's moving." The older man's voice sounded disbelieving. "How much did you use, Ax?"

"Half," he answered.

The older man sounded like he was choking. "Half...what were you thinking, Alexander? You are not indestructible, regardless of what you and everyone else thinks."

"She's a fighter," he remarked simply, as if that explained all. "She took it, and I let her."

"You play too many team sports. We should have raised you as an assassin instead. I told them that, but did anyone listen? Where's she going?"

"To the boy."

"Don't bother, girl," the older man called out. "He's deader than dead."

My mind rejected that notion totally. I kept crawling forward. It was getting harder and my vision was tunneling again. No. Not yet. Just a little farther.

"Ax, stop following her, dammit. This is getting less amusing. The suppression field won't remove our faces from the memories of the officers should they see us. And don't you dare use more magic for her! No!

Dammit!"

A hand touched my back, and then I was next to Christian, vision suddenly clear, dark tunnel pushed away, my hand wrapped around his limp one, still warm. Oh, God. Oh, God.

"It is too late for him," the boy whispered. The other man's voice was swearing loudly in the background. "Bringing back the dead like this is forbidden. This is all I can do for you." His breath, at the nape of my neck, was warm, his voice soft.

My vision was tunneling again—the shot of clarity having come from outside me. "No." It sounded like my voice, but a croaked, cracked thing under the blaring sirens, which were growing louder. I could feel no life, but there was something else in my brother's hand, something that tentatively brushed me. I could feel him. I squeezed his hand. Please.

"I am sorry for your loss." The hand at my back gave a sympathetic pat, then lifted and the tunnel came rushing toward me, faster, blasting, before everything went dark.

Chapter Two

DAYDREAMS AND NIGHTMARES

I LOOKED AT THE winged creature I had penciled in my sketchbook. Since the "accident," my hand kept recreating its pattern. Why I felt compelled to doodle the same image over and over would have freaked me out, if I had the emotional capability for it.

Three therapists in six weeks had been unable to convince me that Christian's death had been an accident. The next in line, scheduled for next week, would have no better success. The doctors kept saying that my imaginings were a result of head injuries, and that I shouldn't be concerned with "dreamscape memories."

I was obsessively concerned.

Especially since people seemed to remember that I was "crazy" now, but not exactly why. Not a single therapist, not even my parents, could repeat the events of that night back to me twenty minutes after I told it. And none of them seemed concerned about that fact.

But at least the men in black had not reappeared. Not in the hospital, and not afterward. No one possessing strange powers had.

I looked at the winged creature—a hybrid of a bird and snake. Not quite a phoenix, not quite a dragon. I wiped at it with my thumb, smudging the shading, then looked down at my otherwise perfectly unblemished hands and curled my long fingers in.

The authorities could try to convince me until the end of time that there had been an electrical explosion that had blacked out the city. But I had seen the pinched looks on the doctors' faces when they couldn't explain why I'd been covered in blood and not sporting a single scratch.

I had searched through every volume in the public library and browsed a thousand websites on magic, secret government conspiracies,

"Awakenings" of all types, and a dozen different meanings of the words "ordinary" and "feral." Nothing matched my experience. Nothing felt right. But the answer to what happened that night was out there somewhere, and I would find it.

Besides, the boy's words—Alexander's words—flowed through my dreams at night. Bringing back the dead like this is forbidden.

Like this?

My pencil tip broke. I took a deep breath, then another, and let the calm vibes of the art studio wash through me. My only haven. It was the only classroom that didn't have a rose glued to an empty chair next to mine. Christian had elected for study hall during my art period.

I took a deep breath, retrieved a pen from my bag, and turned to a blank page in my sketchbook.

The Homecoming Game was next week. The new quarterback was supposedly decent, but I hadn't attended any of his games, and I didn't plan to attend any in the future. Students were still weeping about Christian, yet they were excited for the game and dance, and I couldn't understand any of it.

People walked around me living their lives, while I watched them as if they existed on a TV screen.

I felt...totally removed. My second therapist had whispered to a colleague weeks ago that I was suffering from some sort of raging delusion, mixed with clinical apathy, in order to deal with the loss of my twin.

But it was easier to stay silent and unnerve the therapists than to release the sobs that stayed locked in my chest, rippling there, pushing.

My pencil moved and Christian's braided leather band slid along the desk and paper as my wrist dragged it along. The world had stopped turning the moment I had awakened in the hospital, asking for Christian, and receiving the horrific response of silence from my parents.

Then the world had turned without me.

I was stagnant. Like Christian's room or his locker or his classroom chairs. My connection to the world was gone. There was something about me that was different from everyone else now. And until I could figure out how to undo the past, no pathway would reconnect me.

I hated it. I hated choking back cries at the most random of times. I hated feeling powerless and without direction. I hated turning to speak to someone who wasn't there, accidentally setting a place at dinner in front of an empty seat, calling for someone who would never answer.

I hated the knowledge that never again would I be able to talk to my best friend.

The pressure of my thoughts seemed to resonate under my skin.

Chapter Two

The drawing grew darker and more violent as I traced over the lines, undoubtedly leaving indelible indents on the pages below. I gripped the pen, pressure riding beneath my skin, and repeatedly outlined the little black figures screaming in Munch-styled pain. They stared out at me in anguish, moans slipping from their lips. I could almost hear their choked and building sobs.

Then they started running across the page, shrieking in agony and tearing the ink from their cheeks.

Literally running and screaming across my paper.

I dropped my pen and slammed my hands down, catching the pen under one finger.

The girl on the other side of my large worktable was bent over her work, ignoring me. Focusing on her sketchpad and drawing without care.

I stared at the fall of her wavy hair, similar to my own—but hiding someone normal beneath.

Black motion on the page forced my eyes down again. Then the pen moved, slipping out from beneath my finger and rolling to the edge of my desk.

Small inked fingers splayed to each side of my hands. My heart hammered harder. I could feel the paper pushing around the edges of my fingers, tiny inked digits trying to lift mine. I closed my eyes and swallowed. Breathe. In, out, in, out. I smoothed my hands across the flat paper. Normal. I took another breath and looked down.

No inky fingers, no movement. The figures were once again standing in frozen torment.

Okay. Sure, no problem. I felt lightheaded. My pulse was racing, and the beat of my heart thumped through the veins of my wrist. I looked to where the feeling concentrated. Dots of henna brown were forming a vague pattern across the pulsing skin. The creature I couldn't stop doodling was taking shape on my flesh.

I looked up. The girl across my worktable was staring at me, eyes pinched. Her expression was a familiar mixture of horror, pity, and accusation, as if she was sure I was two moments away from slitting the skin I'd been staring at.

I had heard the rumors. Quiet Little Florence Crown had become Mad Ren Crown. That covered in his blood, I had killed Christian, the fury of my psychotic rage causing me to blow the entire utility lot. Or, it had been a tragic accident that had caused my mind to snap due to his loss. Rumors of my insane ramblings had spread quickly at school. Why the specifics of my ramblings—concerning magic, electricity, and men with weapons—were never remembered, and hadn't spread online, was a mystery I didn't have the energy to care about anymore.

Even the people I had been friendly with had that mix of expressions when they looked at me. I chose to stay far away from them most of all. It hurt more.

Half a person.

I was half a person now.

My fingers curled, my veins pulsed, the henna brown dots darkened.

I pictured a paper bag and my cheeks caving in and bloating out in its depths.

Christian's voice yelled in my head, "Breathe, you idiot!"

Breathe. Right. In, out, in, out.

The henna dots faded to a light freckle.

"Miss Crown. Lovely work," an accented, luxurious voice said from behind me. Mr. Verisetti's long fingers placed a wrapped toffee next to my sketchbook. "Keep it up."

He moved around the table and said something in a low voice to the girl. She blushed, averted her gaze, then gathered her things and moved to another table. I shakily unwrapped the toffee and shoved it into my mouth. As soon as it touched my tongue, the smooth bottom layer melted. I closed my eyes. The rich, smooth coat settled in my mouth, then the next layer melted. It was like ocean waves riding over my tongue and softly crashing in my ears. Calming and settling me.

There were no worries. The other students had stopped watching me. And the only magic that existed was in Mr. Verisetti's toffees. Even our cranky calculus teacher loved them.

"I desire your help with something, Miss Crown."

I looked up at Mr. Verisetti, and the classroom lights caught on the small gold cuff around his upper ear, the only jewelry he wore besides a wide black band around his left wrist.

I checked my wrist reflexively. It was completely clear. I crossed my arms tightly, tucking my hands and wrists firmly beneath. Another layer of toffee melted, and I let my arms relax on the table, and let worries drift away.

"Sure." I liked Mr. Verisetti. Everyone liked him. And he never called me Florence like some of the other teachers. He either used the very proper, Miss Crown, or Ren, the nickname Christian had given me long years ago. "What do you need?"

My eyes wandered to the collection of prints that he had hung on the wall after he had replaced our old instructor four weeks ago. They were nice, simple pictures of flowers, gardens, and natural wonders.

But weirdness suddenly hit and the prints swirled and became strange and fantastic. Moving like stylized videos—brush strokes lingering like tracers as teenagers violently battled each other with blasts of colored light and strange objects, while others raised zombies and storms. Hints of a magnificent hillside university landscape with fields of poppies and wildflowers vied with the scorched earth, death, and destruction of the foreground.

"You have earned the glorious job of mixing paint."

I ripped my eyes away from a print of a girl standing over a boy on a field, restoring his life force—his back arched and his arms flung to the sides, caught in the stillness between death and life. It was hard to breathe.

Mr. Verisetti was observing me with a smile. "Glorious," he said.

Another layer of toffee melted.

My lips lifted in automatic response. It was always easy to smile at Mr. Verisetti.

He chuckled. It was warm and rich, gliding along the surface like everything he did. With his dark hair, smooth skin, and golden eyes, it was hard to guess his age. I thought thirties, but had heard all sorts of weird opinions from others—everything from being in his late teens to early fifties, as if he was whatever the person wanted him to be.

"True glory," he said. "The greatest artists are masters at mixing. Masters mixing for their masters."

Despite his urban hotness, Mr. Verisetti loved to speak in old-world terms. Masters and servants, mentors and patrons. Giving up one's soul to art.

"You don't want me to use a tube of Hot Pink Glitter Extravaganza?" I joked, feeling better—relaxing my tight shoulder and neck muscles. Art class served as my daily Prozac now.

"Definitely not. We will use these." He carefully placed eight dishes of crushed pigments in front of me and a jar containing what looked and smelled like linseed oil.

Excitement sparked. "You want me to mix paint from scratch?" Something in me strained at an invisible leash in exhilaration.

Maybe Mr. Verisetti would let me do a quick landscape after completing my task. My eyes moved to the prints on the walls. Maybe a fantastic hillside town? Maybe a girl raising the dead? Excitement thrummed within me at the thought, and I leaned forward with my elbows on the table.

"Yes." The conspiratorial look in his golden eyes reinforced my thrum. He placed a flat glass surface in front of me, then added a bell-shaped glass muller and spatula on top. Two other glass surfaces were placed to the side. "Interested?"

"Most definitely." The oil kit I wanted to purchase weeks ago... I hadn't been able to ask for the supplies after returning from the hospital, even though my parents would probably have purchased anything I had asked for. The emotional need had lodged somewhere between my overwhelming guilt and despair.

But now...the fervor to create a picture of resurrection from scratch was beating inside of me—heavy drum beats accelerating to a frenetic meter.

"Patience, patience." Mr. Verisetti's voice was soothing, but pleased. "These particular pigments will combine in whatever way you specify. Mix your first choice onto this." His hand passed over the square glass surface. "Trust your instincts each time a decision forks before you. How does each color make you feel? For what might a color be used? Create the visual story and stir in the essence, matching the consistency of the medium to the narrative behind. Lay the groundwork, Miss Crown, for the manifestation of a magnificent...Awakening."

The air felt heavier, the thrumming became a steady beat that swirled the air around it like a finger poking through a curl of steam.

Something about his words made me pause, but another layer of toffee melted, and I let the unease dissipate as I relaxed again. Mr. Verisetti was examining me closely, so I nodded quickly and began. I made my first pigment choice quickly and felt a thrum slide down my arm and into my fingers as I poured a small dollop of linseed into a crater of pigment, then carefully folded the mixture together, spreading and lifting with my spatula. The ache of loss flowed red.

I considered the other pigments and made a second choice. The departure of the other part of my soul spilled gray. I added a third. The loss of my very identity, so wrapped in another being, was a motley green. Sprinkle, pour, stir, consider, release. Far better than any other therapy techniques I had tried; the task discharged internal energy that had been plaguing me since Christian's death. The kind that had kept me awake night after night.

Discharging, but bringing with it an intense canvas of white in my mind.

My thumb dipped to the painted surface almost absently. I examined the swipe on my finger, longing running through me. I wanted to wipe my thumb across a blank page, form a circle, form anything.

Mr. Verisetti had been a godsend to me, but for some reason denied me the opportunity to paint, and strangely, I hadn't been able to pick up a brush at home. The desire to ask for a canvas formed, then stuttered on my tongue, hanging there between my parted lips. The urge to paint itched under my skin. Dried paint flakes buried beneath and needing water and brush to free them. But for some reason I couldn't utter the request.

My eyes slowly drifted to my sketchbook on the table, and my thumb automatically extended. A circle...

A cloth intercepted my thumb before it hit its goal. "Let me help."

I looked up to see Mr. Verisetti examining me, a smile hovering at the edges of his lips. He held the cloth around my thumb.

"Some of our greatest artists exploded and died before finishing their masterworks. The loss pains me. If only they might have exploded properly. Afterward."

I wiped the paint off on his cloth with a quiet thank you. The cloth was damp and the paint seemed to suck right off my thumb. I shook off the strange thought and concentrated on his words.

"Exploded?" I tried to recall any artist who had combusted. I couldn't come up with one. The sounds of the other students intruded into my thoughts—their scratching pencils and quiet murmurs. I had forgotten there were other people still in the room.

The edges of his eyes creased and his lips curled upward, as he carefully wrapped the smeared paint into the cloth. He leaned forward, as if sharing a secret. "Their artistic self exploded."

"Oh." Self-destructing artists weren't an uncommon thing in history. All that lead poisoning.

He put the cloth into a plastic bag, then placed it on a high shelf. "Such a shame. All of that passion and energy has to be funneled correctly. Make a misstep and boom." He signed with his hands. "Artist and earth chunks everywhere. With nothing big enough even to piece back together or use."

I smiled in response to his entreating grin and dramatics. "That sounds dire."

"That is why a good artist must find the right...mentor. Are you interested in destroying the ordinary, Miss Crown?" He leaned toward me in the same conspiratorial, playful way. His eyes seemed oddly cold, though, intensely focused. I blinked, and they were warm again. "Destroying this world and creating it anew, even should it bury you in darkness?"

"Will it bring my brother back?" The words wound from my tongue and released into the air.

I couldn't believe I had just said that. But the last bit of the toffee unraveled and melted and I relaxed into my seat. Mr. Verisetti never gave me pitying glances or uttered useless clichés about time healing all wounds. He just accepted the strange things I said, without judgment, in the same way Christian had.

I wanted to do anything to make him happy.

He smiled. "Keep mixing, Miss Crown."

But it took a moment to make my hand obey. Distrust...no, trust. A headache crept along my temples and a bitter taste replaced the lingering toffee for a moment. I forced my hand to move. Forced my thoughts to my brother. The paint in front of me turned an odd lavender shade. Just this side of being identified as brown.

It was a moody color. Nostalgic and sad. Haunted and trapped.

I used the glass muller and pressed harder, thinking of Christian, of my failure to protect him, of death and the afterlife.

I stopped grinding abruptly. My mind—and the heavy, sure beat of my pulse—told me the lavender was done.

With my spatula, I collected the paint into the center, then slid the glass surface to the side. The bitter taste in my mouth grew. I lifted one of the two remaining glass surfaces and mixed pigment and oil into a pile of garish orange paint to match the taste. The mixture thinned and thickened as I added linseed or pigment. I ground with the muller to coat each particle, trying to find the right consistency, constantly feeling it was a hair off. That everything was slightly off. Another toffee appeared next to my hand, and I quickly unwrapped and placed it on my tongue.

Sated and relieved, I finished the orange.

Mr. Verisetti usually encouraged purely primary colors in warm and cool shades to start a palette, and even while allowing for a dollop of black, he would say with a slow smile, 'Better to mix your own black, for there is no true black in nature.'

We had always used manufactured paint on our palettes, though. When an artist made paint from scratch, maybe she could start with whatever hues she wanted.

The sprinkles of lapis lazuli heavily called to me, so I dumped the lot onto the last glass surface. Crushed lapis lazuli made ultramarine paint, the pinnacle hue of the old masters. I added a bit of the crystal that looked like crushed glass and a spoonful of paraiba tourmaline, producing something exciting and exotic swirling within the oil.

Just like the boy's eyes...

Pressure gathered under my skin, and I stirred harder. I stared at the colors mixing beneath my hand, a charged reflection of the mix inside of me. Magic. It was like there were little zaps of static beneath my skin, whirling around, seeking an outlet.

"An interesting choice," Mr. Verisetti said, as he observed from his position in the chair across from me. One of his fingers reached across the worktable and tapped mine, and the electricity settled. "I have only seen such a color twice."

I would have considered the tone of his voice sinister, if it had come from anyone else. I struggled for a moment, my hand stilled above the paint, as something outside of me tried to suppress the negative thought.

Chapter Two

"Almost ready," he said soothingly.

A layer of toffee melted, and so did my unease. Mr. Verisetti picked up the last glass surface, and rose from his chair.

I looked down at my sketchbook. My pen was in my hand. A butterfly was emerging from a cocoon. I blinked at the pen. When had I picked it up? The butterfly emerged fully and quivered weakly inside the paper. Its wings grew stronger and steadier, and soon it was fluttering all over the page, hitting the edges, looking for a means of escape. I could almost feel the puffs of air on my fingers.

I looked up to see the reactions of the other students, but they were all frozen over their projects, unmoving. No, that couldn't be right. I wiped the back of my hand across my eyes, then slipped from my seat and headed over to the art racks. I pulled out an old canvas.

A self-study. I used to love doing self-portraits—delving into the deep recesses of my mind and determining how to present emotion and thought on canvas.

The darkening afternoon shadows made the sketched features lackluster. I wanted to make the penciled long hair reddish brown—maybe add a few happy gold highlights. To make the colorless eyes a festive teal with a ring of sapphire, instead of dark and empty. I wanted to paint a smile on my face. And at the same time, I couldn't see placing anything there other than the strained, haunted look of the sketch.

Need.

There was an easel next to me. A sudden addition worthy of my shifting dreamscape.

I pushed the canvas in and turned to the easel. A fresh piece of paper was pinned at the top. There was one unmarked tube of paint, one toffee, and two pieces of charcoal in the bin—one a pencil and one a raw chunk.

I picked up the toffee, turning it in my hand, then dropped it to the floor, my mind rejecting it. I wasn't sure why, but in that moment I knew I wasn't going to eat toffees, ever again.

I lifted the raw piece of charcoal. It felt strange in my hand, as if something were just slightly off in the texture. I stroked a stripe of black down the page, bisecting it.

Two figures quickly took form on the left side. I saw those lone figures in my head even as my hand worked. One figure was forever gone outside of sketched representation, and the other still wretchedly existed in life six weeks later.

I looked to the right side of the dividing line and saw I had drawn a box. Ornamented and alive. Sooty and vibrating. As if I could reach over, dust it off, and open the lid. I reached toward it, my fingers still wrapped around the charcoal stick. The lid moved. Just a crack of an opening, but an opening was there now where it hadn't been before. And suddenly, despite the insanity of the thought, I needed to see what was inside.

Paint it. It was a whisper of a voice in my head, but I nodded along—yes, of course that is what I should do. I could almost taste the linseed. Without taking my eyes away, I blindly reached for the tube of paint, and energy shot through me as I touched it. Ultramarine blue with a charged edge squeezed out onto two fingers. It was the mixture I had made, but with something—glistening and extra—added. I didn't spare a moment to grab a brush. I had to get paint on that box right now.

I had finally come unhinged, and I didn't care. There was something alive in the deadened paper world that contained a representation of my brother.

My loaded fingers reached for the paper. The sketched box resonated with anticipation, golden light shooting out around its edges. Just one more inch to the paper—

"Glorious," a voice whispered.

My hand jerked, and the paint flew in a wide arc as I swung to the right in terror. Mr. Verisetti wiped the paint from his cheek in one easy motion, then flicked it. No lingering smudge of paint marred his skin.

I knew him—he had been my favorite teacher since he had begun teaching four weeks ago—but in the strange zone still holding on to me, there was something otherly familiar about him as he examined the paper. Or perhaps, familiar in an other way.

"Glorious," he repeated.

"Um, yeah." I inched away. This man I had considered both my savior and friend suddenly seemed anything but. It was as if I straddled two worlds and saw both—where he was charming in one, and deadly in the other.

At a run, it was about a dozen steps to the door.

He smiled, a nice full smile. It was charming and brilliant—and edged and dangerous. The image of him wavered between the two.

"Do not be afraid, Miss Crown. I am anchoring you." He waved a hand in an aristocratic manner. "You'd likely be dead otherwise, or locked in a mental ward. Though, you are a fascinating subject, I wonder if you might spontaneously create a portal to another layer of the world."

"Right." I cast a quick glance around the room. There were students sitting at each workspace, but every one of them was unmoving. Frozen mid-movement.

"Without a single bit of knowledge or training, you anchored your brother for weeks." I jerked at the mention of Christian, and Mr. Verisetti smiled. "I find the anchoring beyond interesting. Perhaps it is a twin thing. Perhaps it is you."

I took a full step back to get a better line of escape around the tables to the door, and tried to cover my actions with a neutral smile. I could barely force the edges of my lips up.

In both images his smile turned into something more satisfied. "You are seeing me truly now? Of course you are. Excellent."

I took another step back. In movies, when men cornered women, the men were usually hideous in some way. Showing their evil on their skin or in their expressions. Mr. Verisetti looked angelic, except for the intensity of his eyes, and the gold cuff at his ear that seemed to brighten suddenly. I felt an answering electricity—the hair on my arms standing on end—in reaction.

"Don't you want to see what is in the box?"

There was something mesmerizing about his voice that circled around me, but it was only an echo of whatever spell I had been under while drawing, and I pushed it aside. My heart thumped loudly in the unnatural silence of the room. "What box?"

"The one in the painting." He motioned toward the piece I had drawn.

"That's charcoal."

"Ah, yes, the one you were about to paint."

"Right. Listen. Have the piece, if you want it." I actually didn't want him to have it. There was a part of me that said mine in a vicious voice. "School is almost over. My parents will be waiting for me outside. They'll probably be in here to get me any moment now." I tried not to concentrate on the fact that no one in the classroom had moved an inch during our entire conversation.

He laughed lightly, his attention divided between the picture and me. "Clever caterpillar. Clever butterfly." His voice had changed. It was like a long sweep of a loaded brush, curling about a canvas with never ending shades of red.

He tilted his head, looking at the ceiling. "Your father is indeed texting you right this moment to tell you not to walk home, that he will pick you up, and your mother is planning to leave from work soon. Worried and distrustful now, aren't they? It was easy enough to put traces on them, when they were connected to someone like you."

I experienced that feeling of bone-deep fear that only something exceptionally scary produced. Cold rushed down my throat and hardened in my stomach, freezing all my organs, making it hard to breathe.

My phone vibrated once in my pocket.

His smile grew.

I wondered if this was what a heart attack felt like—this non-breathing sort of heart failure. "What do you want?"

"I want you to finish your picture. You've been starving. And I've been dangling the dish of cream for weeks now instead of letting you drink. I can't be sorry, alas. Not for such delicious torment. Especially when it is all the more potent when one such as you breaks through on her own. More painful as well, but such is art." He smiled. It was lovely and terrifying at the same time.

"I don't understand." I could handle my own break from reality. But a psychotic break in a guy who outclassed me by a foot and a good hundred pounds? Not good.

"No, of course you do not." He looked back at the piece on the easel. "A little dark treasure waiting to bloom. It has been a great delight to watch you these last few weeks."

"Okay." I chanced another step backward toward the door.

"I adore ferals." His fingers lightly swept a table as he took a step closer. "Draining them dry is such a delight. All for a good cause, I assure you. And with you—double the delicious torment."

The cold in my stomach turned brittle.

"Here, in your natural element...I could simply sit for days and watch in wonder. Alas, that I have a mission far too important, because watching you...the words escape me..." His other hand went to his chest, and he bowed his head.

I took that as my cue and ran.

I was fast—I had practiced ten million passing drills with Christian, running patterns across our yard in order to make him the best. I dodged desks and chairs, hand outstretched for the door. My hand struck an invisible barrier, fingers crumpling inward toward my palm, then my shoulder, head, and hip hit an invisible wall and bounced me back as if I had run into a giant wall of clear Jell-O. The gross kind with the hard top.

I turned quickly and put up my hands. Betrayal tasted like bitter toffees.

"I can't let you leave yet. I'm sorry," he said, not looking sorry in the slightest as his mouth quirked invitingly again.

I couldn't respond. I didn't know what to say. There was some sort of force field at work behind me. Magic. A vision of electric arcs hit me, and I clutched my head as pain exploded in my skull. My newly crazed teacher was moving closer, one swaying step at a time. All of the colors and shadows around me drew into a vision of dark El Greco lightning, threatening.

He cooed like I was a small lamb. "Don't be frightened. That just won't do. And you are developing a resistance to the toffees." He reached into his

25

pocket to grab—a knife, a gun, duct tape?—and I scrambled for anything I could see. I grabbed a pair of scissors on the table and thrust them in front of me.

"Stop!"

He held his hands out. No weapon. Nothing sinister. Only pieces of pocket lint. I could have dropped the scissors, so heady was my relief, but my fingers stayed tight around the handles. My unmoving classmates sat frozen in their seats around us, eyes down.

The lint lifted and swirled and I could only watch, strangely detached, unable to move with the unnatural wall at my back, as the lint swirled and settled over me, covering and embedding small hooks into my skin like some strange glitter.

There was a pull, starting in the top layer of my skin, then the pull became a wrench that spread through my veins, my bones, diving, swirling, sucking. A pull, then a tug. I shuddered as it rippled through me. Something was being taken from me. I tried to grab whatever it was, but the feeling flitted away, swirling into the air like a reflection of the lint. A deep breath released from my lips. Then two. I shuddered, then grew still.

I looked at my shimmering arms. I felt light. Unencumbered. As if the hooks were pulling all feelings of fear—current and past—right from my flesh and dissipating them into the air.

Terror...did not exist. I could think about Christian and my emotional pain, but it was as if it was someone else's life and misery that I was observing.

"Don't you want to finish your picture, Ren?"

I did. I did want to finish my picture.

"You've hurt yourself." He touched my hand. I hadn't seen him move closer, but suddenly it didn't frighten me. "Let me help."

I looked down. There was a trickle of blood where I had cut myself on the edge of the scissors. The thin rivulet of blood trailed along a path of glitter. The pain hadn't registered. I had been too desperate for a weapon and too scared to think of anything else. Mr. Verisetti's fingers wrapped around the scissors, too.

But I wasn't scared anymore.

I squeezed my eyes shut. I wanted to finish my painting. I wanted my brother. I wanted to go home. I wanted to let go of the scissors that were still clasped in my fist. Why couldn't I release the scissors if I wasn't scared?

The ground beneath me shook.

He moved back quickly, letting me keep my grip. "Bravo, little butterfly." There was a smile in his voice, even as he kept his distance. If I wasn't scared, why did I feel relief? The shaking stilled.

"Most stubborn of you to fight the Dust." He smiled, but didn't attempt to come near me again, as if he had sudden cause to be wary. "You beat the toffees, but it will take you far too long to beat the Dust. Should you survive, I definitely will refine my tests on you. Oh, don't look at me that way. It is far better than what the Department will do to you, should they figure out what you are."

"Who are you?" My mind clinically said that I should be scared in this situation. Like a portrait missing its background—a face floating in empty space. But without the actual fear, my other emotions easily overtook conscious thought. My unchecked desires pushed into control and displayed the possibilities of what I could accomplish without fear.

He smiled, a wide mysterious smile, and the intensity in his eyes grew. "Who am I? I am no one and everyone. But don't you want to finish your piece?"

No. Yes.

No.

"Look at you fight. I ache to push the boundaries of such aggression and submission, regardless of the consequences." But he maintained his distance. He looked back to my picture and cocked his head. "But time hastens all, and for now, I think there is enough to entice you without resorting to other means. Such a hungry soul. And you were twins. Those fools should have captured you both alive."

The tube of paint was in his hand and not mine. With his finger, he smeared a swath of glittery electric blue onto the figure of the girl twin on the left. The color spread to all areas of her dress, as if absorbing the white space. The strange color was like the second paint I had mixed, but it contained an added shimmer of something. Something almost alive. A color edged in silver and gold.

"I am tempted to keep you, even though it would go against all of my plans. If you learn the pleasure of exploiting such power, though, I just might," he said as he dabbed on a bit more of the color. "On your own, I am sure you would have created something magnificent for your Awakening—perhaps destroyed the entire eastern seaboard or created a monster from the pits of hell—and I will dream of it, I will. But alas, I must guide this so that I obtain what I must have."

The figure started...dancing. Her long, white dress whirled outward from the page, flinging white smoke into swirls that appeared to leave the paper entirely. This did not seem to surprise Mr. Verisetti, and I could see his eyes following the motion. I was not alone in my craziness. Or not crazy at all.

He cocked his head, still watching the girl. "Your lavender mix was truly exceptional, and I ached to use it, but this blue is distinctly apt for what I require. A warrior's hue. My heart weeps for what might have been, should we have prolonged this experience another week." He watched the figure twirl. "I might have procured God's own sword."

The girl in the sketch tried to get the boy figure to dance with her, but he remained motionless. I wanted him to dance too. Needed it.

Golden light illuminated the edges of the girl's dress.

"Ah, yes. There you go, butterfly. Perfect," he said. He was suddenly touching my wrist, tucking a stone under my brother's leather band, securing it against my skin. "There is never a force quite as fierce as an Awakening. You possess quite a stubborn will—it amuses me—and I never let opportunities slip by."

He smiled at me as he stepped back again. "I will confess, here in this moment, that you will never remember, that I have some fondness for you. Art will always be my first love, and you, my dear, will be a dark goddess among artists. Should you survive, it will come in quite handy in the future to have learned your habits and weaknesses."

I gave a stiff, negative shake of my head.

He put a hand to his chest. "Glorious. Now, as to your other concern..." He looked to the paper, to the motionless figure of the boy. He smiled, a beautiful, edged smile. "We shall see."

Gold glinted from his ear cuff, and it felt like molten gold flowed through my limbs in response, weighting them, then bursting into brilliant gold sparks, glitter staining everything in my vision.

I followed his line of sight and everything in me suddenly focused on one thing. I wanted that boy to dance.

The girl whirled in her gold-edged dress, leaving the figure of the boy behind. She twirled closer, reaching out from the paper, and hooked her hand over my arm, pulling me inside, amidst the paint and charcoal into a world filled with—

Blackness cleared from my vision. I had...what had I been doing? I stood with heavy scissors gripped in one fist, feeling no fear at all. Just wrongness. And it felt as if I had been gripping something in both hands for a long time. My joints hurt with the effort. My wrist burned. My eyes pulled to the clock on the wall. The bell would ring in five minutes.

Five, not fifteen?

I shook my head trying to clear the lingering fog, yet I kept my grip on the scissors. Dried paint crowned every fingertip. What had I been doing? I pushed at the fog in my mind. There was a man in front of me, putting a box into his pocket and smiling at an easel.

"Even something vulnerable like a sapling or chrysalis can be extraordinary given the right purpose, butterfly."

I followed his eyes to the picture. It too was wrong. A figure of a girl stood in front of closed drapes holding a potted sapling in her hands. Patterned, circular portals shaded with a dimensional edge were the only adornment on the draperies. No box, no second figure, and no color present anywhere. Yet my fingertips were stained blue.

The man smiled, as if I had voiced my thoughts aloud.

"Who are you?" I asked.

The question was wrong. God, what...? I pushed as hard as I could against the fog.

"I am the man with the answers to all of the questions you don't even yet know to ask."

I pushed harder. Hard enough, that I felt something tear around my mind.

There was a loud boom outside, and the other students started moving again, but I couldn't look away from the man in front of me. His smile grew. "Ah, conceit, my ultimate weakness. You ripped right through and exposed me. Delicious. But far too late for them."

Tumbled blocks of memory and information re-formed into a whole, bar one smoking black spot. Mr. Verisetti held something large and dark in his hand, a wide mysterious smile curling his lips. "No time to test further. Do keep hold of that marvelous piece of art."

He dropped a wide, round, black circle to the floor. It stuck like a suction cup thrown with great force. "They'll be here in five minutes. You should really run. Or else they will take that which I have allowed you to keep—your life and magic. I left a bit in the container since you did so well." He stepped forward, one foot hovering an inch above the black circle, the other at its edge. "Do remember my generosity. Until next we meet, butterfly, I look forward to the havoc you will wreak."

He slid forward on his planted foot, not quite making a hop, not quite taking a step, and his body fell into the black hole. The edges of the black circle pulled in quickly toward center, slipping across the still completely intact tile, as if the circle had been a thin blanket covering a gaping hole, and weight was forcing the entire blanket down and pulling the rest of the earth around and above it to close the hole. Intact floor tile remained as the circle rapidly pulled to its own center, sealing itself to a point over the top of him like a pod. Mr. Verisetti disappeared into the earth without an iota of displacement.

The last bit of black circle disappeared without a sound.

Only a light scorch mark remained, as if something round had burned the tile, then been dragged, flaming, to center. I held the scissors tightly in front of me.

Chapter Two

"What is she doing now?" I heard the whispers of the students, who were moving around once again.

Your life and magic. Magic. I gripped the scissors harder.

The door of the classroom burst open, and a boy ran inside, furtively looking in all directions, then at something in his hand.

I looked back to the spot on the floor where my teacher had disappeared. I pushed against the feel of the hooks still buried in my skin. I demanded anger. I demanded terror. I demanded betrayed sorrow.

"Hey, where did Mr. Verisetti go?" another student said, craning her head. "Did she kill him too?"

"Verisetti?" The new boy said in alarm as he stopped next to me. He looked my age, but I had never seen him at school. The jacket of his tailored suit was slightly askew, his gray eyes sharp. His dark hair and silver-rimmed glasses mirrored the black and silver of his pinstripes.

He looked terrified, but squared his shoulders, held out a device and made a sweeping motion with it over the black spot, as if he were scanning the space. He kept sending quick glances between the door of the classroom and his device. None of the other students were looking at him.

It was like I was in a painting by Magritte—normal objects assembled together to form a surrealistic whole. Except, the boy next to me should be wearing a bowler, not a beret. And carrying an apple, rather than a computer tablet.

The boy's face brightened. "I knew it. I knew one could work here. Ha. Suck it, Rational Engineers' Club. The Department can suck it too."

He bent down and scraped a residue from the black scorch mark, collecting it and placing it on a violet-colored tablet device. Then he ran the device over the spot again, pushing buttons. "Three more minutes and this place will be crawling with those bastards. Come on, come on, a little more. I'm so going to win the competition this year. Record keeping first, though. What's that terrorist's full name?"

He touched beneath his ear and his eyes lit. "Oh, right."

He cleared his throat and pushed a finger to the tablet. "On this day, I, William Archenwald Tasky, report that I have found traces of portal pad technology in the First Layer. The name Verisetti was mentioned by an ordinary boy. This leads me to conclude that Raphael Immanuel Verisetti might be involved, given the criminal circumstances. Bookmark this report under Will Is Always Right."

He looked smug as he quickly tucked his tablet into an inner pocket. "Suck it."

I wanted to feel smugness too. I wanted to feel fear. I wanted to mourn the loss of my brother again. I pushed at the feel of the glittering hooks embedded in my skin.

A few tugged, gripping in a last effort before releasing. A light layer on my skin lifted free, leaving me clean and raw, where exposed. I shivered.

The particles streamed into the air, hanging there, as if seeking a new target.

Will looked up suddenly, his eyes going wide at the particles. "Dear magic." He fumbled in his jacket and pulled out the tablet, the pocket liner coming with it, sticking out in a cloth triangle.

He pushed a button, and the lint moved in a sudden burst of air straight into his tablet. He pushed another button, and his jaw dropped at whatever he saw there. "Docile Dust? This day has been the best."

Along with anger and sorrow, a sense of relief seeped through me. The last remnants of the Dust released from my skin and swooped into Will's tablet.

I rubbed my left arm and my fingers brushed rough edges. I slowly looked down to Christian's band, which was brittle at the edges and burned clear through in spots. I carefully touched the damaged leather. I felt suddenly numb. Numb in a far different way than I had under the Dust.

Will pushed something on his tablet. "Two minutes remaining."

I scrubbed my free hand over my arm, but didn't take my eyes away from the space where Mr. Verisetti had been. My delayed fear response had firmly tagged Mr. Verisetti as the most dangerous element in my current situation and put nerdy, unknown Will on the waitlist.

"Docile Dust?" I asked, a little too loudly.

"Who is she talking to?" a student whispered.

Will looked at me and blinked. "You can see me?"

"Yes?"

"Are you an expat?" He blinked at me some more, then suddenly looked cagey, eyes darting around. "Are you from the Department?" He edged away from me, then swore and looked down at his tablet. "It shows I still have a minute and a half."

He hit the edge of the device with his palm as if it was on the fritz, then turned and started walking swiftly toward the door.

"What? Expatriate from what?" I called, my feet moving after him. He had used the word magic and he clearly knew more than I did. "Do you have a Department of Death?"

"She did kill him! I knew it!"

"Crazy."

"Absolutely nuts."

The whispers were everywhere now.

My whole body tightened, the environment around me fully registering.

Before, they might have simply ignored me when I wasn't near Christian, but I had been fair game for weeks now...and had just put myself in active persecution territory. I kept a grip on the scissors and grabbed my bag, quickly stuffing everything from the easel inside. My eyes kept track of Will as he maneuvered around students without touching them and pressed buttons on his odd-colored tablet.

"Wait!" I ran after him. Everyone hurried out of my way, but no one looked at the stranger in their midst as he quickly ducked through the classroom door and started running. I picked up my pace too, pulling the sleeves of my sweater down as we headed for the front doors of the school.

"Wait!"

The bell rang to signal the end of school, and kids came streaming out of rooms chattering about an earthquake.

"Please wait!"

Will suddenly stopped and turned toward me, eyes sharp, one hand clenched in his pocket. "You aren't a Fed?"

I breathed heavily and tightened my grip on my bag. Relief and apprehension mixed. "Not last I checked, no."

His shoulders eased, and he removed his hand from his pocket, letting it hang loosely at his side. "Of course you aren't. And you aren't a terrorist." He looked at his tablet. "Come on then, we only have a minute to get clear of here."

Will put on the black beret as we exited the building. I clutched my scissors. If I found out I was being hunted by some crazy Black Ops artists' colony or a technologically advanced prostitution ring that needed art students with mental problems, I was going to go down fighting.

Will looked down at his tablet as we reached the now heavily populated sidewalk. "The rumors are so right. This Layer is rich with illegal goods."

"Layer?"

He gave me an odd glance. "Yeah. You know, five layers of the world?" He scrolled his tablet. "It says Docile Dust is only supposed to subdue and inhibit, not cause memory loss."

"You are magical."

"Yes," he said slowly, as if I was the slow one.

"How do you bring people back from the dead?"

He blinked. "You do an organ enchantment."

Painful relief slipped through me. "You know how."

He shrugged. "The basics. Resurrection experts are a dime a dozen, though, so I've never studied it." His eyebrows creased. "Wait, how old are you?"

"Seventeen. Take me to one. I'll pay you." I'd do anything. Whatever had just happened in the art classroom would be completely worth it, if I got Christian back.

"You're feral," he said as if just realizing a secret of vast import.

I yanked the scissors into a threatening position. That word had been tossed around the night Christian had died too.

Will held up his free hand. "Whoa. My family supports feral rights." His eyes went wide, and I followed his gaze to the students giving me a wide berth. They were staring at me and pulling out cell phones. No one was looking at Will.

"Put those down," Will hissed, indicating the scissors. "You aren't even close to being cloaked."

Mechanically, I shoved the scissors into my bag and swallowed as I took in the expressions on the horrified and disgusted faces around me. So this, then, was what rock bottom felt like.

I turned abruptly and started walking quickly. Maybe I could outrun the pain.

"What is he doing here?" Behind me, Will's voice was so full of astonishment, that I turned to see what had caused it.

A man dressed in pinstripes and glasses was running toward the doors of the school. He carried a clear aura of authority, even while sprinting, but no one looked at him as he passed. He reminded me of Mr. Verisetti in an indefinable way.

I balanced on the balls of my feet, ready to run. "Is that your Dad?"

Will held secrets that I wanted, but he was also a part of Mr. Verisetti's world—the world that had killed Christian.

Will looked down at his suit. "No. Pinstripes are all the rage right now," he muttered, blushing.

On the street, a black SUV shot past us, did a quick U-turn and screeched to the curb. Will immediately pushed me out of the center of the gawking crowd and into a crush of kids waiting for a bus. Everyone was looking at me, and no one was noticing the very obvious black ops vehicle or the boy with the beret who stood at my side. Three men rapidly exited the SUV.

Another man exited more slowly, menace trailing him. All of the men wore black. Black sunglasses and soulless expressions adorned their faces.

Frozen. I was frozen. Frozen physically and emotionally.

"We have to go." Will pushed me into the crowd. "Now."

"Hey, watch it!" a boy said, as I tripped over him, my body completely unresponsive.

The thin man who had exited last yelled to the others, who were striding up the walk toward the school. "Find Verisetti. Put traces on everything."

Will pulled me behind a low wall of bushes that defined the edges of the school grounds. I tripped over him, already off-balance, and my bag dumped on the ground.

I mechanically started scooping things back inside. "Who are they?" I asked woodenly. They weren't quite the same as the men who had killed Christian. Those men had seemed far more wild and far less organized, but the feeling of personal danger was the same.

Will tucked my art notebook into my bag, then grabbed the sketch while craning his head around. "Department spooks. Bad news. Just stay here until we can make a break for it." He held out the sketch to me.

The tips of my paint-stained fingerpads curled around the paper, touching the girl's dress within. The paint seeped from my fingers into the sketch. The girl in the picture began swaying. She smiled, set the sapling down, and began pulling the shaded white drape on the right slowly to the side, exposing darkness in the middle of the sketch.

"What is she doing?" Will scooted closer, pulling the paper back out of my grip in order to examine it. "I didn't realize you were an art mage."

Anxiety seeped through my wooden state as I watched him. Alarm gripped me. "Let go of that."

"Okay." His fingers loosened, but a charcoaled hand reached out from the sketch and gripped his forearm. Will's eyes widened, and he finally released the paper fully, but it was far too late. The hand yanked back into the paper, taking Will's arm with it. His whole body followed, just sucking, absorbing, him in. Schwoop. Right down to his strange black shoes.

Gone, like everyone in my life.

The freed sheet of paper caught a breeze and gently drifted to the sidewalk. I stared blankly as it finally came to rest a few feet away. A student stepped on it, issued a quick apology, picked it up, and handed it to me.

I blindly took it. People were passing by, pointing and giving me wary glances. Me. Not my hands which held the paper that had just sucked someone inside.

I gripped the paper without looking down. Perhaps it would suck me inside too. Make me disappear completely as well.

I finally looked down. There was a different figure in the sketch now. The girl in the white dress with the sapling was gone, but a male figure, drawn in broad, harsh strokes, looked pretty freaked out as he dashed around, banging into the sides of the sketch.

I lunged forward and grabbed a sophomore passing on the walk, then held the sheet in front of his face. "Excuse me. Could you tell me what you see?"

The sophomore looked scared. "A guy and some curtains."

"Is the guy doing anything?"

"Doing anything?"

"Do you see him moving?"

The kid backed up, then bolted.

I looked back down at the lone figure in the sketch—complete with a little beret—his hands splayed out against the paper, facing me, banging his palms as if against a two-way looking glass. His features were slowly turning from harsh strokes to the more refined ones of Will.

I tentatively reached out a finger to touch his hand.

"Ren!"

My head snapped up, and I saw Dad's car at the curb. He was leaning into the passenger seat and waving to me through the open window, just like he had done for weeks now—leaving work early so that the three of us could awkwardly sit together—broken—for early dinners during "happy time" when the October sun was only just starting to set. As if the dark wasn't more comforting now.

I looked back down at the sketch. Will looked completely freaked out. I looked back to the black SUV where the thin man stood with his arms crossed, eyes narrowed on the school entrance. I hurried to Dad's car.

"You didn't text back," he said as I scooted inside. "I didn't know if you had decided to start walking. Good thing you didn't," he said in a too-hardy, joking manner. "Weather events are getting crazy again."

I hunched down, casting a quick glance behind my seat and through the rear window. "Sorry. Lost track of time."

"What have you got there?" he asked.

He reached for the sketch, and I couldn't contain my yell. "Don't touch it!"

He pulled his hand back, shocked.

I swallowed again, pulling it completely out of his reach. "It's done in charcoal. It will dirty up your nice shirt."

"You trying to say your old dad is afraid of a little dirt?" His smile did nothing to lighten the dark circles under his eyes.

"No, course not." They were going to pressure me again to take those drugs—I could see the intent forming in his expression. "Let's go home." I took a deep breath and dredged up a smile.

But the car stayed in park and he examined the drawing I had plastered against the door—as far as I could get it away from him without turning it face out and risking it swallowing the car with us inside—and nodded sagely while tapping a finger to his lips. "The transcendental aspect of the curvature of your lines is a sterling representation of the Circle Movement. Startling. Brilliant."

"Dad. Let's go."

"What? Are you going to tell me there has never been a Circle Movement? Should I have commented on the symbolism of your hat choice instead?"

"I really want to go home. Now. Please."

"Okay, okay." The lines around his mouth tightened, but he checked his mirrors and shifted into gear.

I watched through the side mirror as we pulled away. The thin man was scanning the grounds. Fifty yards away, his eyes seemed to lock onto mine through the mirrored glass.

We turned the corner.

The tightness in my chest was overly constricting as I watched Will look over his shoulder to the dark sliver exposed by the slightly ajar drape. "Do you see anything wrong or weird about this picture?"

"Aside from the beret? No?"

The word came out more as a question, and as if it wasn't the picture that he was trying to decide was wrong and weird.

I looked to the side mirror. No strange cars seemed to be following behind.

Will's mouth pinched tight as he shifted sideways to keep both of us and the sliver between the drapes in view. He was watching the slivered opening in an increasingly wary manner. Had I conjured up some freaky nightmarish daydream about Mr. Verisetti? Had everything from the time I had entered the art classroom until the time my sketch fell to the ground been a vivid, complicated imagining? Were the lingering traces of such a dream still on me?

Check her wrist.

The memory of the words made me look down. Christian's band was half destroyed on one wrist. And on the other, strange henna brown pointillist dots now formed what looked suspiciously like the sapling that had disappeared in the sketch.

I thought about balling up the paper. About taking the therapy drugs. Letting them make me forget everything.

I pressed my knuckles to my forehead trying to push against the ache growing there. I was breathing too hard; my Dad was going to stop the car any second.

"What do you say we stop for some fries on the way?" Dad said as he changed lanes. "Your mom is making something healthy again."

We were away from the school. No one seemed to be following us. I nodded, focusing my gaze on the sketch again. There was something moving behind the drapes. And there was a boy trapped in front of them.

Even if this was all the crazy in my head finally manifesting, maybe my brain was telling me how to release my fear of another person dying. Or was allowing me to save someone and feel redeemed. I closed my eyes. If I saved Will, maybe I'd gain some unpronounceable psychotherapy resolution.

Dad pulled into the drive-thru, trying to make jokes about Mom's reaction as he ordered three large fries.

I desperately wished for my brother. He would understand. Be able to help. My parents thought me unhinged with my tales of Christian's death.

I had no one. I was on my own.

We finally reached home, and I exited, gripping the sketch, watching as Will repeatedly checked his pockets with his finely drawn charcoal hands, pulling things out and stuffing them back in.

"Roger, that had better not be French fries I smell!" But Mom's joke came out all wrong. High and stringy. I'd bet the Picasso original I would someday own, that someone from school had already called her about either my behavior in art or on the sidewalk.

"Too bad!" Dad's lighthearted reply was equally tight, as he shrugged out of his suit jacket. I clutched the sketch to my chest and stared up the darkened staircase toward my bedroom.

"Sweetie." Mom appeared in my peripheral view and her hand went to my forehead. "You look feverish. Are you well? Should I call the doctor?"

Or the therapist.

Dad appeared next to her, dark circles deepening. "I thought you were just in your zone thinking about your artwork."

Hoping. He had been hoping I was just in my zone. And not dwelling on our missing fourth.

"Are you unwell? What is wrong, Ren?"

I loved my parents. Our family had been an awesome foursome. But now we were a very awkward threesome. They vacillated between holding on to me too tightly and trying to give me space. Holding on too tightly and pushing me away. Holding on too tightly and looking at me with ill-concealed censure.

"Nothing." I had to clear my throat to get the whole word out. "I'm fine. Just tired. Everything will be fine."

Will had confirmed that there was a way to bring someone back from the dead. Hope swelled painfully in my chest that my words were true. I repeated them as a promise.

"Everything will be fine."

Chapter Three

FINDING THE RABBIT HOLE

I STEPPED INTO MY ROOM and closed the door, my stomach grumbling over the abusive way in which I had just shoved my dinner into it. I stood in the darkness for a moment, before flicking on the lights. My carefully wrought walls greeted me, overwhelming and crowding me, instead of providing the haven I desperately needed. I concentrated on the section directly across from the door and took a deep breath. The figures, creatures, and odd shapes remained stationary.

Half of the north wall had been completed during my Picasso cubist period, the other half during my obsession with pointillism and Signac. The transition between those two was...interesting. Demanding that the eye blend color versus elements. Christian had deemed me mad.

I wondered if his statement hadn't been a little true.

The other three walls and portions of the ceiling were a testament to other periods, some short, some longer. Impressionism, Renaissance, Baroque, Surrealism, Art Deco, Pop, Minimalism, Modernism. I looked to my latest period that covered the door to my closet. It was different from the others. It looked more like the designs on the draperies in the sketch— black-and-white patterned circle portals and paths, shaded to create a three-dimensional edge. As if I could enter to find Christian down one of those tunnels. The entrances to Heaven and Hell inside of my room and life.

I looked toward my nightstand and the photo of the two of us that rested on top. I curled my fingers into a fist, then loosened them one digit at a time. I could feel the energy in my skin hum.

I took another deep breath, sat, and unrolled the sketch, clipping the paper to my tabletop easel. Will was crouched defensively in the corner furthest from the slivered opening between the drapes. As soon as he saw me, he jumped up and made large motions with his limbs. The beret was off and stuffed in a back pocket, his dark hair was disheveled, and there was a large tear in the right pinstriped sleeve of his jacket. That hadn't been there earlier. He had been immaculate.

"Are you real?" I couldn't help but whisper.

He replied—a long string of words that were completely silent, but I got the gist through his motions.

"Okay, okay, you are real. And, er, I'm thinking you want out of there?"

Will started pantomiming and doing charades, motioning to me to draw something on the paper.

I looked at the painted walls around my room. Nothing moved there. Okay. I could do this.

He pointed to the tear in his sleeve, then gave me the sign to hurry up. I picked up a pencil, reached forward, and sketched a needle and some thread.

Will looked at me with an expression I could only catalog as contempt bordering on hysteria. He then reached forward, and with his shirtsleeve, wiped clear the lines I had drawn. Unnerved, I set my pencil down.

He motioned to my bag. I glanced down to see the charcoal there. I picked up the thinner of the two pieces—the charcoal pencil. It felt odd in my hand, just as its chunkier counterpart had. Perhaps there was a reason for that.

I re-drew the needle and thread with the thin charcoal. One second after I finished, the lines lightened to a dark gray and fell to the ground at Will's feet. There was a gravity field inside my drawing?

Sure. Why not?

Will didn't even bother to look down, so obvious was his distress. He crossed his arms, causing the rip in his sleeve to grow. He seemed to be taking deep breaths. Finally, he poked a finger at the charcoal pencil, then thrust a finger at his own chest.

I poked him with the pencil. The action forced him back a step, his midsection burrowing in with the poke. The drapes rippled behind him, as though the motions had produced a breeze, and the shaded circles drawn on them slowly rotated, as if they were pinwheels affected by the same wind. His eyes widened, and he backed away from the nearest circle.

I blinked, then touched the needle and thread bundle with the pencil tip and focused on moving them. They inched jerkily to the side, the motion becoming smoother as my motions became surer. The charcoal left only a faint trace of gray, and within a few seconds, the farthest point of the line began to disappear, creeping along the rest of the line toward my implement, as if I was drawing with water. I lifted my pencil and the disappearing line caught up and evaporated completely.

I looked at the end of my pencil, then back at the sketch. Will was wide-eyed as well. He pulled out his tablet, pushed a button, looked frustrated, and shoved it back into his pinstriped jacket.

He pointed at my pencil, then pointed at himself with one hand, while the other mimicked writing.

"Oh." I drew him a pencil. As the tip of my charcoal lifted from the paper, the drawn pencil turned a lighter hue and began to fall inside the page. Will caught it before it hit the sketched floor.

He immediately wrote "uoyeraohw" on the invisible wall between us.

I tried to pronounce it. "Uoyeraohw. Hawaiian?"

He crossed out the letters, cheeks turning a shaded gray in embarrassment, then in a very stilted way wrote, "Who are you?" in the other direction, though, the "r" was still backward.

"Ah." Two way glass. Right. "Write normally. I can read backwards, now that I know what to expect." I nervously ran a hand through my hair. "I'm Ren."

"Ren, you okay?" I jumped, but then realized the voice had come through my bedroom door.

"Uh...just video chatting, Dad."

"Okay." Feet moved down the hall. It was a testament to how much they wanted to believe I had someone to video chat with.

I examined the drapes for a moment, then nudged the panel on the right so that it overlapped the other. Immediately, some of the tension released from Will, though he still cast it a narrowed glance. He started writing again.

I'm Will. Did you create this drawing?

"Yes." I bit my lip. "I think so." It hadn't looked at all like this before Mr. Verisetti had interrupted me. But all of the lines had been styled as if by my hand.

Can you remove me, please?

I reached toward the drawing, ready to be sucked inside, but my fingers crumpled into my palm as they hit a solid surface.

Will's shoulders drooped. Then he looked up sharply, motioning to my charcoal, then at the space next to him. I put the tip in the spot indicated. Will tried to grab hold of the pencil, but his hands slid right off, as if there were a thin layer of slick liquid on the charcoal.

Will peered at my fingers, then lifted his pencil to write.

Paint?

I rifled through my bag, but the tube of paint from the classroom wasn't inside. I bit my lip. The tube must have fallen out with the rest of my things. I hadn't paid attention to anything else after Will had been sucked into the sketch. I grabbed for a tube of Cadmium Red. No, too much like blood. I picked up yellow instead. But when I set it to the page, the color slid off like I was painting on wax paper.

Unnerved, I wiped the yellow from my desk with a tissue.

Where is the blue stuff?

"I think it fell out of my bag," I said softly.

Will's shoulders drooped again. He tried to write something, but the paper wasn't all that large, and his writing had filled the wall between us.

I drew an eraser—a really large one. He gamely began erasing.

I chewed on the end of the charcoal pencil and gagged. I wiped my tongue on the back of my hand, then sorted through my messy desk until I found a large plastic top. Christian had bought them for me years ago.

I stared at the top for a moment, then put it on and slowly started chewing the plastic. I drew a square table and straight chair for Will to use. A little moon and three stars took shape on the white wall to the left side of the closed drapes as I doodled absently. "How did your sleeve get slashed?"

Are you sure the paint isn't in your bag? Please concentrate.

I hated being told to concentrate when I was doodling—as if I wasn't actually thinking. The moon brightened on the page.

"I'm sure. What is behind the drapes?" Looking at them made me anxious. "Do you know?"

No. You are the creator of this world. Don't you know?

"No." My voice fell to a whisper. Not knowing, deeply upset me. I took my memory for granted. I remembered every image I had ever seen. Why then could I not remember my own drawing...?

The stars began twinkling.

He crossed his arms, frowning off to the side.

Yeah, join the club. I hated me too.

One of the twinkling stars hardened, then shot toward Will. I pinned it automatically with my pencil, my reflexes saving him. Will overturned the table and ducked behind it, narrowly avoiding the other two. The crescent moon, however, had other ideas, and winged its way like a boomerang around the table. I quickly pulled down the star I was holding so it fell to the sketch floor and put the tip of my pencil in the path of the boomerang, spinning it around. It rotated and whacked into the sketch wall.

Mouth agape, I stared, pencil still pressed to the page. Will peered over the edge of the table, gave me a wide-eyed look, then righted the table. He removed the stars embedded in the tabletop and examined them.

"Sorry," I whispered.

He shook his head and wrote, What you feel makes a difference in here. I can feel the change. Like a weather mage manipulating winds—focus and intent are a large part of magic.

With my pencil pressed to the page, as he wrote the words, the letters rearranged themselves so that they were written forward for me.

Focus and intent.

I rubbed the back of my neck. Will could feel the change? Was that why he had been frowning? Because he had felt a change in the air?

Since Christian's death, I had become so used to people being disappointed in me, that I interpreted everyone's emotions as dislike now. Depressing.

The circles on the drapes began rotating. I quickly blanked my thoughts, and they stopped. I needed to...change my attitude.

"I need to figure out how things work in there. Are you hungry?" I had scarfed down dinner in five minutes flat, then quickly excused myself, saying I was going to study in my room for the rest of the night, but Will hadn't had anything to eat.

Will looked depressed as he wrote. Yes. Thirsty too.

Not good. I had never been great at those pet games where you had to electronically keep them alive. They always took time away from drawing or from helping Christian by passing footballs or deriving equations together.

"Request?"

Chicken. Simple. Cooked. Focus. Concentrate!

The last was underlined twice.

I tried to concentrate very hard as I drew a chicken breast and glass of water. I could almost taste the chicken and feel the cool water on the back of my tongue as I drew. But I forgot to draw a plate, so the chicken just sort of thumped down on the table.

"Er, sorry." I quickly drew a plate, knife, and fork so that I didn't have to see his expression.

Will's first bite was tentative, but then he began eating in earnest, nodding appreciatively.

I sat back, relieved.

Relieved, until a giant spiked tentacle—like a long, flexible branch of a demonic tree—slithered through the drapes, opening them a crack, and wrapped around the chicken and table, crushing it all and dragging it away. I stared, mouth agape. Three more tentacles shot through, one toward Will and two toward me, denting the page outward. I thrust away from my desk and fell back in my chair, hitting the floor hard and breaking the charcoal pencil in two. I grabbed the exposed half-piece and scrambled up. Will was using his knife and fork to ward off tentacle one, but the other two were slithering around him menacingly.

"Ren, are you okay ?" Mom yelled.

"Fine," I shouted at the door, trying to block the tentacles with my charcoal tip, while hunching over my desk. It was a lot harder fighting the tentacles than fighting the stars and moon had been. This new threat seemed outside my control.

"Are you sure?"

An especially malevolent-looking tentacle, armed with a spike at its tip, lunged toward Will, who dove to the side. I hurriedly drew a messy rectangular shield in front of him. The creature's spike dented the shield, then hurtled it's spike at it again.

"Yes, Mom!"

I tried to layer shields around Will, boxing him in and the tentacles out. One slipped through.

"It sounded like you fell." Mom's voice was closer now.

Red splattered the black-and-white page. Will let out a silent scream that echoed deep within me. God, I couldn't let someone else die. I scribbled a wall between Will and the branch tentacles, shading the wall quickly with my bare fingers.

"Ren?"

A tentacle slithered over the top.

"No! No, Mom!" I threw it off the wall with my pencil tip and quickly drew and shaded a higher wall. I nearly sobbed. Why hadn't I thought of creating the wall first? I frantically tried to bandage Will as the tentacles continued to batter the wall. "I'm fine!"

Will was leaning weakly against the wall and there was blood dripping to the floor from beneath my poorly applied bandage. I drew him a sword, far too late. And a medical kit. I concentrated very hard on what would be in one as I drew it.

"Are you sure?"

I swallowed my sob. I had had practice. "I'm sure! I just saw something awful on the Internet."

One of the tentacles battered its way through.

"Can I get you anything?"

I sliced through the tentacle with my pencil. Black spewed from both ends. Like hissing snakes, the other two rose in outrage, then lunged toward me. They batted against the barrier between us, denting out the paper.

I furiously sliced them. My eye caught on the needle and thread lying in the other corner. I sliced off the tentacles at the barrier of the drapes and quickly sewed the edges together with haphazard penciled stitches. The now-single drape rippled, as something blasted against it from the other side.

I concentrated on retracing the stitches and closing all gaps completely.

Chapter Three

The single drape went suddenly still.

"Ren?"

Shaking, I stared at the wreckage inside the picture—broken table pieces and shields, sliced tentacle chunks, puddles of blood—and tried to remember what she'd asked me. "No. No, I don't need anything. I'm fine, Mom. I'll be out in a minute," I called, my voice a little high.

"Okay." She sounded uncertain.

My fingers were cramping and stained with black, and I realized I was panting.

Will was shakily trying to open the medical kit. I held my free hand over my mouth and drew an already opened one.

"Your dad is asking me to make a run for ice cream. Sound good?"

That meant she had heard the half-sob. "Yes. Please." I watched Will sort through the supplies. I drew a bowl of water and some sterile cloths, then fixed the broken arm on his glasses.

"Okay, I'll be back in fifteen minutes, sweetie."

"Okay." She had to hate the closed door. I blinked back tears. Get yourself together, Ren.

I righted my chair with shaking fingers. "Are you okay?" I could barely whisper it to Will, as I heard Mom's footsteps reluctantly walk away. Will had sorted himself out quickly. I had a feeling that danger wasn't new to him, but being helpless was. His injured left arm was now supported in a sling.

He looked at me in a resigned sort of way, then found his pencil and wrote, Yes.

I couldn't stand the silence anymore. I reached down and drew a megaphone. Will's face was blank for a moment, then his expression brightened and he picked it up. "Good thinki—"

I slammed my charcoal-covered hand over him as his voice yelled into the loud speaker.

Words emerged in an incensed muffle. Footsteps creaked downstairs but didn't stop.

"Sorry," I whispered.

"It is doubtful anyone ordinary can hear me," he said in a moderately loud monotone. "But you can try and fix the level."

Electricity was running through me, making me sharper. I connected the megaphone to his lips, funneling the tube down drastically, hoping that would lower the volume. Then I flicked the megaphone away with my smudged fingers. Will rubbed his mouth, but when his voice emerged, it was a normal volume and he didn't need the megaphone to speak.

"Well..." He looked himself over, tweaking his sling. "This both sucks and is also the most exciting thing that has happened to me in weeks. The research potential is astounding. I wish I could take notes." He looked longingly at his tablet, before shoving it back into his inside pocket. "I'm definitely taking an art magic class as soon as I return to school."

"You go to a school that teaches magic?" I kept my voice low. If overheard, my parents would assume I was still video chatting, but I didn't want them to hear my actual words.

"Of course."

"Do they teach you how to resurrect people?"

He looked at me strangely. "Medical majors definitely learn. Hey, can you draw some ibuprofen?"

He swallowed the tablets I drew, then asked for a few more supplies, and even though I had to search the Internet, I very carefully drew everything he requested and kept my thoughts focused. My desire for the items to function seemed to go a long way for them to function properly within the sketch world.

I felt incredibly guilty and responsible. "Um, are you still hungry?"

"No," he said decisively.

"Right." I laughed uneasily and collected the smaller piece of the charcoal pencil from the floor, shakily removing the plastic chew cap from the top and sticking it on the other piece. The tip was getting dull, so I sharpened it while trying to pull my thoughts together.

I couldn't keep my eyes away from the bloodstains that had dried to a brown crimson—the only color in the sketch.

I rubbed my free fingers together and forced my gaze to my walls. Dungeons, dragons, magic, and mayhem were included in all stylistic forms. Christian had particularly loved anything pertaining to swords and sorcery, so I had included them in everything. He had been so confident that he had roped in everyone around us—even those who had thought it uncool—to liking the magical. He had been the storyteller. The voice that could lead anyone. Ruling the world with a scepter in hand.

"Witches and wizards, sorcerers and sorceresses," I whispered.

I thought of Mr. Verisetti's prints in the art room—of the boy reaching to the heavens, and the girl reanimating the dead. My gaze moved to the photo of my brother and me on my nightstand. Our arms were slung around each other's shoulders.

"We prefer mage, actually, as it represents both sexes equally." Will was cleaning up the space, moving debris into a corner with his good arm.

"Oh. I like that. Mages, then." I attempted to help, but none of my many erasers worked. And Will's eraser inside the sketch was equally ineffective. It seemed that if I drew it, it was permanent. I tried to focus on deleting things through "magic," but that didn't work either. The piece seemed creation specific.

But what had happened to the items removed by the tentacles?

"Maybe I need to buy a magical eraser?"

He shrugged, but nodded. "Could be."

I suggested lifting the drape and shoving everything behind it, but Will wasn't willing to chance opening them even a little. As I moved everything to the corners, he started fashioning weapons by taking broken table legs and making clubs. The sword I had drawn for him was tucked in his belt, close to his side. He kept touching it.

Will picked up his beret, looked it over carefully, and dusted it off.

I chewed on my pencil top. "What's with the beret?"

He looked chagrined for a moment. "It was the only garment in the cloaking closet at the checkpoint."

I couldn't stop a smile. "Seriously?"

"It took a lot of wheedling to obtain it, so I can't really complain. The ironic thing is that I had to argue for it legally. People think this layer of the world is generally magic free, but today just proves how many illegal items are here." He shrugged. "As long as the hat is on me somewhere, it hides me from ordinary sight, and initially, that is what mattered in this foray."

He tucked the beret into his back pocket again and withdrew a black trivet from his jacket. It appeared identical to the one that Mr. Versetti had used. Will threw it on the ground and tossed a piece of wood at it. He looked frustrated when the wood bounced off.

I shifted uncomfortably, feeling cold. "What is that?"

"Portal pad. Probably better that it doesn't work in here. Should something go wrong, it's doubtful you could get me to a qualified mage in resurrection time."

"What is resurrection time?" The words were almost incomprehensible; I said them so quickly.

"Ten minutes post death is allotted for resurrection. Not enough time for the soul to separate." He looked, considering. "Akin to someone being paddle-shocked on an operating room table here."

I leaned forward. "Allotted? But can a person be resurrected later?"

"Necromancy is considered a black art."

That wasn't a no.

"Ren?" My Mom's voice jolted me from the conversation.

"Coming!" I checked the defense measures I had put in place for Will. They were solid. I hurried to the door, cracking it open. "Yes?"

Mom tried to peer behind me. "Ice cream?" She held up the cup.

"Great! Thanks!" I took it, shut the door, then hurried back to my desk.

"Ren?" she said through the door.

"I'm doing great, Mom!" I was doing pretty well, actually. I was going to get Will out of there, and he was going to take me to a necromancer.

I set the ice cream to the side and focused on the drawing. "So, let's get you out of there."

"Great." Will gathered up a few things around him and leaned forward. "I'm ready."

Ten minutes later as flowers kept blooming beneath his feet wherever he walked, he looked less enthused. "You have no idea what you are doing."

I chewed on my pencil top. "Nope. I'm going to make it so you can do magic. Maybe then you can get yourself out."

He perked up. "Great!"

Twenty minutes later as cheerful pixies circled his head and lightning bolts alternately flashed from his new "orb," he stared at me in a manner that said I was dead to him.

"Does Mr. Verisetti's magic work like yours?" A shudder went through me, and it took me a moment to realize it was the first time I had said his name outside of school. I had always followed my urge to call him Mr. V when I left the school grounds. Come to think of it, I had never heard him called Verisetti outside of school...ever. That freaked me out a bit.

"Raphael Verisetti is a mage, if that is what you mean. An extremely dangerous one. Smack on the top of the ten most wanted list. Speaking of which... Why do you know him?"

Will asked the question with concern, but his gaze wasn't judgmental.

Fierce warmth rushed through me.

But I didn't want to think of Mr. Verisetti. Betrayal was still toffee-sharp on my tongue. "I don't know him." Anything I had thought of him as a mentor and friend had been a lie. "Maybe I could give you a magic glove that channels your magic."

I thought long and hard, then drew one to fit his hand. He pointed it at the pixies, which gasped in shock, then grabbed the orb and flew toward the drapes, sobbing. Will looked chagrined. The pixies disappeared into one of the three-dimensional drawn circles on the drapes, then the glove flew from Will's fingers, raced toward the same circle, and disappeared within. We stared at the circle, then at each other.

"Should I draw another?"

He considered it. "Not now, though I might make one when I get out of here. Magical gloves are a commodity begging to be improved upon. But it only worked on the things that you had just created while thinking about how magic might work. It didn't work on the other stuff." He pointed at the debris around him and hugged his sword closer. "Maybe we can attach your intent to the base creations of this world, though."

"Okay."

He pointed to my closet door. "You really haven't been to the magic world before?" At my negative response he looked bemused. "That looks a lot like the transport system in the main depot."

I looked at my door—at the winding black-and-white tubes and tunnels funneling around and through each other.

Will held up his black trivet. "Portal pads are just one of the ways that we travel. They only work in the Second and Third Layers of the world. Well, until today when one worked here in the First." He waved a hand at my unspoken questions about layers. "Another time. Let me tell you about portal pads."

He leaned forward, eager to proceed. I could recognize a fellow nerd, and knew he was about to embark upon a five thousand-word explanation.

He seemed to read my reaction correctly, as he suddenly blushed. "Okay, let me sum up."

I smiled—another time I would be interested in the full dissertation. As he described how portal pads worked, I drew a copy of his portal pad trivet on a separate piece of paper, under his supervision. Since I had seen Mr. Verisetti use one, I followed the explanation well enough.

"Magic is all about using the four cornerstones to produce solid results: intent, focus, knowledge, confidence. Send something through the portal while willing it to reappear."

I drew a feather and let it drop onto the trivet pad. The pad sucked over the top, enveloping it, then it disappeared into the floor of the paper. I blinked. A moment later a black circle appeared on the ceiling and the feather fluttered down and out. The trivet made a suction noise, detaching from the ceiling, and plopping to the bottom of the sketch.

"Yes!" Will's hands were against the barrier of the sketch between us, expression enraptured as I drew. "I can't believe it worked the first time. I wish I could make notes. Where did it go? Did you just let your subconscious magic will it through? Or did you have the feather cease to exist before you willed it to exist again? Or did you create a pocket of space in the sketch using the fibers of the paper, like an insane Origin Mage might? Or was it something else entirely? I need to study art magic more. Send a gopher through, then tell me what you were thinking."

I blinked at Will, but gamely drew a gopher. The gopher sniffed at the trivet, then looked out at me as if to say, no way. It toddled off the screen. Concerning.

Christian would tell me I needed to draw a gopher with more gumption.

And maybe it needed to jump and not just step onto the pad. What if only half of its body made it in?

I drew a little platform above the trivet, then drew a tiny nose-twitching gopher with little stubby legs, and a big belly on a tiny frame. He looked ready to go, but I strapped a hat with earmuffs and a chin strap on him, just in case, then doodled a pair of goggles over his eyes. I accidentally wedged the edge of a goggle into a socket, and a paw reached up and nudged it into place.

The gopher gave a salute then shuffled out onto the platform on his back legs. I halted him with my pencil tip and drew some shoes. He tucked his gopher paws against his sides, then gave three little grunts as if he were counting.

"Aiyeeee!"

He jumped into the air and plummeted straight down, shod feet out, like a scuba diver jumping off a bridge. The trivet dented down into the floor of the sketch, sucking the gopher halfway in. His little gopher belly-roll pushed up over the edge for a moment. He sat there, suspended, then he was sucked down as the trivet swallowed him whole. The trivet closed over the top of him, then disappeared into the white of the floor.

I waited with dread for a choked little gopher squeal, but there was only the steady hum of Will murmuring, "Awesome," over and over. A gopher had just disappeared into a sketched oven mat and the only thing to mark the event was a small burn mark in the white floor of the sketch.

The seconds ticked down as the time that the feather had appeared came and went. Then suddenly the ceiling pad appeared and so did the gopher, falling through the air. I caught him with the tip of my pencil and lowered him slowly to the sketched ground. The gopher raised his arms in triumph. Just like Christian after completing a touchdown pass, but with far stubbier limbs.

"Yes!" Will said. "Okay, draw a pad in here."

But the pad cracked and shattered in Will's sketch. Will blinked at it. "Ooookay. Try again?"

Five more attempts yielded the same result. None of my sketched portal pads worked in Will's world. After some serious discussion with Will about alternate forms of travel, I tried doors, tethers, rips, windows, mirrors, and keyholes. All of the lines would crack and break as soon as I formed the intent to release Will from his prison.

On the other hand, since I tried each mode of transport in the practice sketch first, gophers were dropping, diving, squeezing, and sucking through portals and gateways in their created world like small mad beasts. Little "Aiyeee!" yells punctuated the air.

I tried to change my emotion. The gopher sketch turned into a serious, marching battle formation. I then thought happy thoughts and flowers bloomed and the rodents did a series of can-can style kicks, before pirouetting and leaping into portals.

Next, Will suggested drawing gates, water pools, tubes, pipes, and pockets. Gophers swam and slid. But as long as my intent was to port Will out of his sketch, nothing stayed whole on his paper long enough for a field trial. Will swept the last of the broken charcoal lines into the now-towering pile of trash in the corner.

He became more energized and excited the more we failed. As if the entire process was the best thing that had happened to him—excluding the imminent death part.

"Back to materials," he said. "That blue paint. Energy in, energy out. Paint in, paint out. Some magic only works to the reverse of what was put into it." He looked at me expectantly. "We need to retrieve that tube of paint that got dropped."

I didn't want to go back to school.

Will's expression was full of hope. I looked down at my hands. "My parents installed an alarm system downstairs a few weeks ago."

They hadn't even been able to look me in the eye the day it had been installed—weeks too late in their minds. I looked up to see Will's hopeful expression disappear.

"I..." I swallowed, then shook my head, unable to look at him.

I flicked off my light and took a deep breath, then crept to my door and opened it a crack. A broom was propped next to my door. Mom had been cleaning again. She didn't even put the supplies away anymore, knowing she'd just start scrubbing everything she could reach again the next day.

I could hear her sobbing in their room even though the volume on their TV was almost loud enough to drown out the sounds. I slumped against the doorjamb, head resting uncomfortably against the wood, listening to my strong mother cry herself to sleep.

As the sounds grew weaker, I closed my door softly and walked unsteadily back to my desk. "We'll go in thirty minutes," I said quietly.

Chapter Four

UNWISE ACTIONS

THIRTY MINUTES, a sheet protector, and some safety pins later, Will and his sketch were attached to the front of my black hoodie, and I was slowly removing the screen from my non-alarmed second-story window.

I tightened the straps on my slim black backpack. It would allow me to move quickly and avoid getting stuck going in and out through the window. The porch roof was a few feet to the side of my window and about five feet lower—an oversight in my parent's alarm installation. Using a chair to balance my arms in a strange push-up, I stuck my legs backward through the window, then pushed out and lowered myself down. I could hear Will swear as the protected paper crumpled a bit when my chest moved over the frame. I dangled for a moment, holding on by my fingertips, then swung my legs over to the porch. As soon as one black moccasin touched, I went with the motion, pushing upright.

Getting back inside the house would require a leap and some extra arm strength, but I'd worry about that later.

I took in a deep breath as I stood on top of the porch and looked out into the dark, silent night. It wasn't the first time I had been out past curfew. Over the years, I had accompanied Christian on everything from post-midnight capture-the-flag battles to TP'ing houses. But I had never been on a mission without him.

"You still with me?" Will asked, voice muffled by the sheet protector. We had debated the merits of puncturing the sketch with a pin and had decided attaching pins through the holes of a sheet protector was the better alternative, even though the barrier muffled Will's voice.

I took another deep breath and held up my thumb in front of the sketch on my chest to wordlessly communicate a positive status, then made my way slowly to the edge where I'd have to jump down to the deck.

My moccasins made no sound as I landed. First mission accomplished, I put up my hood, tightened the straps on my pack an inch more, then took off into the night.

"You live in a creepy neighborhood," Will said as I jogged along the wooded path behind our house.

I hesitated, then held up a thumb in front of the sketch again. The rest of my hand was wrapped around my closed utility knife. The trees had never seemed creepy before the night we'd been attacked. Now shadows jumped and parted everywhere.

It was a fifteen-minute walk to school. Jogging, I made it in eight, with one hand wrapped around my can of pepper spray and the other around my knife.

The sidewalks in front of the school were brightly lit, which threw darker shadows farther out. The wall of bushes Will and I had stumbled behind was not near a light. My gaze darted in every direction as I quickly made my way toward the shrubbery. I crouched down with the bushes at my back, the sound of my short, quick breaths filling my ears.

"Ren?" Will asked, his voice concerned.

I gave Will a wordless thumbs-up. Pull it together, Ren. Reaching back, I withdrew my flashlight from the open side pocket of my pack.

With my flashlight stuffed between my ear and shoulder, I rummaged under the bushes. Sitting between a familiar brown hair clip and ballpoint pen, was a plain white tube of paint with a blue smudge around the lip of the cap. It shone brightly beneath a gnarled branch.

My fingers clumsily closed around it.

"Yes," Will crowed. I could almost hear him dancing about. "Let's get out of here."

I pulled my small backpack off of one shoulder and unzipped it. I nudged the charcoal pencil aside and heard it tap against Christian's lock pick set in the bottom of the bag—mine had been confiscated by my parents in the hospital while I had been comatose. Luckily, since they hadn't known we'd had one set, they hadn't known we'd had two. I dropped the tube in along with my other forgotten items and moved the gopher sketch so that I could zip the bag back up. The gophers were still zipping and zooming about.

"You. Hold it."

I jumped at the sudden voice and the heavy Scottish accent. A large man, dressed in black was quickly advancing down the sidewalk toward me. His brows were furrowed as he looked down at some sort of scanning device in his hand.

A device just like the one Christian's killer had held. I crouched, frozen, staring at it.

"Run," Will yelled.

The man reacted to Will's muffled shout, narrowed his eyes, and pointed the scanner at me. A light shot from the sketch on my chest and impacted the man's scanner, sending it flying through the air. I scrambled backward and the gopher paper fell to the grass. The Scottish man didn't waste any time going after his scanner, though, and he threw something in his hand at me instead. I dove to the side, rolling with the motion, and came up behind a tree.

Like playing paintball—except there was no Christian to flash signs to, telling him the best field positions. And, again, the enemy wasn't throwing paint.

A bolt of green shot past and a chunk of the tree three feet to my left exploded. At the point of impact, a net stretched nearly invisible tendrils through the air, then slowly collapsed to the ground when they found nothing but wood chips in their embrace. I couldn't catch my breath, so I clutched my pepper spray with tight fingers.

The ground shook all around us.

"A kid?" The heavy Scottish accent sounded irritated. "They left me here for a kid? Well, come on. Whatever little trick you have there won't work for long. I can just destroy that tree too—give you a good concussion or worse. Don't make this more difficult."

"Do not go," Will warned in a low voice.

"Whatever you've done wrong, they'll work it out with your parents, after your questioning." When I still didn't move, his voice changed perceptibly. I could hear the soft crunch beneath his feet as he slowly approached. "You don't want to get me irritated. Every capsule that you make me waste costs a hundred slaw, and I'll rip each loss out of you."

I peered around the other side of the tree to see him reloading something, my rodent sketch at his feet. Blue seeped oddly from the edge of the rodent sketch, the color growing fainter and blending in as it spread across the page threads. I looked down at my fingers. They were clean. But I had touched the lip of the tube...and the blue smudge at its closure.

The man smirked at me and stepped forward. "There now. Just come along and—"

The edges of the paper crumpled around the sides of his boot.

Schwoop.

I pulled back, harsh, unforgiving breaths issuing from my chest.

"What is happening?" Will's voice was stressed. "Why aren't we running?"

An owl hooted, and the area grew brighter as lights popped on in the houses across the street from the school. I could hear voices yelling down the street about an earthquake and lightning strike. I peeked back around the tree. Only the paper remained. I turned fully so Will could see. "I think...I think I gophered him somewhere."

Will was silent for a long moment. "Well, I do believe, I feel better suddenly." I looked down to see him smirking at the other paper. "Hurry, go look at it."

I slowly walked over and cautiously glanced down at the paper that was now completely blank save for the gopher platform.

"Where do you think he went?" I asked, unnerved.

"I don't—"

"Aiyeee!" A gopher made of paper dropped from the sky. An animated gopher made of paper. If a gopher could have a silly, happy grin, this one did.

"Holy—"

"Grab the sketch, quickly," Will said, his voice high. "And the gopher...paper...thing."

I didn't waste any time thinking and scooped up the sketch. The paper gopher started to merrily toddle off, but I grabbed him and stuffed him in my pocket.

"Aiyeee!" Another paper gopher dropped from the sky, this one wearing goggles and shoes and doing little twirls. I nabbed him as he hit the ground, then stuffed him in my pocket too. My pocket started moving.

"Get us out of here," Will said. "If the Department spook falls out of the sky too, I want to be long gone."

The last intent on the paper had been happy transport. The ridiculous image of the Scottish man wearing the gophers' euphoric grins flitted through my mind. I threw the crumpled paper into a trash bin three streets over. Will hissed at its loss, but instinct urged me to toss it. The paper gophers had stopped moving in my pocket.

Another block over, a good-looking man around my parents' age walked down the street carrying a handheld device. There was something familiar about him. He looked around, eyes peering into the shadows where I was hiding. For some reason I knew his eyes would be blue, though not quite ultramarine. The older man from that night. The uncle. I started to rise.

"Stay down," Will hissed.

"But—"

"Shh! Don't let him see us."

The man finally moved away, and I slipped through a park—a longer route, but less likely to be populated.

Will stayed silent for five more blocks. "Is he gone?"

I looked behind me for the thousandth time. "Yes. Why? Maybe he could help us." He had helped last time. Well, actually he hadn't wanted to help me at all, come to think of it. But reluctantly, he had let his nephew do so.

"Not likely. He's one of the Dares."

"Is that a cult?"

He snorted. "A family. An old, powerful family. High society. Prideful. They stay out of public politics and barely leave their private island, but like all of the old families, they play deep games. None of them works directly for the Department, but my dad said they occasionally send family members to infiltrate organizations. That one looks like a hunter. Probably hunting Verisetti. One of them goes to Excelsine—my school."

Alexander. Was Alexander Dare my savior's name?

The fractured conversation from the night of Christian's death wound through my mind. The Dares had checked my wrist. I looked at the sapling drawn in clear brown lines. The dots that had been there before were now smoothly connected, and the sapling looked bigger. That night might have gone differently with the Dares—for better or worse—if, instead of clear skin, this had been on the inside of my wrist.

"He'd scan you at the very least, and...there is something weird about your magic," Will said. "I don't think most art mages can trap people in sketches. That's a pretty rare skill, I think. That isn't good news for us."

"Thanks."

"Hey, it's just as bad for me at the moment. I can't trust that guy not to simply lock me in the family library vault and enslave me in this black-and-white prison for all eternity." Will cocked his head, eyebrows raised. "I'd be tempted to keep me for testing purposes."

"What are you, a mad scientist?"

"Someday, I hope."

"Great." I shook my head. Just what I needed. Another me. "We have three more blocks, and you're freaking me out. By the way, how did you perform magic from in there? Something hit that guy's scanning device."

"Yeah...that...wasn't me. I don't know if I mentioned it, but I'd kind of like to get out of here as quickly as possible."

All told, even with the stop, we made the fifteen-minute trip home in six.

Chapter Five

REALLY UNWISE ACTIONS

I LOOKED AT THE CLOCK blearily and cradled my umpteenth Coke. The time steadily showed 5:32 a.m., then the final number blinked to three. Will and I were taking turns watching the draperies in the sketch. I had set up Will with an alarm clock and some cymbals while he stood watch, but even then, with the sketch lying on my pillow, I had woken in a panic every fifteen minutes thinking he had been impaled or eaten. He had had no problem dropping off to sleep, though, after I'd drawn garlands of bells over the drapes and tested to make sure they worked. The sword rested beside him on the bed I'd drawn, and his hand was wrapped around a knife under his pillow.

I didn't know whether it was from too much sugar and caffeine in my system, or something else, but the energy under my skin had steadily gone from a trickle to a torrent, raging through me, seeking an outlet.

Will and I had tried the paint, but a single dot had caused the circles on the drapes to start rotating, and battering to commence behind the drapes—forcing them outward, as if by punched fists. I had quickly captured the spreading dot in a container. It had taken all my focus and intent to do so, and the energy inside of me was raging to get out. The battering and rotations had abruptly stopped. The container now sat in the corner across from Will. We would figure out how to test it in the morning. The blue dot inside the container looked as if it were waiting.

The tube of paint was calling to me and freaking me out in equal measures.

"Ren."

I started violently, looking around me. That had been Christian's voice.

"Christian?" I whispered.

No one answered.

A good panic was steadily working its way over me. I was sure Will had noticed, but neither of us had said anything aloud about my last piece of magic charcoal being worn to a nub after all the interim drawings and failed experiments. Using a regular pencil, I could eke out the barest of sketched movements—producing little half-alive automatons—but it was obvious that I wouldn't be able to fight off anything magical with a standard No. 2.

The responsibility for Will's safety was not something I was ready to deal with. I wanted Christian back.

I rolled off my bed and lifted the paint tube. It vibrated in my shaky fingers.

"Help me."

I closed my eyes tightly together. Christian's voice. I clasped the sound to my heart.

"Help me."

I sneaked a peek at Will, who was sleeping soundly, his back gently lifting. I wondered at the depth of his sudden sleep. Wondered if perhaps I had magically influenced his snooze in my sketched world.

All for the better, at the moment. I couldn't take this anymore. I would make something work.

I picked through the mountain of papers covering my desk and finally decided on a simple one—a detailed sketch of a butterfly. It reminded me of the one I had drawn earlier in the day, battering at the edges of the paper. It reminded me of Mr. Verisetti calling me that very thing. That thought made me more determined. I threw the clothes that had been hanging over the top of my small standing easel to the floor. My whole room was a sty. Had been for six weeks now—in contrast to my mother's suddenly pristine world. But I knew, as long as I kept the clutter within the boundaries of my room, my parents wouldn't say a word.

I clipped the paper up and, after another quick check on Will, squeezed a bit of the shiny ultramarine onto my fingertips. I rubbed them together, marveling at the strange glittering of the charged hue. So like the eyes of the boy who had saved me. I ejected a dollop into a small cup attached to the side of the easel. I chose a short flat brush from my scattered collection, and dipped it. The first small sweep on the paper produced an echoed feeling of heat inside of me. I stopped and examined the paint. It glittered. Waited. That was absurd, but I felt the streak of paint was waiting for something.

I dipped my brush and spread another streak. Everything lit inside of me.

It was almost hard to breathe. Painting the butterfly was quick. The paint was alive, pulling together to darken the lines, making a strange sort of electric pop art piece. I rubbed my finger lightly along the surface. My fingertip brushed something soft, and the edge of a wingtip bristled up onto the page.

I stared at it for a long moment. At the three-dimensional protrusion coming out of my piece—a protrusion not created by glue or paint buildup. I stroked my finger a little more carefully around the edges—an archaeologist carefully brushing sand and soot away from my find. With every touch, more was revealed. When I had the edge of a wing half exposed, it started to flutter.

I jerked back. But the fluttering became a heavy beat.

Working with the blue insect, I pried and willed more of it to break free, and it worked hard, determined to do so.

A final, giant flap fully disengaged the butterfly from the paper, popping it out. It landed awkwardly in my hand. I slowly rotated my hand watching the feathery edges move, feeling the gentle beat of its wings. I set the butterfly carefully on my table and stared in wonder. It had worked.

The butterfly straightened, as if strengthening its frame, then beat its wings fully, lifting into the air. It flew around unsteadily at first, then with greater strength. It landed on my windowsill, which was still open to the night. Its wings flattened, then folded gently as it seemed to consider the night. Then it launched itself, fluttering and disappearing over the edge and into the dark.

Life. Created. Alive.

I lurched forward. With my clean hand, I pushed the papers on top of my desk aside. Some fell to the floor and others shifted to bury everything in their path. I paused only when I came to a canvas near the bottom. I tugged the half-finished image of my brother free.

I had started it in pencil. The perfectionist part of me said that I needed to finish it in pencil. But the need in me said, Paint. Now.

Blue was an odd choice for a portrait of my brother. Yet, my fingers squeezed more from the tube and the first brush of paint was intoxicating.

I paused to look at the tube, lying there so innocently. Mr. Verisetti had used me to create this. How? And why?

Don't you want to see what is in the box?

I blinked at the thought and gripped the brush. My breath hitched. My knuckles turned white. The paint glistened.

I looked at the picture, at the features that with each glowing brushstroke seemed to come more alive. Really alive. And the electric knot inside me grew.

I made a tentative swipe. Then another. I felt the pleasure in the paint.

Easily framing and forming the other side of my twin's face in broad strokes. Every swipe increased my feeling of purpose. Determination and desire filled my motions. Every time a line connected with another, the intersection...glowed for a moment, then transformed into whatever color I imagined it should be. I could almost see the skin of his hand.

I reached out to touch it, and my fingers dipped into the canvas, into a pocket of space that shouldn't exist, and touched the edges of something soft. Cool skin. I couldn't breathe—I could feel him. I could feel skin I hadn't touched in six weeks. My fingers automatically tried to wrap around, but the paint was drying and the softness was turning brittle, repelling my fingers. My hand came free of the canvas and the spell broke, shattering what was in my hand, spilling what now felt like the ashes of paint chips to the floor.

I stared at my hand, covered in beautiful, unnatural blue. The digits curled in. I had felt Christian.

I touched the canvas again, but it was solid. No hole or magic vortex in sight. But I had felt him. I had.

I had.

The edges of my vision tinged gold, and I plunged my brush into the paint cup and forced blue onto the canvas again, the edges of the brush splattering the canvas before I outlined him once more. The canvas glowed, and I thrust my hand in, the untainted white of the sheet rippling around my wrist like a vat of splotched milk. Skin. I gripped and frantically pulled, trying to wrench my brother from the canvas, but only paint drops and chips spilled free.

Again.

Everything else grayed out around the brightened space of the easel. Dip, brush, thrust, nothing. Dip, brush, thrust, clasp a strong wrist, nothing. Dip, brush, thrust, skin, nothing. Over and over, drops fell from my hand, the remnants drying and crumbling on the floor, resting amongst the other drips and chips and sobs.

Dip...dip, dip, dip. I picked up the paint cup. Splatters only. I picked up the mangled, flattened tube.

I looked at the splatters on the wall next to me. Like a giant blue beast had been slaughtered against it. How many times had I reached into the canvas and yanked my hand out? I just needed one more time. I was certain. I wrapped my fingers around the tube.

"Please, please, please." I whispered, squeezing the dead tube. "I need just a little more." I didn't know who I was asking, begging. "I know I can do it."

"Ren!"

Chapter Five

I whirled around to see Will banging on his side of the sketch with one hand, a horrified look on his face as he fastened on the armor I had created for him earlier—complete with pinstripes. I could suddenly feel the paint coated on my cheeks. Dripping from my skin. Some truly feral warrior in a jungle of canvas, cubist lines, pointed colors, and deco blocks.

"I can do it," I told him, beseeching. "I just need more paint like this. Where can I get more paint like this?" I had the paintbrush gripped in my fist, shaking like a junkie demanding her next fix.

"Ren—"

The building electricity within me exploded with a hiss. "Where can I get more paint?"

His gaze went past me, widening. I followed it...to the drawings on my walls. The dragons, the vines, the parties and battles. The cubist lines and deco blocks. The birds and beasts and abstract things. Stick figures and realistic portraits.

And now magic paint in a warrior's hue was on one of those walls. And I was vibrating with energy and intent. To make things live. A Renaissance woman started screaming as a gryphon dive-bombed from the sky. A stylized female Don Quixote dressed in knightly silver rushed in with her gleaming helmet and sword and stepped in front of the other, fending away the giant beast as the woman in the flowing gown gripped her desperately from behind.

Oh, no.

I dropped the paintbrush and grabbed the charcoal nub and lunged to help Knight and Renaissance. But near them, the impressionistic lily pads were winding up a bridge and over a couple standing there. They curved around their necks. I slashed my nub through one of the lily pad vines, and it fell to the floor. Others replaced it.

I slashed again and again, and yet similar events were happening all around me. Geometric blocks smashing, modern art squeezing, and old masters piercing. I could never get to everything in time. The savagery escalated, the carnage multiplied, and I could only watch in horror. I needed an eraser, but I had created mostly with paint and ink and I didn't know how to hit undo.

The festive party scenes and whimsical things I had drawn were being consumed by the destructive elements I had also created—sharp mirrored edges, harsh lines, unforgiving borders slashing through their softer counterparts—the balance left unchecked with too few knights and protectors and far too many victims and predators.

I used the nubs, then the charcoal remnants on my fingers, and then I had no more charcoal. I had no more paint.

I sank to the ground, sob unable to release, as everything around me died, dripping and seeping together into a morass of sickly brown at the base of my walls. I clutched Will's sketch, but forced myself to view the last moments of the others, to watch the last one standing on top of the brownish murk that was trying to suck her in—the female Don Quixote in her silver, knightly armor. She had made it to the end, surrounded by the fallen compatriots she had tried to help and the predators she had been forced to kill, covered in paint and pen splatter. And then she fell to her knees and landed face-down in the mud, once-fluffy hair spilling from the back of her helmet in tangled, wet strands. Then she too was absorbed into the endless brown landscape. All lay shattered and still on my walls. The ecosystem collapsed.

Will was quiet. He reached out a hand to me, then let it fall back to his side.

Then his eyes drifted toward my fingers touching the page. The paint splatters on the backs of my fingers had moisturized, then joined together, running down to my pads, unnaturally spreading into the sketch, through my drawings around Will, soaking into his environment. The jar containing the paint dot rattled, the dot jumping around, wanting to join the spread. The circles on the drapes started to rotate— slowly and ominously.

And I realized I had no charcoal left.

Will's right fingers curled tightly around the hilt of his sword, his left around the knife. He looked at me and gave me a tight smile. "Go to the coffeehouse downtown and talk to the women working there. Don't tell them you are feral. Just say you need some help. Then go directly—"

The bells on the drapes gave a cacophonous clang, as razor-sharp roots came piercing through each swirling circle portal.

Chapter Six

DEADLY ASSAILANTS

"NO!" I YELLED at the paper. I heard something crash down the hall.

The roots flew directly toward Will, spiked and deadly. I was about to watch him die too. Gold light lit everything around me. I let out every sobbing emotion I had and thrust a hand into the sketch.

"No!" Christian's yell echoed mine.

My hand and wrist disappeared into the paper and funneled down, smaller than Will's in the sketch, and twice as ineffectual. Putting my minnow-like fingers into a fish bowl filled with predators. A root flayed the skin from one knuckle, then batted my hand to the side. My whole arm jerked as my hand was thrown into the sketch wall opposite Will.

Will was battling and doing a great job of it. The sword fit him perfectly—exactly as I had envisioned it—and he obviously knew how to use one. But there were too many opponents, just like on my walls—and these opponents possessed some of my magic, whereas Will possessed none here—I could feel the reflection of the opponents' magic in my sketched fingers, the echo of my own electricity—along with what felt like tinted gold. Raphael Verisetti.

I could hear footsteps running down the hall.

Root-like protrusions behind the drapes were pushing the drapes forward. Trying to push the swirling portals against the "glass" of the sketch.

Christian's voice continued shouting, crystal clear with my gold-enhanced senses. "Get back, Ren! Stop!"

"Ren, open this door!" My mom yelled hysterically, jangling the knob.

Will removed five roots from action in one swipe, but the slash left him open and a bright flash zinged from a swirling circle and struck him in the chest. His chest armor exploded, and the shock wave knocked him off his feet. Something large was moving behind the drapes, coming toward us. Something with far more presence and magic than the roots.

I thought of Mr. Verisetti with a second feeling of betrayal, and a vivid memory of him twisting his hand, a smile upon his lips, bloomed from the darkness. I flicked my wrist in imitation, and three of the roots severed. I didn't waste moments playing with this new ability—I simply battled my way through.

Christian screamed for me to stop. I would not let Will die too, though. I'd die first.

"Ren! Open this door! Roger, I can't open it!"

The house started to shake. The patterned circles on my closet door opened into mouths of malevolent intent, black tunneled holes stretched behind them, and the vision of my parents bursting through the door and into danger forced cold certainty to my thoughts.

No. No.

This time I would make it work. Gold lit everywhere.

"Ren, please! Please, open the door!"

"Move, Catherine!"

"Ren!"

I latched onto Will's arm—firm and warm beneath my stained hand—and used every muscle and desire I possessed and pulled. Will came diving out, knocking me to the ground, and flattening me in a tangle of limbs, a chair, a sword, bits of armor, paint and charcoal flakes, and a lot of swearing. Golden light flashed everywhere again. My closet door roared, then it and the house stilled.

"Why didn't you save me, Ren? That was my magic."

Christian's leather band burst into flames, burning my wrist as it disintegrated into ash. The picture of him lined in blue paint erupted into unnatural flame next, bright blue with gold-tinged smoke, gone within seconds. Small bursts of flame, like match strikes, sparked around us—every drop of blue paint exploding, extinguishing, then leaving a feeling of emptiness behind. Only my old, dead, normal acrylic paint was left seeping on the walls in mixed brown agony.

Christian's voice was silent. Gone. I could feel a tear spill over. I had lost the bracelet I had retrieved from the man who had killed him. The container. Oh, God, no, of course that was what it had been. And even the canvas containing the remnants of paint was gone.

A loud sound impacted against the door as I tried to breathe. I struggled to see through the teary blue-and-gold film over my gaze and Will's shoulder pressing my nose into the floor.

Chapter Six

My parents burst into the room, then stood there, in the doorway, stunned, as if what they were experiencing was so out of their realm of understanding that they didn't know how to react.

I had no idea what or who they could see. Therefore, I was the only one distantly relieved when Mom whacked Will with the hallway broom.

Chapter Seven

CONVERSATIONS OF THE EXTRAORDINARY

WILL AND I WAITED in the kitchen while a thirty-something year old man named Phillip Marsgrove, a dean at Will's magic school—and, unnervingly, the pinstripe-clothed man who had entered my school a half-minute ahead of the Department men—spoke with my parents in the living room. Or rather argued, as my parents were in complete disbelief about the existence of magic. Three voices battled in mumbled discord as I pressed my ear to the closed door.

"There is a suppression field in place that makes anything with the whiff of real magic hard for an ordinary person to remember. Visions or experiences float away like daydreams. Daydreams where you are lost to the real world for small periods of time are indicative of episodic exposure to magic."

I had been exposed to a lot of magic then.

"Why suppress us? Or separate us? It sounds like we could benefit from magic too."

Mom was angry, her voice tight and deadly.

"There was a reason for the Split."

Will was leaning against the island's white granite counter top, punching in all sorts of things to his tablet. Occasionally, he would pause and touch a spot beneath his ear. "Recording the adventure in my field journal," he had said, when I'd looked at him in question.

I wandered over to the other side of the island, touching the burned skin of my wrist, then picking at the bandage encasing my hand. I had felt Christian there under the paint, but his image hadn't animated like the butterfly had. Was there different magic in play between the sketches? The butterfly sketch and Christian's portrait should have been the same. Why had I been able to pull out a butterfly—and Will—but not Christian? Especially with remnants of his magic encircling my wrist. How did I recreate the circumstances of the first two?

Had I lost Christian completely with the loss of his band?

I didn't want to think that. I reached over and tucked in the loose edge of the bandage around Will's hand.

"Thanks," he said, smiling and pushing his glasses back onto the bridge of his straight nose.

It was strange, but I felt responsible for Will. I had never felt responsible for anyone other than Christian.

I had been an awkwardly balanced child, and a late talker—little things would catch my attention, and I was apt to run into walls and slip down stairs while daydreaming. Colors and shapes and objects had been so vast and incredible that I'd tripped over my own tongue trying to describe the wonderful things I was seeing. The sentences and constructs in my head never seemed to make it into coherent phrases.

Christian had always stood between me and the people who had tried to poke fun. He'd knocked down and scrapped would-be bullies, then told me to keep drawing. Had encouraged me to take all the time I needed to explain the thoughts running through my mind.

I shook my head. It had not been hard to concentrate my energy on my brother in return and to make sure he succeeded in whatever he wanted to do. Running thousands of drills and devising play strategy with him had been the least price. And he'd lock me into my room, if I went too long without drawing, and tell me to do something "artsy." There wasn't a normal lock I couldn't pick, and he knew it, but the protective gesture had allowed me to relax. Drawing made the world make more sense.

But the world was making no sense now. I looked at the inside of my left wrist, just above the burn. The picture there had changed again and now showed a bloody ax. Still drawn in brown, but the dripping splatters on the edge of the blade were straining toward red. An executioner's blade.

I touched my own bandage and swallowed hard, trying to shut down my emotions.

"We can get healed in the Second Layer," Will said. "If you think your parents will let you go?"

I needed more magical charcoal. I needed more paint. I wasn't going to get either here. "If they don't, I'll go anyway."

Will nodded slowly.

"Tell me about necromancy."

Will looked nervously at the closed door to the living room. "Black magic is illegal. It demands a price. Don't let people hear you talking about it. If you have even a whiff of dark magic aptitude, the Department puts you on the Watch list."

"But you said resurrection experts are a dime a dozen." I forced lightness into my voice, then turned and filled the teapot. I didn't look at him as I said, "I was just curious."

"Were you?" Will's voice was soft.

I turned back to face him, crossing my arms tightly without answering.

"There is a statute of limitations. We did a whole unit in primary school on mental counting and time tracking in order to anticipate the time frame. We are also trained early to abandon resurrection efforts, if the ten minute period has passed. They say bad things start to happen once fifteen minutes have occurred. And there are all sorts of thresholds in black magic. One month, two months, four months."

I watched Will's face carefully. "What happens when you die?"

Will rubbed a hand through the back of his hair. "I haven't died yet. But it seems to depend on the person."

Will shifted categories suddenly in my mind. He moved from Code Red Ally into a category labeled something closer to Normal Friend. I wasn't quite sure what to do with the latter, so I pushed it aside for the moment.

"Ninety-five percent of students die on campus, though, so you might find out. And we have the best libraries. None of the other universities come close."

The tea bag dropped from my fingers onto the granite as I stared at him. "Ninety-five percent?" So much for the thought that I might attend Will's school. There was no way I was going to survive that statistic. Not alongside kids who had been using magic since birth.

On the other hand, death would allow me a different kind of search.

"They get resurrected." Will's expression was earnest. "Ten minutes is a long time. Though, there are people who die for good. They go eleven minutes or their injuries are so severe that they can't be resurrected. It happens every once in a while at school."

Will's reassuring tone warmed me. The Normal Friend category was a nice one.

I needed to seek out other sources of information, though. I nodded as if I accepted the topic as closed, and picked up the teabag and dropped it into a cup. The counters were spotless—Mom made them so each day. And the reason why she did so only firmed my resolve. Mom's voice rose in the other room, as did Phillip Marsgrove's. Marsgrove had shown up within two minutes of Mom hitting Will with the broom. I wondered how he had gotten here so fast if porting wasn't something that could be done normally in the non-magic world.

"Where is the magic world?"

"Oh! Right on top of this one. Layers, you know. In the Split, four magical layers identical in geography to the first were created directly on top of this one, using most of the world's available magic. Leaving this—the First Layer—a normal, non-magical safe haven for people without magic abilities. Course, that was three thousand years ago, so most places look different between the layers now—due to weathering and construction from different species and kingdoms."

"Like giving the same assignment and paints to five different artists."

Will smiled. "Sure. The Second Layer is pretty in tune with this one, lots of mages travel or live in both—sharing, taking, or modifying technology— but the Fourth Layer, for instance, is for magical creatures and beings and looks completely alien. The Fifth is pretty unstable. And the Third Layer,"—he shook his head, expression hard—"much of it is barren wasteland now. But Layer History 101 is required at school. That class is all you'll need for understanding the layer system unless you want to specialize in layer physics and dimensions."

Will seemed to be of the opinion that I would be attending school with him. But I was stuck on the non-magic aspect. "But magic works here."

Will shook his head. "There is magic in the earth, of course, that seeps through all of the layers. But magic use here is suppressed and fiercely restricted. You can perform magic with a bottled container and a use permit. If you don't have a permit, they send hunters after you. Once you are in the system, all magic use shows up on the Department's grid." He cocked his head, eyes agleam. " You aren't in the system yet. Crap. We should have run from your parents and gone on a road trip. There are a thousand things I can't collect here without using magic. Stinking museums and alarms. Why the devil did I call Dean Marsgrove?"

He thumped his forehead against the granite.

Did that mean I had only been able to do magic here because of Christian's bracelet?

Will's cheek kind of rolled on the counter so that he was looking up at me forlornly. "We could have kicked ass. There are small time users living here, people who read fortunes and things, but they have to get a license and the Department regulates that stuff, and small timers can't get me in the really good places without ordinary people noticing. Devices that work on ordinary people are fiercely restricted."

I thought of the students frozen in class. "But—"

He sat up, elbows on the counter, chin sunk into the palm of one hand in an I-just-watched-my-true-love-ride-away fashion. "The dean will never let us get away with it now. He must have taken care of the Department, though, since they aren't here arresting us."

"Weren't you doing magic here?"

He shook his head. "My tablet has a two month permit for passive research and collection use in the First Layer, but no active magic is allowed. If I used magic on an ordinary person or used it in an aggressive way, the tablet would immediately immobilize me."

"How did you get that permit?"

He cleared his throat. "Hey, do you want to see the battle competition from last week? I have it queued up."

"Ren."

I managed not to jerk my head around as Christian's voice sounded in my mind. I touched my burn in relief and anguish. His tone sounded different, half-cunning, half-protective, but it was him.

I tentatively sent out a thought. Christian? Please, please answer...

A full-color, incredibly detailed, rotating hologram burst out of Will's tablet. The hologram view swept a field, and I caught a momentary glimpse of thousands of feet—directly below the edge of the field. I immediately leaned closer, examining the landscape in more detail. This was the exact backdrop in some of Mr. Verisetti's paintings. No wonder the backgrounds had always looked strange, like the earth was rising. The school was on the side of a mountain. "This is campus?"

"Yup. The seventeenth circle's hippodrome to be exact. I like the twentieth circle's amphitheater best myself. They do a student-teacher war there once a year. Marsgrove frequently wins. No one knows why he won't teach combat classes."

My brain rapidly worked on what "circle" meant in the context. Circling around the mountain?

Students wearing black duster-type cloaks adorned with silver buckles fought fiercely using staffs, rods, swords, marble-sized bombs, and other indistinguishable objects. One boy stood untouchable in the middle of the field without a weapon, familiar Last Judgment blue eyes barely sparing a cold glance at the next challenger in front of him—nor the one sneaking up at his back—as lights shot from his palms and fingertips, his arms performing a deadly dance.

Michelangelo would have loved him.

Will was saying something about avoiding mages who wore three rings, but I couldn't hear over the pumping of my heart in my ears. I stared at the hue of the boy's eyes and watched as he annihilated everyone around him. The hologram avidly focused on him.

I had no memory of his face, but I knew those eyes. I knew him.

My fingers were reaching out without my consent, and I snatched my hand back before Will could notice. Combatants were spread like rag-dolls on the ground around him—though none were within a ten foot radius. Apparently, none had gotten that close.

I looked at one of the fallen challengers. Could magic sew an arm back on? I hoped so.

"Who is that?" My voice sounded far away, seeking confirmation of something my senses didn't need confirmation on.

"Huh? Oh, that's Alexander Dare, combat mage. Best on campus, and that's saying something since the Academy encompasses ages sixteen to twenty-two. Considered a prodigy. Even beat Marsgrove last year when Dare was a second year. The combat mages all call him Axer for good reason. I'd, uh, stay away from him."

I looked at Will. "He's not nice?" His banter with his uncle had been cocky, and here in this vision he was clearly dominant and seemingly ruthless, but he had healed an unknown girl. He had given me one last moment with my brother. I didn't care if he turned into a man-eating troll every Sunday, I would never forget that.

"Old Magic." Will rubbed the back of his head in a gesture Christian had used frequently when imparting bad news. "Which as I was saying—"

Voices rose in the other room.

"Send her to Miss Angelie's School for Girls, then!"

"You misunderstood. That is where we send the new thirteen- to fifteen-year-olds who qualify for mage training. Your daughter is seventeen."

Will shook his head at me. "Boarding school," he whispered.

I lurched forward and pushed through the door. "No way. I'm going to Will's school."

And Alexander's school. And the place straight out of Mr. Verisetti's painted images of resurrection.

Everyone stopped talking.

Mom's shoulders were stiff. "We will decide where you are going, Ren."

I looked at the prim and proper Georgian manor rotating in their hologram field.

"No."

I remembered being thirteen. It had sucked. I had permanently and safely embedded myself in Christian's shadow.

Screw safe. I needed access to those libraries. And the resurrection experts Will kept teasing me with. I wasn't staying here—in the skeleton of my previous life—but I also wasn't going to some boarding school where I'd be tucked in at nine each night.

"No, you won't decide," I said more forcefully. "I am going to Will's school. You can support me or you can oppose me. I will still go. You didn't believe me when I told you what happened to Christian. You are going to believe me now."

The side table started shaking. Framed pictures started clattering against the walls. A piece of crinkled paper on the coffee table lit gold and a black stain grew from the middle. My mother's favorite wooden statue of a girl laughing, her head flung back without care, flew over and was sucked inside the paper. I despised that statue. Drawn on the paper, a little platform stood above the statue as it splintered on the sketch floor.

Shocked, I froze. That was my gopher sketch.

I looked at Phillip Marsgrove, who was trying to appear relaxed even as his hand hovered near his pocket. Glasses and pinstripes were similar to Will's, but his gray eyes were arctic. When he had first arrived and assessed me there had been horror and revulsion in his gaze. The same expression was there now.

"Your parents did not have the ability to believe you," he said stiffly. "That is a consequence of the suppression magic. They will believe you now. And now that the spell is broken, they will remember all you had been trying to tell them."

My parents' expressions were stricken.

Phillip Marsgrove and Raphael Verisetti had the same intent focus to their gaze. But whereas Mr. Verisetti looked upon me as if I were an adored pet, Phillip Marsgrove looked upon me as if I were the neighbor's rabid dog that he was in charge of putting down.

Something outside of my control flowed over me and emotions twisted within me. On the table near Marsgrove and the gopher sketch, the stems of the flower arrangement curled and twisted together, strangling—a reflection of my feeling.

"How did you get that?" I demanded, pointing at the sketch.

"I thought you said magic couldn't be performed here?" Mom demanded. It looked as if she was trying to put distance between us, pushing against the cushions at the back of the couch. "What happened to my son?"

"Magic can't be performed by a normal mage unless he has an exorbitantly expensive stash of separated magic at his disposal," Marsgrove said in a clipped voice. "Powerful magic occurs when a mage's powers first awaken, and I assume your son's powers were awakening when he was killed. Some try to...harness that power. Normal mages cannot use their own magic here. And only specialized law enforcement mages are permitted to use devices in the First Layer."

All eyes turned to me. The burn on my wrist said that I no longer had a stash of magic to draw upon. Well, so what. Maybe there was some embedded in my skin or something.

Marsgrove's gaze said otherwise. Ok. Fine. I had known for a long time that I wasn't normal. I had just thought I was a little more human abnormal.

Mom's eyes focused on me. I could see fear there. It pinched my stomach. A thick candle flew toward a picture of Christian and me on the wall and cracked the glass. The candle thumped to the ground.

Silence stretched, then the picture fell as well, shattering on the floor. I darted forward and snatched the gopher sketch, holding it against my chest.

"I'm going," I said softly.

"Ok." Mom's voice was strangled.

Dad's was only slightly stronger. "Yes."

I felt a tendril of something wrap around me and extend toward them.

"Great," Marsgrove said, as if we had all agreed. There was noticeable relief in his voice, as if we were now bound by the decision, and he had just been waiting for such an outcome to occur. Marsgrove popped a black wrist guard out of his tablet, and handed it to me. The wide wrist cuff felt like some form of flexible metal and looked identical to the ones worn by Mr. Verisetti, Marsgrove, and Will.

He popped what looked like a magazine out of his tablet next and handed it to Mom. A thick volume was handed to Dad. "Here's a brochure on the Academy, and a primer discourse on magic, physics, and the layer system. You have a week with the primer text, then it will be loaned elsewhere. Only the two of you will be able to read the brochure and the primer."

He collapsed the hologram and began packing up. "You will remember the words of the text, and can discuss the information freely between yourselves since you were spelled together, but you will be unable to speak them to a non-magic user."

Mom's eyes narrowed. "You spelled us?" The magazine-sized brochure dangled from her fingertips, as if she held a poisonous snake in her hands.

"No. Magical objects have their own properties that can bespell non-magic users. Same with magical places. As I said previously, mages cannot work magic in this Layer on non-magic users. Unless we have a magical device that allows it,"—he pointed to the thick primer—"and then, even that will register on the grid, which is constantly monitored."

So how had Mr. Verisetti frozen the students in my class? Why had no magical law enforcement people responded to that? Mr. Verisetti had made it a point to say that I had caused him to be noticed when I'd pushed against the dust.

"How many devices are there?" Dad asked.

Chapter Seven

"Few." Marsgrove stood. "Read the discourse. Miss Crown, Mr. Tasky, show me the other sketch."

I startled, having forgotten that Will was behind me. I didn't meet his eyes as I led them to my room, leaving my stunned and broken parents behind. I would fix things. They would be happy. We all loved Christian best. I had to stay on target.

Marsgrove took a few moments to look around. His gaze rested on the muddy brown color on the lower section of my walls—where all the paint had run down to collect together and dry.

The sketch was resting on top of the mess on my floor, where it had fallen when I'd pulled Will out. Marsgrove reached for it. Six inches from touching it, he snatched his hand back, as if he had been burned.

He stared at it for long moments, his back to us, then he turned to me. His revulsion was carefully hidden, but I could still feel it. "First things first. Draw an X over that," he said, pointing to the gopher sketch in my hands. "Concentrate very hard on the fact that you don't want it used for anything ever again."

"Did you dig this out of the trash? How did you find it?"

"Draw an X," he said, with forced patience.

"I used all of the magic charcoal."

His nostrils flared, and his lips tightened together. "Use your finger and concentrate. Destruction should be easier than creation for you at this point."

"What do you mean?" I asked sharply.

"Do it." He looked scary all of a sudden. I could believe that this man might waste someone in a fight.

The X worked like a water mark, disappearing into the page. I felt the sketch settle, lifeless under my intent.

He took the sheet from me and ripped it into eight pieces before putting the pieces in his pocket. "It is important that you do not utilize such skills again until you can be taught how to use them properly."

I was going to pull Christian out of a painting as soon as I found more magic paint.

His lips tightened as he observed my expression. He looked at Will. "Did you see magic supplies anywhere else in this Layer?"

Will stared at Marsgrove for long moments. "No, no supplies. What—?"

Marsgrove held out a tablet that looked a lot like Will's, only Marsgrove's was black. "You will not speak of this incident with anyone else."

"I will not speak of this incident with anyone else without Ren's permission."

Marsgrove looked displeased at the additions, but nodded sharply. "You are dismissed."

Will hesitated.

"Mr. Tasky, may I remind you of your tenuous position? And that you deliberately misrepresented your research permit allowances?" Marsgrove's voice was silky and dark, impatience underlying his tone.

Will bit his lip.

Marsgrove's eyes narrowed. "Oh, for magic's sake, I'm not going to kill her after you leave. I'm going to enroll her."

Will looked down at his tablet, then perked up as if the device had told him that Marsgrove's words were true. He gave me a wave. "Ok! See you at school, Ren. And thanks for the awesome adventure." He sounded like he one hundred percent meant it too.

Sudden anxiety overtook me. "I...ok, but don't forget to eat."

Will's cheeks turned scarlet, but he grumbled something and disappeared down the hall, walking peculiarly.

It dawned on me that I hadn't seen the sword I had drawn for him in some time. It had popped out of the sketch with him, but I hadn't seen it since he'd disappeared into the bathroom after my parents had calmed down. He had changed into some of my brother's clothes, which had been slightly too big for him, and he must have tied the sword inside a pant leg, and worn the armor beneath the sweatshirt, since that too was missing. No wonder he had remained standing in the kitchen.

Why was he hiding it?

"What is going on?" I asked Marsgrove, all pretenses gone along with Will.

"You are a mage of interest," he said, eyes cold. "Until I have further information, that is all you need to know. Where did you get your supplies?"

He gingerly picked up the empty, flat tube of paint, expression displeased as he examined it, then carefully put it in a plastic bag in his pocket.

"Will already told you. A man named Raphael Verisetti—my art teacher for the last four weeks—gave them to me."

"Did you make any of the supplies?"

I didn't answer for a moment, something in me arguing against answering in the affirmative. "Possibly the paint."

He showed no surprise at the answer, as if he had expected it. "What did you give him?" His stare hardened.

"What do you mean?" The unease that had overtaken me when I first realized I couldn't remember the landscape I had drawn in Will's sketch struck me again. I could remember most everything I read, which had always made classes easy, but my memory for images was unbreakable. Not remembering what had happened with my drawing was distinctly unsettling.

"You painted something at your school. With Raphael involved, and seeing the magic you have already created, I can guess what you are." His gaze was dissecting.

"What do you mean, what I am? Some feral beast thing?"

He gave a short laugh, devoid of humor. "What did you create and give to him?"

"I saw you at the school, right before those other men arrived," I said, ignoring his question, unnerved by his words and his reference to Mr. Verisetti by first name. "What were you doing?"

His eyes narrowed. "Mr. Tasky said residual paint on your fingers activated the drawing."

"I asked what you were doing at my school."

"As it turned out, I was cleaning up after you." He tossed the butterfly sketch onto the table. It was the one I had created in the classroom after mixing the paint. The butterfly was still fluttering around, but its wings were badly damaged, like it had been beating itself against the sides of the paper repeatedly. "Do you know what the Department would have done with that, if one of them had managed to carry it back to the Second Layer? They would have used every resource searching for you, instead of Ra—" He cleared his throat. "Verisetti."

"Why?"

"I answered your first question, now answer mine. What did you paint for him?"

"I don't know," I whispered. "I don't remember painting."

Marsgrove looked frustrated and irritated. "What did Verisetti last have in his hands?"

"A box." A box that had been an exact replica to the one in my initial drawing, but had not been in the latter version. I pulled my lips between my teeth.

Marsgrove was watching me carefully. "And a portal pad?"

I shrugged, trying to ease my anxiety. "I guess?"

He took a step toward me, menacing. "This is not a joke."

I tightened my fingers and realized I had somehow grabbed the art room scissors and had them thrust out in front of me. Energy pulsed under my skin and muddy brown paint started dripping down my walls.

He crossed his arms and took a step back. "Draw an X over the insect."

I looked at the butterfly pitifully beating its half-broken wings. "I don't want to kill it."

"It's not alive."

I opened my mouth to say that the butterfly that had escaped a few hours ago had been very alive. Even the paper gophers had been animated for a short time. But I shut down the sentences before they could emerge from my mouth.

Holding the scissors firmly in my other hand, I put my finger against the sketch and stroked the edges of the butterfly's wings, soothing its battered appendages. Energy leaped into my finger and out through the tip. The butterfly stopped its sluggishly frantic motions and its wings folded gently under my stroking finger.

The energy continued to flow, and the beat of its wings gentled until stopping altogether, stilling the image on the page. The energy settled, resting in the tip of my finger, sorrowful.

I felt a tear slip down my cheek, and I hurriedly wiped it away with my shoulder.

"Good. Now do that to the other one." He motioned to Will's sketch.

"No." I wasn't doing it again.

"Yes."

"No." The paint started dripping from my walls in double time.

Marsgrove's hands formed into fists at his side, his lips pressed tightly together, but there was an odd gleam to his eyes. "Do you remember anything else being removed from the artwork?"

Will seemed to trust Marsgrove, and yet he had not revealed his possession of the sword.

I could hear the steady drip, drip, drip of the dead old paint. "I blacked out." It was true, and there was no reason for me to tell him about Will's sword.

"Don't trust him." Christian's voice was sharp.

Marsgrove looked at his tablet and gave a grim nod, then his eyes went to the top of my head. "Verisetti put a spell on you."

Christian? Christian! But he didn't answer.

Marsgrove's words made me nervous, as did his expression. "Can you remove it?"

"No. The spell is tied to your heart. If I tried to remove it, it would kill you."

I swallowed and put the scissors down. "Ok, do it."

His eyes narrowed. "What?"

"Can't you just bring me back?" I could try to latch onto Christian, wherever he was in my mind.

"No."

I scratched Marsgrove, dean of irritation, off my short list. There was now only one person populating it. Mr. Verisetti.

"Don't ask anyone else to remove it either. For one thing it denies any ordinary human the ability to mention your name to a mage or within one's hearing—it works like the First Layer suppression spell on ordinary humans, except this spell works against mages. I have been searching for you since yesterday. Even knowing how Verisetti uses spells, and hearing all about a crazy student at your school, without Mr. Tasky's call, I wouldn't know you were the...feral. Nor would I have remembered the crazy student portion except as a throwaway piece of chatter."

I stared at him, absorbing that information while sending out call after mental call to my brother, begging him to answer.

"There are...advantages to leaving it on. I have spells that will work with...his." His eyes were pinched. "Of course, it will make you even more vulnerable to Verisetti. You will either gain a benefit from the curse or be cursed twice over."

As long as I could still die and be resurrected a thousand times, I didn't care. It gave me more chances to find Christian. He was out there somewhere. He had called for me.

I nodded.

Marsgrove smiled, but the smile didn't reach his eyes. "Let me see your tattooed wrist."

I automatically looked at the executioner's blade. It seemed to be fading, though, and if I squinted, I could see what looked like a stylized phoenix blooming beneath it. I looked up to see him examining the ax.

"Feeling bloodthirsty? Or did you betray someone?"

I hugged my wrist to my chest and pressed my lips together. "It's an emotional indicator?"

"The images can do anything from display a depiction of a mage's last major magical event to providing an indicator of emotion or special skill. Mages cover them to avoid revealing things they don't wish to disclose." His non-smile turned into a smirk. "Don't ever show anyone your wrist."

Betrayal should only bloom when you trusted someone. Marsgrove's actions made me angry.

"Put the cuff over it," he said.

I stared at the smooth black metal, distrust high. "What is it?" I could feel the energy pulsating within it. The magic.

"Put it on. It does more than hide your design. It will control your intentions until you can do so by yourself. I'll put other necessary magics in it later. Wearing one is mandatory in the Second Layer."

I didn't want to put some magic bracelet on, especially one given to me by someone I didn't trust—someone obviously repulsed by me.

"Put it on, Miss Crown, and I will give you a shield set that will make you the envy of your peers."

Did I need shields?

"And you will feel better." Marsgrove's voice and expression suddenly held pity. "It's not your fault you are different. You can work hard to overcome your origin."

His voice had turned compelling, urging me to follow his instruction. I pushed against the unnatural feel of the persuasion.

Marsgrove looked surprised for a moment, then thoughtful, his voice turning neutral. "The loss of control downstairs with your parents, the magic now dripping from your walls... Those were and are small events only because I have a magic inhibitor in my pocket. When I leave, there will be no inhibition. You could inadvertently kill your parents with a snap of your thoughts." He snapped his fingers.

I immediately put the cuff on my left wrist, his words ringing true. The cuff wrapped itself around and sealed together. The raging torrent under my skin muted, slithering around, frustrated, poking to find an opening.

The cuff was solid, but it moved fluidly with the shifting of my skin, staying in contact with my wrist at all times. The feeling it provoked was both terrifying and relieving—different parts of me reacting to different parts of it.

I tried to take consolation in the weight of it replacing Christian's leather band, which was now lost to me.

"Now, hurry up and pack. No furniture, just clothes and essentials. There are nine weeks remaining in the term." His voice was brisk, and curiously, the revulsion was almost completely absent. "I'll be back in three hours to pick you up. If you have too many items, I'll weed through them and toss things at random."

I touched the cuff again. I couldn't find the opening.

Chapter Eight

INTO THE RABBIT HOLE

I PACKED AS QUICKLY AS POSSIBLE, with my parents' help. They kept hugging me and touching my hair as we stuffed clothes into trash bags. I was sure I was going to forget all sorts of important things, like underwear, but I would worry about that later.

Marsgrove arrived back before the three hours were up, looking aggravated, winded, and determined. "Where is the sketch?"

I pointed to the table.

His eyes narrowed as he took out a pair of black tongs and a thin white document box. Using the tongs as if the paper was hazardous waste material, he carefully placed the sketch inside and sealed the box.

He breathed an audible sigh of relief, then started shoving my clothing bags into a piece of paper. I stared at him, suddenly wondering why my sketches repulsed him, since he had a similar object himself. I reached toward the storage paper, but he yanked it away as if my leprosy would spread. "It's priceless. Don't touch it."

I curled my fingers into my palm.

He brusquely handed me a turquoise. "Put this in your pocket and leave it there."

I slowly stuck the rock in the small pocket of my jeans.

Marsgrove gave my parents a two-way journal that connected to one he gave to me and said that maybe I could visit at the end of term.

I took off to check last minute items and spaces in my room as they discussed school fees. He was trying to convince them that magical education was free in the Second Layer for everyone under age twenty-two. I was all for this seemingly magical way of bypassing fifty reams of scholarship and admittance forms.

Chapter Eight

And then it was time. They hugged me as if they didn't think they'd ever see me again. It was all too fast. I took one last glance at my parents, who were clutching each other, and said a soft, "Goodbye."

I'd be back, I mentally promised. With Christian in tow.

~*~

Thirteen minutes later, we entered the twenty-four hour coffeehouse near my high school. I scratched the skin near my new wrist cuff.

The ladies at the counter were helping customers. Mages living in the First Layer, Marsgrove had said, on the quick walk here. They looked like normal humans, just as they had every time I had come. But now I knew they were other, and I could see the cuffs I had dismissed previously. It made me nervous, where I had never been nervous here before.

"Go sit."

Marsgrove's quick glances around us and at his tablet were starting to freak me out. Following his instruction, I hunched over a table at the far end of the shop. Few customers were sitting. Just a guy with a Stetson, a girl with a thousand orange bangles, and a couple smooching in the corner. None of them looked magical. Though, who knew? The Stetson could be a cloaking device, the bangles might jam someone's hearing, and the lovers might turn into frogs at any moment.

Marsgrove ordered two double layer mochas. His cuffed arm rested on the counter. One of the women glanced at the cuff, but the other was clearly flirting as if she knew or recognized him.

As soon as he had the cups, his eyes met mine and he jerked his head toward the bathroom hall. He handed me a cup as soon as we were alone and out of view. I looked nervously around the hall. There were three doors—two with standard restroom stick figures and one stating authorized personnel only. I shifted on my feet and the shimmer of a fourth door slid into view. Then it abruptly disappeared. I leaned back just a measure, and again, like a mirage, or a perspective anamorphosis where I could only view the desired image from one particular angle and location, it came into view once more. The image looked like water steadily flowing between two panes of glass.

That had to be the entrance. I opened my mouth to ask Marsgrove, but he waved me off.

"Hurry. Drink up. You have to absorb magic in order to see the door and to get out of the First Layer," Marsgrove said in a low voice. "Only registered establishments have permits."

I shifted position again, and the waterfall door slid into view, like sidewalk art presenting another world in a single perspective. I could see it already, or at least the thin edge of it, but I followed his lead and drank from my cup.

Seconds later the waterfall doorway pulled into full glorious view.

"Lucky to have a shop with a permit so close," I said nervously, as we moved toward it.

He snorted. "Shops are everywhere. And they don't all sell coffee."

Without pausing he walked right through the cascade. I took a deep breath and followed—butterflies battering against my stomach, knees slightly knocking.

A light mist swept over me.

A closed, industrial-styled hall with twelve doors and a large trash can was on the other side. There was some form of writing above each door, three of them were written in glyphs I had never before encountered.

Marsgrove threw his cup in the trash can, so I followed suit and parted with mine as well. I tried to remember what Will had said about traveling. Pinch or absorb into another layer; port or ride within the layer. Which meant I was in the Second Layer—another dimension of the world—right now.

As Marsgrove approached a nondescript door, I looked above it and the text shimmered into readable words—Main Depot.

He opened the door and I carefully stepped through after him...and right into something straight out of one of my black-and-white patterned three-dimensional designs. I now knew what Will had meant when he'd asked me if I'd ever traveled to the Second Layer Depot. I stepped forward, entranced, and the door shut behind me. It opened again, admitting a man who had not been in the coffeehouse or hall. Which meant he had come from somewhere other than the coffeehouse, but had entered here using the same door that I had. No wonder Will was such a travel maniac—how cool were the possibilities?

Tubes crazily looped in the cavernous sky. Colors and objects whooshed through the clear pipes that overlapped and curled around each other like the rats nest of wires at the back of our old stereo system. One of the largest tubes was whooshing things through faster than the others. I could barely make out tones as each shape flew past.

A woman flew by on the back of a stork. A man passed riding what looked like a mechanical spider. Two kids shouted from atop a flying carpet. It was madness. Wonderful, chaotic, magical madness.

I turned to ask Christian how we were going to snag one of those carpets, the first word already curving my lips.

But the space next to me was empty.

Of course it was. I pressed a hand to my ribcage, trying to stop the pain from spreading. Would I ever stop doing that?

Christian? I tried reaching out again to the voice that had spoken in my mind, but no voice answered.

I clenched my eyes closed, then opened them and strained to focus on the sights in front of me. Dozens of arches peppered the landscape and led into domed rooms labeled with descriptors like gates, threads, pools, shimmer pinches, steps, archways, doorways, sheets, and planes. Signs pointed to long, dark hallways with other words—glimmer travel, vertical transport, plate transfer.

The letters on the signs shimmered as my eyes passed over them, then cleared into readable text.

A long line of people were queued up in front of a large dais where people were throwing down portal pads, then disappearing into their depths.

"Thinking of what you gave him?"

I turned to see Marsgrove looking grim. He was tucking items into his pockets. A hat, a bracelet, a handkerchief—none of them had been on him in the coffeehouse. I looked behind him and saw a stand labeled "Checkpoint." People were swapping things over the counter with a harried, bald-headed man who looked like he should be wearing a visor and taking bets. There was a large liquid pump behind him.

"No, I wasn't thinking of that at all."

"Come on. Let's get this over with." He walked under a sign saying "School Transport," and I quickly followed. Inside the room were nearly fifty doorways. The one labeled Excelsine was an interesting combination of classical Corinthian columns wrapped in vines twisting toward Gothic. Marsgrove used a skeleton key in the lock.

A gorgeous atrium of modern architecture spread before us and a woman in a crisp business suit nodded at Marsgrove as she walked by, heels clicking. Unexpected. I looked behind me at the busy depot station, then stepped through to the new world.

The atrium was wide and open, and a long ramp spiraled upward along the rectangular edges of the walls. Doorways dotted the sides of the wall to my right. Groups of students were gathered in front of dozens of the doors. Others passed by carrying bags and packs, and their clothing occasionally, remarkably, changed from one outfit to the next, rippling like waves.

Hanging in the middle of the atrium was a giant compass surrounded by five concentric silver rings, each rotating in various directions around the ones inside it. The edges of the rings were rippling in an asynchronous, nonuniform pattern as well. The inmost ring lay mostly flat, with just a bit of a slow ripple. The outermost one was wildly changing, even in its thickness.

A smile started to unwillingly spread my lips.

On the floor, directly beneath the enchanted gyroscope, was a large stone with Rosetta styled carved markings. The view through the windows showed the building edged a large circular grassy space. Hundreds of students lounged on the grass. Endless sky appeared through spaces between the buildings across the grass circle. Were we at the top of the mountain?

"Turquoise." Marsgrove motioned with his hand.

I blinked, then dug the turquoise nugget from my pocket. As soon as it left my fingers, words on signs grew hazy and people started speaking in languages and tongues that I had never encountered. I hadn't noticed it before now, but had everyone in the depot been speaking English?...or had I just been hearing English?

"Give me your finger."

I held out my hand, and quicker than I could react, Marsgrove punctured the tip of my pointer finger with a small knife that was glowing blue. I tried to pull my hand back, but he held firm.

"Hug the Shinar Stone and press your blood against it." He pointed to the large engraved rock in the middle of the atrium floor.

People were passing us, and the only second glances were appreciative ones toward Marsgrove.

Unnerved, I walked awkwardly over and wrapped my arms around the rock, bloody finger pressing into its surface. I held the position for a few seconds, then decided that I had provided a good enough sideshow. As I let go, the writing on the stone grew brighter, shimmering, and a nearly invisible layer of something pulled away with my movement, then snapped from the rock and settled on me. The writing dulled to stone-cut gray again. I walked quickly back to Marsgrove.

A girl passing said, "Toot oreet wamput," to her companion. Something in my brain shifted. Then shifted again, like tumblers slotting into place.

"It is my favorite parufferie," the other one answered, her shirt changing from red to blue, then back again.

I blinked. I could understand her. Though, what was a parufferie?

Another tumbler scraped and slotted.

"They sell the best perfume," the first girl said in clear English.

I almost stopped walking. I had hugged the Rosetta Stone.

Marsgrove was doing something complicated with his tablet.

"I can understand everyone," I blurted out.

And I could see students throwing balls of colored light where I hadn't been able to before.

"I can see magic."

"Of course you can." He continued fiddling with the tablet. He didn't seem as elated as I was at the suggestion that magic truly might be able to do anything.

"Anything." Christian's voice sounded relieved. But not as relieved as I was to hear him. Christian? He didn't answer.

"You'll have to renew the enchantment again in a few months, or learn how to see magic without aid." Marsgrove didn't sound as if he cared which I chose.

I looked around me in renewed anticipation. As soon as I raised Christian, I was going to do some serious learning. I watched as a woman walking across the atrium cast a jet of red at her feet. Immediately, she started moving at least forty miles an hour across the floor, disappearing down a hall.

Magic could do anything.

"Yes," Christian crowed, before going silent again in response to my flurry of mental questions. Why couldn't he answer me? If he would just answer—

"Good. You are now enrolled as a student." Marsgrove made a sweeping motion with his hand. Something settled on top of me like a liquid shell, then absorbed. He repeated the motion three more times with lips pressed firmly together. "This will have to do so you can't paint, just in case."

The man was a lunatic. I was totally going to paint.

He turned on his heel. "Follow me."

We entered a room containing seven arches, strode through the one second to the left, and emerged onto a section of flat grassland about three football fields long.

A grassland that then dropped sharply about twenty feet to lay flat for the next three football fields of land, then dropped again—giant terraces continuously spreading and descending thousands of feet, buildings of all varieties, styles, and sizes clumped together in places, open fields in others.

And the view...

The mountain was awe-inspiringly huge.

If the Tower of Babel existed, surely this was it. Or an anti-Tower—a strange enchanted fortress where people spoke in thousands of tongues yet still understood each other.

I breathed in a deep gulp of air. A fortress without altitude sickness. Boys played a football-like sport one terraced level—no, what had Will called them? Circles?—one circle down from us. A perfect sport for Christian. Euphoria bloomed. Soon. Soon.

The mountain was surrounded by expansive flat plains and towns

84

stretching out for miles. I could see clouds surrounding mountain tops in the distance, but none lingered here, making the view utterly unspoiled and fantastic.

My feet had slowed, trying to take in the visual thrill. Marsgrove motioned impatiently in front of another arch. "Hurry."

I kept waiting for him to say, "I'm late, I'm late, for a very important date."

That arch led us into a cozy Midwestern street. I blinked. It was almost too normal after seeing such a wondrous place earlier, but the mountain still stretched high above. A look down showed more mountain below, so we were still on Excelsine, just nearer to the bottom. Maybe this residential area was where students lived?

Everyone walking by was a businessperson, a parent, or a small child, though. Maybe this is where professors lived?

We eventually turned onto a slate path leading to a lovely two-story brick house.

"Through here."

I followed him inside and was surprised by the warm tones and stylish decor. The man obviously had money, although he was in need of a housekeeper. The house was immaculately clean in some places, irreparably cluttered in others. Marsgrove unlocked, then poked through a large wooden secretary. He grabbed a few items, then started climbing the stairs.

When I didn't immediately follow, he turned and said, "Come on, then," with a harried wave.

He walked into a bedroom, opened the closet door, and stepped inside.

I stepped over the threshold of the room, wondering where the closet might lead. The thought fled as a weight pressed down upon my cuffed wrist, then spread over me, constricting—like a fish caught in a net then hauled to land. I bent over, trying to catch my breath. The closet door slammed closed, as well as the door behind me, and I could hear a lock engage.

I closed my eyes, betrayal quickly pressing upon me again, as I breathed heavily in the pinched air. I was so stupid. If Marsgrove hadn't been acting so much like the White Rabbit with a tablet instead of a pocket watch...

The weight of the air lifted and I backed myself against the wall across from the door, eyes searching for weapons. There was a bed, a desk, an armoire, a black box attached to the wall, a wall screen, and some full bookshelves.

No scissors.

"It is the best I could do on such short notice."

I looked up to see Marsgrove's face, peering through a little barred window in the door that had not been there previously.

"Let me out, now," I said. I would even forgive him the joke, if he did it right away.

"It is for the best, really. For you." His face was almost sympathetic. "I can't let you loose on the world, but I also didn't take you to the Department. The man in charge makes Raphael look like a gregarious border collie. And my cousin...she would dissect you in an instant. Raphael runs free with whatever tool of mass destruction you gifted him with—in the midst of the treaty negotiations. I'm darkly tempted to circumvent Raphael's spell and yank the information from you, but he would have put in protections against me. Better for you not to be in the world at all, but matters have gone beyond that."

I swallowed my emotion with difficulty. Crying hadn't yet helped me deal with Christian's loss, and it wasn't going to help me now. "You told my parents you were taking me to school. I felt the magic of the oath. You told Will you wouldn't harm me."

"And I fulfilled my pledge, all of it. You are here. You are not hurt. You have extremely enviable shields, as promised, you just won't need them. You are enrolled as a student. Your class transcript, however, is blank until you have a start date, which you never will."

Will had stressed the idea of intentions mattering in magic, but Marsgrove had just taught me that words held power.

"Food will be delivered through the black box. Read, watch television, look out the window. Draw with the ordinary pencils in the desk. Magic cannot be performed inside this room, but too, no one can feel you here. Nullified." I could feel the net of the energy—magic—around me. "There are suppression and encapsulation fields on the room. It will protect you from yourself and also from anyone else. No one but the two of us can be in this house."

"I don't need protection, I need out. Now." I thought of Will's comment on time thresholds existing with black magic. "You can't keep me prisoner."

"You have no idea what is happening in our world." His expression was dark. "And I have no time for explanations. I'll check on you in a few weeks. And maybe I will teach you magic someday. When you will be useful, and I can control the risk."

He said it as if he expected me to understand. I stared back at him without response.

"Your belongings are in the closet, which you will be able to access in ten minutes. There is a bathroom and laundry through there as well. You can talk to your parents through the journal, but they can't get to the

* Into the Rabbit Hole *

Second Layer, even should a mage serve magic to them—which they won't.
Your police will never believe anything about magic due to the suppression
spells, and if the Department hears about them causing a fuss, they may
decide to dispose of them, then come after you. Keep those things in mind
when you decide what you are going to tell your parents tonight."

I swallowed down my hatred and just stared at him.

"Yell, if it makes you feel better. Throw something at the door or
windows. They are unbreakable. You can see and hear the outside from
here, but no one can see or hear in. Think of this as a...vacation. A soothing
field will kick in soon—or immediately, if you just accept it. Watch
television—that screen has a channel specially hooked to First Layer
programs. Teenagers like that kind of thing."

I continued to stare at him without expression, seeing that it unnerved
him.

"I'll check on you after the treaty negotiations are finalized. When the
danger won't be as high, and I won't be missed." He left quickly, and the
barred window closed, the wood threads reaching out to entwine and pull
themselves together, the iron becoming part of the grain. I heard the front
door close.

I touched the stomach of my long-sleeved shirt—the fabric covered my
tight camisole beneath, which secured the smooth paper of Will's sketch
against the skin of my stomach. A No. 2 penciled copy rested in
Marsgrove's document box. The best decision I'd made so far this
afternoon.

I wish I had trusted my unease in all other areas. I checked the large
black box and found a wrapped sandwich, a carton of vegetables, and a
glass bottle full of pink liquid.

There was no need to bang on the window or yell. I believed Marsgrove.
And I could feel the magic net already trying to stroke my skin and hair,
soothing. I also believed that with the cuff and the room spells and my
general lack of magical knowledge that I wouldn't be able to escape by
magic. I looked out the window, which had a view into the mountainside.
Craning my head, I could only see two circles up, the mountain towering far
higher than my view allowed.

Examining the desk supplies, I calmly opened a box of large paperclips
and began to unbend two. I wasn't going to let that soothing field turn me
into a vegetable. I shoved the comforting touch away, and it backed off.
But I could feel it there, waiting.

I inserted my paperclip probe into the keyway and nearly jerked my
hand away as the tumblers and pins audibly began to spin independently of
each other—at variable speeds and in various directions. The end of my

rake touched a pin, then the plate. The lock chomped down and bit my paperclip rake clear through, then spit out the loose part.

Staring at the sheared piece, I was suddenly glad I hadn't waited the ten minutes to get my pick set out of the closet, or my best rake would now be lost to me.

Bending another paperclip, I tried again. Since it took about half a second for the spinning to start, I took a guess that this was a protective measure, and that the correct key would not engage the spin. If I touched a pin without setting it, then touched anything else, the chomp would engage. If I pressed my torque paperclip in the wrong spot, the chomp would engage. It took me ten precious paperclips before I had a reasonable starting schematic drawn in my mind.

I had neither time nor paperclips on my side.

The door lock required me to rethink how a lock might work with magic—or at least with a magical creator—involved. The lock had the standard five pins, but the spinning was variable on each. Sometimes the first one spun clockwise at a rate of one turn per quarter of a second. Sometimes it spun counter-clockwise at a rate of one eighth of a second. Thankfully, there seemed to be a preset of the same six possible speeds on each of the tumblers. In the silent room, I tuned my ear into hearing which one was in play at which distance from me, and focused on figuring out which pin I needed to set first.

Two days later, I opened the door. The force that had been weighing down on me immediately spread out into the hall, the break in the net making it extend, looking for a way to connect its broken edges back together. As the net expanded, the force thinned and grew weaker. Combined with exhaustion and ongoing stress, the relieved pressure left me weak and shaky.

I waited by the front door with a fireplace poker and kitchen knife in my trembling hands for an hour, in case Marsgrove had somehow been alerted by the stretched magic.

Hugging the weapons to me, I started to realize why Will, after feeling vulnerable, might not have wanted to part with the sword I had drawn for him.

"Ren. Help."

"Yes. Just tell me how." But he was silent once again, and something that had been bothering me forced its way out, "Did you know about magic before?"

He had seemed as surprised as I was that fateful night when his fingers had started to glow. But how had he known about magic when he yelled at me the night I saved Will? Had he learned it in death?

He didn't answer, but whatever freaky things Marsgrove had done to me hadn't blocked out his voice, and I had to count that as a personal victory at this point.

I waited a few more tense minutes by the front door, then tiptoed back into the bedroom and grabbed everything from the closet, dragging the items downstairs, where I felt safer. I could feel the bedroom wanting the magic back, and I had the feeling that closing the door would suck all the magic back inside, sealing it again.

The lock on Marsgrove's secretary desk was simple. Ordinary and very similar to the one my parents had on theirs. It was obvious that he was used to using the magic on the house to do his warding. If others weren't allowed to enter the house, then there was no reason to truly lock anything inside of it.

Anything other than me.

The desk was littered with all kinds of Academy seals and papers. The drawers and slots also contained many interesting things—like his sweet storage paper, which was delicately propped in its very own wooden slot.

Smiling, I withdrew the storage paper and started loading it with my bags, setting each one on top and letting the magic of the paper pull them inside. After a moment of consideration, I tossed in the other items on Marsgrove's desk, which included a stack of money, numerous papers, a book on protection fields and one called "Primer on Magical Control."

I fought the notion of staying at the house while I figured out my plan of attack. I couldn't risk it, and I couldn't go home. Home was the first place Marsgrove would look, and going there wouldn't provide the answers I need to revive Christian.

I'd go back to the Depot and try another door.

~*~

It took dozens of failed bounce-backs on arches—arches that numerous passing mages swore went off-mountain—before I accepted that one of Marsgrove's spells prevented me from leaving Excelsine. My eight foot tall prison had grown to six thousand feet. After traveling all over the mountainside through different random arches, and even unsuccessfully attempting the crossing of two bridges across the river circling the base, I finally got a person to point me to a small inn a few circles up. I didn't spend time admiring the view or gloriously mixed architectures anymore.

The man at the inn counter greeted me politely in English. I watched his lips. It seemed like he was actually speaking English.

"You ok, kid?"

I was so tired and strung-out that I didn't think so, but nodded anyway. I fumbled the strange-looking bills I had taken from Marsgrove's desk onto the counter, hoping the amount was enough, and the man looked at me in sympathy as he took a few and pushed the rest back to me. Runaway, that look plainly said.

"You need any help, kid, you just let me know, ok?"

"Yeah, thanks." No way.

I locked the door to my hotel room, propped a chair under the knob, just in case, plopped down on the bed, and started a list in the notebook I had packed. I put "Get off this rock" at the top.

"Help me."

I pinched my lips together and with two dark strokes, crossed off the item I had just written. I dumped out the contents of Marsgrove's magic paper, and started rifling through his things. An unused administration packet was part of it—for me, I thought darkly—along with a missive begging for a solution to the "Olivia Price rooming situation," and three packets of transfer students who had withdrawn enrollment due to "security concerns." There was a note on top to "investigate familial ties."

I looked through the administration papers and the brochures, chewing on my lip, and turning over ideas. One propagandist paper proclaimed— The best libraries and resurrection experts in five layers!

Student population of fifteen thousand, read another.

Marsgrove had said he'd be back to visit me in my prison in a few weeks. Which meant, for those weeks, the one place I knew my jailor would not be was on this mountain. Whereas Will and a bunch of magical knowledge would.

I needed real shelter first. Though the innkeeper had only taken a few bills, I had a feeling that was due more to the pity on his face then the real price of the room. If I was going to stay at an inn or hotel, I was going to need to figure out how to make money, which would mean giving adults information about me.

I had hopped all over the mountain after escaping Marsgrove's house, and estimated that there were at least two hundred thousand people living on Excelsine. The mountain was unevenly divided into three parts. Students were on the generous top portion, the thinner middle section was composed of some weird gray swirly area that caused my wrist cuff to pulse anytime I got close, and adults—professors, shopkeepers, and the like— ruled the bottom levels. I'd stick out far more if I stayed down here, and I wasn't going to find a solution to any of my problems by hiding out.

Hopefully I could find Will on campus.

"Yes, help me."

I scratched around my wrist cuff and stared at the paper that stated that the Olivia Price rooming situation had been deemed "unstable" and there was a request to revisit a new roommate the following term.

Most of the official papers from Marsgrove's desk were approved by someone named Johnson. I carefully filled out a few documents, traced his signature, then used Marsgrove's seal, which matched up perfectly to the ones on the papers.

I opened the primer on control but exhaustion sealed my eyes closed. That night I dreamed of Christian dying, of my own death, and of ultramarine eyes staring at me from above.

Chapter Nine

OLIVIA PRICE

I AWAKENED EARLY and began the arduous climb up the mountain. Alone on the path, I had ample time to think. Equal amounts of apprehension, excitement, and terror flowed through me, and I began to second guess my decision.

A soft, comforting whisper wrapped around me. "You can do this, Ren. You're strong and capable."

Hearing Christian spurred me on. The journey suddenly seemed less lonely.

And before I knew it, stretching across the flat grass of the fifth band near the top of the mountain—and encircling the entire mountainside—was the mammoth nine-story structure straight out of Ancient Rome that was referred to in the administration packet as the Magiaduct, or more informally, Dormitory Circle.

A stone columned arcade lined the lower level, providing coverage for students walking from door to door. Symmetrically spaced between the entrance doors were gateways, allowing a tunneled path to the other side of the building. From the second floor skyward, the building was an unbroken wall of ancient multicolored stone and glass. In the morning light the façade glowed and shimmered, alive with color. If I survived the day, I would lovingly admire its classic architectural magnificence tomorrow.

With a cocktail of emotions stirring inside, I walked beneath the nearest arcade arch, passed a group of students laughing together, and approached a door. Apprehension. Excitement. Terror. The number thirty-two was carved into the stone above the wooden door, bright in the rising sun. I continued on to the right—hoping that walking counter-clockwise decreased the number count—past another stone gateway and to the next door. Thirty-one. It was a hike between doorways. The administration packet had mentioned thirty-six nine-story "dorms" each housing four hundred students, solidly ringing this level of the mountain.

People were running on top of the Magiaduct. Some of the workout gear was rather strange-looking, even from this distance. But the evidence of a track indicated you could at least move from one dorm section to the next at the topmost level.

I continued on until I reached the heavy wooden door beneath the stone-carved number twenty-five.

Nothing ventured, nothing gained. I swallowed hard and opened the door.

I had expected the interior to be stark and medieval, but the lower-level meeting and study area was fresh and bright with white slate floors and cream walls. Rich walnut furniture and comfortable sofas and lounge chairs upholstered in rich burgundy and forest green were scattered about in conversational pods, giving the room a warm and inviting feel. The area was a bustle of activity, with students entering, loitering, and exiting.

I climbed the nearest staircase and found room fifty-two on the second floor. I took a deep breath, hoisting my papers more firmly in the crook of my arm, and knocked.

No answer.

I knocked again, then leaned casually against the wall and inserted one of Marsgrove's straightened paperclips into the lock to see if a chomper engaged. No answer, no chomp.

Relief nearly unbalanced me. No one was inside and the lock was completely standard, thank God. I could have it scrubbed open in ten seconds. Two students engaged in a hot debate passed me.

"Social theory is important," the girl said.

The boy shook his head. "Brute force will always win. Magic is might."

I knocked on the door again, trying to look like I wasn't loitering, and discreetly pulled out my favorite rake and torque wrench from my brother's set, knee pressing my papers against the wall so that I could use both hands.

The door yanked open and a chilly voice said, "Yes?"

My papers spilled to the floor as I jumped away in surprise. I quickly bent my fingers around the pick and wrench, shoving them back along my wrist and up into my shirt sleeve. I cleared my throat nervously.

Potential new roommate Olivia Price was dressed in a tailored black and gray dress that looked very severe on her tall, thin frame. I couldn't help a glance at my own clothing, feeling more than a little out of place. But other students had been dressed in a wide variety of styles, especially the students whose clothing continuously changed form. More than a few people had been informally dressed in First Layer fashion.

I was fine. Normal looking and totally as if I belonged, I tried to assure myself.

I bent to collect my papers, then pasted on a bright smile and held up my forged documents. "I'm your new roommate."

Her hair was pulled tightly into a bun as severe as her clothing, and rectangular black glasses perched on the bridge of her very straight nose. She smiled down at me, but there was no humor in her eyes. "Are you?"

This now clearly qualified as a complete introduction failure. I tried desperately to keep my face calm and smiling. It had been a stupid plan. Thoughts tumbled through my head on how to nonchalantly extricate myself. I'd figure out something else. I had six thousand vertical feet of space to work with.

"Come in, then." She stepped back, a clear invitation to enter, despite the cold amusement decorating her features. I hesitated over the threshold, then walked inside.

The feel of a net descended and I lashed out with my arms, thinking that I had once more let myself be captured. But the magic gently pushed my limbs back to my sides. It swirled inside me and pushed against the cuff encircling my wrist. The net stroked me, then gently dissipated.

I squirmed, feeling suddenly like I was in the right place, then realized the austere girl standing silently in front of me had to think I was certifiable. The skin around her eyes tightened, loosened, then tightened again, as if she was surprised, then displeased by something.

I cleared my throat. "Hi." I tried to remember my cover story, as well as how I could admit to having gotten the room wrong. "Sorry. I just transferred from—"

"That is your side." She pointed to the empty bed and desk on the window side of the room.

My thoughts and words all crashed together. "What? Really? I mean, yes, great!" The feeling that I was in the right place intensified, then slowly dissipated.

There was a curiously blank look to her expression, all tightness gone. As if she had no emotional reaction to me at all anymore. "You stay on your side, I'll stay on mine." And with that, she turned to her desk and an enormous tome that was placed there.

"Oh. Er, thanks." She hadn't even asked me my name.

I quietly walked to the empty desk on the far side of the room. The energy that had been capped by Marsgrove's cuff was restless now, pushing and leaking, as if it had tasted freedom for a moment and now refused to be denied. The room's magic hummed around me.

Well, that had gone pretty well, actually. Totally antisocially, but having a roommate who didn't care what I did was exactly what I needed.

Loneliness pushed. I shoved it back.

I dropped my papers on the desk, then pulled Marsgrove's storage paper from under my camisole where it had been pressed against my back. Just in case I needed to travel quickly, I wasn't taking any chances. The storage paper was ingenious. There were a number of shelves drawn inside, and I had figured out last night at the inn that I just needed to concentrate on the item I wished to remove in order to have the proper shelf slide forward. From there, I could pinch and remove the desired item.

Putting things in and taking them out provoked a weird feeling inside of me, though. As if the paper knew I wasn't its true owner, and though it was reluctantly willing to let me use it, it issued a vague feeling of chastisement each time.

I had tried briefly to use Will's imprisonment sketch as a storage option, but the paper had remained impassive beneath the paperclip I was trying to insert. When I had willed it to accept the paperclip, the paperclip had detonated into a million fragments.

There had been a distinct feeling of disdain emanating from the sketch afterward. I was either truly certifiable, or I was going to need to embrace anthropomorphism in a more acute way.

I concentrated on Marsgrove's paper, then pinched and removed the overnight bag I had packed in the inn. Everything else would stay in the paper until I was more secure in my location. A sound alerted me, and I turned my head to see Olivia looking at my paper, a strange expression on her face.

"What?" Too late I realized that Marsgrove had called it priceless. But Mr. Verisetti and I had created one—somehow—and I had zero magical intelligence. Surely others existed.

Olivia's eyes narrowed on the paper, then she turned back to her giant book. Alarm spiked the energy residing under my cuff, and it started pushing.

If the storage paper was that valuable, I was going to have to figure out a way to secure it. I stared at the desk. I pictured a locked security box with a big, fat, unpickable lock.

There was a sudden whirling sound, and I stumbled back in alarm, hands up, as I stared at the desk.

The legs, desktop, and braces were breaking apart and hooking around and up, over and around, morphing into the locked security box I had been imagining.

The desk...was a Transformer.

Chapter Nine

Whoa, whoa. The energy escaping around the cuff was delighted. The first chapter of Marsgrove's primer had touted meditation. I tried to shift my mental image of the locked box into the calm peeling of rose petals. My desk legs changed directions and began to take on a distinctly floral shape. Olivia's writing motions slowed.

I put my hands out, trying to signal the desk to stop, but the stem wrapped around my arm. "No, not me, you. Stop!"

The desk became a stop sign, a boat, a bird, then a disembodied foot, flattening me to the ground. I struggled, fingertips just clutching the edge of my overnight bag and pulling it toward me, as the foot pressed harder. Olivia sat with her back to me, ignoring the whole thing. I shuffled through the administration packet, giving a grunt as the foot found and pressed a kidney. Why not a kitten? My desk turned into a roaring lion resting on my back. Oh, dear God. I frantically shuffled through the papers, fingers horribly sweaty as the lion batted at my hair. I madly read through the paper titled "Room How-tos."

"Reset!" I yelled.

And then I was awkwardly wedged under a normal, unexciting four-legged desk once more. I allowed my head to drop to the floor. Olivia's pen scratched her page, loud in the sudden quiet of the room.

My hand holding the paper dropped too. Thank God the administration papers had been in my overnight bag. I gracelessly extricated myself, read the instructions, and finally got the coding right. The desk became a nice normal workstation with a tabletop easel similar to the one I had at home. I made sure to utter "Set" twice, just in case.

I looked at the time to see an hour had passed and gave a strangled laugh, cheeks burning. "Uh, sorry about that," I said to my roommate. "We didn't have these at my old school."

Olivia, who was still writing, didn't respond. Her back was turned to me, as if a new roommate spending an hour trying to make her desk work was nothing out of the ordinary. She hadn't even spared me a glance, which made the episode a little less embarrassing, but seemed beyond weird.

Maybe everyone had this type of trouble? Somehow, I doubted it.

I walked to the window, determined to do something safe and normal for a few minutes. The room had an extraordinary view down the mountain, instead of up toward the higher levels. Strange animals hopped in the trees, and little explosions rocked a building a half-mile away. Sparks and lightning shot jets of fire into the midday sky. There were thick clouds a few levels below and massive shapes dove through them. I couldn't believe my roommate hadn't chosen the window view. But her crisply made bed was across the room and it was the bare one that was pushed up against the

96

outer wall.

"Is—ouch!" I jumped as something zapped me. I turned to see Olivia staring over the top of her glasses in disapproval.

"I don't like to be disturbed." She turned back to her tome.

I stared at the back of my new roommate's tightly bound head, then looked back out the window. The jumpiness that had been my constant companion since I had entered the coffeehouse days ago wouldn't settle. My last therapist would say I was suffering from anxiety.

I took catalog of my new illegally-obtained room. It was Spartan. Two beds, two outwardly normal-looking desks, two bureaus, a cupboard and three large mechanical box contraptions. Olivia's side was neat and pine-fresh. If it weren't for her books, there would be nothing personal on her side at all. And the types of books—with spines bigger than my head—weren't what I would have normally called personal.

I thought of my walls at home—before I had killed them. They had been completely cluttered. If I stayed here more than a week and didn't temper my usual stress relief activities, Olivia was going to be in for a rude shock.

I was bursting with questions on everything from how to get off the mountain to how to raise the dead to how to work any spell. I couldn't ask those, though, if I wanted to appear normal. But I could ask her a general question. I waited for her to close her giant book and to set aside her journal.

"Do—ouch!"

She set down the sharp little metallic rod that she had used to zap me again. "I don't like to be interrupted while I am changing tasks."

I rubbed my arm. "Do you like to be spoken to at all?"

"No. You should refrain."

I reminded myself that this was a good thing. It was like hiding out in plain sight at an inn that just happened to have an ornery troll who lived in the corner but didn't speak.

Ornery cat. Troll had my imagination conjuring pictures of her eating former roommates.

She disappeared into the bathroom, which I had also quickly cataloged as utilitarian, and I leaned my head against the window. I didn't want to unpack, just in case, but it was going to look suspicious if I did nothing.

I made the bed. I would be sad to lose my cozy sheets and Guernica comforter, but I had learned the hard way six weeks, four days, and nine hours ago that things were replaceable, people weren't. I put a few changes of clothes in the bureau and set up my toiletries—also disposable—in a free nook above the sink.

Chapter Nine

The picture of Christian and me at the beginning of summer was soon perfectly squared on the windowsill next to the bed. A photo of the four of us at a family wedding, and another of us after one of his football games, went up too. None of these were disposable, but the originals were on the server at home. And I needed the comfort.

I looked at Will's sketch. The drapes were still there, but the rubbish in front had disappeared at some point when I hadn't been looking. I propped the heavy paper against the wall near my pillow.

But as much as I wanted to crawl under my covers and never emerge, I couldn't afford to hide. I had to find the answers I needed in order to resurrect Christian.

Olivia started edging around the room, gathering things, flicking her wrist to call things to her. She obviously had to depart, but was reluctant to leave me alone in the room. This made me feel better, somehow. If she had been worried about me earlier, she'd have just run out and gotten a...police mage, or something...to arrest me. Her actions spoke more of a long-term evaluation of what harm I might be capable of inflicting. She did a number of complicated things to her stuff before she left. Probably warding me against poking.

Stone-faced and unblinking she left, and I began poking.

The first two mechanical boxes ended up being some sort of refrigeration and reheating units. I decided to label them strangely with words like "fridge" and "microwave." The last one was a black box similar to Marsgrove's. Some sort of delivery unit?

I checked out her neat stash in the cupboard. There were a lot of "Magi Mart" labels.

I could see the papers on her desk and notes on her bulletin board. All of the notes were perfectly squared and visible. I didn't need to rummage through anything. One of the notes said "Rule the World" in perfect block letters. I blinked. Underneath was a list in shorthand code that I couldn't make sense of.

I decided not to touch anything on her desk after all.

But I needed to learn the door lock, so I could enter quickly, as if I actually possessed a key. Scrubbing was the fastest method for easy locks, but the sounds were like...well, like you were illegally picking a lock. If Olivia were inside at the time, then game over.

I opened the door and poked my head out. I waited for a pixie-like girl to walk by before I wedged my foot into the opening and curled my hands into place, forcing my muscles to relax as I figured out which pin had to be set first, then which second. Three, Four, Two, Five, One. I stared at the brass placard on the door that read fifty-two and attached the order sequence, as well as the physical memory of what force needed to be applied to the torque wrench, to my mental image of the placard.

It would take me six seconds to open the door now. With a little practice, I'd get that down to three. Magic locks or physical scanners would have screwed this plan from the get-go.

I curled up on "my" bed and looked out the window. Groups trudged past below, people laughing and talking, engaged in normal relationships and activities. Happy. Silence stretched around me. Even if I'd been a real student, entering midway through the school year sucked. Groups were well-established. I had seen it all over campus as I'd frantically dashed by.

Loneliness sat in my gut, as it had for weeks now, morosely staring at me.

Whatever. I didn't need friends. I needed Christian.

I pulled Marsgrove's paper toward me and retrieved two journals. Sitting on top of my Guernica bedspread, I sketched the day's events into my personal journal, logging the emotion and actions in pictured form.

I closed my journal and looked at the clock on the wall with its weird hands and inscriptions that made no sense. It was similar to an astronomical clock, but there was a "shift" hand and an "enchantment" hand and the signs of the zodiac doubled to twenty-four. I wondered who had dreamed up the zodiac first—people here or people in my Layer. I opened up my phone, which was gamely keeping time in airplane mode. There was something that vaguely resembled an electrical outlet in the wall near my desk that I would have to test at some point, if I wanted my cell to continue ticking, but I'd wait until I absolutely had to test it.

By comparing my phone with the wall clock, I guessed that noon would be the Sagittarius at the bottom.

Ok. I just had to adjust my metric and figure out how to tell minutes—the disc in the middle maybe? I looked around for some sort of wizard phone and a phone book. It would be really handy to call Will right about now, but I had no idea how to even begin that kind of search. I could try hanging out in front of the dorm, but what if his dorm section was on the other side of the mountain circle?

"Help me."

The plaintive call hurt. It curdled my insides with the knowledge that I wasn't able to do anything to stop the pain. It was past time to gain that knowledge.

I pushed the administration documents around until I unearthed a brochure for the Student Center. It proclaimed itself to be a one-stop spot for new students, for students seeking information on changing disciplines, and for internship searches. The building was located on the sixth circle, which meant it was close—one level down from the dorms. I could walk that. Thank God, for if it had been on the, like, twentieth circle, it would have involved a hike of three thousand feet or attempts at thirty random arches.

I gathered my things, securing the storage paper and Will's prison paper onto opposite sides of my torso again. Everything else went into my pack. I'd grab a bunch of papers and guides from the center, then hurry back here to sort through everything.

Shoulders hunched tightly, head lowered so as not to make eye contact, I walked down the first section of stairs. As I rounded the landing, uproarious feminine laughter caused me to raise my head. A boy was levitating up two steps at a time, with his hands steepled in front of him, and a group was cheering him on.

I was really going to have to stop calling them people. Mages.

The map showed the Student Center location to be down a staircase from the highest numbered dorm. I walked until I reached Thirty-Six, then descended the staircase nearest to it. It was quite steep, and I could see movement flashing past me on the right. Some alternate form of transport that I couldn't quite make out. I really hoped no one veered from their path, because I wasn't going to feel the impact until my guts squished out on the stone path at the bottom.

The flashing didn't seem to be present on the field of the sixth circle below, but I hurried across the perceived trajectory of the path, just in case. This part of the circle had a well-groomed grassy field. Large enough to play a regulation game of football.

A low stone wall had been built into the mountainside and would make a great spot for watching and cheering.

"I like it."

My breath hitched at the warmth in the mental thought and the familiar, affectionate delivery.

"Out, out, out!" He then said in a singsong fashion, which was decidedly more unnerving and very unlike my brother.

I picked up my pace until I reached an Art Deco building with a placard that said "Student Center." I quietly entered. The building was large, but no one seemed to be seeking information. I breathed a sigh of relief that I was alone and started browsing through the brochures on the shelves. The front was set up as a sort of welcome center akin to the ones we would sometimes stop at when we drove over a state line. The room extended back in an L-shape that I couldn't see beyond.

I started pulling useful and interesting titles—Welcome to Excelsine, Warping Techniques, and Traveling the Mountain.

"Just flex it!"

I froze at the voice. Clutching my traveling guides and intro brochures, I peeked around the corner of the "L."

A girl with short black hair and a distinct Erté vibe—sleek, stylish, and outrageous—that perfectly matched the architecture, stood behind a desk, looking down at a device and bopping along to some inner playlist. She looked to be about seventeen too and just as short as I was. She drew her fingers along a card on the desk, and sang, "Flex it day, flex it night, hit that mage, oh, just right!" One finger touched the skin underneath her ear and she tapped three times, as if adjusting the volume of music I couldn't hear. "Just flex it!"

Her head bobbed back and forth, and she grabbed the card she had been touching and shoved it into the open slot on the thin top edge of the device. She clicked the card into place, her head still bopping left and right and her body following along with the movement. When she turned in the midst of a bop, I blinked to see a large hardbound book on top of her device. She flipped through it, then held a finger down, and I could see a faint trace of blue. She pushed the thin top edge of the device, and the book disappeared as the card ejected. She deposited the card back on the table and shoved in another.

Something must have alerted her to my presence, because she looked up sharply, eyes narrowed on my position. Eyeliner drew itself around her eyes and angled out. Rose red painted her lips. She looked down at the brochures in my hands and her expression transformed.

She was suddenly beaming and spreading her arms wide. The eyeliner and lipstick disappeared, making her look younger again. "I'm Delia!" Her hands clapped together.

I nodded slowly, stretching a smile, uncertain. "Hello."

She seemed to be waiting for something, some kind of recognition, and when I didn't give it, her smile grew. "Wonderful." She skirted around the desk. "You are new, you are smart and magically talented, and you have come to the right place!"

My bullshit meter started ringing, but her big eyes were shining with sincerity.

"I just stopped in quickly. I really need to run," I said.

"No!" She plucked the brochures out of my hand, placed them on the counter, and guardedly looked behind me toward the door. I did too—we were still alone.

"The authorities are a bunch of flingweasels around here," she whispered. "The really good places are on the secret list. Hang on."

Flingweasels?

She leaned over the front of her desk, rifling through papers. While she wasn't looking, I snatched the brochures from the counter and shoved them into my bag. "Here it is!" She handed me an illustrated map. "It's only for the upper six circles of the mountain—the cartographer graduated last year before he could do more—but this will allow you to get anywhere on the most important levels, quickly."

Near the Student Center, the map featured a patch of green labeled "Blarjack" with a note beside it that read, "Pops out near the entrance to the cafeteria." Another location nearby indicated a tree with a flashing "Entry", and when my gaze hit it, the map whirled to a drawing of an obelisk three layers up that said "Exit."

I let my eyes scan the map, watching it move in coordination with my gaze and zoom forward on a section whenever my eyes stilled. Setting my finger down on a section froze the map so that my eyes could freely take in everything in view at leisure. Once I let go and looked away, the map zoomed back out, resetting. My fingers itched to make something like this. "Construct map" etched itself right below "create a storage paper" on my list of future art studies.

"Thank you," I said sincerely, watching how the map world tilted.

Controlling magic sucked, but art magic rocked. Magic had killed my brother, but magic was going to bring him back. Mages created great items, but also sought to enslave. This world was a study in contrasts for me so far.

"No problem. If you just use arches, you still have to walk miles. Totally screws with the hair, especially if the weather mages are messing with the humidity on one of the circles."

"Oh, thanks."

She clapped her hands together. "I have so many things for you," she gushed. "When I arrived tonight, I didn't know I would get the chance to influence the life and goals of a new student! Do you have any questions, anything at all?"

She looked expectant. I took a chance. "What do you do if you are...blocked?"

"Your magic?"

"Yes."

"Oh my goodness, how horrible. Horrible! But don't you worry, dear." She reached over and patted my hand. A green bracelet sat atop her black cuff. "I have just the thing."

I thought of the strangled flowers in our living room and the murky paint dripping from my walls. "Will it help with control too?"

"Oh, now you have to go to the meditation class tonight. And learn everything. This is perfect timing, the universe seeking to guide you! To rearrange your chakra, your chi, your twining vines! It is a must for anyone wanting to connect with their magic on a deeper level. Mandatory."

She gave me the address of a building she said was near the cafeteria, and thirty minutes later I was toddling out of the center loaded down with documents Delia had pushed into my hands. She had repeatedly grabbed any brochure that I took off the shelf, saying that I needed the "good stuff." I had managed to sneak in a few of the brochures, though, darting around to do so while she was unearthing the next thing in the back. I wondered if I could figure out her hours so that I could return when she wasn't working.

Will was normal. Well, there was that mad scientist vibe, but he was mostly normal. I really hoped he was the standard and that all mages weren't as strange as Olivia and Delia. Or as diabolical as Marsgrove and Verisetti. Maybe playing with the forces of nature made one peculiar or unconscionable.

The map Delia had given me was dead handy, though. I watched it bounce around and decided to try the Blarjack portal to get me up near the cafeteria. Magical meditation to get my magic unblocked sounded sensible, and if it was a session, I could hide unnoticed in the back. I needed to start somewhere. I tucked the map and my papers into my bag and stepped toward the portal.

Chapter Ten

CULTURE SHOCK

- ✓ MEET SOMEONE WHO gives me a sweet map? Check.
- ✓ Enter roped off patch of greenery based on sweet map? Check.
- ✓ Find out said patch sucks me through the ground and ejects me into a deep swamp—which turns me green? Check.
- ✓ Realize "Blarjack" is a seaweed-dripping swamp monster? Check.
- ✓ Swim at Olympic pace then throw myself over the swamp bank? Roll down subsequent hill? Check and check.
- ✗ Hatch scary little Blarjack babies from my toenails in three days? No check. *Yet.*

A little sign next to the pond said "Blarjack—Danger Level Two."

I was really, really hoping that almost getting eaten by Swamp Thing was the worst thing that could happen in a Blarjack pool, because I was dripping swamp snot, and the goo that was still on me was *moving.*

I wiped feverishly at my face, arms, chest, and legs, breathing shallowly through my nose. My bag was water resistant only, but there was no way I could open it now to check the damage. I desperately wanted to check the sketches under my shirt, but likewise didn't want to infect them, in case they had made it through unscathed. My current camisole was made of wicking fabric, so it was possible they had survived. I tried to laugh. It wasn't emerging right.

A boy on a unicycle peddled by, cackling madly, billowing sleeves straight from the Old Testament outstretched as he tried to keep upright. He glanced at me, then pulled his arms up. All of the goo and green swept from me up into the air in two arcs, as if he were parting the Red Sea, then, with a downward thrust of his arms, crashed to the ground around me. A little Blarjack goo hopped its way back onto my shirt and I vigorously shook it off. I could have sworn I heard a tiny, "Noooooo!" as it fell to the ground.

"Thank you!" I yelled after Magical Moses as he peddled by.

He lifted a hand in a backwards wave, then promptly zapped some poor sap walking down a flight of stairs further down the path with a slim bolt of lightning. The boy tumbled to the ground.

The cackling continued as the unicycle zipped left and disappeared from view. A girl with a red tablet raced after the unicycle. The fallen boy brushed himself off, muttering expletives, and continued on his way.

I blinked. Ok. Glad I had gotten the helping hand, instead of the hindering one.

I quickly rose and moved away from the Blarjack goo, which was trying to recollect. I stepped onto a flagstone path between buildings that led to what looked like the pinnacle of the mountain. I...needed to learn how to shield myself against magic. Marsgrove's shields obviously sucked like everything else about him. But meditation class experienced a big, fat mental slash on the list, as well as any other suggestion uttered by Delia.

Emerging from between the buildings, I was immediately assaulted by yells and screams. A thick group of mages running toward me abruptly parted, like a school of fish slicing in two directions to escape a predator. A rhinoceros charged through the middle. A rhinoceros...on a mountain?

I pressed my hand against my forehead. Maybe...maybe I had hit my head? Maybe Blarjack water caused hallucinations?

A few fleeing mages tripped their fellows, before darting into the spaces between the buildings to the right and left of my position. The unlucky people went sprawling and were immediately trampled. Five feet from impaling a doomed mage, the rhinoceros disintegrated into what looked like...Skittles. A million little rainbow hued rocks hit the flagstone path around the doomed mage with a clatter.

People were yelling, but I decided to...walk away. I stopped at a low stone pillar to check my sanity, and more importantly, my backpack. Damp, but not ruined. I touched my stomach and heard paper crinkle. Relieved, I did the same with my back. I'd have to check them thoroughly later, but I felt a little better.

I dug out the travel map—the *real* one—from my bag. The flattened top of the mountain, which formed Top Circle, was behind me. Located along its perimeter on the map were the cafeteria, the Administration Building, the Student Union, and several classroom buildings. Here, as with Dormitory Circle, the architecture had a great deal of Roman and Greek influence, but there were also two modern glass buildings, two of the Collegiate Gothic variety, three Neo-Georgians, and other forms intermixed, some decidedly odd—most notably, a large Gypsy tent, a colonial log cabin, and a geodesic dome.

The map indicated the long classically columned building where students were exiting in droves was the cafeteria. It took up the entire northern side of Top Circle.

Hundreds of flags were mounted on the buildings surrounding Top Circle, flying in every direction, defying physical wind conditions. Movement swirled around the flag poles and my breath caught.

Dragons the size of eagles soared into the air—lithe, graceful, blue, green, and red forms undulating on the winds, which seemed to be swirling in all directions. Other animals flew in the airstreams as well—familiar looking birds along with creatures straight out of the imagination of Hieronymus Bosch. Jets of fire and blue wind flared upward from the edges of the immense circle of grass in front of me. The winged creatures ducked and dodged and caught the jet streams and twirled up, up, up, into the clouds.

"I like them," Christian said warmly.

"Fly free, free, free!" emerged high and tinny directly on its heels.

"Dragon Wednesdays are the best project the weather and tech mages have ever done together, frankly," one student said to another as they walked by me.

"We'll see if you still think that the day one of the big guys decides to come play."

A small dragon caught a flare of blue and shot upward. He executed a smooth backflip over a cloud, opened his jaws and roared. Blue flame pierced through an adjacent cloud, bursting it out in the middle, sucking around the edges, and flaring like a nuclear mushroom, then rained white and blue sparkles on the grass.

I looked at the immense expanse of grass and the people lounging and playing on it, unconcerned or tickled by the unnatural shower. They looked like normal college students, except for the jets of color that they too played with and released. One girl spun a ball of red into the shape of a cat with her hand. It bounded across the grass, then dissipated into the air in a projection of fire and light. Her skirt turned the color of the firecat, projected flames licking down from it.

I hunched against the pillar, feeling completely exposed—a mouse in the middle of a swarm of hawks. At the far end of the grass circle were a bunch of guys playing a rugby-esque sport, propelling a ball by magic. Colors formed a comet tail as the ball was passed or kicked. A guy raced down the field toward me with one arm outstretched overhead, and made a fantastic one-handed catch, hauling the ball to his chest. He turned, backing up a few steps as he taunted the guys down the field. Christian would have immediately recruited him.

My feet started toward him. I stopped abruptly, troubled, as a group walked between us. The tug to walk to him was almost overpowering. Disturbing. He turned suddenly, brows creasing as he searched the groups of people streaming out of the cafeteria and onto the walk, and I forgot how to breathe as he suddenly seemed to zoom into view and my eyes met ultramarine blue for a moment.

Another large group of girls walked between us, breaking the unnatural zoom and eye contact. The view of him was imprinted in my mind, though. He was dark, athletic, and wind-blown, sporting the echo of the smirking smile he had worn upon making the catch—the kind that appeared only on the faces of guys who were totally convinced of their own skill.

I took another step, then cursed and stopped. I pushed against the overwhelming urge to walk to him.

His smirk slipped fully into a frown, he turned, and threw the ball. A loooong way. He had to have used magic, but I couldn't see any tendrils as I had with the others. He ran back into the thick of the pack and a number of the guys rallied around him.

I couldn't see the color of his eyes anymore, but that shade had been haunting me for weeks.

I tried to concentrate on the other players and to still my traitorous feet as I shakily walked past, hugging the edge of the path, and trying to think of other things over the sound of the blood pounding in my ears. Christian would assuredly want to try this sport after I got him ba—

A boy screamed, holding his throat, then leaned forward and projectile vomited blood all over the field. Spells flew, and players took hits hard enough to cause someone to wake up three days later, drooling. I skirted the steps and picked up my pace, but couldn't prevent a last look at Alexander Dare, who was standing with his arms crossed at the edge of the pile-up, looking down at the bodies and blood in amusement.

I felt curiously blank. I wondered if this was what people meant when they mentioned culture shock.

~*~

I took the long way back to the dorm, eschewing magical travel, walking down the circular levels. By the fourth circle I was sweating profusely and willing my feet to move faster, like the lady in the Administration Building had. Nothing happened. I concentrated harder. Rose petals peeling, rose petals peeling. Nothing. I sucked at being a mage. Rose petals! *Rose petals!*

A hole opened up in the middle of the air with a loud boom and my shoe exploded from my foot. The shoe sailed right through, a perfect goal, then the hole closed with another boom.

I had just blown my shoe from existence.

As people strode nonchalantly by, I stood motionless, contemplating nihilism, then began to hobble back to Dormitory Circle with one bedraggled left shoe and three holes in the sock on my shoeless right, ignoring everything around me. I tried to make myself feel better by imagining my shoe balancing on top of an electrical line somewhere in First Layer Kalamazoo.

Limping over the stone walk leading down to the fifth circle steps, I tried not to make eye contact with anyone. As I stopped to dislodge pebbles from my sock, my eyes traveled past a storefront sign that read "Magi Mart."

Olivia had all of those foodstuffs labeled with the name. My stomach rumbled.

I shuffled inside hoping they didn't have a "no shirt, no shoes, no service" policy, otherwise I was going to have to argue the merits of one shoe and one sock.

The store was tiny. She had gotten all that stuff here? I could see a box of Cheerio-looking cereal on the shelf. Safe. Weird, though, that there was only one. In fact, there was exactly one of *every* product on the shelves. I reached up to get the nice, safe box of non-Cheeri—

"Ow!" I rubbed my arm where I had been zapped.

"Don't touch the displays," a bored, half-dead voice said. Likely to match the bored, half-dead guy at the counter up front.

Great. So I was supposed to magic the box or something? I'd probably blow the store off the face of the mountain. I carefully considered my hunger needs versus the guilt of mass destruction. It was close, and hunger was starting to edge ahead.

A dead sigh emerged from behind the counter. "Press the button and the product will appear in your basket."

I looked around for a basket.

Nothing.

I switched my thinking around, looking for a basket that wasn't really a basket. Just like my desk was really a super-transformer.

My eye caught on a stack of cards on a ledge near the window. The cards were printed with the image of a wicker basket. I picked one up and examined it. It glowed briefly, then returned to its brown hue. I looked back at the display and carefully pressed the button under the cereal. A frisson of energy went through me and down my fingertips into the card. I looked at the card to see my previously empty basket had a rectangular yellow box placed neatly inside. I stared at it. The image zoomed up to hologram above the card in all its bright yellow glory. My fingers promptly released the card, and it dropped to the floor.

I looked around and hurriedly picked up the card. Damn magic-startle-reflex.

I started populating all sorts of things—way more than I actually needed for the night, but it was fascinating to feel and then watch the items appear. And...I had no idea how to remove one—pushing the button again simply populated my basket with one more of the item—so I ended up with a basket so overcrowded that I imagined my card was starting to bend.

I took my card up to the register. "So, uh, how do I get the items out?"

Dead sigh. God, up close, the guy even looked like a zombie. "Place it in the slot in your room's delivery box then tell it to appear."

"Ok. Thanks." That made me a little nervous. My eye caught a display of a pen and pencil and my pulse jumped. The pencil was labeled "Layer 2 Pencil." "Is that a magic pencil?"

The guy stared at me. "Yes. Munits or credit?"

I quickly populated the card with three pencils and three pens. "Munits?"

Dead sigh. "Magic units. That will be twenty-five even."

From my pocket, I withdrew a few soggy bills from Marsgrove's roll.

Dead guy looked at me as if I were both gross and an idiot, then gingerly handed a bill back. I kind of wanted to ask him if he or his family could give me any tips on raising the dead, but kept my lips shut and put the card in my pocket and took my change.

I didn't know if the card or delivery box included refrigeration, so I hurried back to the dorm, quickly picked the lock, thankful Olivia was still gone. I stuck the card in, excited, and throwing my hands out like Magical Moses, I told my groceries to appear.

And appear they did—exploding into a hodge-podge of mush, mash, goo and pulp all over the ceiling, walls, and floor.

Immediately, a little self-cleaning device in my desk whirled out and got to business. I heard the trash can next to my desk flush.

I rounded up the food products that had survived and quickly ate a completely normal tasting burrito. After crumpling up the paper and wiping my hands, I sighed, then fished out some cleaning products from the bathroom and got to work on the surfaces that hadn't been cleaned. Magic kind of sucked.

Knock, knock, knock.

I put down the spray bottle and carefully pulled the door open an inch.

A good-looking, uniformed guy with smooth, dark skin and closely-cropped hair stood on the other side. He had a royal-blue tablet similar to

Will's violet one.

"Florence Crown?" He had a nice deep voice and a trustworthy vibe, but *he knew my name.*

"No, thanks. I'm full-up on candy and magazines." I started to close the door, but his foot wedged between it and the jamb.

He pointed his tablet at me through the space, and his deep voice took on an edge. "You are making this worse on yourself, Miss Crown. You just performed a Level One Offense. You either open this door fully or my tablet will vaporize you."

I opened it quickly. I had seen both Will's and Marsgrove's tablets do some freaky things.

He pulled the tablet back and clicked a few things on the screen. "Just kidding about the vaporization. Squad joke. But blowing up groceries is prohibited, as the delivery mechanism can react in a volatile way, so I'll have to punish you with impunity."

My heart leaped into my throat.

He smiled. "I'm just kidding. This is a first offense, and let's keep it that way. Be a good citizen, Miss Crown, or else. Do you run?"

I couldn't tell if he was completely serious or having me on. He stood between me and partial freedom, so I decided to treat him as serious. "Yes?"

"Great. Were you headed anywhere soon?"

"The library?" That seemed a safe destination—populated and normal.

"Good. Run to one of the libraries and run back." His tablet dinged. He smiled. I tried to smile back, mentally tightening the straps on my pack. I had just been tagged. How long did I have before Marsgrove found me now? The boy gave me an encouraging look. "You say, 'I will run to a library and back, by my magic I so do vow.'"

I repeated the phrase, plotting out my next move. Something wrapped around me, squeezing briefly just like in the administration building and when I'd first entered the dorm room. Magic testing and settling.

"Great. Make sure you do so or you will regret it. Have a nice day!"

I nodded quickly as he turned and walked back down the hall, tapping his tablet. I shut the door, threw everything except my bed linens and toothbrush into Marsgrove's paper, and ran outside. Standing at the front of the building, a pressure started to build in me. A painful cramp made me bend over briefly. I was hoping this was the punishment magic instead of Marsgrove doing something freaky to me from somewhere. Another cramp rolled over me.

I concentrated on the travel map and willed my magic to pinpoint my location and take me to the library by the fastest route possible. It snapped into place, like a freaky paper GPS.

I started running, following the dotted path on the page.

I knocked over a trash can, then stopped to right it—full body cramp.

Climbed a wall—too slowly—zap, zap, zap.

Bounded two fences with limited liabilities but had to dodge bushes that reached out to ensnare my shirt, which slowed me down—double cramp.

Ran through the middle of a practice field—got yelled at—social pain only.

Overturned another garbage can—left it. Guiltily circled back around to pick it up—light zap.

When I experienced remorse, the pain lessened. Interesting, but irrelevant in my current panic.

I vaulted the last impediment, and brushed a banana peel from my leg in disgust as I ran to the giant steel building in front of me. It reminded me a little of the mechanical spider I had seen walking in the Depot—all slim silver limbs crossing, beams supporting each other in diagonal and crosshatched fashion. I checked the map one last time to make sure I had the right place and breathed a sigh of relief.

Opting for the "fastest" way had obviously been the wrong thing to ask. Being a feral mage kind of sucked. I should have asked the map for the "best" way to reach the library.

I'm sure this was another one of those training things that normal mages were taught from birth—or at least for the two to three years at prep school—how to ask questions of and to magical objects and creatures. Visions of genies and lamps and frogs and sphinxes combined with dire warnings and consequences in my mind. Who knew what Aladdin might have become in this stinking world? And that frog prince? Probably a total bum.

The library building was...enormous. My skin tingled as I ran over a stone seal embedded into the walkway. A sign on the door shimmered, then read, "No chaos magic may be performed on textbooks under any condition—up to a Level Four Offense."

I slowed down—no zap, no cramp, no pain. I leaned over, resting my hands on my knees as I surreptitiously looked around. I couldn't see Marsgrove.

My punishment seemed to be fulfilled by crossing the seal so close to the entrance. I could run somewhere else on the mountain now, and keep running, or I could enter a place overflowing with knowledge and try to figure out how to free myself.

I slipped in behind a group of mages.

A sea of desks, support beams, and open staircases spread before me. In contrast to my emotion, the space was brightly lit and optimistic; the lighting almost jaunty. Across the space, mages were flipping through books and taking notes by hand or with wands and small scepters, circling hands and cursive loops over papers, and plugging cards into readers similar to Delia's. Some desks were pushed together and people were animatedly talking to each other, yet quiet stretched over the whole room. Obviously an enchantment of some kind.

There was no evidence of a help desk.

I watched as students climbed and descended the various staircases. The floors above were made of glass—both clear and frosted—making the view visually terrific through the geometric layers that were formed. Most of the students descending the staircases were carrying cards. I jogged up the nearest staircase. No one on the first floor was going to help me unless I was prepared to start shouting insanities.

The second floor had a far different floor plan. Wall after wall jutted out from the sides, others formed cross sections in the middle to create large industrial partitions. Smaller nooks and crannies were set up between some of the walls and cross sections and contained cozy chairs. Students stood in front of the walls, manipulating pages and occasionally protrusions—pages blazing past, as if the walls were giant tablet computers. Fully-formed books slid out with pages printed by magic.

I perched uncomfortably on a chair and withdrew my journal and the single Layer 2 pencil that had survived the magical unpack explosion. I started drawing a snare for Marsgrove while surreptitiously and carefully watching a student's fingers manipulate a wall. Nearly all the books on her wall featured a woman dancing with magic.

Each time she touched a cover on the wall, out slid a faint rectangular outline that bloomed into a fully-formed book that she could flip through. She nodded at one finally, her dark brown hair moving like a silky curtain, let the book slide back into the wall, and swiped the picture toward the edge. A card popped out of a slot at the end of the wall. As she walked away with the card, the wall turned to plain frosted glass once more.

With the card in hand, she climbed a staircase to the next floor. I flipped my journal shut and followed. The third floor was a maze of white rooms that contained frosted floors. I watched her enter one and shut the door. A little green light blinked over the door and a timer beneath it indicated one hundred twenty. I discreetly checked out a few others. One timer read ninety-three. Another read forty-two.

Next to those rooms was a singular room with a red door. A red light shaped as a skull and crossbones hung over the threshold. The number fifteen in red was unblinking below it.

Continuing on, I tried to get up to the fourth floor, but ended up on the first floor twice, then the second floor before I stopped trying. Magic portals in the library? Great. Possibly useful as exits though. I sketched them quickly in my journal.

Three adults wearing black business suits strode down the staircase from the third floor and toward the steps behind me that lead to the first floor. I pulled my hair forward and concentrated on reading the bulletin board near me, keeping my back to them, but my senses open. Papers were attached to the board by little white dots of swirling magic.

"Art Expressionists—join us for chats and workshops on all things artistic! Thursdays, Cancer Rising, 14 Rubens Hall, Third Circle"

"Want to advance rare mage types and creature rights? Or are you a muse who just wants to be seen for yourself? Come to a meeting! Eighteenth Circle, 3rd and Evergreen, on Tuesdays at Libra Rising."

"Sniffer training—suss out undesirables under the guidance of mages with fifty-five years of combined experience."

I waited for the adults to descend to the next level before I darted over to a wall.

Luckily, using one was easy. I flip-flip-flipped through books, keeping one eye on the nearby staircase. Having a search up on the wall did serve to make it visible to anyone walking by. Since I was thinking of the snare drawing I was creating, I accidentally channeled both gophers and prisons into my mental search, and subsequently out through my magic. That meant that my current search results showed gophers imprisoned or on trial.

Likely a pretty sketchy search wall, if someone were to walk behind me. A sad little picture of a gopher with its paws around the bars of a cage, peering out, made me swipe the book to the card slot, though. If I figured out how to free an imprisoned one, maybe it would want to live with me.

Clearly, I was not meant for people friends.

I tried more searches—removing spells, death magic, magical tracking, feral mages, art magic—and popped out card after card. The cards felt like smooth, thin plastic—envelope sized, with rounded edges.

I grabbed my cards and took the stairs two at a time to the third floor and the white rooms.

White walls, white floor, white ceiling. I had the sudden thought that I had been led into a trap finally by the guys in the white jackets. A little unnerved, I entered anyway, and closed the door. In the wall were eight small slots, one large slot, and a red button. I looked at the cards in my hand. They would fit in the smaller slots. I wondered what went in the larger one.

A small, neatly written sign above said "Recommended: five card maximum." I looked at the nine cards in my hand, shrugged, and looked for somewhere to put four of them. It was odd that there wasn't a table for materials or a hook for bags. I decided against the floor—I'd likely step on them knowing my luck—and tucked unlucky cards six and seven into my back right pocket and eight and nine into my left. Hopefully, I wouldn't accidentally sit on them later and blow my jeans from existence.

I plugged in my first card and heard a whirring noise suspiciously close to my ear. A breeze slid over my hand. I plugged in number two and both the whirring and breeze increased. I paused. Should I just go with two? I had no idea what was going to happen. But my front pockets weren't really card sized, so I inserted the rest. A light pounding began and I felt the beat on my skin.

I looked around waiting for something else to happen, but the pounding just steadily continued. I looked back at the panel and pressed the button.

The compressing feeling of the cuff...*popped*. And the energy trapped beneath drove forward in a great wave.

A layer of air around me sucked toward the panel, then my world was suddenly filled with light. A corona of light flew toward me in a beam that shot out a grid in all directions. Like all of the stars in the universe had shot toward me and were now surrounding me. I took a step back and the system followed.

Another light shot from the panel, but more focused and intense this time, and a line zipped around me, shooting right, then right again, then up, then right, framing me, and building around me, connecting the stars in some places and leaving them free in others. I watched in fascination, turning my body and craning my head as the beam of light wrapped, re-wrapped, and overlaid in a geometric web.

A second beam joined the first, but took a different path, intersecting with the first stream at some places, mapping new areas in others. A third light shot out, then a fourth and fifth, all intersecting to form an intricate, complex pattern surrounding me. The individual lines became less sharply defined and more twining as they joined together, hiding parts of their brilliance in curling loops. As if there were secrets that had to be literally unraveled from the coils.

I touched one of the intersections and *felt* the magic. The point zoomed closer.

"Cross reference of the Mad Mage and Sergey Kinsky. The reference in Text A refers to the explosion and subsequent death of the Mad Mage. Text D refers to Kinsky, but using almost the same language and style. It is within a realm of 85% probability that the reference is to the same person. At least two other texts to cross reference and validate is recommended. None of the other texts in this grid contain similar subject data. Turn twice to experience Text A. Three times for Text D."

I didn't so much hear the voice as feel it. Know it.

Holy...*awesome.*

I quickly touched another point.

"There is a fierce disagreement between Text A and Text C on the aspects of rare mage types. Text A has a very small piece that agrees with Text C on origin mages, though—saying that it is still considered in the best interests of the world to enslave them. Points in common, against, and with judgments are provided. Turn twice to—"

It was strange, but I could see tiny lights blinking along the zoomed portion of the line. As if I could access the actual pieces of that statement. I touched one.

"A separate reference text has not been provided, so the word fierce is used in the context of Mage Manual of Style CMXI. Fierce—the disagreement of more than 75% of points and opinion."

I touched another.

"Points in agreement between Texts D, E, and F are as follows—when trying to rid oneself of an enchantment, it is best to—"

I touched another.

"It is within a 50% likelihood that—"

I touched a little to the right of that.

"Likelihood is defined by—"

I waved a hand along the line, and the grid rotated. I pulled my hands together, and the entire grid grew closer together, zooming out. Spreading my hands made it larger. I grabbed one point with my finger and drew it to another point, then pushed.

"Cross referencing the Mad Mage with Toilet Habits of the Fligobbony Tribe. Both had the unusual practice to—"

I bit my lip and pulled another point to the intersection.

"Adding in Gopher Mating Rituals gives one point of familiarity. Brushes. While the brushes of the latter two refer to grooming, the Mad Mage used his as a primary weapon when pai—"

I pulled my hands out and grabbed another point, then another.

...preventive spells could be nullified if a mage was under a chaos field.

Chapter Ten

...a litter of ten gophers would form three pair bonds.

...rare mage types were either highly celebrated or aggressively feared.

...art mages couldn't bring things out of their art that hadn't been put in.

How had I pulled out the butterfly?

...embedding larger objects into smaller objects required the manipulation of universe space, which was extremely dangerous and difficult.

Point upon point upon point responded, until the grid started to look more like a web, and I became increasingly tangled within it. The red button glowed. I pushed it, and the whole thing vibrated then snapped back into original formation.

Harsh breaths filled my ears.

I started again. The more I selected, the more I had to select. I had come in here for...for something. What was it?

A gaming system? There had to be one for this room. I had to get my hands on one of those cards. Christian would love them.

"Ren. You can help me."

Yes. I could help. I could do *anything*. I attacked harder, trying to figure out how to turn, shape, and work the information grid. I'd bet there were a thousand tricks and endless ways to do it. Like living inside of one of my graphic patterns or on a Mobius strip. This was the answer to my prayers—exactly what I needed.

I couldn't remember what I needed it for, but I needed to find it—the answer, the end.

Ping.

Ping, ping.

Ping, ping, ping.

I distractedly checked the red button at ten pings in a row. It seemed fine. The sounds were coming from outside the room. Annoying. I had work to do, and I could feel that I was close to the core of the intersections and what drove them. Maybe I could figure out how to generate this type of system away from the library? Harness the magic? What if I could imbed it in a painting? A grid of knowledge that could be visually shown. How would I—

PING.

I used a little magic to push the distracting outside sounds away when they became a steady siren. I could almost hear voices now too. I pushed harder, trying to absorb the information I was seeing and tasting.

116

A new stream of magic tapped me. It had a warmer, smoother feel to it, than the annoying pings. I shuddered at the brush of it across my skin. But I was getting off target. I batted the titillating magic away sloppily, using a pinwheel motion I had seen a man with golden eyes and a golden ear cuff do...sometime, somewhere...and concentrated again on deepening the intersecting points of the texts and figuring out how it worked. The smooth magic tapped harder, a bit of a vibration to it this time. It seemed annoyed. I slapped it in mirrored annoyance.

Then the magic came at me *hard*. Startled, I nearly lost the thread, but managed to push back just as hard, dulling the grid for a moment, which irritated me. I heard someone swear. The magic probe strengthened, and I pushed equally, giving an extra twist to my shove. I had seen that too somewhere, in some place filled with electric ultramarine-blue paint. The audible swearing grew more violent and a vision of a winged snake popped to mind. I paused on the image...what...?

A hand thrust through my magic field, breaking all my threads and shocking me stupid. The back of my shirt lifted, and I left my feet, as I was yanked from my new world. I hit the ground hard and different types of stars twinkled through my vision. My cuff felt heavy against my wrist again.

"What the hell?!" I yelled, as soon as some air worked its way back into my lungs, reality seeping back in much more slowly.

"No, *you*, what the hell?" a voice said.

I had to really concentrate to get my eyes to uncross in order to see two very irritated faces staring down at me. Ultramarine blue swam into view, and the vision of something winged—the creature I hadn't been able to stop drawing for weeks—burst through the cloud covering my mind.

I shut my eyes hard and blinked again. The vision of the creature was gone, but ultramarine blue eyes remained in a face that was Michelangelo hot, even with my eyes crossed. The second boy's face above mine was unexceptional, the visage of a guard statue that didn't stand out in a line. Unexceptional, but furious.

"Of all the stupid, fathead stunts!" Even his voice was pissy.

I had no idea what pissy, unexceptional guy was talking about, and I was still sorting out my vision and reality, but—"Fathead? Seriously?"

That seemed to anger him more. Unsurprisingly, because I was good at saying the wrong thing without Christian nearby.

Wait. Christian? I rubbed my head and reality returned fully—thrusting back upon me like a sudden, intense migraine.

Hot guy—no, Alexander Dare—looked mildly amused, but he was also staring at me in an intense, considering way. Like I was a strange breed of Chihuahua he had never before encountered. I could feel the heat in my forehead, chest, and the back of my neck—the sweat gathering. I had the feeling I was in trouble. It seemed a sound notion considering I hadn't two clues to rub together about this place or magic. I wondered suddenly if Marsgrove was waiting somewhere to the side, handcuffs in hand.

"You are in so much trouble," the pissy guy said. I needed to stop calling him that in my head. He looked about nineteen or twenty, a student then.

"Sorry. Who are you?"

He seemed offended by that too. "I am Mr. Peters. And *you* are in trouble. You overextended your time by two hours."

"Oh. I hadn't realized there was a queue." There hadn't been any kind of a line when I'd entered. And dozens of the rooms had seemed available.

"That's it. I'm charging you with a Level Two." He pulled out a sunshine-yellow tablet.

"What? Why?" I asked, alarmed. What would a Level Two make me do? Run to the bottom of the mountain and back?

Dare straightened and looked at the other guy. "Take it easy. She didn't even raise an alert." He pointed at the yellow tablet.

I stared at him. His voice...

"She magically attacked me! And you! She magically attacked *you*."

Dare looked suddenly bored. "Yes, so?"

The eyes matched perfectly, and I would *never* forget that voice. Without a doubt, standing above me was the guy who had saved me. Healed me.

"She...she can't do that! The handbook says overusing a reading room is chargeable. Offensable!"

I didn't think that was a word, but I kept my lips zipped and cast a nervous glance around looking for Marsgrove.

"With what is going on right now, you are worried about someone extending a reading room session?"

"No, of course not." Peters stood tall. "But this is how the big timers start out—as small timers. If we let them get their start doing petty crime, soon they will be moving on to bigger jobs." He looked at me as if I was already contemplating a slide to armed assault.

"You," Alexander Dare said in his chiseled voice, pointing at me.

"Yes?" My voice squeaked in response. If Peters could use the word offensable, I could describe a voice as chiseled, just like the rest of the guy standing over me.

"Was that your first time in a reading room?"

"Yes." I nervously ran a hand over my hair. "Sorry?"

He turned to Peters, brow raised, arms crossed. "You are going to charge a first term sixteen-year-old on a reading room violation that didn't even register?"

Seventeen! Almost eighteen!! Vertically challenged!!!

Peters gave me a disgruntled look, as if I had stolen money from his pocket and there was nothing he could do about it.

"You saw the time was extended on the room and decided to intervene, Peters. Admirable. You helped a student in need."

Peters *preened.* "And I appreciate your assistance in this matter, Mr. Dare."

It was as if someone else actually saying his name out loud forced everything to overwhelmingly intersect, like the points on the grid. I opened my mouth, a heartfelt thank you on my tongue. *Thank you for saving me, for letting me have that last moment, for—*

I closed my mouth with a snap, swallowing the words, but not the sentiment.

He gave a short nod to Peters, a strange glance to me, then walked away.

I found myself staring at his rear, unable to help myself. Because of the glimpse of him on the field, I could recognize him from this angle too. That strange pull strained as he gained more distance.

I wanted—needed—to know what exactly had happened that night with my brother, but I couldn't very well follow him and say, "Hey, you know that ordinary girl you helped many weeks back? Surprise! Feral! Illegal! Thanks for your help that night, now please tell me everything. Oh, and don't enslave me, ok? Thanks!"

"You are lucky to be all in one piece," Peters said darkly, as soon as he was gone.

"Oh? You like to assault people?" I rotated my right shoulder forward where I had been grabbed and yanked. Marsgrove hadn't shown up, I had just had a wonderfully awkward exchange with the guy I had been dreaming about for weeks, and I was starting to feel pluckier. "I feel lucky."

"You should. Mr. Dare had to pull you out."

It made sense that Dare had removed me, not Peters. His voice had caused me to pause in subconscious recognition. I rotated my shoulder again. Being tackled by a hot guy still hurt. He had snapped through my magic like I was a twig too. I remembered how he had looked on that hologram field. I was thankful I was still alive.

"It will be ok," a soothing voice said. I looked over to see a girl standing ten feet away, her appearance matching her soft voice, before my eyes slid to the right, away from her.

A little of the ire went out of Peters, but he continued to stare at me, as if unaware that there was anyone else standing near. "The only reason I'm not charging you is because it wouldn't look good on my sheet. But next time, you'll get double." He gave me a dark look, then strode off.

"You can wear a zap timer—to wake you up next time—if you want," the soft feminine voice said.

I looked back at the girl. There was a dreamlike quality about her, conjuring visions of sand and veils. She smoothed a hand over her dark hair in a self-conscious way, and I realized she was the girl I had followed initially. I had watched her hands, her searches on the wall, and her path direction, all while thinking about being kidnapped at any moment by Marsgrove. I hadn't actually paid attention to *her*.

Her dreamlike quality made my eyes slip past her again. I tried again, and once more my eyes drifted to her hands before I forced them up to her dark brown eyes for a full second. Aching emotion tightened the skin at the edges of her eyes. I fixed my gaze upon her eyes and concentrated hard. *Intent, focus, knowledge, confidence.* I could do two of those four and fake a third. I wanted to comfort her. My cuff pulsed, and a little thread of magic pushed past, escaping.

She snapped into view—a doe-like work of Raphael with her blended sand beauty. Raphael, the old master, not the betrayer.

"I remember hearing beeps. Alarms?"

"Yes." She smiled, hope in her expression. "A reading room is fueled by the user's magic, so it is quite usual for newer users to get entrapped. Two hours is a long time for most people, especially depending on how many books you engage."

That might be why I was feeling so tired. Had Peters said I had extended the time two hours? Did that mean I had been in there for four hours?

I suddenly realized that the four card disks from my pockets were broken on the floor. I picked up the pieces. "Oh, no."

"The cards are recyclable." She lifted a delicate shoulder. "Students can take them out of the library to use in personal readers, so they get lost and destroyed frequently. They won't work outside of campus wards, though. Were you using those four in the room?"

"No, the sign said five, so I used five and put these in my pockets." For once, I was glad to have followed a rule. Though...there were *eight* slots...and hell, what was that big one for? An *Ultimate Tome of Magery*?

I pushed a hand against my forehead and the headache splitting it.

"Would you like help?"

"Yes." I gave a short laugh. My therapists would be delighted at my final capitulation.

A warm hand touched my forehead and the headache just...seeped out. I almost closed my eyes, so good did it feel. The hand touched my shoulder next and the pain seeped out as well.

"Wow." I looked at her. She pulled her hand back and swirled it gracefully, making two loops, then picked up one of the broken cards. I could see a light glow of orange transfer from her fingers to the card. The card shattered into a dozen pieces.

Another sweep of her hand scooted the pieces into a pile, then the pile swirled up and into a trash bin.

Handy.

She must have noticed my envious glance, because she tilted her head, her loose dark hair flowing with the movement. "There are practice rooms in the ninth circle battle building. You can buy a guide at the bookstore and learn all sorts of things that way."

I blinked.

She smiled. "Mages tend to be a 'try it first—read the instructions only in dire circumstances' people. But if you were that fascinated with a reading room, you might like the practice rooms located on the ninth circle. You must have a good amount of natural magic to have repelled Alexander Dare even a little."

Ah. That was what that considering look had been then. Curses.

"And using five cards in the room for four hours..." She shook her head. "I can't help there, unfortunately. You will probably sleep through your morning classes tomorrow."

As I was a vagrant currently, this was unlikely.

She touched a spot below her ear and her expression fell. "I need to go." She rose, but didn't move for a moment, reluctant. "Good evening to you." She started to turn.

"Wait, I'm Ren. Thank you."

"I'm Nephthys." She smiled, hope in her expression again. "It was nice to meet you, Ren."

My name had just tumbled from my mouth, even though intelligence and preservation instincts said that I should keep everything about me bland, blank, and unmemorable.

She walked gracefully down the hall, and I touched my shoulder and head, which were completely pain free.

I spent another hour at the library, looking over my shoulder for Marsgrove and unsuccessfully trying to reach the fourth floor. A tug had started in my gut, though, and was spreading and starting to make me uncomfortable. The image of the dorm room kept popping into my mind's eye, as if the tug wanted to lead me there.

I collected three dozen cards from the wall before I finally gave in to the tug. I approached the ground floor door with my arms full of cards, just in case I needed to drop them and sprint away. Ever since I had been falsely beeped leaving a library as a child, I had been cautious exiting them.

I stepped through the door warily. Relief swept me as I gained a few paces of freedom. The tug loosened, as if it was pleased. But as I walked through the courtyard, a stomach cramp made me buckle over in pain. Bad Magi Mart food? Another cramp hit me, this one more debilitating. A girl in tight pink leggings and a painted-on tank jogged passed.

Oh. *Oh.* I needed to run back to the dorm. It appeared magic had a keen and vicious memory. I really wondered what the Level Two Offense Peters had wanted to give me would have required.

After a couple of stumbling steps, the cramps eased, but once I got a jog going, the cramps receded completely. I tried to stuff the cards into my bag, jog, retrieve my map, jog, and watch where I was going at the same time. It took me twice as long to jog back, but the new route took me past one of the campus bookstores. I reached Dorm Twenty-Five, slapped my hand upon the front door, just in case, then doubled back.

The cramps were gone, but the dorm tug immediately showed its displeasure, which meant I had to be dealing with two magic enchantments.

I jogged back to the bookstore, blinked in wonder at the flying books, and with Marsgrove's money, I purchased a card reader and a number of nifty blank auto-sorting notebooks from the peppy and helpful clerk.

I returned to the dorm at a jaunty pace, eyes still sweeping for Marsgrove, then entered the building, ready for anything. But the door to room twenty-five was unlocked and Olivia was the only inhabitant. The tug abruptly settled. She gave me an unreadable look, before burying her head in her bound book again.

I made a quick sweep behind the shower curtain—and as surreptitiously as possible, under the bed—before going back and locking the door to the room. "Uh, are you in for the night?" Should have asked that first.

"Yes," came the short reply.

"Me too."

No response.

"I purchased a ton of cookies from Magi Mart. They are beside the box. Feel free to have some."

Olivia's gaze drifted to the cookies, then abruptly turned back to her desk. "Thank you," she said curtly, as if she was upset she had looked.

I settled onto my comforter and looked out the window to the softly lit ground and shaded trees below. When I could no longer justify sitting on the bed with my jacket, shoes, and pack still on, I reluctantly shrugged them off, but kept everything close.

I opened my new reader and read the instructions, which echoed the actions I had watched Delia undertake earlier. I shook my head and spread out my library cards. I had gotten a book on magical meditation. Far safer than attending any sessions Delia had suggested.

I carefully slipped the first card into the slot. There was a tingle in my finger as it lifted from the edge of the card, and I swallowed as I felt the amazing pull of magic under the cuff. The magic reluctantly responded—which was almost a surprise after the torrent the reading room had allowed. I rotated my forearm, examining the cuff. I was going to have to put removing it at the top of my research list. Finding out what magic the reading rooms were made of—or called forth—became a mental bullet point underneath.

The image of words appeared on the reader, then real pages flipped out from right to left, settling in the middle, then disappearing back into the screen, displaying page one like an e-reader. I touched the page and wished for a real book again. Blue light gathered and the frame of a book rose up. I rubbed a page between my fingers. It felt like real paper. I stuck my nose into the pages. It even smelled real. I gripped a chunk of pages and flopped them over.

I touched the page and wished for a flat screen again. It complied. A real book one moment, flat like an e-reader the next. I called back the real book and imagined turning twenty pages. The pages turned, then settled again—twenty pages forward. I held my finger down and focused a search on the word death. It flipped five pages, and the word glowed blue. Thin lines of blue striped the rest of the book, indicating more search results, and one thick latter chunk of pages glowed with the color.

Perfect.

I looked over at Olivia buried in books with eight inch spines. Why didn't she have a reader? A reader was a poor substitute for a reading room, but far superior to both regular books and electronic, seeing as it combined the two aspects.

I yawned, scrubbed a hand over my eyes, and fished through the cards to find *Time Lines of Death*. I quickly consumed the text, which was full of alarming opinion. No one had ever been successfully resurrected after four months. Mages were arrested and imprisoned if they were found practicing resurrections at *thirteen minutes* post death. Everything from heavy fines to imprisonment was given for eleven and twelve minute time frames.

Seeing as my brother had been dead for nearly two months now, none of this was good news. But I had anticipated such roadblocks, and they were merely words on the page.

"Ren, I need help."

"Help, help, help!"

Chapter Ten

But yet again he wouldn't answer any question I posed. I curled up into a ball on my bed and pulled my journal with the massive to-do lists against my belly. I would do whatever it took.

My eyes immediately started to close and I vainly tried to keep them open—what if Marsgrove showed up?—but exhaustion pulled me into the abyss where Christian hung in chains.

Chapter Eleven

PAIN...TING...

I WOKE ABRUPTLY, hand reaching for Will's sketch. Olivia was in her chair, working, as if she'd never gone to sleep. Marsgrove wasn't standing over me. No handcuffs circled my wrists.

I wiped the back of my hand over my eyes. I had made it through the night unscathed. A little notch of hope peered out from my Pandora's Box of emotions.

Breakfast consisted of unexploded Magi Mart food—burritos and muffins, since the faux-Cheerios hadn't survived the magical unpack. It all tasted...normal.

My after breakfast activity consisted of sketching—each draft becoming easier to animate than the previous one. Hopefully, I could get these working, then I could move ahead and activate the snare I had planned for Marsgrove. I attempted to place paint on a sketched gopher that was prowling and sniffing a patch of sketched grass. The paint was from a store-bought tube from the First Layer, so I wasn't expecting much, but I needed to see if paint brought into the magic world became magical.

So far, it had just stuck to the hindquarters of the gopher, who was vainly trying to lick the Phthalo Blue off.

Knock, knock, knock.

Olivia didn't make any move to answer, so I walked over to the door. A girl with three ponytails stood on the other side holding a tablet and wearing a pressed uniform. Not good.

"Florence Crown?"

"Yes."

"Level One Offense. Illegal substance use."

I stared at her. "What?"

"You triggered a Level One Offense." She shook her head. "Drugs are bad for you and there are mages who can help. Now—"

"What are you talking about? I'm not using drugs." That was the last thing I needed in this world.

She frowned at her tablet. "You are telling the truth. Hmm... What were you doing a minute ago?"

"Drawing and painting. With...paint." No. No way. "Paint purchased legally at a store!"

The girl looked apologetic. "I bet someone put a hex on you. There are a few going around that mimic administration spells. Get yourself checked at the clinic. Unfortunately, the justice magic still needs to balance the infraction with a punishment, as it is insisting you are guilty. But I can make it painless this time, I think. Do you have any suggestions?"

"Er, I could run?"

"Great! Run aimlessly for a half hour. You can have until the end of the day to do it."

Aimlessly?

I nodded, but she continued looking at me expectantly. What was it the boy had made me say? "Er, I will run aimlessly for a half hour, by my magic I so do vow?"

The magic wrapped around me, squeezing.

"Great! And get checked out, ok?" She tossed over her shoulder, three ponytails swinging as she walked down the hall.

But a clinic wasn't going to do me any good—some mischievous student hadn't put this spell on me, an official had. Marsgrove had put some sort of spell on me so I would get in trouble if I *painted*. I remembered his muttering, though I hadn't paid much attention at the time, absorbed with the visual world around me.

He had made it so I couldn't even use store bought, non-magical paint?

I closed the door. Maybe...maybe he had just cursed the stuff in my bag? Yes, that had to be it. I walked quickly to my bed and unearthed the campus map. I needed an art supply store. I was brimming with intent and the map zoomed to a building on the third circle.

Twenty minutes later, I entered the main art building, which looked as if it had been half-constructed with tongue depressors, twine, and crystals—held up entirely by dream magic. The other half was constructed using some sort of melted stone and bulged pods. Winding pathways suspended by magic, and bridges that spiraled as they stretched from one side of the building to the other made up the atrium.

I wondered if Gaudí had been magical. Seemed likely.

At the far end of the atrium, the art store brimmed with light and energy. My feet moved faster. I could feel the pull from here. Lovely magic that spoke of creation and promise. My hand curled around the serpent handle and pulled. I stepped forward.

Wiewiewiewie!

I jumped back. Everyone in the store turned in my direction. The door shut, and the alarm stopped ringing. It took a few moments for people to turn back to scanning shelves. Someone walked from behind me, opened the door, and walked through. Nothing.

Taking a deep breath, I opened the door and stepped through.

Wiewiewiewie!

I turned and strode quickly away, shoulders hunched, cursing Marsgrove with each step.

My steps slowed as I noticed an older art student painting the winding suspension bridges above us. He was squeezing paint from a near empty tube. I hurried over.

"Pardon me, can I buy that tube from you?" I pointed at the one that only had a few drops left.

He blinked again, then screwed the cap back on and held it out silently.

"Thank you," I said fervently, relieved beyond belief when no alarm sounded. I held out a munit.

"Seriously, kid, keep it." He was looking at me with pity. I was ok with that at the moment.

"Thank you again." I stuffed the munit back in my pocket. "Does this do anything...specific?" I was going out on a flyer here.

"It's light-induced paint. Brightens and twinkles." He pointed up. "Great for interiors."

"Did you make it?"

"No."

"You don't make your own supplies?"

He shrugged, but thankfully didn't find the question odd. "Don't need to. Store grade supplies work well for me. I'm not working toward a mastery."

I nodded, putting it on my mental research list. "Ok, thanks."

"Sure, kid."

I hurried from the building, just in case I tripped off another alarm. I walked down a level, just to make sure, then sat on a patch of grass. There was no view here, the grassy area was surrounded by buildings tightly clumped together, but I didn't need to draw anything special. I quickly sketched a pond and a starry sky, perfect for twinkling and reflections.

My fingers shook as I uncapped the tube. I touched my finger to the lip, and the barest bit of milky paint transferred to my finger pad. I touched it to one of the stars, willing it to spread through the sky and reflect onto the pond.

Nothing happened. I lifted my finger and a dot of milky white remained stagnant on the page. There was a vague twinkle in the drop, but no spreading. No magical connection of lines.

What—?

"Florence Crown?"

The tube tumbled from my hand and plopped on the grass. A boy wearing a uniform stood in front of me. No. "Yes?"

"Level One Offense. Illegal substance use."

I shut my eyes.

Two hours later, I finished cleaning the entrance hall to the biology building near the grassy valley.

I flexed my back. The magical grime stripper I had been "issued" chased dirt around. At first it had seemed fantastic, like watching frames of the Sorcerer's Apprentice in real life. But after two dozen squirts, I had quickly comprehended that fantastic was relative, since I had to corral and contain the dirt that my squirts were freeing. And since I had no clue how to do magic, I had chased dirt for two hours, while mages had walked around me snickering and doing little effortless whirls of magic to sidestep the mess. At the twentieth snicker, my cuff had nearly vibrated off my wrist and I'd abruptly blown the entire swirl of filth through a vent in the floor.

Grumpy and pissed didn't quite do justice to the violence of my current thoughts. I decided to do my running punishment to work off some of the rage, but even thirty minutes later, dodging nuts thrown by some kind of weird tree monkeys on the third circle, a little growl still escaped.

Painting was the only way I knew how to bring anything to life. I had *felt* Christian. I sure as hell had watched that butterfly fly away. With art, I could focus, concentrate, intend, and *do*. It fulfilled those stinking cornerstones of magic, and everything.

And it had been taken away from me.

I could sketch, sure. But for me, so far, paint was the life-creating medium in this world.

I was stuck with zero knowledge of anything else magical, working from the ground floor up. I narrowed my eyes as I marched into the dorm, looking like a sweaty chimney sweep. Well, I would be learning magic extra quickly now, wouldn't I?

I managed to undo the dorm room lock in quick and precise fashion. Olivia didn't look at me as I walked past, but I saw her nose wrinkle.

A long, hot shower—while only touching the two knobs that I could identify as hot and cold—made me feel a lot better. I sent a quick note to my parents in the journal, noting details about the magnificent landscape and architecture in the Second Layer Depot, how a mage enters the Depot and school, the interesting things mages could do—like making magical fields for specific purposes—and how I was looking forward to telling them all about it in person. I kept it brief, and tried to leave out anything alarming. On the other hand, if needed later, they had some basic information to put together.

I stuck in a little note at the end asking Mom to find out how I could finish high school, either doing assignments that I could turn in or getting a GED. My parents would approve. It would give Mom something to focus on. And I might need it, if I ever found my way out of here.

I quickly accessed the books I had on death and death magic, looking for alternative plans. My time was ticking already. *Dealing with Magical Loss* and *Grief and Grieving* were quickly put aside as they contained information for coping, not action. *Pain of the Black Arts, Why the Soul Separates,* and *Guide to Resurrection* were more promising.

The latter was by far the most explicit, as it provided actual instructions on how to raise someone within a ten minute time frame post death—although most of the instructions required other knowledge, like "locate magic nucleus" and "create a spinning enchantment."

All of the authors agreed that customary techniques didn't work after fifteen minutes of death. They hotly debated the moral repercussions of the time frame between ten to fifteen minutes.

No one debated the two to three month time frame.

"Ren."

"Shh, it's ok," I whispered quietly.

I read through the books quickly, putting the important pieces into the mental map I had created to remember everything. The mental black paint bucket labeled "Consequences for Christian" now contained the following information based on the books—bringing souls back hurt them, once a soul separated it was at peace, and souls that *were* brought back didn't always come back right.

In the mental forest green bucket labeled "Consequences for Ren," I had a significant main item—black magic demanded a physical price on a scale starting at fatigue for the least of the rituals, moving to blood and body parts, then ending with soul death for the truly abhorrent. In addition, there was a magic sacrifice commensurate with the ritual. This meant that successive rituals performed immediately were magically impossible and needed to be separated by a minimum of three days to ensure personal safety. I chewed my plastic cap, then noted in the margin, "Plan for one day between rituals."

The contents of the red bucket labeled "Time Line" that I had started to populate last night had grown larger.

"Ren...don't do it."

"Ren, help me!"

Christian's splitting personality was a concern I didn't need. I shakily tucked my hair behind my ear and drew two stars next to "plan for one day between rituals." I would do what needed to be done, because my brother was not at peace.

In fact, maybe the books were wrong about other warnings as well. I made a note to locate the story details on the failed four month resurrection.

But even if everything the books said was correct, it didn't matter. My brother needed me.

"Ren."

"Shhh," I whispered. "Yes."

There were a hundred different things I needed to learn—laws, paint making, getting around magic restrictions, ferals, layer dimensions, prisons, art magic...

"Maybe even a guide to getting along with one's roommate, if they have one."

My hand flew to my mouth. I wasn't sure what would emerge, if the sound trapped in my throat escaped. That was the Christian I knew.

I took a deep breath. One thing at a time. One thing at a time.

"Free me."

"Yes," I whispered. "Of course I will."

"I will have my freedom!"

There was a handy ritual for determining a soul's state of peace. A minor type of séance that only required intense focus through repeated words and motions. The text said to fill up on energy first, whatever that meant. Food was going to have to suffice, unless I needed to suck someone's essence out Dark Crystal style. I was hoping for the food option.

It seemed like it might be a bad idea to get more Magi Mart food, plus I needed to save what money I had. I chewed the top of my plastic pencil top. The administration packet said the cafeteria was free for all students.

Rubbing the back of my neck, I argued the merits of getting a part-time job and subsisting on Magi Mart food versus going to the cafeteria.

I looked over at my roommate's stiff spine. "Would you like to go to the cafeteria?"

"No." Olivia's reply was abrupt and cold.

I gave myself a quick pep talk, verified the location on my map, and headed off on my own. Soon, I wouldn't be alone.

Chapter Twelve

THE CAFETERIA

I LIKED WALKING, but climbing up the mountain was a lot more taxing than going down, and after huffing and puffing for thirty minutes, I gathered my nerve and located an arch on the Academy-sanctioned map that propelled me up three circles, then another that popped me the remaining ones to the cafeteria.

The nice feature about arches was that when I looked at them, the interior of the arch showed the view *through* to where it exited. The area around the arch was normal, and walking around one was just like walking around any other large stone structure, but the interior clearly showed a different landscape. It was a lot easier to trust arches, since I could make sure I wasn't entering a swamp or another equally unpleasant hazard.

Top Circle was as populated as it had been the previous day, so I hurried through one of the two dozen doors leading inside the Corinthian-columned cafeteria building, like a mouse scurrying through a barn full of cats. I prepared for a wailing siren of *wiewiewie*, but no alarms pegged me as an intruder.

Ten feet in, I found my feet glued to the floor and my lips parted—the symptoms of another shock, as I'd experienced so many times since I'd entered this world four days past. Someone bumped me from behind. I murmured an apology as my feet took me forward to the balcony's edge.

Since the building stretched almost the entire length of Top Circle on the northern side of the mountain, I had expected it to be enormous. What was unexpected was that the northern wall of the building—the one I was facing—was made entirely of glass, and that the dining hall was multi-tiered.

Dropping down were four long tiers with hundreds of tables on each level. From my view up top, looking down and across the tiers, they were all seemingly *full* tables, too. The massive glass wall consisted of a single pane—obviously architecturally magicked—which displayed a jaw-dropping view of the north face of the mountain and miles of land stretching out from the base.

Enormous chandeliers hung at appropriate distances above each tier, making the ones hanging above the bottom tier look like tangled glittering gold hooks at the end of deep sea fishing lines. Staircases and ramps striped the tiers vertically and diagonally, in an organized Chutes-and-Ladders fashion.

The smell of freshly baked bread permeated the air, and pleasant crowd chatter filled my ears, but it wasn't overly loud—some sort of sound dampener or spell like in the library?

I swallowed the taste of fear, and dragged my gaze back to the top tier. It was filled with dozens of food lines and hundreds of machines.

I numbly got in line behind a group of mages, hoping we were in line for actual food. As I shuffled forward, I gazed out across the hall. It was overwhelming. A part time job and Magi Mart might be a better idea.

No. After Christian's death, I had sat by myself in the cafeteria every day. I could do that now. I wasn't afraid to sit by myself, though it would feel...obvious. Like people were staring and wondering.

I forced my eyes away again and saw that I was inching closer to a line of food that was being served by magic—food whizzing onto people's plates—and less by staff in white uniforms. I did a double-take on the two thin people with ten tiny eyes who were serving at the end of my line.

Ok. I'd deal with that when I got there.

The line east of me had a periwinkle border. My line was bordered in chocolate brown.

I watched the students ahead of me push the buttons in front of the buffet-styled containers. One push and a half-fist sized portion of food was magically delivered to a plate. Two pushes doubled it. I said a little prayer of thanks that I didn't have to actively perform magic, and chose a little of everything—most of it identifiable. Chicken, veggies, fruit. The first ten-eyed person smiled widely and deca-blinked at me, before offering some potatoes. I gamely accepted, praying I wouldn't do anything weird, and smiled back as the potatoes whizzed onto my plate. The other ten-eyed person offered something that sounded like "caniopidas." I politely declined and added the word to the "look-up" list steadily growing in my head. I also made a note to explore other races in the magical world.

Maybe I could find an explanation for the creature once tattooed on my wrist. I scratched my cuff against my hip, hands gripping the tray in continued panic.

There was no scanner at the end of the line, so I walked slowly to the railing, looking down at my doom.

There were obviously formed groups everywhere I looked. Magical cheerleaders in uniform? Check. Various sports teams? Check. Alexander Dare sitting at a large circular table full of other athletic and deadly-looking types? Check. So much for me never seeing him again.

Irrelevant. I sure as paint wasn't going to sit at that table.

I forced my gaze away, again, and continued my observation, my palms starting to feel slippery on my tray. Two adjoining tables below me were filled with charts laden with incomprehensible symbols, and the diners were yelling at each other and pointing to the graphs. Scientists? Check.

Another table was full of students playing handheld devices with a projection coordinated in the center of the table. Gamers, check. And, wow, I had to try that. There were tables with people arguing about politics and rights and resolve. Activists, check. I looked for an art table, hoping, but didn't immediately spot one. The tables stretched on and on. At a school of fifteen plus thousand, half of the student population seemed to be here. I made a mental note never to come at this time.

There were no empty tables anywhere, just empty chairs scattered here or there. The tables near the end of the ramp to my left seemed to be populated with more eclectic mixes. I nervously gripped my tray. I would cautiously approach one of those.

"You can do it."

Easy for you to say, I thought back at him.

Christian would have approached any of the tables and fit right in. Christian was the master connector, an extrovert. People loved him. I was a number two, an introvert.

I had always been the number two to Christian's number one. I was the one who observed people and examined peripheral events while he charmed and conversed. I had always provided the extra pieces of information he might otherwise have missed—the details and shading, decoding the symbolically painted sky, and whether it showed a portent of doom or the rolling calm following the storm.

My palms were now actively sweating. I needed him back. And yet, I needed to *get* him back. Heller's Catch-22 looped in my brain.

Oh, for the love of...*Buck up*, I yelled at myself internally.

I heard Christian laugh.

Before my courage deserted me, I made a beeline for the ramp on my left and let it take me down to the first tier and one of the tables with empty chairs.

I had made friends with Will, right?

However, in my mad dash and pressing anxiety, I somehow chose an all-female table which included a few girls decidedly of the popular variety.

"Hi," I said brightly, cursing fate and panic. Three of the girls looked at me blankly, two frowned, and one gave me a piercing gaze. She opened a container of juice, and I noticed her hand had three rings on it.

Oh, crap. I had no idea what that meant, but when he had been showing me the hologram, Will had said something about avoiding three-ringed mages. I had been in an Alexander Dare induced haze at the time. Not good.

"New?" She asked in a lilting voice. The other girls gained more interested expressions, as if scenting blood in the water.

Not good at all. I managed a small laugh as a number of responses ran through my head.

Just transferred!

No, just thought I might meet some new people!

New to this table.

But any further conversation would reveal me for how very new I was, so I stood there like an idiot, leaning over the empty chair, butt poking back, slippery fingers gripping my tray, and wished I had stayed in my room after all.

Then the sketch of Christian, smoking and broken upon my floor, sapped of its life-giving paint, came to mind. I *needed* to survive in this world.

My magic reacted, swirling suddenly from under my cuff—and all I could think was, please, oh, please don't blow the Homecoming Queen from existence. My eyes rose almost automatically and pulled to the right and amazingly I saw a familiar boy working his way along a second tier ramp. Will was walking, light almost shining around him, and I felt like my suddenly broken lifeline had been given an extension.

"Oh, no. Sorry about the interruption. There is my lunch date. I thought he said to meet him up here. See you around, I hope!"

I made a very poor and obvious strategic retreat, and didn't look back. There were fifteen thousand mages at this school. They'd never remember me.

Will was slipping into the crowd as I dashed down to the next tier via the closest ramp—a ramp that was unfortunately leading in the opposite direction that I needed to go. It took a concentrated effort to keep an eye on him. How did people find anyone in here?

I lost sight of him for a few moments, but then saw him sit at a table, still glowing with an internal light. I once again was a complete pillock and quickly darted forward. There were several empty spots at his table. I took a deep breath as I drew closer.

"Hi. Um, I was wondering if I could join you."

I got a couple of "great, new person coming to ruin our group dynamics" looks. Will just looked surprised. I gripped my tray. I could handle being told no. I braced myself for the rejection.

"We are discussing our group project for Transcendental Physics in Politics," one of the guys at the table said condescendingly.

"Sorry. Didn't realize. I'll just—"

"No, it's my fault," Will said quickly. "I asked Ren to join me for lunch. I forgot."

A warm rush of feeling swept me.

Another one of the members looked at Will. He looked half-starved and there were circles beneath his eyes. "That is exactly your problem, Tasky. You lack a brain sometimes."

"Better than a conscience," Will shot back.

The conscience-lacker sighed heavily. "Just sit, whoever you are. We will talk over your head, then you can continue on your lunch date with Tasky."

"Er, ok." At this point, I'd take it. I put my tray down and settled into a seat.

One of the prettiest girls I had ever seen sat down next to me. Or rather, she gracefully slid into the seat. Blonde and graceful—a lithe Botticelli wearing three very conspicuously located rings. Nervousness rushed through me.

"Hot," Christian said appreciatively.

Which he followed up with—*"Such a delicious soul, suck it out too!"*

Christian's voice seemed to be splitting even further. Was he stuck between realms? I started eating quickly. I needed to rescue him before something irreparable happened.

"I'm good, good, good. Worry, worry, worry!"

I ate faster.

Another tray plunked on my other side, and a cute, sporty looking guy sat down. He flashed me a smile and opened his drink. "New?"

I could feel Will's intent stare.

"Er, to this group, definitely." That seemed safe, and my tongue was all but useless in my mouth. I felt Will relax, even three seats away.

"Lucky you. I'm Mike."

"I...I'm ok. Stay, Ren."

I bit my lip, but nodded internally, relieved that Christian sounded like himself and that he was responding to me even a little.

"Nice to meet you, Mike." I held out my hand. "Ren."

"Great," someone said. "Happy everybody's friends. Now if we could continue with study group..."

I didn't have to contribute, thankfully, as the seven people around me bickered and argued and debated concepts I had never heard of. Needing to soothe my nerves the only way I knew how in this situation, I withdrew my notebook and a drawing pencil, and allowed my mind to capture images. I had always sat with Christian and his friends at lunch, drawing and soaking up their theatrics.

I sketched small, detailed pieces of the gorgeous architecture and magnificent view, then lightly blocked in the rest of the cafeteria landscape. I flipped the page and started to outline the people at our table. Only after block shading most of each face, making sure to catch the way the bright light from the massive window mixed with the warmer tones from the chandeliers, did I cue back into the conversation.

"They are scanning cuffs at checkpoints, Camille," said the boy who had rejected me initially.

"Good. Anyone who doesn't wear a government issued cuff has something to hide," the beautiful girl next to me said. Her expression was militant. Perhaps, not so much a lithe Botticelli as a warlike Athena, beautiful and deadly.

"That is not true. Maybe some mages just don't want to be tagged by the government in case the government goes corrupt. Can't very well overthrow a corrupt government if you are controlled by them," Mike pointed out.

Camille stiffened next to me. "That is treasonous talk."

"No, that is speculation and philosophical discourse. Besides, using your logic in reverse, a government shouldn't be wary of an uprising, if it isn't doing anything wrong."

She narrowed her eyes. "Controlling cuffs help mages. They stop crazy ferals from blowing all of us up."

Will looked nervous, but he broke into the discussion. "It wasn't that long ago that similar devices were used for far worse things, though." Will's words had an edge to them. A warning to me not to speak. I obediently started shading again. "And that is why you have mages still questioning how we can limit them."

"Yes, well, you all can use your tiny little outlier of 'a corruption what-if' while I use my real world example of a past origin mage on the loose, laying waste to half of the Third Layer."

"The government—"

"I understand why the resistance doesn't want cuffs," a girl said in a strong voice on the other side of the table. "My Awakening was extraordinary. But once the cuff was on, it felt like I was empty again. It took three years to achieve even a tenth of the magic level of my

Awakening."

I looked at my cuff. So...Marsgrove hadn't done anything extra diabolical to mine?

"The more adept you are at control, the easier it is to access your magic through the cuff," Camille said stiffly. "It compensates for you." Her tone clearly said that she found the other girl lacking because of this.

A variety of expressions crossed the other girl's face, then she smiled, though it didn't reach her eyes. "I wouldn't give up the feel of my Awakening for anything. It was extraordinary. You old magic types completely miss out."

So...non-ferals had a cuff in place from birth? Maybe I could still get Christian resurrected with mine on, then. Maybe I was starting in the wrong place.

"We miss out on nothing. I trained myself to be exceptional, and all that effort makes *me* extraordinary," Camille replied.

I pulled my pencil along the lines of her face, edging it with more dominant strokes.

"Definitely hot," Christian mused. I kept myself from rolling my eyes only at the last moment.

I paused for a second and embraced the feeling. How long had it been since I had done that?

"Allowing mages—especially rare types, ferals, and those who don't practice real control—to be free, encroaches on the civil liberties of the rest of us," Camille said. "Such mages pose real dangers, and I for one do not want my law-abiding family in danger because some wild beast can't contain his urges."

I wondered if she thought sitting next to such a person might be contagious. I calculated the proximity between our elbows.

"Not this again," someone muttered.

"Dangerous when uncontrolled, but late-blooming ferals tend to be powerful, which gives them a political position. It's what I've been saying all along," Mike said, pointing his fork.

"And we have diverged from the physics aspect of class again," a boy across the table said, obviously annoyed. "In order for the Third Layer terrorists to succeed in either taking over the First Layer or collapsing it into theirs, they would need to use a series of very complicated enchantments, only *one* of which we've discussed."

"Or they would need a new weapon."

"Like what? Everyone knows you would need either a port mage to allow the equipment through, or an origin mage to bend creation entirely. Five port mages exist, and they work for the Department and are accounted for. The last origin mage blew himself up three decades ago."

The first boy put a small disk in the middle of the table and a hologram burst out, showing a senate-styled chamber and many delegates arguing.

"You can see it there. Look at Lorenzo's face. He knows something. The Third Layer bastards have something. Everyone *knows* Lorenzo is a terrorist, and yet there he sits free as a bird."

The hologram showed a close-up of a distinguished man who did indeed have a smug smirk, but my attention was caught by the pin-striped man across the aisle, who was staring hard at him in displeasure. Marsgrove.

"This is happening now?" I asked, absently, barely aware of speaking at all.

The silence was absolute for a moment. I looked up to see everyone staring at me.

"What she means is do you have the delayed transmission or the live one?" Will said, giving me a small negative shake with his head.

"Oh. This was the Sagittarius Resting broadcast," the boy answered.

No clue what that meant—maybe the Sagittarius at the bottom of the clock?—but I just nodded and kept silent. The group continued its squabbling, while I stared at the hologram. Shots of Marsgrove were frequent, as he made statements at a large podium and was featured with many of the others who spoke.

"Two more weeks of negotiations. I can't believe I took this class during the term the Third Layer decided to enter talks."

Two more weeks. I had two more weeks.

"Could go faster," someone said. "They still haven't disclosed the reason behind their sudden decision to negotiate."

"No way, they are going to draw this out until the last brutal minute."

I tried to put all of the information I was hearing into a temporary holding-bucket in my mind so I could analyze and categorize it later. But when one of the group members rose to get ice cream, I followed suit, needing a break and hoping magical ice cream machines would do something neat, yet non-threatening.

I could use a pick-me-up. I didn't want to think about political whatsits or when Marsgrove would return or discussions that spurred ennui and rage. I just wanted to learn what I needed to bring Christian back. After that I could be *normal.*

Disappointingly, the ice cream machines looked more normal than I was. No delightful ten-eyed creatures serving, just machines with handles emitting a distinct chill.

The choices in the first machine were Banana Swirl and Magic Raisin. I wasn't fond of raisins, but Christian loved them. Maybe they'd make me feel better.

And maybe I'd love magic raisins. Did they come from magic grapes? Or was it magic mixed with raisins? I reached forward to find out as Camille stepped next to me.

"I saw your sketch of the discussion group. You are talented."

"Oh, uh, thanks. It's not finished. But you make a good subject." Ok, that sounded weird.

She tilted her head, accepting the compliment in a way that didn't come across as narcissistic. She was simply very sure of herself. "Thank you. Do you do commissions?" Her voice was rhythmic and feminine and strong.

"I...haven't?"

"Well, if I saw more of your work, I'd consider hiring you for a portrait."

"Thanks." I tried to accept the inherent compliment half as well as she had and failed miserably as I shifted on my feet.

"You didn't say anything during the discussion. Are you an advocate?"

I looked her over cautiously. They had discussed physical constructs, Third Layer terrorism, controlling cuffs, ferals, and repressive governments. I wasn't sure which advocacy I was supposed to be for or against with that question. "I am all for keeping the world safe."

"Good. Speak up next time, guest or not, or people will assume you are on the side of integration."

"Got it. Thanks."

She pivoted and walked away.

I decided maybe I'd do the Banana Swirl after all. Just in case magic forced me to be stranger.

When I returned to the table, only Will remained. The cafeteria had steadily cleared out, and there were now many vacant tables. I glanced up at the astronomical clock hanging on the eastern wall and made the mental note to come at *this* time tomorrow.

He raised a brow and sent a pointed glance up to the ice cream machines, which were visible from the table. "Making friends with Camille Straught?"

"You know I like to live dangerously." I took a bite of my ice cream. It was good. The banana and the cream flavors tasted fresh and real. "What's her story?"

"She's a combat mage."

I blinked. "Seriously?"

"A good one too."

"Huh. She looks like a fashion model." The Athena vibe grew stronger. Or maybe I'd go back to the lithe Botticelli image, but splitting her own

139

clamshell in half with her bare hands.

He shook his head. "Don't run afoul of her. The Straughts desperately want to be considered an Old Magic family, but are only three generations removed from Magie Nouveau. New Magic. They compensate in a somewhat draconian manner."

"Lovely."

He nodded. "Our groups were assigned by the professor; otherwise we'd never cross paths. My advice is to walk the other way when you see her—or any of her minions. Any of the Old Magic users or their clubs, really." He waggled his fingers. "Three rings."

I tipped my spoon to him. "Shall do." I wondered if she usually sat with that first table of girls I'd blundered across.

Taking another bite, I watched Will write something in his notebook. I looked around, but the tables near us had emptied. "So that thing about the cuffs? It's not just me who is blocked?"

He looked surprised for a moment. "Oh. No. It's too easy to make things happen here. What do you do if you want a turkey sandwich and, all of a sudden, start thinking of live turkeys? A sandwich with a live turkey sticking out might appear. Then you might think of King Kong, and you'd have a fifty-foot turkey gobbling everything."

I stared at him, scoop of ice cream halfway to my mouth, and thought of my dormitory desk. That was exactly how my brain worked. "So, the cuff is stopping me from making King Turkey?"

He nodded. "Most people don't think or conjure that big, but the cuff stops you from the brief wistful or vengeful thinking the mind naturally evokes. Course, if you really, really want a King Turkey, and have natural skill with creation magic, you might get one. You're a good candidate for that, what with the gophers and all. That type of magic usually doesn't last long, though, unless you can fill in all the pieces to make it somewhat real. Then you just suffer the consequences. Someone made a rampaging rhinoceros yesterday. It was full of candy and rage." He shook his head. "A piñata spell gone bad."

My mind was suddenly envisioning a rhino full of Snickers, fully forming it into vectors, rotating it around and shading rough skin in, chocolate growing inside. Each piece of the rhino moved in order, like a robot testing its parts—toes flexing, neck shifting. I slid my gaze to the right, half expecting a rhino to come bursting through the giant pane of glass.

Nothing.

My magic lay completely dormant beneath my cuff. Caged. I mentally assessed the feeling. Magic had slipped out when I had desperately wanted a solution to my cafeteria table dilemma. Magic had slipped out when I'd concentrated intensely on a locked box in my room. Magic had slipped out when I'd gone past sane chasing dirt particles.

At the moment, magic hummed pleasantly, but uselessly, beneath my cuff.

Will must have read my face. He smiled. "And...no rhino. You should try the practice rooms. You can make all the crazy stuff you want in there without penalty. Helps you get in touch with how your magic works. And buy a guide. A guide will help you identify and modulate your output. The more you can control it, the more your cuff will let free. Cuffs aren't sentient, but they 'trust' more if you can stream your magic in certain ways. Get the cuff to work with you instead of against you. That reminds me." He put his hand in his pocket. "I've been carrying this around for days now, hoping to see you."

He looked nervous, but handed me a familiar leather band. I felt a little like I had the day I had fallen off the jungle gym in third grade. Wondering why I could no longer breathe.

"It isn't the same one, obviously," he said, voice uncertain. "But I...I saw the look on your face when you looked at the burn on your empty wrist..."

"It was my brother's." My voice was barely audible as I mechanically reached for it. It was a perfect replica. Made by magic, obviously. And there was a *feel* to it. It almost felt like Christian. Like a melding of Will and Christian.

"I...er, I did a quick workshop in leather spells." He looked around quickly, lowering his voice further. "And, I used a spark off the sword to capture some of your magic for its creation. I also inserted a spell to help you with basic knowledge. A basic knowledge encyclopedia will ping your consciousness when a topic is raised. Then you just have to tap into the database. You can put other stuff in there too. Useful." He tapped the side of his head.

"Thank you," I whispered, barely able to speak as I put it on.

He cleared his throat and did that male thing Christian and Dad sometimes did, where he rubbed at his hair, intent on changing an embarrassing subject. "So, it's good to see you. How are you adjusting?"

I cleared my own suspiciously tight throat. "Splendidly."

He smiled. "It's crazy here, isn't it?"

More glorious and terrifying, but I nodded to him, touching the bracelet. "So an old magic club? What clubs are you a member of?"

He looked surprised, then shifty. His caginess caused me to smile. My magic adored Will. I touched my new bracelet again.

"What makes you think I'm in any clubs?" he asked.

"Aren't all the cool kids?"

He looked around, then leaned forward, pushing his glasses up. "There are all sorts of secret groups around here. You just have to keep your wits about you and your senses open. They tend to find you, rather than the other way around."

I blinked. "Ok."

He smiled. "I have a feeling you'll be in more than one."

I picked up my spoon again. "Can you be any more vague and mysterious?"

He put his fingertips in the air and little jets of blue flame sprouted off each. His glasses filmed over. "On the fifth day of searching, you will find your calling in the large oak of the wild wood."

My spoon dropped into my bowl. "I demand to know how to do that. Can I shoot lightning bolts too?"

Will started laughing, and the three thousand pound weight on my shoulders abruptly felt twenty pounds lighter.

Chapter Thirteen

ADVENTURES IN CAMPERY

WILL WALKED WITH ME to the bookstore, showing me a handy tree portal on the way, that shot us down the roots of one tree, into the roots of another, then popped us from the trunk two circles down. "Sister trees joined by the same root system," he said cheerfully.

He had classes all afternoon, so we made a date to meet at the library that evening and he waved as he trotted off. I had to figure out what to share—or leave out—about Marsgrove. It was a threat to have any personal contacts, but everything in me rebelled at pushing Will away.

I castigated myself for a moment, then stepped inside. There was a stand just inside the bookstore's entrance that immediately caught my eye, a large sign marked "NEWS" hung above it. On a pitiful little shelf near the bottom was a plastic card labeled "News Feeder" that would fit into my reader. It was deeply discounted, if the multiple slashes in the munit price were anything to go by. Above it were hundreds of packaged round stickers labeled "Frequency Tweaks" in a far bigger and more eye-catching display. The display featured a picture of a smiling girl pressing the soft skin behind her ear.

I lifted the discounted news card, ignoring the other stuff. The last thing I wanted was to have more people chattering in my head. I could keep track of Marsgrove with my obviously ancient technology.

"Free me."

Yes.

Books, devices, and articles were marching in precise order down the aisles, then flying up and onto the shelves. A perky clerk was orchestrating the work with a baton.

I found the guide shelves easily, thanks to another well-lit display. A number of different guide constructs greeted me on the box covers—a cheerful woman with a plume, an adventuress sporting a coiled whip, a businessman with a wand and an oily grin, a Buddhist monk with flying yin-yang discs—there were too many choices.

I decided on the "self-selecting" guide package. The advertisement stated it would work on the fly to tailor the perfect guide for the user "at activation," as specified per the warnings. I had always trusted my intuition. I'd trust it and my magic for this.

The guide package was expensive and used up a good amount of my remaining munits. But Will had seemed confident that this would help me, as had Nephthys, the girl from the library. It would be well worth the price if I succeeded in getting around the cuff limitation so that I could get around the paint restriction, so that I could get around the laws against necromancy.

Everything in my current life seemed to revolve around how to free myself from bindings.

I needed to succeed in this world.

"You will succeed in whatever you choose to do, Ren." A warm rush of magic followed.

"Conquer everything! Enslave them." The warm rush cooled at the sound of the voice I had dubbed "Evil Christian."

The practice rooms were located on the ninth circle in the Kratos Battle Building—a huge domed compound with thick steel and concrete walls and ceilings. When the apocalypse occurred, I was coming here.

At the edge of the ninth circle was the swirling, misty area I had avoided during my frantic hop around the mountain when I had been trying to leave Excelsine. A thick veil of smoke hung evenly along an invisible edge, preventing me from seeing inside. My cuff tightened, as the mysterious area called to the magic flowing beneath it. *Come, enter, be mine.*

The map called the area that comprised the tenth through twelfth circles the "Midlands." Unlike anywhere else on the mountain, there were clearly marked warning signs along the invisible edge, making the barrier visible by the very nature of the obstructions. Arches were systematically placed to transport mages from the ninth to the thirteenth circle, completely bypassing the swirling smoke.

I took one last glance, and entered the compound. The door shut behind me in a definitive way, sealing the wall there completely. The long, tunneled hall was empty, and eerily silent. Candles flickered in clawed Gothic chandeliers that hung from the ceiling. I had thought that maybe I would hear the sounds of battle—the clang of swords, the cries of agony, and the shouts of victory— but, it was the kind of silence poets attributed to the aftermath of battle. I could almost feel the newly dead hovering. The place gave me the creeps.

I hurried into the first available room. Lights flickered on, illuminating rich brown walls and a brown ceiling and floor. I could either think of the brown as dried blood or something better. I made the mental rhino schematic I had been carrying with me abruptly fill with Hershey bars. The door shut solidly behind me. Three deadbolts simultaneously engaged.

I nervously looked over the simple instructions that had come with my purchase. Plug the cartridge into the wall, then let the magic do its work. The program was designed to interface with my conscious mind, subconscious needs, and magic, and choose the form and personality of my instructor. There were hundreds of instructor templates included—based on real people—that could be combined with my personal needs in order to tailor my guide. A picture of a floating Sifu with a long beard and tendril mustache was on the cover. Very tranquil, meditative, and powerful.

I plugged the cartridge in and the whirring sound I had experienced in the reading room revved its engine.

My subconscious chose a shaved-headed, big-chested, tree-trunk-legged, total hardass, who liked to wear seventies-styled workout shorts, one-size-too-small white t-shirts, and tall athletic socks. A guide who liked to shout dire warnings and weird animal curses.

Apparently, not only was I not Zen, but I was in need of magical boot camp.

"As Marcus Draeger, I was brought into this world, ordinary-born, at the age of thirteen," he barked. "And all those born mages were the enemy. I conquered them! You will call me Lieutenant Draeger, as I'm going to make a soldier out of you, Cadet Feral. You will not be squirrel meat! You *will* give those born-tos hell."

I blinked at him, then eyed the cartridge in the wall and the distance I'd have to cover in order to remove it.

"Swear it, Cadet!" He leaned in, towering over me, looking completely real. A magical construct that might be able to pulverize me in here.

"I swear to give everyone hell!"

"Excellent." He waved a hand and three crates appeared. "While you are in here, everything is real. You will experience everything as reality. Inside of these walls, you can find your true potential, if you work hard."

He blew up three wooden crates, then put them back together with magical military precision. Enthralled, I watched the network of blue lines on the walls bend, then snap back together with each explosion.

"Give it a try, Cadet. *Will* the crate to blow."

I looked at the crate nearest to me, held my hand toward it like he had, and *willed* the crate to explode. Nothing happened. I shook my hand and willed harder for the crate to explode.

"Turkey giblets! You have to want it, Cadet!"

I thought of the night Christian died. I wanted my brother back. Electricity lit within me, running down my arms.

The crate rocketed back and blew a hole through the side of the room, then through the side of the next room. I heard someone shout. I shoved my hands in my armpits and willed them not to blow off my arms.

"*That* is what would have happened if this room and that cuff didn't encapsulate your magic," Draeger said. He drew his hand downward through the air and circled back up again. Tendrils of rock and wire from the top of the hole in our room reached down as materials from the bottom reached up, stitching themselves back together, tendrils twisting and connecting, then smoothing into a sleek, unblemished brown wall.

"So I didn't actually destroy the wall?" I asked nervously.

"You did not, Cadet. You destroyed the *thought* of it under a different condition."

"And the yell?"

"The mage you would have whacked three rooms over. This compound works on moment to moment spec. Allows you to virtually battle others in the compound, if you have the right cartridge."

I gave my cartridge a nervous glance.

"You are feral, Cadet. Means you have access to a large magic well and the desire for its use, but that you don't know turtle pellets about what to do with it, all bottled up inside. We'll get that worked out," he said with relish, then blew up three crates in precise order, assembling the previous one as the next exploded. "I have a good feeling about you, Cadet. Your brain doesn't work like most people's."

Great.

"I like it. Structured, yet highly imaginative. And you've got good innate control of yourself." He peered into my eyes. "But you absorbed someone's wild magic, and it mixed inside you, muddling things. We'll find your bottleneck," he said with relish, uncaring of my shock at his words. "Don't you worry."

"How do you know I absorbed wild magic?" I put my hand to my chest.

"Knowing your physiology and experience is what I'm programmed for upon activation. My personality, wisdom, and background are modeled after Marcus Draeger, but your magic gives me life as this." He waved his hands over himself. "Structurally, I was part of you at the moment I was conceived here; yet, now I am separate. This allows me to know you without knowing exactly what you will choose to do from moment to moment. You now have a hundred more experiences than you had five minutes ago, and each experience you gain will tweak your future choices."

Warmth bloomed under my hand. Christian was with me. And I would *do* this. I would pour his magic right back into him.

But Draeger wasn't observing my metaphysical moment, or maybe he just wasn't programmed that way. "Intent, focus, knowledge, confidence! Those are the keys to magic. You need all four to be proficient."

I was going to be *more* than proficient.

"Here, you will be able to access amounts of your magic that you will not be able to outside. And I will be able to control that access to a certain extent."

I rubbed the skin alongside my cuff as he conjured a beautiful bottle, or the image of one, between us. It bulged then exploded, fragments dissipating into sparkles, then falling to the floor. Elements whirled and things shattered and reformed in the air swirling around him.

In the center of the room, a dozen small blocks stacked themselves perfectly one on top of another as Draeger concentrated on each. "Meditation and centering will help you, as will going back to basics. Learning like a child does, one block at a time. We will work on your focus first, which is the point that the other cornerstones build or flow toward."

He swiped a hand and the blocks clattered to the floor. He indicated that I try.

Focus. Focus. Using pure force of will, two blocks rose and banged together, then dropped noisily.

Draeger said nothing, just watched me as I breathed heavily and tried again. Focus, bang, drop. Focus, lift, bang, clatter.

I repeated the movements. Focus, lift, bang, drop, focus, lift, clatter, drop, focus, wobble, smack.

Twenty times. Focus, lift, bang, drop, focus, lift, clatter, drop, clatter, drop.

Thirty times. Focus, lift, bang, rattle, smack, clatter, drop, bang, focus, lift, wobble, whack.

Forty times. Focus, lift, bang, drop, focus, bang, focus, rattle, focus, smack, focus, lift, focus, drop, focus, clank, focus, clatter, focus, focus, rattle, focus, focus, focus, drop, focus, focus, focus, focus, *boom.*

A block exploded and slivers of wood flew outward in slow motion. My attention centered on the remaining blocks as the splinters continued to spread through the air. Unacceptable. *I would not fail.*

I took a deep breath. *One block lifting, hovering on top of the second, fingers bracing the sides, smoothing and settling them perfectly into place.* One block at a time. Focus.

I touched my chest, where Christian was with me. My singular focus. A block wobbled and rose, stacking unevenly atop another, pushing slowly into place. I concentrated on the next block, my complete focus on it and the topmost point of the small stack where it would be placed, just as a child would. Electricity, energy, *magic*, flowed through me, responding, soothing.

Everything fell into position internally, zeroing in on that one movement. Like being in the zone. My art zone, or a music, or sports zone. A lovely combination of focus and emotion, making me feel as if I was doing exactly what I had been born to do.

I wanted this feeling forever.

"Excellent, Cadet. The cornerstone of focus is incredibly important. Your magic *wants* to be used and always will. Can't put the grizzly back in the cage! But you need to figure out how to focus with a switch of your mind."

He ran a simulation that produced a lovely trunk. Gorgeous lines of color crisscrossed the space, some of them startlingly intense and others bleeding and blending. The trunk itself was a masterwork. Brilliant gold-and-rose-colored lines swirled out and billowed around it like some sort of Pandora's Box.

"Magic at its clearest levels, Cadet. Magic lines—wards, leys, old spells, and new enchantments."

My brain kept thinking "pretty" in a looping pattern.

"Mages with excellent control can channel magic that is crystal clear to most eyes. The more skillful you become at picking out even the slightest hue change, the better off you will be in magical situations."

Each drill threw out a new beam of color, and I had to identify its basic feel and hue before I got zapped.

Identifying the basic "feel" of the beams left me floundering and I got zapped...a lot. Christian would excel at this, though, and only when I thought of him could I correctly identify the feel of the beams every time. Luckily, on the color side, I had a bit of an edge. I could identify the differences in color and texture rather well. Turquoise, lapis, cobalt, teal, sea-foam, ocean. A tiny variation in hue made the color look entirely different to my eye.

Draeger set up the simulations to run in tandem. Beautiful things grabbed my attention and distraction nudged me physically off center, pushing me out of the zone again and again. Blocks fell, and fell, and fell some more.

I wiped my forehead. "The books suggested picturing peeling rose petals, drops of water, sand grains falling, flames dancing," I said. None of those things were working for me.

His gaze was penetrating. "Magic is not a one size fits all boot. Some mages learn and express through logic, some through movement, some through introspection, others through rhyme, and everything in between. Find the image and focus that works for you. That is your homework, Cadet. Look to your strengths. The goal here is for you to connect with your magic. Magic is about self- discovery. Let's begin again."

I tripped from the brown room in a wondrous daze four hours after entering. I had memorized everything he had said, so I could absorb it later. Tips, tricks, basic knowledge. Failing a task had made me more determined. I would learn *everything*. I would master everything. I would get Christian back.

Outside, the world seemed brighter even as dusk was taking hold.

A group of students carrying staffs, swords, and wands walked past. A mage rolled two metal balls around his palm as he walked and talked. My eyes pulled ahead to a figure entering the swirling gray smoke of the Midlands. Alexander Dare's form was swallowed completely mere seconds later.

The pull tugged, but I turned in the other direction, back up the mountain. I juggled my bag as I walked and withdrew my reader and the news card. Easy enough to operate with its channels and menus, a live feed of the treaty negotiations was prominently displayed on the first page. I selected it. Only a minute later, I could see the room. I could see Marsgrove. It looked as if none of the participants had moved since the last time. Good. If they stayed in those seats, unmoving, for the next two weeks, even better.

I jumped to the fifth circle by way of three arches, then surveyed the mountains far in the distance. The thrum of magic was a pleasant buzz in my veins. I felt as if I could fly.

I focused on the teeniest, tiniest drop of paint falling from a mental paintbrush into a glass of clear water. The paint drop spread inky tendrils through the water in my mind's eye, sending magic flowing through my limbs in reflection. My administration map lifted out of my hands and wobbled in the air. Yes. *Yes.*

"You are doing well."

"Now get me out of this hell."

I checked my reader's news feed—Marsgrove still in place—then gave Christian a firm mental nod.

Chapter Fourteen

PLANS

MAGIC WAS TIRING—making me fire on far more cylinders than I was used to. I yawned and flipped through a few texts on magical meditation. I pushed them aside twenty minutes later. There were too many things vying for attention in my brain for me to meditate.

I *had* to learn magic. I had to be good at it.

While finishing off a Magi Mart personal pizza, I looked at the sketch I had framed the night before. I had stared at it while falling asleep—hung so near to my pillow. The room lights glinted off of it, giving it a soft inner glow.

I brushed off my hands then grabbed the black auto-sorting notebook I had purchased for my necromancy research.

Olivia rose and her starchy schoolgirl outfit rippled to be replaced with something older and even starchier. She disappeared with her bag a minute later.

I looked over the ritual that would determine if Christian's soul was at peace, then got to work. Three candles from the bathroom were placed in a triangle formation on a ceramic plate to represent "enlightenment." Potpourri was scattered around the edges for "essence." The "writ of the deceased"—an obscene postcard from Christian when he'd been at football camp last summer—went in the middle.

I started the chant, focusing on the ink of Christian's slanted letters. Suddenly the ink swirled, fire lit, and I was bodily ejected from my bed and thrown into my desk.

Whack.

Swearing, I rubbed my shoulder and dragged myself back over to the bed. I blew out the overturned candles before they could ignite my bedspread. The picture of the smirking model wearing a skimpy Speedo had been obliterated. I shakily turned the charred fragment over. The joking text from Christian was gone. Only a single two-letter word in his handwriting remained.

No.

Christian was not at peace.

Grief was sharp as I collected the ashes of the postcard he had jokingly sent to me months ago. I'd get new notes from him soon, though. I nodded sharply. Full steam ahead.

Delving into my reader, I found I could access some of the main library collection through a centralized server. But the fourth floor library texts were only accessible by hand, and many of the second floor wall books were accessible only by card. It was as if students were being herded to the library if they required more information.

I dove into the books available on the server. There were some crazy practices involved in bringing someone back from the dead. Rites and rituals involving ashes, pits of fire, goats, bells, circles, talismans, bloodshed, and earth. Some of the darker ones entailed copious amounts of blood, consumption of rotten food (to simulate the flesh), and eating flesh itself.

I gagged, but dutifully transferred the knowledge from the reader to the notebook via the spell interface. It copied the words neatly in my handwriting.

Speed reading over the items that weren't directly related to my goal, an advertisement at the edge of the page caught my eye.

Black Magicks Unlimited. Loosen your stiff! Reanimate the dead! We do it all! Ten percent discount* on your first visit!
*Ganymede Circus branch only.

I stared at it. Could it be that easy? Had I overlooked the obvious due to all of the insane warnings in the texts? A shop that could bring Christian back—it was right there in their advertisement. I quickly noted the information. Ganymede Circus? I had no idea where that was.

A quick search through the library server indicated information concerning Ganymede Circus was only available on the fourth floor. I wasn't meeting Will at the library for two more hours—an eternity. Time to figure out how to get up to the fourth floor on my own. I threw my notebook in my bag, shoved my feet in my shoes, and started jogging.

Pausing only when I reached the third floor of the library, I examined the ascending staircases scattered around the floor and studied my hand drawn map. I had tried, then noted, a dozen different staircases. None of them had worked.

I needed to watch someone else do it, but few people seemed inclined to go up. It made me a little nervous as to what was up there.

Whereas the floor beneath the third level was glass and steel, allowing frequent glimpses of the second level, and even the first, the ceiling above the third level was thick and opaque.

Staking out a comfy chair that had an unimpeded view of eight ascending staircases, I waited for the first candidate. I pulled out my notebook and began a design for my first storage space paper. Something simple for a first attempt, yet complicated enough to be useful. I shaded three-dimensional shadows around a single bookcase with three shelves. I chewed my pencil cap. I sketched a spinning carousel in the margin and wrote "future ideas" above it.

The idea also made me think of my magic focus. The paint drop was great, but I needed to work the cornerstones together in order to perform the magic I would need. Maybe I could use a geometric construct? I'd ask Draeger in the morning. I planned to spend a serious eight to ten hours in the practice rooms tomorrow.

Movement at staircase three caught my attention. Notebook and bag snatched up, I was out of my chair and padding closer as I watched Alexander Dare saunter up the stairs. Seriously? Was he everywhere? I felt like some kind of weird, unwitting stalker. He paused deliberately on the third stair with his hand on the rail, then continued up.

Ok. That might make sense. Focus, concentration, knowledge, confidence. By the time I gained the third step, he had disappeared up into the mystery of the fourth floor. My eyes closed, and I concentrated on projecting my desire to get to the fourth floor. I *needed* to get up there. Christian needed me to.

In my mind, I rotated a three dimensional box, like the one I had just drawn, with paint spreading around its sides. The image was not quite right, but magic slipped from under my cuff, soothing as it traveled along my fingers and into the handrail beneath. I opened my eyes and a bright light lit the top of the stairs. I hurried up, bypassing an umbrella stand that held a number of carved wooden walking sticks in its basin and helmets on its pegs, and entered pandemonium.

Unlike the bookstore, where books marched in orderly fashion, here books were soaring and diving through the air in a hostile manner, book covers snapping. A mage battled a book that was trying to eat his papers.

Before I could close my dropped jaw, a book swooped down, pages spread open like wings and clamped around my face. My relationship with my brother flip-flip-flipped in my mind exactly like the magically flipped pages of a book that was sucking out my mind.

Sucking out my mind.

I pried it off, and the word "twin" that it was in the process of writing took a sudden dive down the page like a pen that had been yanked away. I thrust the book far from me, freaked out, and it flew upward, circling above me, the words "Magical Family Relationship Collection" on its cover.

Another book swooped in with great, paged wings spread and clamped its pages around my head, boxing my ears. The book sucked, then took off in hungry disgust. I saw the title "Dating Advice" written on its cover. Ok. Disturbing and embarrassing.

I turned and snatched up one of the walking sticks and a helmet. There was something rectangular on the end of the stick, and as I brandished it, the aggressive book diving for me snapped its covers shut, propelling itself back through the air like a squid reacting to danger. I examined the bottom of the stick. An eraser was stuck to the end. I waved it menacingly at another book that looked poised to attack and shoved a helmet on my head with my other hand.

The books circled like vultures, awaiting opportunity.

In a table in the center of the main room, five students were sleeping with their heads on cushions, books greedily sucking out their souls. I watched horrified as helmeted mages walked by without sparing them a glance.

"Save them, Ren!"

"Suck out their souls too!"

Ok. Christian was intact. Well, part of him was still intact. I took a shaky breath and poked carefully around my mind, relieved to discover I hadn't actually lost any memories or thoughts of my twin. So had the book only made a copy of something in my head? And that's what the other books were now doing to those students? I crept toward a student/book pair, bent down, and peered under the pages to see words speedily writing themselves on the mellowed paper.

A passing mage gave *me* a weird look, and I hastily pulled back, then whacked a book that was diving toward the edge of my helmet—as if it planned to knock it off.

Still freaky. Though, if I could get a book to drag a term paper out of my head in the future, that would be horrifyingly useful. I put osmosis on my mental research list.

The books circling my head had alarming titles. *Why Teenagers Look to the Dark, Straying from a Righteous Path, Dreams, Rare Mage Identification, Solving Problems in Unusual Ways, Lateral and Literal Thinking.*

Dreams looked at me hopefully, its pages rippling in a little hand clenched gesture, while maintaining a respectful distance.

"Maybe...maybe later, ok?" I muttered, feeling ridiculous.

It gave a little ripple of its pages and flew up to rest on a balcony above with a fleet of other books, watching and waiting. A black-and-white book perched there tilted toward me, its glittering but unreadable letters piercing me like eyes, as it regally wobbled next to *Dreams*, which sat straighter, then bowed its spine and rippled its pages.

Ok. I was officially disturbed. I waved my eraser stick. "The rest of you, get lost," I told the still-circling tomes, a few of which exuded a far more predatory vibe than *Dreams'* polite request.

Straying from a Righteous Path looked outraged, its spine stiff as it sailed off. The rest followed *Dreams'* path, though, and clustered around the black-and-white book to form a little papered powwow.

I secured the chin strap on my helmet more firmly. I could wonder about my sanity later—the whole experience of the magical was surreal, but felt too linear to be a dream.

It didn't matter. This existence held hope and I was grabbing it with two desperate hands.

Several dozen pedestals dotted the perimeter of the large one-room floor. On each pedestal a book was displayed, surrounded by either a glass case or a cage. Hanging from each was a ceremonial knife in a jeweled scabbard. A jet black cage drew my attention.

As I walked closer, I noted the binding was made from the skin of something striped black and forest green. The title read *The Twelve Black Steps*. There was a tangible dark allure to it. A little like Mr. Verisetti. Another encased book to the right read *Death Magic*. What would one of those books do if it got a hold of me? Suck out my soul for real?

"Don't do it!"

"I...reluctantly concur."

Even Christian's mad alter ego was agreeing.

"I love him," an unhelmeted girl cried, reaching for a pedestal to my right. A book titled "Lovesick" attached to the back of her head.

"No, stop." The other girl—helmeted—manhandled her back from the pedestal, but didn't whack the book off her friend.

They struggled in a pseudo-wrestling stance. "I love him, and I know he only needs a little push to love me back."

"You will get pegged by the Department for checking that out of its case," the second girl hissed. "I'm not letting you."

"I need him." The girl extended a hand toward the hanging knife, still locked chest-to-chest with her friend.

"Getting Constantine Leandred to love you is not worth it. You'll be in the system forever. They check those mages first. They do an automatic check on you the moment you press your finger to the stone. No." She pushed the other girl back two steps. "You are out of your mind anyway. Leandred is insanely vengeful. He'd turn you into a carrot, then feed you to a rabbit, if you didn't get the spell right, and he found out what you tried to do."

"I'd get it right!" *Lovesick* left the back of her head and was replaced with *Delusions of Grandeur.*

I examined the knife. Could I use synthetic blood? Or did it have to be student blood? I thought about the Rosetta Stone episode that had given me the translation enchantment and enrolled me. Likely student blood.

I reluctantly moved away from the pedestal. Marsgrove had made too many references to the people in the Department being worse than he. Will had been freaked out by them too. I'd try Ganymede first, then figure out a way around the blood restriction, if that didn't work.

I wandered around, checking out the floor plan, which was similar to the libraries I was used to in the First Layer. The shelf inhabitants, however, were anything but normal.

There were very few mages on the fourth floor—maybe three dozen in total—and silencing enchantments either didn't seem to be an option here or weren't enforced. Two students at a humongous oak table were arguing loudly.

"I'm telling you, the Third Layer is going to sign the contingency tomorrow. They are backed into the corner on this one. No negotiating power."

"Don't say that." There was a note of warning in the other boy's voice.

"Oh, come on, they can't enter any of the major cities here without being noticed. There are too many patrols."

"All it takes is one of the Ten Most Wanted mages to make an appearance—"

"Powerful, all ten, but in order to do the kind of grand scale damage needed—"

I ducked a book titled *The Joy of Flight* that was randomly doing spirals and loops, and approached a sea of wooden drawers that housed a simple card catalog system. There was no wall or computer system in sight. The fourth floor was technologically backward from the three floors below it and yet a hundred times more overtly magical.

There were helmets atop the cabinets with a sign that said to leave the catalog helmets in the catalog area. I could only imagine how easy a target someone looking through tiny drawers would be to a ravenous book. I rapped the top of my helmet—secure—then thumbed through the drawers in order to figure out the cataloging system and find what I was looking for.

A floor map was posted above the cabinets, and I found the designation that coincided with the map stacks. Ducking out, I walked briskly through the maze of bookshelves and, upon seeing my goal, increased my speed.

"Ack," I gasped, as I crashed into something solid that emerged from the shelves on my right.

Strong hands clasped me, preventing me from falling, but my necromancy research notebook clattered to the floor, pages splayed open.

Ultramarine eyes filled my upward vision.

"Steady there."

His hand reached down to retrieve my notebook, and I dove for it, knocking his hand to the side. I did a little somersault, whacking my helmet loudly on the parquet floor, and came up in a crouch with the open notebook pressed to my chest.

Alexander Dare's amazing eyes filled with surprise, then a brow quirked under dark brown hair which was neither long nor short. "Should I even ask?"

His voice was just as I remembered. Beautifully masculine, deep and edged. There was the slightest bit of humor there now. A book dove at him—*Strategy and Tactics*—and he flicked his fingers without looking, forcing it off its path and straight into a shelf. It crashed, shook its pages, and took off into the air again, then hid behind a shelf, peeking around as if plotting its next move against him. Unsurprisingly, Dare wasn't wearing a helmet.

"No." I pressed my necromancy notebook against my chest more firmly. My actions screamed guilty.

He seemed to be waiting for me to say something more, but I could do nothing but stare at him. Visions of him utterly destroying people in the holograms with an easy flick of his fingers—just like the motion he had made with the book—looped through my head.

And yet, this was the boy who had healed me. Who had expressed his sorrow that he couldn't heal Christian. Who had given me that last moment.

My pulse pounded, my wrist itched fiercely under my cuff, and I was wearing a helmet.

He looked at me oddly. "You are the girl who had the trouble in the reading room. The one who tried to stun me."

I just stared at him like some feral mute recently emerged from a jungle. Preservation instincts were overriding common sense. Luckily, they were also overriding the words that sprung to my lips—*I bet you stun people stupid a lot.*

No. A thousand times no. I clenched my lips together, determined to keep them that way. I somewhat hoped a book would bean me in the face so I could just pass out and escape from my own awkwardness.

He touched his cuff, frowning, then rotated his wrist, shaking his right hand out. I followed the motion. I wondered what design lay beneath his cuff. An image of the bird and snake hybrid shot forward in my mind.

"Phoenix dragon," I blurted.

"What?" he asked sharply.

I shook my head and clamped my lips together harder.

"Are...you ok?"

"No." I was most decidedly not.

"Should I call the librarian?" he asked slowly. "Or help you walk to the stairs?"

I eked out another "No," without saying anything more. It was close.

He watched me intently for several more seconds, and I wondered if he was going to call the librarian—or the men with white coats—after all, but he finally raised a brow and walked away.

My eyes followed him, body frozen until he turned the corner. I slumped against the wall. Wow. If there was a competition for worst communicator in history, I needed to enter.

Unsurprisingly, an adult appeared a minute later to see if all was well. My savior had obviously sent the librarian to check on the unstable girl in the stacks. My capacity to be completely mortified swelled.

After poorly reassuring the librarian that I was fine, I found the information I needed. The arch to Ganymede Circus was located on the twentieth circle, two up from the base of the mountain.

The circus was listed as a "protected area." Highly magical and extremely volatile.

The city map showed the spoked streets of the circus converging into a center roundabout and gave me the location for the entrance arch that admitted mages from "academic institutions" as well as the location for Black Magicks Unlimited.

I just needed to figure out how to get around Marsgrove's manipulation in order to access an off-campus arch.

~*~

I met Will on the first floor, in the midst of the sea of packed tables. He was already seated. The inner light that had highlighted him earlier when I'd panicked in the cafeteria was still in place, making him easy to find. He drew his finger in a pattern on the table, and the voices around us dimmed.

"Rune for silencing fields," he said. "They are standard around most parts of campus; you just have to activate them."

I copied the shape into the general notebook I was keeping for everything not necremancy related and activated the sorting feature to move it into the "green" section, where I was keeping a task list of things to be researched. I included a note to get a book on runes as well.

Will and I chatted about fun and bizarre things—like books that attacked and how the caged ones did require student blood and were dangerous to unlock—until I managed to bring the conversation around to Will's port and travel research.

"So, if there is an arch that is blocked, how do you go about getting through it?" I asked casually. If I could avoid it, I didn't want to tell him that I was Marsgrove's prisoner and on campus illegally.

Will nearly vibrated in his seat as he explained in one big spew, his hands motioning so hard that he knocked his glasses askew on his nose. He took a breath finally. "So, to sum up, you need to find an accelerator to move past it or another magic that will overwhelm or trick it."

I gave him the "keep explaining" sign with my hand.

"Accelerators are difficult to obtain, and tricky to make, but once you have one, you tap the accelerant on the object, then let the magic do its work. Even better if you can make an accelerator box or spider. Device magic is the best—many mages like to pretend to be all otherworldly." He waved his arms around in a mystical fashion. "Me, I acknowledge and celebrate the practicality and brilliance of toys."

He gave his pockets a pat. "You insert the magic during a controlled lab setting, then don't have to worry about point focusing in the field. The tricky part is inserting the right magic. Like your magic paint. Definitely a powerful accelerant. I've been meaning to ask you about it. What kind of paint did you use? I want to buy some."

I rubbed my hand along my neck. "I don't know." I looked around. "I got it from...my teacher."

"Ah." Will put a small plain black device on the table between us. He looked around, then pressed the top. It lit red and he relaxed, but leaned forward. "Tiny bit of chaos magic—it will disrupt our conversation for anyone trying to eavesdrop past the silencing fields. Works for ten minutes. I did a little research on your teacher after I returned. He studied art here."

That made sense—what with the mountain paintings and Marsgrove knowing him.

"I found an old school picture," he continued. "He was standing between Dean Marsgrove and another guy. Chummy."

Will looked like he was expecting me to take the news badly. I shook my head. "Marsgrove called him by first name a few times, so I'm not surprised. Speaking of which..." It was as good an opening as any. "If you could not mention me to Marsgrove at all, that would be great. I don't trust him."

And if Will was ever in conversation with him, I didn't want my name dropped.

Will looked surprised, but said, "Sure. He's a big deal around here, but I only know him because of that research project. He was in charge of my pu—I mean, assignment."

My eyes narrowed immediately. "He assigned you to that project?"

"Yup. Wanted me to look for magical technologies in the First Layer." He shrugged. "It paralleled my own aims. Was what I got in tr—noticed for. I, ah, might have tweaked the parameters for my own purposes, though."

I tapped my fingers, thinking hard. "So, the paint is an accelerant?"

"Definitely seemed to be. Special, though. I'd love to study it. I'm going to do some serious delving into art magic now. Good for conceptualization at the very least, especially if I can gain some rudimentary skill."

I blinked at him and my mental brown paint bucket of "uncategorized" information immediately spit out an item. "Hey, there is an Art Expressionists meeting tomorrow. I have no clue what that is, but do you want to go with me? I'm not exactly signed up for classes yet. Middle of term and all." I tucked my hair behind my ear. "And it might be informative?"

"Sure!"

I smiled at him and relaxed as he returned the grin. Maybe I wasn't the worst communicator in the world after all.

~*~

Well past midnight, and after I had done another practice round with Draeger, I sketched the day's events into my personal journal. Long ago, I had found a quote from Pablo Picasso that I had taken to heart. "Painting is just another way of keeping a diary," it had read. I had used art as my emotional log ever since.

A broken heart led into a book, then morphed out to become a budding rose. Two birds tentatively hopped toward one another, each extending a wing.

My scientific journal was a tightly written database of tests and formulas. My personal journal was all about the emotion. I needed both.

As I finished up my log of the day's events, my gaze wandered over to the sketch that had held Will prisoner. When everything in front of the drapes had been mysteriously cleared, the jar containing the single drop of paint had been too.

But now...

My pen slashed a jagged line up the journal's page as I lunged forward to grip the sketch.

Chapter Fourteen

Now it sat in front of the drapes again, as if something had pushed it out from beneath. Nearly shaking, I put my hand on top of the paper and willed the jar to come out. I *needed* this. I focused hard, thinking of a perfect spot of ultramarine blue spreading into a glass of water, each tendril separating exactly as I wanted it to, then spreading to collect as a single, large focused intent in my mind.

The jar started shaking, then sliding across the sketch floor. The paint inside briefly glowed, then half of it disappeared at the same time that one of my fingers glowed blue.

The small jar popped half out beneath my palm. I quickly grabbed the glass and pulled it against my chest, pushing the paper away, in case it tried to reabsorb my treasure.

The drop in the jar was now only half the size, but it was still *paint*. True magic paint.

Knock, knock, knock.

~*~

Another substance abuse charge earned me a stint cleaning the dark, empty entrance hall. I was so on edge with excitement and nerves that I practically vibrated the dirt into the floor grate.

As Olivia turned off her light for the night, I continued to stare at the jar, now lit only by a faint reflection of moonlight seeping through the blinds. The drop was not enough to paint Christian out, but it might be enough to trick an arch. I gave Will's sketch, propped near my pillow, a stroke with one fingertip, then curled around the jar. I would go in the morning.

Christian screamed in increased agony all night.

Chapter Fifteen

GANYMEDE CIRCUS

I HITCHED MY BAG higher and watched the morning activity around the arch to Ganymede Circus with heavy, exhausted eyes. No one was going into or coming out of the arch, but there were a number of mages in business suits chatting together nearby. A henge of twelve Druidic-styled arches occupied the center square around which walking paths were situated. Excelsine travel seemed confined to static portals, foot traffic, and the occasional unicycle.

The library search had revealed that Ellery Square, the twentieth circle's business district, was an exit portal to major magic spots throughout the Second Layer—including Ganymede Circus—and was used frequently for off-campus activities. Three days ago I had unsuccessfully tried every portal here.

My eyes drew up to the rest of the mountain towering above. Far up, the mountain flashed, and clouds swirled around most of the levels, like some fairy-dusted Mount Doom. It was raining on three levels today, including the fifth circle where the dormitory was located, and though it wasn't raining in the thick middle section that comprised the Midlands, there was something strange about the clouds there, all green and black and swirly.

I shook off the dark pull toward the area and walked to the arch that would take me to Ganymede Circus.

Like the inner-campus arches, I could see through to where it led. The static picture of a five-spoke circus of streets zoomed closer as I stepped nearer. Within a few feet, an opalescent barrier grew over the image. One foot away, the barrier turned thick. I touched it tentatively with my hand. It was impenetrable, just as the other off-campus arches had been.

Taking a deep fortifying breath, and a quick look around to see if I was being observed, I unscrewed the jar. The paint drop vibrated wildly as I reached my fingers inside, then jumped eagerly to my fingertip. I slowly extended my finger toward the opaque arch, allowing the paint to lead me.

There was a crack and groan, then as if I were on a conveyor belt, the barrier pulled me through a dry, milky waterfall and into an antique store filled with things decrepit and strange.

Boca de Vida lions roared on the walls, tapestries with rippling threads billowed, and murmuring sounds issued from mirrors and pieces of fractal art. Odd trees, garden pools, and dozens of arches filled the space.

Turning back toward the arch I had come through, an image of the henge was projected in its interior. Stepping away, the picture zoomed out until it featured only edelweiss in the foreground and an enormous mountain far behind.

A man at the desk didn't even look up as I passed through the store and nervously gave wide clearance to the pools, trees, and mirrors. Who knew where they might take me? I needed to go to Black Magicks Unlimited before exploring anything else.

I opened the door to exit the antique shop and stepped into a different world.

A narrow street full of colorful and bizarre shops flowed into a cozy, roundabout circus that was madly alive. A silly smile spread over my face as I walked. Unlike Excelsine, people here were riding all sorts of crazy contraptions—magic carpets, beasts of burden, little cars, motorcycles, tanks, and flying vehicles. Horns, shouts, and magic flew in the air between mages.

In the middle of the roundabout was a statue of a boy holding a gleaming gold chalice toward the heavens. Nearly invisible tendrils of gold and white smoke lifted from it, then flowed downward, spreading out in all directions. The tendrils seeped into the buildings clustered around the circus, then continued down the spokes and into a nearly clear dome that surrounded the small town.

The buildings here were more crazily arranged than they were at Excelsine. Erected side-by-side were castle turrets, adobe abodes, office buildings and tents. It was as if a drunken man had dumped out the contents of his children's toy boxes, then haphazardly glued them to a large wheel—putting teepees and princess castles together with Legoed units and animal pastures—capping it all off with a giant Tupperware dome. It was bizarre and wonderful.

The store I was seeking was the next spoke over. I would waltz in; get Christian raised, then we'd celebrate in this festive atmosphere.

No more loneliness. No more pain.

I hummed a silly tune as I walked. My daydream was rudely interrupted when a siren shrilled.

"Tremor!" someone yelled frantically and everyone ran. Portal pads were thrown and mages disappeared into the ground by the dozens. Some sprinted toward storefronts, others dashed down the street, vanishing through the walls of the dome. Flying vehicles shot upward, disappearing through the roof. A mage pushed me from behind, causing me to stumble.

BOOM.

A cacophony of sound erupted and colored lights shot from every direction.

The thinning crowds on all sides of the circus started ducking, throwing, and deflecting the magic, chunks of concrete, and earth. Carpets whizzed past, animals shrieked and flew. Beams of light flashed everywhere. Mage after mage disappeared into a portal pad or a store.

Another siren sounded, and I heard locks engaging on the stores to my right.

Not good.

A chunk of rock flew toward me, and I thought of Marsgrove's crappy shielding promise. I formed a gun in my mind and shot my finger toward the projectile. The rock exploded and a light shimmered in front of my eyes. I looked down at my hands and saw a light gold dusting layered over my skin. My shield?

Another boom sounded, and I concentrated on the gold, making it form a thicker barrier. It shimmered more firmly, collecting energy from my intention.

Keeping partial focus on the gold shield, I ran down the spoke and ducked behind a car just before a purple beam shot over my head. Black Magicks Unlimited was directly across the street.

Two mages were dragged into *Black Magicks Unlimited*—torsos and appendages dragged in with them, and moments later disoriented, but *whole*, people emerged, then abruptly ported away.

God, I *had* to get in there.

A huge half-winged beast flew in front of the store, shimmering in and out of sight like a projection without full power. The half-elephant, half-giant vulture suddenly bloomed into full color and form, roared, then started pecking at something on the sidewalk in front of the store. It looked as if some mad person had split two animals down their spines, then sewed together opposite halves.

What the *hell?* I instinctively touched the leather bracelet Will had made for me.

There was a beep and a visual of the animal came to my mind's eye along with a small list of basic facts. Called a sweeper, it was dangerous and always hungry. It liked human flesh and apples and belonged firmly in the Fourth Layer.

I felt competing urges to laugh and hyperventilate. As far as I knew, I was still in the Second Layer.

A bolt of yellow flew toward the sweeper. The animal raised its beak/trunk and heaved a stream of thick indigo. The yellow light became ten feet of solid stone, then shattered on the sidewalk. Three men exited Black Magicks Unlimited and upon seeing the sweeper, one screamed like a starlet in a horror movie, and they all started running and fumbling for their pads. The sweeper roared and stalked after them.

This was my chance.

I shot out from my hiding spot, ducked a yellow beam, dodged a piece of flying debris, sucked in my midsection as a red beam flew by, then skidded to a too-abrupt stop and threw open the door to the shop wedged between a magical tattoo parlor and pawn shop.

The deathly knell of bells signaled my entrance.

Black Magicks Unlimited was a narrow shop with a long stainless steel counter spanning the length, leading to a curtained area at the back. I forced myself to relax and breathe normally. Thankfully, the primary odor was an antiseptic cleaning smell and not the smell of death.

The guy on the other side of the counter looked like a leather-clad biker who had been dead a week already. Nothing on his face indicated what he thought of me.

I put my hands on the counter to steady myself, as another explosion hit and the street outside exploded. I let the explosion settle into aftershocks before speaking. The sweeper had taken up position in front of the store again, licking the sidewalk.

"Shouldn't be here during a Layer Tremor, kid." The man's expression clearly said I was an idiot.

Touching the bracelet deliberately this time, Will's encyclopedia kicked in again to tell me that Layer Tremors happened in areas containing too much magic. The magic needed to untwist itself and the result was always explosive.

Also, layers "thinned" during tremors and sometimes things passed through. The warnings about Ganymede Circus made sudden sense. I wondered how the dome over the city functioned. I wondered if yeti sightings in the First Layer could now be explained.

But none of that was important. This was my single opportunity, and I wasn't going to waste it. "Your sign says you can reanimate the dead."

The term produced images of Christian with giant eyes and a tiny triangle of a nose. And maybe that really concentrated look of anime fierceness as he flew through the air toward a foe. I was feeling a little high.

"Yup. Put the stiff here." The man patted the counter in front of me.

I quickly removed my hands and rubbed them on my jeans.

"I don't have a stiff." Probably could nab one from the street right now, though... Still, my nervous excitement morphed into euphoria again that I was so close to my goal that I was being asked for a body.

He frowned. "No stiff? What are you here for then? Information? I don't do government or university surveys." He spit over his shoulder and into a bucket on the floor.

"No. I mean, I have a...stiff...but he's not here."

"Well, go get him."

"I...now? You need the actual stiff, I mean, body?"

That would set me back. I would have to get to the First Layer and drag back a six-foot two-inch male. Though, I was fairly brimming with the need to do so *right now*.

"What does this look like? A form-shifting shop?"

"Um, no? Er, do I just wrap him in a carpet? A normal one?"

"What do you have him kept in now?"

"Nothing?"

The guy looked at the ceiling, then back at me. He still looked half-dead, but now he looked irritated at his half-success. "What does the guy owe you? Do you need to know where to find the safe?"

"What safe?"

"Do you need information from him? Does he have to apologize for something?"

"Dying?"

"Do you need to talk to him so you will get the last word in?"

"What? No."

"How did he die?"

"He...he was hit with a spell. It overcame him. That night we were pretty far away from help." Like a whole other dimension away.

He gave me a look that delved right into my soul. "That night? The body isn't fresh?"

"Fresh, like recent? No."

His face shuttered. "I can't help you. Sorry."

"What? Can't we just...dig up the body?" I would get gloves and a shovel right now and work out the logistics of getting his remains through a port later.

"Dig up the...how long ago did he die?"

"Seven weeks ago."

"Seven weeks? Young lady, I reanimate the dead."

"I know. That's why I'm here."

"I reanimate them for thirty seconds. Five minutes at most. These things have an expiration date. Seven weeks?" He shook his head.

"What? No, I don't want him to just pop up for five minutes to chat. I want you to bring him back completely."

"Ten minutes post mortem, or not at all. And even if I *did* try to raise a two month corpse, you wouldn't be pleased with the result."

"He'd be alive. That would make me very pleased."

He shook his head. "You could get a zombie wearing your boyfriend's skin."

"It's my brother," I said stiffly, hope rapidly dwindling.

He gave me a brief look of sympathy. "Listen. You don't want to pursue this. Where are your parents, anyway? They should have told you all of this. My advice—and it's against my business profits, you hear, because I could sell you all kinds of crap—is to let him go."

I thought about the books locked in the library cages. I wet my lips. "But what about *The Twelve*—"

He leaned hard against the counter, and so fast, that I took a step back.

"Don't you go learning any of that filth. That's black magic." He spat into the bucket.

"Er, your sign says—"

"*Real* black magic. Not gray-edged magic tricks for the elderly, the thrill seekers, and the susceptible."

"But you bring people back to life. Even if it's for five min—"

"Those that haven't been dead a day. A week at most. Two months? No. You are dealing with a whole 'nother level of dead. And at sixteen weeks? It becomes magically impossible."

"Then at seven—"

"Listen, little lady, you give up a piece of your own soul for the kind of magic *The Twelve* promotes. And it doesn't work out how you think it's going to."

I watched how he said it. I looked carefully at his face, the brittle cracking look to his skin. "You have done it."

He didn't confirm my thought verbally, but he didn't have to. I could read clearly in his body language that this establishment was a dead end for me and that our conversation was over. I had no power or money or abject charisma to wheedle further.

But there would be other shops. And even though my disappointment was harsh, I had more knowledge now. Anything that increased that knowledge was time well spent. If I gained one piece of knowledge from each endeavor, from each bloody hour I spent, it would all be time well spent.

"Ren...I think you need to abandon this plan."

"Free me however you can! Please!"

I had lost seven precious weeks, but the remaining nine started ticking a countdown in my head, overlapping whatever time I had until Marsgrove's return.

"Ok." I nodded, my gaze sweeping the items for sale. There were two books on black magic rites and rituals. "Do I need to give blood or magic to buy those?"

"We are required by law to ask for blood."

I chewed on my lip, then looked out the window and into the street which surprisingly was almost fully re-formed. A few people were poking their heads out across the street. The sweeper was nowhere to be seen. "Ok, hang on."

I ran outside, swiped my finger through a puddle of blood on the walk, then dashed back in.

"I'll take both."

He stared at me for a long moment, and I stared stonily back. Then he put both books on the counter and turned around. I pressed the blood from the street onto the paper and put more munits than the purchase required on the countertop. "Thanks."

"Don't thank me, kid," he said harshly, and thumbed toward the door. "And don't come back."

The bell thudded dully behind me.

I struck reanimation from my primary list and put it in a secondary classification. I might be able to elongate reanimation time through experimentation. Or maybe figure out how to get in a quick session with Christian, while I was experimenting on other things. Get him to say more, so he could help me.

But I needed to reorder my experimentation list based on the need to exhume a body.

In my excited mind I had figured magic could solve any problems. That somehow Christian could just be magicked back and—voila!—be normal again.

But he was buried in the First Layer in a graveyard that I was pretty sure was *not* a magical site. That meant that if I didn't figure out how to pull him out of a painting, I really would have to exhume him the manual way. Shovels and dirt and digging. And I would have to do it myself, in the dead of night, if I didn't want to get into a whole host of trouble. I wasn't sure how one hired clandestine grave diggers. It didn't seem like the Better

Business Bureau would be involved.

People were dragging bodies toward Black Magicks Unlimited again. I sprinted across the street, watching for flashing lights. But the town air and magic felt sluggish now, and people were starting to walk about again.

I walked quickly, listening carefully for any sirens and rapidly checking out the stores as I passed. One proclaimed itself a purveyor of "chemical potions and magical herbs" and another sold magical weapons. There was an art store and a...I stopped. An art store?

My feet detached from the authority of my brain. The uppity tinkling of three bells sounded as I entered the shop. I stared in wonder for a few long moments. For being located in such a crazy town, the paintings were incredible. Full-featured figures were running and jumping and dancing and flying in their frames. One was even singing a dark haunting melody. It was like watching small, gorgeous videos on the walls.

I wondered if they sold storage box spaces here.

"May I help you?" A middle-aged man with a receding hairline was watching me disapprovingly from behind the counter.

"I am just admiring your lovely shop."

But he had that displeased look of a shopkeeper who disliked teenagers, so I moved to the side.

I hated being watched like I was going to shoplift, so I wandered over to a wall filled with art supplies. Maybe I could purchase magical paint here. A smile lit my face. Maybe I would be able to *use* paint here.

A sign ran along the top of the display in bright red letters: *SECURIMAGE Anti-Theft Enchantment Activated.* The enchantment or company must stink if I was still being watched by the shopkeeper, though—unless it was one of those "I have a dog/alarm" yard signs where the person really didn't have one.

Wanting desperately to believe that maybe Marsgrove had just cursed paint already on campus, I scanned the tubes hanging on the wall. There were dozens of different kinds. "Fast acting," "quick release," "multidimensional," "chaophonic," "added texture," "moving pieces." Fascinated, I wondered which one my electrified ultramarine would be labeled as. Some uses were obvious, others not as much. Chaophonic? I suppose it was too much to ask for one that read "reanimate the dead!" on it.

The bells tinkled and a lady in high heels and a stiff business suit strode into the store. She smoothed her skirt and perched a pair of tiny glasses on her nose. "I'm looking for something of exceptional quality. A signature piece. I was told that I could find one in your establishment, even located in such a reprehensible town."

The store owner straightened up. "You have come to the right place, my good lady. The tremors are regrettable, but the magical benefits are keen. We boast the finest collection in the Second Layer. We even have a piece by the last origin mage, Sergei Kinsky. Very rare!"

Sergei Kinsky? That was the Mad Mage guy featured in my reading room grid. I peered over my shoulder trying to see where the owner was pointing. My eyes followed the direction to the edge of a gold frame on the far wall, but I couldn't see the canvas from my position.

The woman looked over her tiny glasses to examine the piece. "Extraordinary. But they should have kept Kinsky in a testing facility permanently. You can't trust people with those kinds of abilities and that type of temperament. Look at what happened to the Third Layer. Such mages must be controlled by others. I carry around a leash device, in case I encounter such mage types, or out-of-control ferals. They tend to go hand-in-hand, more's the pity."

The owner nodded along with the woman's increasingly alarming opinions, murmuring his agreement as I stood there frozen, with my hand raised to touch a tube of paint, and my chest absent of a heartbeat. Leash device?

"I can't deny the quality of Origin works when created under control. Our layer system is a testament to Origin design and power after all. But that was long ago when people knew their place. It is a relief to all that there is no origin mage in existence presently. Thirty years ago, the best thing Kinsky did was to blow himself up. He had started making things freely..." She shuddered. "It's not one of those works, is it?"

The man shook his head rapidly and uttered a loud, "No, never one of those! This was created while he was at the Zantini Institute, under the direction of Mussolgranz."

"Ah, excellent. I will indeed look at the provenance. But at the moment, I am in dire need of a piece for my niece's thirteenth birthday."

The colors around me had started to tessellate, and I was unable to draw enough breath. They didn't know I was feral, they couldn't know. Besides, I was cuffed. That was good enough, right? I repeated the mantra to myself, trying to restart my heart. I needed to get out of here. My eyes pulled in the direction of the Kinsky piece, then toward the door—where I received another shock.

Marsgrove stood outside looking at his device. A mere fifteen feet away from me, separated by a pane of glass.

My breath and heartbeat whooshed back in double time. I ducked my head and pulled my hair forward. Trapped. I looked around for another exit.

"Wonderful, ma'am," the owner said boisterously. "We have a lovely children's storybook art piece over here. Perfect for a budding mage. A master artist mage and master mage storyteller collaborated on it. Very rare. The figures inside make up new adventures and grow and change whenever the enchantments are activated, and they take direction from the activator, if desired. Your niece will feel that she is in on the adventure too. There is a record spell and a reset spell, so she can experience an adventure again or start completely anew. Unless it is requested, the same story is never repeated. Family friendly fare and adventures are also guaranteed."

Such a piece of art as he was describing would normally fascinate me, but self-preservation focused my attention elsewhere. I looked back to the window. Marsgrove was slowly stepping along the walk in front of the shop.

As the owner and customer began haggling over the price, I moved around the displays, hiding myself farther from view. My feet moved to the Kinsky piece without my explicit consent. His portrait of a beautiful woman was Mona Lisa-esque. She appeared to be quietly observing me, no matter the angle of my approach.

Drawn to it, I examined the piece carefully as I moved. My own works were stick figures compared to this artist's Da Vinci scale. The portrait possessed depth and dimension and reality. A little too much reality, perhaps. The woman looked...lifelike. Like Will inside my sketch, but with colored texture and movement. She looked as if she would step from the frame at any moment and emerge in glory. The colors shifted with her movement, catching and reflecting interior light as she moved inside her painted world. Shadows cast behind her, shrinking, growing, and morphing. A living diorama, where this woman was trapped inside. Unnerved, especially after Will's imprisonment, I was unwillingly drawn to the painting.

She put one finger to her lips and urged me forward with her other hand. I drew closer, spellbound, and she smiled. Her hand reached into a fold of her dress and the material moved, rippling the canvas along its path. She withdrew a piece of paper from her dress. The paper grew sharper, and I could almost see the words on it, as she held it out toward me. My heart thumped madly in my chest. The canvas pushed outward as the paper pressed from inside, almost like a finger or object was pressing against the barrier, and I reached forward—

"Stop! Move away from that!"

I flinched at the yell and turned to see both adults watching me. The shop owner was frowning and had taken a step in my direction. "What do you think you are doing? Do not touch that!"

"I'm sorry. She..." No. Everything in me screamed that saying that the woman had something for me would be extremely unwise. I looked back at the painting. The paper was gone and the woman gave a resigned smile, then smoothed her dress and looked off to the left, her face freezing again in profile. I wondered if the First Layer hid safes behind paintings as a reflection of this layer being able to hide things *in* them. "...she is very pretty. Sorry."

I returned to the supply wall and kept my head down, but my eyes active. Marsgrove was across the street now, thank God, still frowning down at his device. *Keep walking*, I urged him mentally. I could hear the man and woman muttering.

"The intoxicating threat of an Origin work." The woman tutted. "Do you have anything hidden in there? You said it was a safe painting."

"Nothing hidden, and yes, it is safe." His glare hardened—I was damaging a future sale. And I was exposing myself—making myself memorable. I tried to breathe normally as he continued talking. "I only demonstrate the security measures and properties if someone past puberty is keen to buy. It is an empty canvas right now."

It wasn't empty. I was sure of that. The cretin just didn't know how to access it. I quietly examined the paint tubes without really seeing them. Marsgrove's storage space, the painted woman's canvas, Will's body...could I store Christian's soul in a painting? Was that what was missing? The reason I had been unable to retrieve him, even though I had felt him before?

My eyes skimmed the cover of a book on creating 3-D spaces. A discordant note rang in my head, but I couldn't connect the warning to anything tangible. Maybe those bold block warning letters in the textbooks were affecting me.

The customer shook her head, muttering about leashing teenagers too, and handed over some sort of credit card.

"A villain is in for a nasty shock if she touches that painting without the owner's permission. A nasty, nasty shock." The man projected his voice in my direction.

The lady and her leash left, and on the other side of the street, Marsgrove was moving away. I grabbed the "multidimensional" tube of paint and the book and hurried to the counter. As long as Marsgrove continued in his current direction, I could slip out and go the opposite way back to the antique shop. Better to get out of here while I had a chance.

The owner looked at me through narrowed eyes, peering at my pockets, obviously trying to deduce how many things I had stolen.

The sign over his head said the establishment took First through Fourth Layer currencies. I put the items on the counter. "I would like to purchase these please."

"They are not for sale."

I stared at him hard. "Then why were they on the wall of supplies?" I wasn't playing this game.

His lips thinned and he snatched the items and rang them up. I had just enough for the purchase. Magical paint wasn't cheap.

Marsgrove shoved his device into his pocket and disappeared into a portal pad across the street. Relief swept through me in a painful way.

The street was becoming packed with people again, as if it had never been anything but.

"So, this will make my paintings three dimensional?" I asked, as the owner put the tube and book in a bag, then thumped the bag down on the counter.

He snorted. "I'm sure your parents will be pleased by your *attempts*."

I nodded and stuffed the bag into my pack. They would be pleased when I brought back their son. And when I became a famous artist, I was going to make sure this guy never got any of my pieces.

As I pushed through the door, my eyes strayed to the Kinsky. The woman was watching me again.

The bells chimed behind me as the door closed, and I stood for a moment on the walk, undecided. No. Nothing good would come of me re-entering. The owner would never let me near the piece in his customer-free store.

I took a quick view of my surroundings and joined a pocket of foot traffic. I tried to keep my pace to those around me, not wanting to attract attention.

I was a dozen steps from the store when I realized the pocket had dispersed, and only one person was striding along in step beside me. And that that someone was Mr. Verisetti. I stopped dead. People moved around us, but my heart had stopped with me.

He turned smoothly and smiled. "But why have we stopped, Butterfly? You haven't yet reached your destination."

I tried to get my heart to restart—surely it wouldn't survive this day—as I quickly checked to make sure I still had the light glow of gold on my skin. Picturing paint and liquid gold, I chanted *channel, focus, channel* in my mind. The gold grew brighter. "How did you know I was here?" I asked aloud.

His smile turned Cheshire. "You wouldn't ask a mage to give up his tricks, would you?"

"Oh my Magic! Terrorist!" Someone screamed two storefronts beyond us, but she was pointing to the opposite side of the street, away from us.

Mr. Verisetti's left hand reached into his pocket. He shook his head and sighed as the identified man across the street starting shooting beams. "They simply do not make minions like they used to. But a little birdie did mention that he would like a favor. This town will make a good demonstration."

He pulled out a handful of marbles and a familiar ornate box, and I started sprinting. I wasn't going to let him dust me a second time or do whatever he had done to make me forget those lost minutes in the classroom. Better to take my chances being blown up.

A bomb exploded in the middle of the street, blowing me into a wall. I crumpled to the walk, ears ringing, vision wavering.

"Now, now," his voice sounded odd through the hollow ringing. "Wait for me, Butterfly, or you might be hurt." He crouched down and easily lifted me, setting me back on my feet. Magic coursed from where his fingers touched and with the sudden sound of a ringing bell, my vision completely cleared. With a sideways flick of his wrist, he tossed a marble into the street and the pavement blew high enough to touch the top of the dome. Two more flicks cleared the street in front of us. I saw other men throwing spells and causing mayhem. Some of them had marbles too.

The thought that Will would like those marbles registered oddly in my dull haze.

A swirling black-and-white patterned circle appeared suddenly in the middle of the air, then burst open. Animals burst from it—hybrid animals, like the sweeper—but these hybrids were tumbling out in rage as if they'd been forcefully rounded up, then ejected. Two sweepers flew out, their single wings unfurling and holding them in the air only one foot from their heavy half-elephant bodies impacting the ground. Their beak-trunks opened, and a horrible sound filled the air. A tiger-crocodile snapped its terrible jaws and leaped. The hybrids ran, jumped, and flew in every direction, mowing down people—or doing worse—as they went.

"Beautiful," Mr. Verisetti said, tossing the box in the air, then stroking it.

People fled, and street chunks fell around us. And the screaming...

I tried to run too, but I was the lone being in the nightmare who couldn't run no matter how hard I tried. I pushed forward, foot by agonizingly slow foot—forcing my way through air too dense for me to move, with muscles that barely responded to my commands.

Everyone else's panic and motion...the sounds...the screams...was a fast and terrible juxtaposition.

Then someone pushed mute. I could see people's open mouths screaming, but nothing emerged. As I moved at an agonizing pace, I kept my eyes forward, too unsettled and terrified to watch their silent screams.

"Mages are so loud and unseemly these days." Mr. Verisetti strolled casually beside me, stroking the top of the box. Every few moments he would stop stroking and wave his hand, effortlessly blocking an incoming strike.

"What do you *want?*" I gritted out the question, pushing my body harder. A tear leaked out as I saw another mage go down silently beneath a rampaging animal. "Why are you doing this to these people?"

"All in the job description, Butterfly. But let's speak about you. Interesting visit to the...art store?"

How long had he been following me? I didn't respond, painfully pressing my lips together.

"The owner and his customer need a bit of a mind tweak, I think." His mouth curved pleasantly, but there was something very unpleasant about the feel of it. "Perhaps I will send one, should they survive. But you exited too quickly—before more interesting matters could take place."

How had no one noticed him in the store? The owner? The customer with her leash? I hadn't, but I wasn't even a week old in this world. I would be dead on the pavement right now, no doubt, if the source of the carnage wasn't strolling next to me.

I looked around for Marsgrove as I continued to gain nightmarish ground, foot by foot, slowly rounding the corner to the circus. Focus. Goal. Endpoint.

Beams were flying everywhere, but whereas the tremor beams had been chaotic and avoidable, these were designed to attack specifically. People ducked and dodged—or not—but nothing touched within a foot of air on all sides of us. Soundless. A vacuum in space.

He tilted his head. "Didn't you wonder at the woman in the painting? Who she is? What she had for you?" He leaned toward me. "I wonder at it."

I inched slowly toward the antique shop and tried to pretend everything around me was a staged Hollywood production.

"I have your best interests at heart. Far more than dear dogged Phillip Marsgrove, who right now is trying to find me instead of helping you."

"It is hard to say which of you I trust less," I said grimly, not looking at him, concentrating on my goal.

I could feel his amusement. "Wise of you. Now, what did the woman have, Butterfly?"

"Nothing. She had nothing."

If anything, his amusement grew. I could feel it as if it were a living thing coiling around me. "Perhaps one day she will have something then. Always good to revisit old haunts. If they are still standing, of course."

"What do you want?" I was so close. I could see the antique shop and the people streaming inside.

Inside my bubble of unnatural silence, I tried not to watch the panicked people who were stepping on their portal pads, their faces filling with horror when nothing happened. Nor the people who were running smack into the sealed walls of the dome. Would the arch still work? I had to try.

I felt Mr. Verisetti poking absently through my bag. Clenching my teeth together, I kept my slow movement going.

"You need true paint, Butterfly, not this drivel."

"I likely won't even be able to use that drivel."

Unfortunately, while my feet were dragging metaphorical cement blocks behind them, my mouth was working just fine. I should say *nothing*.

Suddenly, my feet were leaden, welded to the spot, and Mr. Verisetti was standing in front of me with narrowed eyes. Things silently exploded behind him, like the strange Hollywood set I wanted to pretend this was. He rubbed his finger in the air slowly, then his eyes focused on the cuff at my wrist. "Phillip still remembers how to play dirty, does he?"

He suddenly smiled—his charming smile. It put me more on edge. "Good. But this just won't do, you not painting. I can do nothing about an administrative spell, but I can tell you that all areas of the Academy are not created equally, and some magic can be completely hidden by the truly powerful. Juleston's warding text goes on and on about it for four thousand boring pages."

I tried not to take his bait, but my brain put the reference securely into a memory slot.

"And some professors will be able to halt the restriction, if you can worm into their good graces. I wonder..." He tapped his lip. "What would you do, if I gave you real paint?"

My heart sped up.

He drew his finger down the air in front of me again, then brought it to his mouth, licking it. "Phillip outdid himself on your shields. If anyone other than I had thrown that first bomb, you wouldn't have been touched. I see his fondness for me will never die. But let's improve this set, give a kick back to him, should he try to tweak."

Something rippled over me, hooking in.

"Stop doing magic on me!" I crossed my arms then thrust them out instinctively. Mr. Verisetti's Italian leather shoes pushed back on the concrete, chunks of concrete forming behind as the magic moved against an impenetrable force.

The force of his shielding around us stretched.

He laughed. "Look at you, trying to flee your cocoon. Perhaps you will be ready to fly free soon after all. Though I can't deny you the opportunity to attend school and make...allies. But only allies, Butterfly. Friends get in the way. Easy choices become harder. Then they take all you've worked for and crush it. Betray you with a knife in the back or by drowning you in paint."

"*You* betrayed *me*." The emotion was still there, only a week old. He had helped me get through four horrible weeks of school. Had given me an outlet in art and a mentor who always seemed to know what I needed. All so he could use me when the time was right.

"I'm crushed, Butterfly. I didn't betray you. I just subverted your will. Here, let me make it up to you, you are delighting me." He put his free hand into his pocket and removed a small plastic packet containing what looked like gray sand. He held the packet flat on top of his palm.

I edged away from it—and from the very familiar ornate box that he still carried in his other hand—and realized I could move normally again. Whatever magic I had done to push him away had freed me, at least temporarily, from the slow, nightmarish motions.

I kept my magic and attention on highest alert, waiting for an opportunity to flee. "More Docile Dust?"

He smiled. "Your new ally is a smart one. Though don't become too attached. No, this is an antidote." He gave a lazy shrug. "Now, if *I* want to use something on you, I still will be able to, of course. But no one else will...I'm a little possessive of my acquisitions, Butterfly. I am thinking of adopting you as the dark daughter I will never have." He made a theatrical little gesture around his heart with the ornate box clenched in his palm. "You are so useful to have around."

What is in the box? I stared at the ornate box that had allowed the hybrid animals entrance into the circus. Hazy memories drifted by without an anchor.

I looked back up at him. "Antidote? I don't *trust* you."

"Of course not. I'm entirely untrustworthy. But then I do not claim to be a friend. Friends only provide opportunities for betrayal. Look at those silly children at your high school, afraid of the dark." He glanced at the street, shadows overtaking his countenance. "Allies, Butterfly. We are allies, though you do not accept it yet. Have your school chum—Will, was it?— examine the powder."

It was extremely unnerving that he knew about Will. "So, you are giving me a packet of anti-dust to protect me? Because you are possessive? No."

"You wound me terribly. Delightful. Perhaps I am just protecting my interests knowing what you will do with the item of mine you truly desire." He hummed and a tube of paint, in the same kind of plain white tube as the ultramarine blue had been, suddenly joined the packet in his hand. "A tube of our paint. *True* paint. All for a bargain of a price."

My stomach tightened painfully, and I had to stop myself from reaching for it. I wanted that paint. *Christian* paint. Freedom paint. "What price?"

He smiled. "An unspecified task in the future. Something small. Inconsequential. A Level Two magic."

I *wanted* that paint. An acrid smell filled my nose, and silenced screams filled my head. Christian needed that paint. "A bargain with the Devil?" I smiled thinly. "Swear on your magic as to what you are holding in your left hand and that you are giving me the paint I mixed during my Awakening."

"You flatter me with your comparison and you are learning so well, Butterfly. Already in trouble, I see. Very well, the substance in the packet will protect you against Docile Dust and mid-level controlling magics, but will do nothing more, and the tube in my hand contains paint mixed by you during your Awakening, by my magic I so do vow."

I felt the familiar feel of magic wrapping around us and settling.

"I was so very specific too, Butterfly, aren't you pleased? Now it's your turn," he said, his voice very nearly singsong.

I touched Will's bracelet and quickly scrolled a list of what a Level Two magic was. The scale went to ten. Twos were normal, everyday magics.

I repeated the necessary vow and the magic settled again. Shaking, I held out my hand.

He extended his forth and I plucked both the tube and anti-dust packet, then clutched them to my chest. The vibrations of magic in the tube connected with my magic, humming happily.

I tried not to think about the stark vision of black-and-white chaos and destruction I had seen during the brief touch of our skin.

I had *paint*. Real paint.

Christian's less sane voice crowed exultantly in my head. His real voice remained silent.

Paint that would release me from the prison of Excelsine whenever I wanted to be free. I could study, have a base, then go anywhere. Hop through an arch, paint Christian out of a painting somewhere else, then we'd be together again. I hugged it harder to my chest. We could be free from thinking that the nightmare happening around us was real.

Mr. Verisetti leaned in, looking closely. "You look thinner. And stressed." He drew a finger down again, then made a face. "Magi Mart? No. There is a reason there is only one cafeteria on campus with a student population that size. Going is good for your magic. And hiding out is not the way to make allies. You need to be celebrated. You—"

A strange man came running toward us, and the panicked crowd split around him. His eyes and posture were completely on the offensive, and he looked far more threatening than any other man on the street. He looked eerily similar to the men who had exited the black SUV in front of my high school—and to the man who had been gophered. It wasn't their features or body types, but something about the way they moved that brooked the comparison.

I looked back to the man at my side and revised my statement—far more threatening than any other man *except* Raphael Verisetti. He looked as if he had stepped off his yacht, wearing his expensive shoes, slacks, and loose collared shirt, a relaxed, almost lazy posture, exceptionally handsome golden features...and sporting a smile so cold and evil as he observed the man running toward us that I took an automatic step away.

His dark gold shield—with veins of black—pulsed, then peeled back to rest behind us. He pushed a hand down toward the sidewalk tiles, and the cement rolled in an explosive wave toward the other man, then opened into a mouth that closed over the top of him. The ground and concrete gave a sort of belch, as it shifted back into place.

I opened my mouth, but nothing emerged as my jaw worked. The silent screams around me increased.

"How rude, interrupting our time together," Mr. Verisetti said.

Two other men ran toward us, lights shooting from their hands in deadly arcs. Mr. Verisetti's shield walled me in from behind. I had no way to run.

And I had no knowledge of how to repel the beams. I channeled all of my focus into powering the gold of my own shield, but instinct told me I was about to join Christian.

I just wished I could have made us a family again first.

Mr. Verisetti flipped open the ornate box and it hovered in the air between the spread fingers of both of his hands. There was a tearing sound in my ears as black-and-white swirling holes ripped open a mere two feet in front of us and swallowed the jets into...nothing. My magic pulsed and throbbed, and terrifyingly reached for the hole nearest to me.

He pulled his fingers together beneath the hovering box, waved his wrists, and flung them forward. The power of the energy he thrust was tangible. The holes flipped, zipping shut as if they had never existed as a tear in the very fabric of the air, then ripped open directly in front of the men. Lights shot out from them, striking their targets.

"And the rude shall be punished." He caught the floating box as it fell easily in his left hand.

Bile rose in my throat, and I automatically covered my mouth at the sight of the carnage fifty feet in the distance. The magic from the blasts swirled, then shot upward into the sky. A horrible crack sounded as the dome splintered, spider-webbing out in long, thin lines.

"But I do think I am getting proficient at that maneuver, wouldn't you say, Butterfly?" An opaque chunk of the dome crashed to the pavement across the circus. All of the shop doors blew open, as if their magic had somehow released all at once. "You should move along, Butterfly. There are hunters everywhere, and I wouldn't want them to capture you. That would quite ruin my game."

I could see people running, their mouths open, screaming, but for some reason I could hear nothing past the pounding in my ears and Raphael Verisetti's words. Black swirling smoke, like ink ejected into water, dispersed around us.

"And try not to forget, Butterfly, that when it comes to pigments, there is no true black in nature." He winked and opened a space in the smoke by circling a golden finger as one would cut a hole in glass, then pushing the resulting hole inward with an audible *pop*. He put the finger to his lips in a "shh" motion, then disappeared in a violent swirl of black-and-white smoky dust—the echo of my black-and-white patterned drawings. A moaning sound echoed, as if my magic, and the universe itself, were groaning in displeasure.

Sounds grew in volume, screams echoing loudly and violently in my ears. The notion that Mr. Verisetti could disappear that way...

The memory of sketched drapes flashed.

Crack. Crack, crack, crack.

I lunged for the open door of the antique store and dove through as the dome fell. The lingering traces of the heavy smoke clung to my clothes and swirled behind me. Bang. I could feel the shocks in the ground as the explosion grew closer. I hugged the packet and paint tube to my chest and ran to the mountain arch and plunged through, tumbling into a somersault in Ellery Square. I gained my feet and sprinted. I could hear the arch crack and explode behind me.

People were yelling and screaming. Sirens were blasting.

"Campus lockdown, repeat, lock all off-campus portals!" echoed from every direction.

I ran like my life depended on it, uncapping the paint tube—haunting lavender staring up from its jaws—as I sprinted toward the base of the mountain. I squeezed a drop onto my finger, then jammed it against an off-campus arch whose interior had turned a sudden, milky white.

CRACK.

It blew me back and my hand automatically gripped the tube of paint as I fell. Paint squirted to the ground. The ground shook, a fissure cracked downward under the paint trail, the arch vibrated violently, and a milky rock painted with a drop of lavender exploded outward. I caught the rock against my chest.

Screams grew as the fissure in the mountain opened, splitting violently down toward the water.

I lunged to my feet with the ejected rock and sprinted up through every inner-campus arch I came across. I didn't look back.

Chapter Sixteen

ON THE EDGE

AS I RAN TOWARD DORMITORY CIRCLE, the paper trapped between my stomach and shirt gave a sharp tug. Marsgrove's paper. I slammed a hand over it and entered the dorm. Groups of students were talking loudly and gesturing wildly.

"—Ganymede Circus destroyed!"

"—sweepers, gambits, lockeys, and moonglows ported right into the center of town."

"—the terrorists have a new weapon! The port mages *must* be in league with them!"

"—trapped here!"

"—fifty officials are trying to hold the twentieth circle together! The arch to Lolinet was destroyed too! We are under attack!"

Marsgrove's paper tugged harder and something told me that losing skin contact with it would be a bad idea. I sprinted up the stairs.

Holding the paper firmly against my stomach with one elbow and the painted rock firmly in the other, I clumsily picked the door lock. Thankfully, Olivia wasn't inside to hear my fumbling.

I slammed the door shut with my hip, dumped the painted arch chunk on my bed, and yanked Marsgrove's paper out from under my shirt. It tugged and pulled wildly, trying to rip itself out of my hands. God. Nearly everything I owned was still in there. I slapped my hand down on top of it and willed my things out. Trash bags and boxes immediately started ejecting. The corner of a cardboard box hit me in the temple and I lost my grip on the paper. The freed paper shot toward the floor grate and dove inside.

Breathing heavily and shaking uncontrollably, I stared at the mess strewn around me. Hadn't there been another trash bag? I put my head into my hands and tried to will myself to calm down.

I was no longer a flight-risk. Not even the paint worked now.

And Mr. Verisetti had found me so easily off campus. I activated the live news feed and saw fleeting images of Marsgrove, tight-lipped in the background.

"Negotiations are trying to be salvaged in the wake of today's unprecedented attacks in Ganymede Circus. Diplomats will work through the night to push negotiations forward. Salvatori Lorenzo has issued a statement expressing sorrow over the loss of life claimed by the terrorists, but an unnamed source in his camp hinted that they expect better terms for the Third Layer in light of today's incident and show of force."

The reader panned in just as a familiar paper winged its way toward Marsgrove. If he found any of my items in there, I prayed he would just think they were ones he had forgotten to remove.

It didn't matter. I was here. Unable to leave. I could choose to be freaked out and scared, or I could *do this thing* until I was caught. I would get Christian raised and be ready the next time someone tried to do something to me without my permission. Or the next time someone decided to destroy a town around me.

The dorm starting shaking. I could feel seismic shock waves running through the mountain. I knelt to the floor, touching it with my fingertip. *Please, please, please don't let me have destroyed this too.* The tremors lessened. I placed my palm down on the tile, and everything around me crystallized—slowing like it did whenever I entered "the zone." *Heal, heal, heal.* The rumbling stopped completely.

For several seconds everything was unnaturally silent, then the chatter out in the hall started again. I laughed shakily at the thought that I had tried to tell a mountain to stop destroying itself and for a moment believed it to be possible. Delia from the student center would applaud such self-delusion. I touched my reader in order to tune it to campus news. The professors must be doing something.

Knock, knock, knock.

I approached the door warily. An extremely harried student officer stood on the other side.

"Hell of a morning. And it says here that you racked up a substance abuse offense two hours ago, eluded pursuit, then racked up two more substance offenses in the last fifteen minutes. That adds up to a Level Three." He shook his head. "Listen, kid. There is no reason to use this much, even with the world being as screwed as it is. Get some help. A Level Three is serious. The punishment I'm going to give you allows three days of leeway, but my advice is—do it in the first two, don't push that third day. Maybe some hard punishment will stop you wanting a fix?"

I wasn't capable of speaking anything other than the wooden acceptance response that was required. He handed down my punishment—molted firesnake skin collection on the fourth circle. Even through my numbness, that seemed weird. What the h—

"Take these." He handed over three pieces of paper that had popped out of his tablet. "And be a good citizen from now on."

One paper contained the campus address of a substance abuse facility. The second gave the drop-off address for the five skins I was supposed to collect. The third was a general student advisory that I read as I closed the door.

> Mountain integrity has been assured.
>
> Travel Restriction Advisory : Students may not leave Excelsine unless accompanied by a Department official or the Academy President.

I dropped the paper to the floor. Guarding me or guarding against me? I needed a guard against this *world*. Magic streamed from beneath my cuff as if it was no barrier at all.

The paper at my feet flew over to the fist-sized piece of arch rock that contained the first dollop of paint I had squeezed from the new tube. The paper wrapped around the rectangular rock, covering it tightly, then binding to it. Little arms and legs grew through the rock's sides, as the paper was absorbed into the stone.

My wild anger fled, and I knelt by the bed to watch as the rock waddled around. It picked up a pencil that had spilled from one of my bags and thumped the pointed end down, standing at attention like a small sentry. A guard. I looked at the door nervously, but no one knocked to arrest me for the effects of my wild magic or the paint I had already been punished for.

I reached out a finger and the rock's free hand clasped around the tip, giving it one firm shake, as if we were sealing a pact. It thumped the pencil against the Picasso bull of my Guernica bedspread and stood at attention again.

My magic might leap to my chaotically guarded intentions, but my paint...made things *live*. Creation. Life.

"Me," Christian said.

The door opened and I whirled around. Olivia stopped dead in the doorway, eyes sweeping over the utter mess strewn everywhere.

I waved my hand behind my back, hoping the rock could interpret hand gestures and would stay put. "Uh, I'll just, uh, get this all cleaned up now."

She thumped her books on her desk and turned her back on me.

Shakily, I started shoving things into drawers. I swallowed hard. It felt so permanent. I levitated an empty notebook toward the desk. *Paint drop flowing, powering—*

The notebook burst into pulp, landing on the floor like lumps of papier-mâché splatting. I stared, then tried to levitate an empty trash bag. *Paint drop flowing, powering—*

A trash bag banshee formed and screamed, diving toward me. Holy—!

It fell harmlessly to the floor, trash bag rippling for a moment before stilling. Swallowing, I decided to do the rest of the cleaning by hand.

Even so, my desk tried to bite me. Twice. For no reason that I could deduce other than that I had been thinking of how hungry I was. The toilet tried to swallow me whole when I absently wondered where the pipes went. And I was pretty sure my dresser drawer ate one of my socks when I was contemplating a change in wardrobe.

Throughout it all, Olivia read her books and paid no attention to me. Existing in a world of which I was not really a part.

I felt for Christian's magic mingling with mine, and clasped it to me. Not alone. Not alone.

"Ren, stop hurting yourself."

"Enslave them! Let me free!"

I sat down on my bed and stared at the sketch that had brought me here, as Olivia packed and headed for her next class.

"Free me! Help me."

I closed my eyes tightly and hugged the familiar sound of his voice to me while quickly drafting a sketch of him. My fingers hovered over the lavender tube, but reached instead for the store bought one.

Two minutes later, I closed the door on the second beleaguered looking officer, who had added on an additional skin to my collection punishment.

I looked at the lifeless sketch of my brother and the paint that was smudged along his arm, tossed the useless art store tube in a drawer, and carefully withdrew the lavender paint.

The woman in the Kinsky painting had looked as if with just a little bit of magic, she could walk free. That she could have been real, if the artist had willed it.

"I want you here, Christian," I whispered.

"Yes, do it now!"

"Will...will I be me?"

"Of course you will." I touched a fingertip to his forehead, then stroked it down his cheek, thoughts of our last real conversation in my mind, magic flowing out wildly from beneath my cuff. The paint spread out and along the penciled lines, blooming into the colors in my mind's eye as his skin turned a healthy hue, his hair turned brown, and his eyes brightened to teal. Sapphire slowly circled the irises.

My brother screamed in my mind, making me flinch.

Then his teal eyes blinked.

"Christian?" His name barely made it past my heaving breaths. Every emotion and muscle I possessed clenched, and so many brain chemicals collided together I could barely form thought. "Are you ok?"

"I feel strange." His brows drew together and he looked at his flesh-colored hands, stretching and retracting his fingers. Shadows shifted behind him in the flat sketch.

"Well, you've been dead a while," I said somewhat hysterically.

He looked at me blankly and I hastily added, "You left me."

No. I hadn't meant to say that either.

"It's ok. It's all going to be ok." I could feel the hysteria overtaking me, so I took a few deep breaths. Focus. Concentrate. Brother alive and in sketch. Win!

But the hysteria screamed that something was very wrong.

"I feel strange." His brows drew together and he looked at his hands, stretching and retracting his fingers. "But good strange. Like I've just made twelve perfect passes and could complete a hundred more."

A piercing alarm sounded in my brain.

"It will be ok."

"This is our year, Ren. It's all about continuing a benevolent dictatorship and having fun. And it is time for you to become a general, instead of first lieutenant."

He stopped suddenly. There was a blankness behind his eyes that was wrong. Wrong, wrong.

"Christian?"

"I feel strange." His brows drew together and he looked at his hands, stretching and retracting his fingers.

The piercing alarm finally spit out a full report.

Our last conversation. His actions just as I remembered from that night. The blankness as he couldn't find anything new to say. This wasn't Christian. It was my memory of him.

I grabbed the tube of lavender. I could fix it.

I just needed to get him out of there. Even if he was a not-quite-real version of my brother, I'd fix him afterward. I thrust paint on the paper and tried to push my fingers inside, but it didn't work.

Then suddenly, the top edge of Christian's head *peeled away*. Like a sticker pulled downward from a page, Christian separated, tipping forward and toddling along the surface of my bedspread on paper legs, arms windmilling as his body bent forward and back—a barely two-dimensional cutout.

My lips parted, but nothing emerged. He toddled around unsteadily. The enchanted arch rock helpfully steadied him when he nearly fell over near the foot of the bed. When he tripped back toward the head, only reflexes made my fingers shoot out and grip him before he fell off the bed.

Holding him in my palm, he looked up at me with blank teal eyes.

"I feel strange," he said with his rosy paper lips.

Then he spontaneously combusted, the paper burning quickly. I let the flames burn my hand, unable to look away or drop the ashes.

I carefully put the ashes in a Ziploc bag, then numbly collected my punishment of two more firesnake skins from the same beleaguered looking second officer—bringing my total to eight.

I stared out the window for a long time, the rock sitting beside me.

The same thought tumbled over and over. The woman in the Kinsky painting had looked as if with just a little bit of magic, she could walk free. That she could have been real, if the artist had willed it.

But I couldn't recreate Christian. Unlike one of the art pieces in the art store, where the adventures and characters were programmed to work with one's magic like a *Choose Your Adventure*, I didn't want a fake Christian that I could pretend was real—with my memories of him creating a distorted, real person. I wanted the real Christian, who always surprised me. Who sometimes knew me better than I knew myself. Who did things that exasperated me.

I wanted Christian with his grumpy morning temper and all. I...couldn't trust something I created purely from my magic and mind to be the actual Christian.

I opened the book I had purchased and started reading. It was all about storage theories and the abilities needed to make them. Kinsky was briefly mentioned. I definitely needed to look up more about him later.

But a storage space...

A three-dimensional construct...

A place where I could safely store Christian's *soul*...

If I could trap his true soul, I could then make him a body with which to walk free.

There were a thousand different things I needed to research. A million more than I needed to try. And a billion magical ideas, constructs, and limitations that I didn't even know existed yet.

It was a good thing I didn't have time to question the existence of magic or my place in the world. Because I only had nine weeks in which to succeed.

~*~

I met Will at our predetermined meeting spot—the busy fifth circle west arch that ported to the third circle east area where Rubens Hall was located. I had spent the entire afternoon drafting storage constructs, then had performed a two-hour grid search on soul binding.

"You look tired," Will said promptly.

"Rough day."

Will shook his head as we waited in the line for the arch. "For everyone. Some weird rumors circulating that the mountain almost split. And other things."

I gripped the straps of my bag, holding some of the weight off my shoulders. I was carrying far fewer things, but everything now weighed far more. "Like what?"

"About the weird porting abilities in Ganymede and the identities of the mages involved in the attacks. People are freaking out about an unknown origin mage on the loose."

I could see Alexander Dare and a group of combat mages conferring under the Dormitory One arcade.

Will snorted. "I think they had to up the enchantment levels in the cafeteria to keep everyone calm. Sucks that campus is on lock down. Lolinet Village is locked down too—someone blew an entry arch that in turn destroyed half a dozen others in Lolinet's central henge. The arch from here was one of the ones destroyed. I want to go to Ganymede and get a look—see what was used for porting. The Department is deliberately choosing which parts of the recording enchantments to show the public, so I don't even have an educated guess."

"Recording enchantments?" Alarming. More alarming than calming enchantments even. "Like they have security tapes of the entire town?"

Will nodded. I stumbled through the arch. They would show me speaking to Raphael Verisetti.

"But they must have been damaged by the wild magic involved, or else they would have broadcast them by now," Will said, as he too came through.

Unless they were biding their time. I forced my feet forward. Marsgrove already knew about me. *Keep moving.* "Do you think the meeting is still on for tonight, with everything else going on?" It was a risk for me to go anywhere at this point, but I needed to know everything about productive art magic that I could find.

Will waved a hand. "Course. World is threatened all the time. Every time you experienced a really weird weather event or unnatural sighting in the First Layer, I guarantee something crazy happened in one of the others that bled or shifted through. We are usually the layer that most affects the others, but that is least affected ourselves. The average Second Layer mage is great at pretending everything is normal, but the hard core conspiracy theorists, old magic users, and combat mages on campus will be out plotting tonight, make no mistake."

A bunch of student vigilantes. Likely with Dare as their head. Great.

"They'll open school back up to the outside tomorrow, and no one will care."

I really hoped that would prove true.

We approached the building. I was hoping simply to get through the door without setting off an alarm at this point.

I carefully entered Rubens Hall behind Will, who had launched into a recitation about everything he wanted to learn. No alarm activated upon entrance, though there had been no alarm activated in the art building entrance either. Six adults were talking together near the entryway.

"What do you think he will do next, Lucille?" asked a man dressed in black.

"Do I look like his pen pal, Gregor?" a cool, thirty-something blonde said sharply. She had really great, severe cheekbones. I was totally sketching those later. As if she could feel my gaze, her scathing glance turned in my direction. Her eyes narrowed immediately and there was something strange and unreadable in her expression.

I quickly looked back to Will, who was still counting out points on his hand for what he wanted to get out of the session. I nodded along with point number eleven, then turned my gaze back to the woman.

She was still staring at me—or more accurately, at the top of my head. I felt a little prick on my arm, like something had poked me. Jumping a bit, I rubbed the spot. She abruptly turned on her heel and walked down the hall.

"Did she just walk away from me?" The man referred to as Gregor looked astounded.

Someone snorted. "She walked away from all of us. I can't believe your infatuation is still intact after all this time. Didn't she turn you into a goat last year?"

Someone else snickered. "A *female* goat, too."

Will walked through the door to the lecture hall, not noticing my hesitation. I tentatively stepped through. No siren sounded, but a light brush of magic registered on my skin. My paranoia was tagging everything as a threat.

"Ren, come on," Will said, three steps ahead. "There are two seats on the aisle."

I gave a shaky laugh, rubbing my arm again. "Coming."

I pulled my pack around and clutched it in my lap as we sat. The people to the right of us were holding little paddles. I hoped there wasn't some hazing ritual associated with being an artist.

Will was craning his head, looking around. "It looks like there are a bunch of student-made supplies up front. Do you want to go look?"

"Sure." Maybe they had charcoal. I cursed my tunnel vision which had made me totally focused on paint while in the art shop. I should have picked up some magic charcoal or magical sketching pencils or bargained Mr. Verisetti into throwing some in, I thought darkly. The magic required to animate objects using regular pencils took a massive toll. I had dropped off three times while drafting storage spaces, and woken up with my cheek smashed against my desk and pencil shavings in my hair.

And I was going to hold off on the lavender paint for a bit—until I got a firm bead on Christian's soul. Seeing a figment of my brother had messed with my head.

I needed safe, magical charcoal.

Will was nearly bouncing in his seat. "Let's see if we can get more information on which product does what during the meeting, then go after." He nudged me in the side. "Maybe they'll have good paint."

I clutched my pack harder, feeling for the edge of the tube inside in reassurance.

I forced myself to look around. There were student displays and written materials around the edges of the room. Like in the art shop, pictures and images moved in swirls of paint or in the harsher marks of charcoal.

The emcee took the stage and did a fancy swirl in the air with a paintbrush, producing a red dragon that dripped and dissipated. "Welcome folks! Looks like our timing was right in line with the world's. Excitement! Instead of our regular weekly workshop, we have our biannual auction tonight!"

That explained the little paddles. Will groaned and slumped in his seat. "That sucks."

I nudged him. "We can come back next week." If we weren't going to learn anything, I had a million other things to do—looking up wards and special areas of campus, most specifically.

"Yeah," he said morosely. "But let's give it ten minutes, just in case."

The emcee clapped his hands. "We have our normal displays, informative brochures, and material purchases located in the booths around the room. During break, take some time to browse around and see what your fellow art mages are up to. Never know, after today's events, you might be looking at the work of a future Kinsky."

A number of mages rolled their eyes, though some sat forward in their seats.

Chapter Sixteen

"But first, padded door prizes!"

There was some snickering and the emcee smiled broadly. "We'll have another round of door prizes at the end too. Just by entering this room, one ticket was deposited for you in each bucket, but to increase your odds, you may purchase additional tickets, and tonight folks, we have some wild raffles. Six professors have volunteered a small session of their time. One on one with the professors, folks. Don't wait for the auction portion—the professors go for thousands of munits each. You can increase your chances for the door prizes by buying more tickets until each container is drawn."

Hundreds of little yellow tickets flew from the seats and settled into different containers.

"Great. Let's begin!"

Five professors were prized off in quick succession. They were the adults who had been in the group near the entrance. I took notes on their titles and the information the emcee gave on each. If I could audit larger classes—sitting in without signing up—I could learn without being tracked. I'd go through the class schedule tonight.

"And now here's a real treat, folks, Professor Stevens, master professor of chemistry, materials, and chem-creations has just offered to be part of the door prize raffle. Folks, this is the big time. Professor Stevens rarely takes on personal students, and her sessions go for a fortune at auction, but she is offering a thirty minute session on constructing anything you fancy—legally, of course—to one lucky door prize winner!"

Laughter ensued at the mention of the legality clause and a flurry of tickets flew into her glass globe. It was far fuller than any of the other containers had been. Surprisingly, Will shot five magic tickets into it.

He shrugged at my questioning look. "Worth it. If you aren't majoring in one of her fields, you go through her assistants, and her seminars are always fully booked. I could get all kinds of questions answered." He rubbed his hands together.

A last ticket from the audience wobbled, then settled inside.

The student emcee bowed and waved his hand toward the globe. "Professor Stevens, please draw the lucky mage's slip."

To my surprise, the woman with the marvelous cheekbones stepped forward, pinched and regal, and her hand dipped inside. Two students to the side of me leaned forward, hands clasped together. Even Will looked excited as the professor pulled out the slip of paper and handed it to the emcee.

Professor Stevens must have practiced a penetrating stare designed to make everyone in the room feel as if she were dissecting them, because I felt like she was staring right at me and holding a scalpel.

"And the winner is...Florence Crown!"

~*~

I stood in front of the frosted glass door and tried to breathe normally. So much for not being noticed. My name had been yelled out and the ticket had zoomed into my hand, urging me forward, seeking to fulfill a contract.

I looked at Will, who stood at the end of the corridor holding his purchases and free product samples. He gave me an excited wave. The ticket tugged. I took a deep breath and knocked on the door.

"Enter," a voice said sharply.

I walked just over the threshold and could feel a magical net settle around me, poking, looking for weaknesses. The woman on the other side of the room was looking at a device she was holding.

"Well, come in and shut the door," she said, just as sharply. I shot another quick look at Will, then moved forward with reluctance.

Click, click, click. Professor Stevens was a thirty-something, tall blonde with impossibly spiked heels, cheekbones that could cut glass, and a hairdo just this side of severe. The severity was echoed in every clipped stride. However, when she turned her head to look at something to her left, I could see the wisps of hair at her neck seeking escape. She was like a beautiful and dangerous natural creation by Constable—a veneer of painted perfection underscored by wildness. Thunderstorm clouds caged and leashed only by strict control. Perhaps Constable had known someone like Professor Stevens, and the mixed medium of weather was a representation of that woman.

She stopped in front of me. A very complicated series of emotions crossed her face and were reflected in the pinching of her eyes and a working of the muscles of her cheeks. Her eyes narrowed upon the top of my head.

"I'm, um, Ren Crown," I said, when she continued to just look at me as if she were deciding how to dispose of my body. "I won your raffle, and they told me to come here." I finished the sentence awkwardly.

Her hands reached out, quick as lightning and one set of fingers wrapped around my cuff, the other pressed against my forehead. Her device hovered freely in the air. "Where did you get that shield set?"

I froze, terrified, but was compelled to answer. "Dean Marsgrove placed the shields on me." One thing was very clear—I was ingesting the anti-dust Mr. Verisetti had given me as soon as I was out of here, and to hell with the consequences.

"Why?"

"It was a trade for a task I performed." Truth, though not full disclosure. I had put on the limiting cuff in partial exchange for the shield set.

"Who are you allied with?"

"The Crown family, Will Tasky, and Alexander Dare." Wait, what? Where had that last one come from? My magic felt as if we were allied?

"No one else?"

"No." Thank God, thank God, thank God, no "Raphael Verisetti" emerged.

"What kind of mage are you?"

"A feral one?"

She let go, and I quickly stepped backward, keeping her in view, hands raised in front of me.

She turned and walked to the desk. "You are dismissed," she said, waving me away.

My flight response paused at her dismissal. "Why did you just do that?" My breath was coming too quickly, catching on the words.

"Dismissed," she enunciated, picking up a bag.

"Are you going to turn me in?"

"Have you done something that I should turn you in for?" she asked briskly, walking toward the door without looking at me, obviously intent on leaving. Her dismissal assuaged my panic more than anything else could have.

I looked at the ticket, which had tugged me here, then squared my shoulders. "I want my thirty minutes. The one where my questions get answered. Or aren't you bound by the raffle terms?" Magic seemed to hold people accountable.

She stopped abruptly, her eyes narrowing. "You want your *winning* session?"

"Yes." Obviously, my winning had not been luck. I needed to be careful and smart about this, but I also couldn't deny the opportunity in front of me. Mr. Verisetti's words ran through my head. *Some professors will be able to override the restriction.*

I had always let Christian be the daring one, but since that fateful night, my life had turned into one peril after another and it was up to me to either fold or break down the walls. Grab the opportunity, take the risk.

"I want you to show me paint making techniques. I want to know how to make magical charcoal. I want to know what makes one tube of paint do wondrous things while another produces lackluster results."

"You can find those answers in a textbook."

I could feel Guard Rock pacing at the bottom of my bag. Activated with paint that could make things live. What kind of materials might this woman who was so revered by the students be able to teach me to make?

"I want to know how to make exceptional charcoal and *extraordinary* paint." I wanted to know why she cared about my shield set.

Stevens's eyes narrowed further, and her eyes once more went to the top of my head. "Be at the art vault at sharp Libra Falling tomorrow." She turned sharply, her heels clicking. "If you are one second late, the session will be void."

She opened the door and strode through. Will's encyclopedia beeped that Libra Falling meant ten in the morning, and that falling numbers indicated the right side of the clock as the hand fell toward the bottom. I took a few moments to compose myself—the elation caused by the thought that I might finally be able to use paint was tempered by abject terror of discovery. I walked out to see Will examining his bounty in the hall.

He looked up. "Hey, how did it go?"

"Fine." Terribly fine, possibly with the edge to the terrible part. "I'm meeting with her tomorrow. What's with the zodiac timekeeping, by the way?"

"Oh. That's right, the base translation enchantment doesn't include timekeeping. So you hear what people actually say. There's an update that allows you to choose how you hear things—Capricorn Rising, one p.m., thirteen hundred, etc. The update makes it so you don't have to spend time mentally looking stuff up—the translation magic does it for you. Lots of First Layer born students use it. You can also change how you interpret names and slang. Many people have crazy names here, but the standard translation enchantment normalizes them to something you are accustomed to hearing and allows you to pronounce the name back without you even hearing yourself say something different. Sometimes it's pretty fun to remove that tweak. Want me to transfer my tweaks to you?"

"What does that involve?"

"I just spell my own translator to you. Like an update. But it has to go into your magical subconscious because it takes too much energy and time to do it on the conscious level each time. You'll never get the translations in time to participate in conversations if it's kept in an external device—like in your leather bracelet. But I can port it *through* your cuff so that your magic can check it out first—make sure it is virus free and safe—before it is absorbed."

I looked down at the cursed flexible metal band. I trusted Will. But I think I had hit my magical threat quota for the day. "Maybe...later. Your encyclopedia is awesome, by the way. Thanks for that."

"Sure!" He beamed. "Do you want to go to the library to check out our loot? I want to hear about Stevens."

"Well, the interesting thing about that..."

Chapter Sixteen

~*~

Will and I spent two hours in the library as mages gossiped silently around us. The atmosphere on campus had split into two camps—one of continued loose whimsy and the other of focused paranoia. The latter was extremely unnerving. I felt gazes land repeatedly on me. I hoped it was just *my* paranoia that made my skin crawl.

Will was busy looking for information on the port situation in Ganymede Circus. Luckily, that meant he kept a rolling news feed going. My name and face hadn't made the news yet, so I was hopeful.

"Stop hanging out with him, Ren."

"Suck out his soul!"

Christian's disapproval was about as useful as his psychosis, so I muttered, "How about you tell me how to get you out here instead?"

Silence from sane Christian. *"I told you, suck out his soul!"* from insane Christian.

Used to doing things on my own, it took me a few minutes of mental debate before I passed Will the anti-dust packet Mr. Verisetti had given me. Will, hungry for all knowledge and discourse, didn't bat an eyelash when I told him what it was supposed to be and asked if he would check it out.

"Yes! Absolutely. Awesome."

"Just be careful. I...received it...from a suspicious person."

Will nodded and I let him infer that it had come through the mail system.

I excused myself while Will was inspecting the substance and headed to the fourth floor to research soul separation and soul bonding techniques. With a helmet firmly in place, I batted away the book *The Psychology of Criminal Accessories*. Thank God nobody was around to pay attention to the title—Dare most especially.

But the imposing black-and-white book I had seen on my first visit—whose title I still didn't know—sat atop the upper railing watching me intently.

I struggled with a few other books, until a prick of blood from a paper cut made one settle down. It wasn't one of the caged books, but I was still unnerved. The damage was done, so I flipped through it. I had paint now. And depending on what happened with Stevens, I could possibly obtain other resources. Once I figured out the correct dimensional space, the soul bonding ritual aspects, and how to make a body, I would be all set to pull Christian out.

I felt pretty confident in my dimensional drawing and conceptualization abilities—I was just going to have to tweak them until I found the ones that worked best for holding Christian—so I focused my search on bonding and securing a soul. When I eventually pulled Christian through, I wanted to make sure I got the sane one, and not the psychotic doppelganger. In order to achieve that, it looked like I needed to perform purification and container rituals to secure him properly.

Pertinent information from the books went into my notebook as straight text, while my interpretations consisted of a mishmash of text and pictorial representations which were easier for my brain to decipher quickly.

On the way down the stairs, I saw the girl who had helped me previously—Nephthys—ghosting through the second floor aisles and speaking softly to people she passed. The mages nodded, but otherwise ignored her. She disappeared before I could speak to her again.

~*~

Will and I had discovered the "art vault" was on the south side of the third circle, attached to one of the busier art studios and lecture halls. I woke early, scouted the location, then settled into a small benched courtyard nearby to look at every "material and compounds" text available on the server, just in case Professor Stevens was the taskmaster she presented.

No one entered the vault while I was cramming. At ten to the hour, I moved my position so that I was sitting next to the humongous steel door leading into the mountainside. I scrambled to my feet as Professor Stevens approached, her heels clicking steadily over the cobblestone path without a single stumble.

She barely looked at me as she pressed her hand against the door at ten sharp. Blue energy zipped along the surface of the steel, and the two foot thick door slid inside a pocket. Stevens stepped over the threshold, but I hesitated. The door started to close, and I quickly darted inside. In for a penny, in for a pound, at this point.

The single room of the vault was only about five hundred square feet in area. Stations and equipment were set up along the sides with an island in the middle. There was no discernible source of light—no windows, no candles, no bulbs—and yet it was fully lit. Furthermore, there were no shadows. I didn't even cast one as I moved, which was a little freaky.

Stevens moved toward a station. "Your minutes start now. Crafting requires power, creativity, and control. Anyone can make a charcoal pencil." Professor Stevens cut her hand through the air. "Any mage can shove magic at an object. True craft comes from the ingredients you use to create the medium, what magic you put in, and the process you undertake."

I hurried over to watch her, thinking of the words Mr. Verisetti had used when I'd been mixing paint. I nodded to her even though she wasn't looking at me for a response.

"You put magic in the instrument, then you extract the magic later—forming a direct conduit for your intentions. Injection and extraction can be done in a thousand different ways. But the connection between your internal magic and the object magic is what will bring success. I despise adequacy. Anyone can be adequate."

Glass boards, material supplies, and oddly shaped tools flew from around the room and gathered on the island counter between us in a flurry of magic. She stabbed a sharp, manicured nail into the steel of the counter. "Make paint."

My heart picked up speed.

I opened my mouth to ask for direction, but at the last second clamped it shut. No, that was not the way to proceed here. Christian had always won over people with charm and interpersonal skill, even when he barreled past their preferred boundaries. I only had simple honesty and observational skills. "Thank you for giving me this opportunity, Professor Stevens."

Her expression was still cold, but she tilted her head and gave a short nod.

I took a deep breath and dipped a fingertip into the linseed, then touched a lilac pigment with my fingertip, waiting expectantly for the campus police to arrive. But no one knocked on the vault door. I pulled the almost-paint along a piece of waxed paper at the side. Still no knock. Excitement gathered under my sternum and surged upward. I could paint here. *I could paint here.*

"What are you doing?" she snapped.

I moved a glass board closer to me, trying to hide my fierce smile as I tucked my chin to my chest. "Getting a feel for the materials, Professor."

I started mixing, and quickly realized that silence and concentration earned points with her. She started to give me sharp tips and pointers as I worked. I soaked them all in, trying to absorb everything while injecting that desire into the materials I was mixing.

After another quick test of my ability to freely touch paint—real, mixed paint—the twin urges to crow and panic gripped me simultaneously. Go time.

"Can students rent time here, Professor Stevens?"

"No."

"What about the time when the space isn't in use?" No one had entered all morning.

"Inconsequential. Only mages with clearance can open this space. And if a cleared mage is not present, anyone attempting to perform active magic would be very sorry."

I took my hands away from the mixture and touched Will's bracelet, scrolling through the active and passive magic topics until I found what I was looking for. Studying wards was considered passive magic.

That meant, if I could study the vault magics, I could recreate them somewhere else. My first library search had yielded the knowledge that preventive spells could be obscured under a chaos field. I took a deep breath.

"Is the vault made of chaos magic, Professor?"

She had been examining my completed mixtures, but now looked sharply at me. "Yes. Are you finished with that mixture then?"

I hurriedly picked up my tools, trying to keep my mind on the task while I also mentally starred the engineering class I had previously added to my uncategorized mental paint bucket. I created a new bucket—a nice turquoise—and populated it with Professor Mbozi's Engineering 101.

"These are all adequate as base materials, Miss Crown, but I thought you wanted to make *extraordinary* paint." Her voice touched the edge of derisive as she examined me.

"Yes."

She stared at me hard. "Then do each step as if it is the one that matters most."

I nodded and started again. It was a good thing I had crammed before entering. Magic materials worked differently. I took a deep breath and thought of magic filtering through the paint, making it flow in my mind.

Mixing pigments, binders, fillers, and solvents wasn't hard. Mixing them while adding magic at each step was. Making each step a magic-filled process.

Pigment dust poofed everywhere. Linseed oil sprayed every surface. Flour, milk, chalk, and clay mixed together, making the whole place look like some mad bakery. And I was going to need to look into an anti-turpentine hair cleanse.

It was nothing like mixing for Mr. Verisetti. But then, there had been those toffees...and the heavy, zoned atmosphere...and my suppressed awakening magic...and, hilariously enough, emotional support. Also, I was quite sure he had magicked each mix after he'd collected them from me. Added the "extra shine."

I was adding magic in each step. But unfortunately I blew the magical brains out of each substance every time.

"You have to put just the right amount of magic in or you will fail every time." Stevens didn't yell, but there was a very disdainful, sharp edge to her words. "Twenty milliliters into the ochre pigment."

"How—"

"Twenty milliliters. Now."

Chapter Sixteen

I thought hard about what twenty milliliters looked like in a beaker, shot that vision at the mixture in front of me, and promptly blew the whole thing skyward, splattering it over the ceiling like some alien goo that had dripped through the tiles.

Stevens, I learned quickly, was fabulous at shields, and my shield didn't give a hoot about messes. So, whereas I was covered in drippings along with the once pristine floor, she just stood there, completely untouched, tapping her stiletto-clad foot.

I had always prided myself on being competent. But when I needed to measure twenty milliliters of a substance, there were tools that could be used, like "spoons" and "beakers" and "scales" and the oh so obvious "measuring cup."

"Is there a measuring device for magic?"

"Yes," she said icily. "There are many. But they are for those who seek no skill at the craft."

Maybe that was my problem. I had always thought of chemistry as a science, not a craft. Or maybe my problem was that this wasn't chemistry.

"Twenty milliliters."

"Can—"

"Now."

I shot my magic out and was dripping dark yellow sludge two seconds later.

"Again. The calcite this time."

Frustration created a discordant harmony between stiletto heels tapping and my ears buzzing.

Twenty milliliters, eh? I'd create twenty milliliters of—

Boom.

I blew a hole through a giant kiln and a table, white powder puffing the air.

I stared, horrified—she was going to kill me—and quickly reached out and pushed all of my focus into making the objects whole, just like Draeger did in our pseudo room. *Knit, knit, knit.*

The kiln snapped back together, as did the table.

I didn't risk a look at her, I just concentrated that same focused energy—rotating a picture of a beaker filled with twenty milliliters around in my mind. I shot the *image* of the measurement at the umber pile and felt my magic crisply respond and follow.

The brown flakes sparkled briefly, then the odd light rested. The pile of pigment was now *vital.*

I backed away, afraid my heaving breaths would scatter my hard work. I chanced a look at Stevens, who was watching me.

Her eyes were unreadable. "Adequate," she said, then looked down at the materials. "Which pigment speaks to you the most?"

My eyes slid to the pile of beautiful blue. "The lapis-lazuli," I reluctantly said.

"Why?" She surveyed me.

"Crushed lapis-lazuli makes ultramarine pigment." My voice lost volume at the end of the sentence. I cleared my throat. "The old masters used it for portrayals of power and importance, literal and figurative."

"Do you crave power?"

I started to answer in the negative, but stopped myself. "I suppose, a bit, yes. I crave knowledge. I crave the ability to put forth every vision I create. But leading people, no. Not that kind of power."

"What do you see when you focus your magic?"

"Paint flowing. A beaker appropriately leveled with magic."

"Do it again."

Keeping track of the feeling of how my magic had crisply responded and modifying the image depth according to her instructions, I was able to inject the right amount into each subsequent pile. Mostly. I made a mental note to buy a set of measuring tools so I could memorize the image of each level.

The more I exercised those images, the easier they would attach to my magic. I could feel it. And used with my paint drop image, I might be able to make a real go of this magic control thing.

I wiped at the dried and drying pigments painting me. I feared what was going to happen when I stepped out of this room. Thirty campus police officers might be standing on the other side.

I rubbed my painted hand. "Professor, why did you care about my shields?" They hadn't much saved me here.

She looked at me as if I'd said something inordinately stupid. "You should have been able to throw off my probes yesterday, with that kind of shielding." She motioned sharply to my head. "Yet you let them sit. What use is having a physical shield at all, if you let it dangle from your fingers, useless?"

I needed to power them constantly? I made a note to look it up. "Can everyone see the shield—shields?"

"No." The skin at the sides of her eyes tightened, as if she hadn't meant to say that. "You can't even see them," she said condescendingly.

I looked down at my hands. They were covered in streaks of umber, sienna, ochre, cobalt, and white. I tried to separate the colors from my hand. A thin, very thin, hue of gold outlined my hand for a moment, before disappearing from sight again.

A bolt of something shot toward me and I reacted, calling and shooting twenty milliliters of magic into the gold layer over my hand, lifting it in front of me.

The bolt bounced off. I blinked and watched Stevens easily wave away the reverberated magic.

She crossed her arms and sighed. "You have the stupid combination of attributes I seem destined to attract. Intuitive, determined, chaotic, and reckless. But denying talent is stupid, which I'm not. Meet me here at the same time tomorrow."

She waved her hand and the pigments, binders, fillers, and solvents encasing me whooshed into the grate in the floor.

I blinked at her, shocked at both my squeaky clean state and that she was allowing me another session. "Tomorrow is Saturday."

She gave me a hard stare.

"Thank you," I said quickly, still in shock. "I'll be here tomorrow."

She opened the door and motioned me out. The sun was directly overhead, which meant I had extended my time with her by at least an hour and a half.

I turned to her. "I'm sorry, I—"

"Tomorrow." She strode away.

No officers were waiting for me. I had just made paint. Stevens was going to teach me. I had just *touched* paint. I had passed her tests. I had just found a place I could *paint*.

Maybe...

I dug out my supplies and drew a quick sketch, then bypassing the lavender tube, I pressed a fingertip of store-bought paint to the page. An officer appeared two minutes later, tablet out, shaking his head at me. Another firesnake skin was added to my tally. I now had to collect nine.

But amazingly I hadn't been penalized for my actions inside the vault. The officer could have added a hundred skins and I'd still be flying high.

Nothing was going to stop me now.

Chapter Seventeen

THIEVES, PYRAMIDS, AND FIRESNAKES

I CHECKED TO MAKE SURE my headless rock was still holding his pencil and pacing in my backpack, protecting the lavender paint tube I had tasked him to guard, then set off for the fourth circle.

Fortuitously, I ran into Will—who was surrounded by an increased golden glow, making him easy for me to pick out of the crowd. He cast a quick look around us. "I'm on my way to class, but I have something for you. The substance is exactly as described. I tested it against the dust, then converted it to liquid form. I tried it last night." He grinned, then handed me a capped glass. "And I'm still alive. If you want to risk it, drink it all in one go. It tastes pretty gross."

I downed it before I could second guess the decision, then shuddered. "I think the word you are looking for is vile." I could feel the mixture spreading inside of me. I really hoped I wasn't swiping one horrible predicament for another. I used my tongue to swipe all lingering traces past my taste buds as quickly as possible.

He snickered at my facial expression and waved as he jogged off to class.

A student officer popped up minutes later, intercepting my route to the fourth circle. For once, I had actually earned a substance abuse infraction. I wondered if Will had gotten one.

"You have nine firesnake skins to collect?" The officer shook her head, aghast. "I'm not adding more. But there is a note in here that you've racked up too many of the same offense. I am required to take the substance."

"What?"

The empty glass container flew out of my bag, into the air, and off down the mountain. I lost sight of it when it zipped between buildings one circle down.

"It was sent to the Midlands processing factory for recycling."

Speechless, I clutched my bag, checking to make sure my rock and paint were still inside. I shakily zipped it. I don't know what I would have done if my paint tube had been taken. I held my bag against my chest, as if she might take it from me too.

Blood would be shed.

"Just so you know, that's going to happen from now on. Please get some help. But more firesnakes?" She grimaced and shook her head. "I'm not adding more. Here, do some cleaning."

I quickly cleaned the building indicated, bag straps uncomfortably tight on my shoulders, still unnerved by my near miss. I was going to have to be absolutely sure of my warding from now on before using the lavender paint.

Something in me was illogically relieved by this.

I trudged off to my next punishment. The girl's reaction to the firesnake collection made me nervous. It was weird enough that I was going to collect snake skins, I hadn't thought of *why* I had been assigned such a punishment for an upper level offense.

Touching Will's bracelet and thinking about firesnakes produced an image of beautiful opalescent serpents breathing fire.

I mentally scrolled the stats. High level of camouflage ability. Favorite food source—mice turtles. Level Three Danger. Human death occurs twenty minutes after an untreated bite. Non-magicked exposure to freezing temperatures causes skins to shed spontaneously. Unnatural shedding makes them angry.

With great reluctance, I picked up a large bag of ice from Magi Mart.

Dragging the bag of ice behind me, I approached an unfamiliar section of the fourth circle. A patch of trees with red and gold leaves lit with an internal fire that was a little too beautiful and singular in the otherwise green landscape surrounding it. I slowed my steps, the feel of an invisible net tightening around me.

The "pavers" a few yards in front of me rattled and stilled. A vague outline of a thin tail curled into the grass. Then another nearly invisible snake weaved slowly over the blades of grass near the walk, hissing. Only the odd reflection of its scales was detectable, as it successfully camouflaged itself as it moved. It would be a lovely challenge to paint such a beautiful creature changing color in such a rippling, seamless fashion.

Fire streamed out from its tongue in a thin line as it hissed again.

A tree to my left was surrounded by sharp and exotically beautiful flowers and plants. Now that my eyes were growing accustomed to the sight, I could see a serpent lazily draped from the branches and another slithering through the rose vines webbing around the trunk, only careful observation and the fluttering outline as it stretched itself gave away its position. A strange mountainside garden of Eden with venomous guests.

And there wasn't a single shed snake skin anywhere that I could see. I checked the walking paths in the distance. Students were strolling a few hundred yards to the east. I could see a group of combat mages, and a familiar head of black hair. I could only hope that someone *else* would assist me when I died from a snake bite. If I woke up staring into ultramarine eyes, I was going to start thinking fate was seriously against me.

I paused on the thought, then dug out my campus map and queried the location of the nearest "clinic." During the last few days, I had observed too many mages deliberately trip their fellows into the path of danger to trust the goodwill of strangers.

Sighing, I popped open the bag of ice at the perimeter of the red and gold trees. The firesnake area was abnormally warm. Thankfully, the weather mages had placed a chill on this circle today, so just outside of the firesnake area it was at least thirty degrees cooler. If it had been balmy like the sixth circle currently, my ice plan would be in deep trouble.

Bouncing an ice projectile in my hand, I gauged its weight, took careful aim and threw. Whack. The snake turned red, hissed a stream of fire in my direction, and spontaneously expelled its skin. The skin curled over the branch, then dropped softly to the ground. Unlike the other snakes, this one stayed a pinkish red, no longer blending into its environment.

Ok, that hadn't been so hard. Though, all of the other serpents were now staring at me, eyes red and enraged. They all started slithering toward me.

Ok, ok. Calm. Calm. One skin down, eight to—

A tall boy with brown hair that was slightly too long strolled by and lifted the fallen skin from the area that was now clear of snakes, since they were all writhing toward *me*. The boy continued strolling.

"Hey. Hey! That's my skin!" I yelled, but the firesnakes were moving toward me faster now.

He threw an obscene salute over his shoulder and kept walking.

"Constantine! Leandred, wait up," a short blond boy called, huffing as he ran toward the thief, giving the red and gold trees a wide berth. "I want to talk to you about procuring a—hey, is that a firesnake skin?"

I could see them conducting a transaction—selling *my* firesnake skin—but I couldn't see the thief's face, his hair blocking my view. And the firesnakes were fast gaining on my position. I grabbed a handful of ice and darted to the left.

I powered my shield as much as I could, then prepared my black mental paint bucket to gather data on what death felt like. I prepared my ecru bucket to search for information on Christian while I was dead.

Two hours later, I was still miraculously alive, but my throwing shoulder was sore. I had discovered that firesnakes could *air glide*, and I had a dozen bruises and a grand total of four shed skins—not counting the one the thief had taken.

But I was getting a good workout evading "tackles" and my adrenaline was fiercely flowing as Christian alternately crowed at my hits and cursed my misses. It felt like we were in the backyard throwing, catching, and evading invisible opponents again. If I missed a few of the easier shots because I wanted to clasp the feeling of this to me, no one would know of my weakness.

The sudden reverie was a weakness, however, and my inattention allowed a firesnake within striking range. Its jaws opened.

A pencil jabbed past my cheek and into the snake's mouth. The snake snapped through the pencil, but the moment gave me time to evade the second strike. My shield repelled its fire spit. The animated rock in my bag leaned over my shoulder, his rock legs hooked into my bag strap, his rock hands brandishing and shaking the remaining half-pencil at the snake hissing from the branch.

I blinked at the dangling rock, patted him on the top of his...rock...and set him upright.

I made quicker work collecting the other skins, though it still took me four hours to secure the full amount. I deposited nine in a mailbox at the address specified and tucked an extra into a plastic bag in my backpack. As irritating as the theft of the first skin had been, it had taught me a valuable lesson about what things might be worth.

I proceeded directly to the battle building and activated Draeger.

He crossed his arms. "What's wrong, Cadet?" he barked.

"I need to learn everything," I said, shucking off my backpack. "I want to know how to—"

A square opened in the wall and my backpack zoomed inside. I lunged after it, but the wall closed, and my hands smacked solid marble. "No, no!" My paint, my rock, my snakeskin—my *paint*.

"Ease up, Cadet. You have high level prohibitory items in your bag that aren't permitted in here while the wards are running. Your bag will be returned when you deactivate me. Now, let's—"

I yanked his cartridge from the slot. The wall square opened and I grabbed my pack, breathing heavily until I sorted through the contents and was satisfied that everything was still there. It took a solid minute before I was able to reactivate the cartridge. Draeger appeared, and my bag zoomed back into the holding cell.

"Cadet, we need to work on your fear," he said pointedly.

"I just threw ice cubes at snakes and dodged vipers for hours because I don't know how to do a—" I waved my hands "—material collection spell, or whatever."

"Turtle socks! Relying on magic to fix your problems is not a good long term strategy. Some good ducking and diving never hurt anyone. Let's go!"

Draeger observed me for an hour, tapping his lip even when I exploded an entire wing of the complex. I winced to hear the screams. All a simulation, all a simulation...

"Your limiter has been slightly loosened. Strange. But it's not at dangerous levels. If you ever find yourself out of control and in trouble, Cadet, sink into the earth. Bury the part of you that is overflowing or connected, and let the earth take care of things. Got it? All of the layers are part of an intricate network, and even in the First Layer, the earth is filled with life magic."

We practiced in a dirt pit I had exploded into existence during an earlier exercise. We worked for four hours, which partially removed the shaking, jittery feel I had been experiencing since returning from Ganymede.

Afterward, as I clutched my successfully returned bag to my chest in relief, I didn't think my fear of failure would be so easily removed.

The visualization technique of paint spreading wasn't working as well as it had previously—my control was far poorer than it had been before my limiter had been loosened. I suspected whatever Mr. Verisetti had done to me was the reason for the alteration.

I exited the battle building and my gaze strayed momentarily to the Midlands. I withdrew my reader, and after checking the time and class schedules, I headed to the engineering compound. Slipping into the designated classroom, I took a seat in the back of the large lecture hall and chomped an energy bar.

Alexander Dare sat in front.

Class was awesome. Professor Mbozi, a man with very dark skin and a very muscular frame, was an excellent speaker and made every concept sound exciting. I remembered Will talking about how much he loved his classes.

Everything the professor did was magnified so that even from my seat at the rear of the lecture hall I could see as well as if I was sitting up front. I watched Dare scroll the air in front of him. I'd have to figure that out later. I just sat and absorbed and watched the holograms—and Dare.

Mbozi suddenly frowned and put a finger under his ear, then motioned to Dare, who gathered his things and strode from the room. Strange.

But his absence made paying attention far easier.

Chapter Seventeen

Mbozi told everyone to construct a simple ward box that we would use for the exercises. Even though the other students' boxes were far more grandiose—and it was obvious that I was in some upper level class instead of the beginner class I needed—I was ridiculously pleased with my miniature result as I pulled the last line of it crookedly like a beginning weaver interlacing her last thread.

My box wouldn't hold anything bigger than a fly—and wouldn't keep out anything but a fly—but it was functional all the same. All of that studying was paying off. A few more ten hour sessions and I'd have the equivalent of Persian rugs on the sides.

Energy zipped along the lines of Mbozi's box hologram, keeping the image sharp, as he explained the exercise in further detail. Frowning at the zipping energy, I opened my reader and pulled up a magic primer.

Focus, concentration, knowledge, confidence. The cornerstones of bending magic to my will.

Something Draeger had said was brought to mind—"Some mages persist in thinking two of those concepts are the same and never try to rectify that mistake, relying on their cuffs to compensate. Squirrel brains! *Concentration* encompasses measurement as well as the tightness of one's control."

Maybe in order to gain better control I needed a different way of mentally channeling my magic.

I tapped my fingers on my desk watching the changing holograms that had roses, animals, and objects encased in each box. The boxes were examples of warding designs, but I might be able to use something similar *mentally*. Four sides for four cornerstones...no not quite...four parts building one construct...maybe...

I pulled a pyramid to mind, letting it rotate—considering how I could use it.

The apex would be focus. The point of the pyramid rotated and became prominent in my mind's eye. My focus could be blunt or razor sharp. I made the apex of my pyramid as pointy as the tip of a needle. Ultra focused.

Something very blunt, on the other hand...I let the tip dull, rounding it. Uncontrolled detonation and destruction. I might need to use that someday too. I practiced working with the point.

The edges extending from the focal point...they would embody concentration. Measurement and control. I widened the pyramid, then stretched it and made it taller. If I could make the magic travel farther or shorter, in greater quantity or smaller than maybe...

I made the pyramid thinner than thicker, trying to imagine the amount twenty milliliters would require.

The base of the pyramid...well, that would be knowledge. The foundation that everything rested upon.

Confidence was my non-static element. *Movement.* Zipping magic. Confidence would be what sent the lines of concentration flowing down the rays to my focus. And the rays...I could abrade them to coarse sand or polish them to smooth, slippery marble.

Confidence promoted movement in all aspects of life.

I projected the vision of the pyramid in my mind into the air. Magic flowed unchecked toward it and I had to forcibly hold my confidence and concentration. I forced sand along the rays.

Intuition and instinct supplied innate confidence. Made things easier, faster, more effortless. Excitement built within me as the concepts drew together and the construct pulsed.

I rotated the pyramid in my head, assembling pieces one at a time, and tested a zip of movement. Magic *wanted* to be quick. The visual representation mirrored my mental one. I watched the movement, then shot my magic at the focus.

A rose bloomed from my desk, bright fuchsia and perfect.

I smiled and without thinking, blunted the point of the pyramid. The magic detonated. Half the mages in the class jumped to their feet. Roses started blooming on every desk—twining, fat buds that were flowering ever larger. Students exclaimed. Mages began casting. One boy gamely plucked one and gave it to the girl on his left as his other wrist was entwined.

The blooms reached the ceiling. The professor's eyebrows rose toward his hairline, but he did nothing to stop the magic. A number of students started fielding blasts and setting up small containment areas. The professor crossed his arms and watched, calling out praise or chastisement.

Blooms broke through the ceiling as roses that hadn't been contained banded together—Jack and the Rosestalks stretching to the sky. Professor Mbozi tapped a pointer against his beefy arm as he watched the chaos. "I'm growing irritated, mages. There is no reason I should be reminding you to try one of the mass containment spells I lectured about two weeks ago. They require four people as corners, so make friends with your neighbors, quickly. I'm going to leave all of you here to be suffocated, if I don't see some results soon."

I gathered my supplies and ducked out of the room before anyone could peg me.

But...my magic had worked. I smiled fiercely. I had found the image I needed. I headed back to Draeger to do some practicing. I'd have Christian out in no time.

~*~

Chapter Seventeen

Professor Stevens watched me with pinched lips and a raised brow as I grinned at her the next morning.

I was still riding high from my new way of controlling magic. Last night I had practiced until I'd dropped, then giddily made my way past my disapproving roommate and flopped into bed. I had put in another two hours of practice this morning.

"Good morning, Professor!"

I just needed to remember that my natural desire to master a skill was not always an asset. I needed to learn just enough to be able to raise Christian in a timely manner. Then I could delve subjects to my heart's content.

"Be content now, Ren."

"Raise, raise, raise! Danger, danger, danger!"

Stevens briskly magicked a set of supplies, sending everything in the room dancing. "Have you ever made charcoal?"

"Only accidentally." Christian had been fond of fire.

She handed me a blank research journal and a light wooden tool case with slots. "If you are a serious student, you will record every result. Let's begin with vine charcoal first."

I gripped the journal to my butterfly-filled chest and nodded.

We hand-cut and burned different types of woods over different types of fires, and I watched through a pair of clunky, magic-enhanced goggles as a thin tendril of spring green wrapped around the wood and over the fire in tight, perfectly spaced loops. Stevens's magic settled like a clinging vine, then the green seeped into the burning wood. A very faint shimmer of green caught the light when the charcoal cooled.

"You can cover your charcoal with paper, wood, or other coatings, but unless you specifically create those too, coverings will separate your internal magic—that which is in your skin—from the instrument. You will get more powerful results the closer you are to the weapons you wield."

I blinked at the wording, but nodded.

The next three hours were filled with experiments. We used different methods of burning and magic infusion. In some attempts she had me infuse the natural wood with magic, on some I had to manipulate the time and space of the spirals, and in others I injected the magic as the wood cooled. I furiously scribbled down the process and results in my journal and carefully labeled each product in the slots in my new tool research case. I made a column to record the results of my drawing attempts with each piece.

All in all, my creations ranged from poor to adequate, but I ended up with thirteen knobbly charcoal sticks. I was rather stupidly thrilled, and my sloppy grin had to convey such.

Stevens rolled her eyes. "We will be working with graphite, clay, and wax tomorrow. Research firing techniques and come prepared."

She held up the last piece of charcoal she had created and looked at it critically under the light. It was coal black, but it shimmered, as if something white was trapped inside. She handed it to me. "Use this one for the next week as a control sample."

I twisted her charcoal pencil between my fingertips, and it caught the light, sparkling, as if it contained fairy dust. I could *feel* her magic in the filaments of the charcoal. Zipping along, then soothing down. I couldn't wait to try it. I imagined holding a Stradivarius would feel like this to a violinist.

"It's beautiful," I said.

There was something strange about the expression on Stevens's face as she studied the pencil. "I had a lot of practice many years ago making those."

"Oh." The tone of her voice made the atmosphere suddenly uncomfortable. "Do you have an artist in your family?"

"No." She turned abruptly and strode to the sink and began washing her hands.

"Do you draw, Professor Stevens?"

"No."

It made me wonder for whom she used to make charcoal.

~*~

Olivia entered our dorm room soon after I returned with my newly crafted supplies. Her steps slowed, and she looked around suspiciously, delicately sniffing the air for a moment, before giving my sloppy grin an expressionless look in return and sitting at her desk.

I had hoped that the charcoal pencils would work well. They were performing beyond my expectations.

Gophers were leaping and shaking their tails all through my sketchbook.

But though they could skirt around each individual page to the backside, I couldn't get them to port from one page to the next. The urge to make it work pressed, but I reined it in. Christian first. Creative curiosity gratification later.

I turned the page and examined a clean sheet. If materials were so important...I should probably look into making my own sketchpad paper too. I put it on my mental list, then set about drawing the three-dimensional box I had designed. It started rotating beautifully minutes later, the charcoal channeling my intention with ease. A three-dimensionally envisioned and shaded box sketched on a two-dimensional paper space.

Chapter Seventeen

But a hundred jabs later, and the paper was still two-dimensional. I still couldn't stick anything inside. I could make the things I drew *inside* of the sketch use the boxes—like gophers nesting within—but I couldn't insert anything from my physical realm or withdraw anything from the sketch realm.

The book I had purchased from Ganymede Circus said that making storage spaces had been accomplished in the past, but that it necessitated particular talents for manipulating universe space—far outside the knowledge and talents of the regular mage. The descriptions were shady on that account.

Whatever. I had seen the magic in action and wasn't one for accepting defeat because someone told me something was impossible. Will, the Department's hunter, the gophers, the butterfly, Marsgrove's storage paper. Not impossible.

And impossibility is what those books said about necromancy too. That spirits were at peaceful rest. I could clearly hear Christian's pain, nullifying their words.

I was sensing a government conspiracy against knowledge and personal advancement. Marsgrove was surely in on that.

I chewed my lip, then grabbed a plastic cap and happily stuck it on the end of a newly made knobbly charcoal stick. I started gnawing the cap, comforted by the familiar action. The freed butterfly in the First Layer had been drawn with pencil, but I had used paint to activate it. And the gophers had only come out of the sketch—and the hunter had only been sucked inside—after the drop of paint had absorbed. Same with Guard Rock and the Christian paper-doll. I had no idea about Marsgrove's storage paper, but it seemed likely an infused propellant had been used there as well. Something that gave life or bound space, or both.

I could hear Guard Rock pacing under my bed, defending the premises with a new pencil. I wasn't sure what I was going to do when Olivia discovered him. I had told him to remain under there and be inconspicuous, and he had saluted with his stick. But he was a...rock. An animated one, but still, I was pretty sure I hadn't willed him either an advanced brain or personal survival instincts in my uncontrolled thought about guarding.

"Save me."

"Free me."

I needed to try a drop of paint. The good stuff. But I couldn't risk losing the tube. What I needed was a way to *try* the drop. I needed a chaos field like the one around the vault in order to paint for real, but if I could just get a *drop* onto a paper, I could do smaller item tests in the comfort of my

210

room.

I dug out all the class notes I could find on the server for Professor Mbozi's classes, and containment fields in general.

Three hours later, Olivia looked like she might start posting reminder notes titled "Murder Roommate, Hide Body," if I stayed in the room any longer trying to figure out how to set up a small containment field then put a drop of paint on a paper without using my hands, magic, or intentions. I had used up the non-magical paint tubes I had brought from home for the tests—each had been taken in turn—and I had racked up five more offenses.

My sixth was awarded when I attempted to turn my desk into an unbreakable barrier box around the paint and my hands.

The sixth law enforcement student aimed his tablet at me and the tube of crimson whizzed to him. He looked at it in consternation, just like all the other officers had. He held the tube as if it must be filled with flesh-eating bacteria instead of paint.

"Your items will stop being confiscating as soon as you are clean for two weeks straight."

Well, that was unlikely to happen.

"Ren, I think I want you to stop."

"Ren, you need to free me!"

I looked at my roommate, who was making a career out of pretending I didn't exist. I wished I could ask her for advice. On things like hiding my illegal status while still gaining all the knowledge I lacked. On things like making a containment field to hide my prohibited projects. On things like hearing my dead brother's fractured soul calling out to me, discrediting every text that said he was somewhere peaceful.

But I just was not born for interpersonal relationships. That was why I had a twin.

One more test...

Knock, knock, knock.

I spent the rest of my Saturday and much of Sunday morning working off the punishments I had earned.

Sunday afternoon, as I was coming back from soul studying at the library, I suddenly found myself pushing through a Jell-O force field as all hell broke loose freely on campus around me. Two people near me pressed their fingers underneath their ears and screamed in loss.

A second town in the Second Layer had been destroyed.

I mechanically watched the news reels in my room. An event that happened only on my reader—black-and-white swirls in the smoke prefacing the destruction in the replayed reels. The black-and-white swirls were intimately familiar, and I didn't know how to process it. The sudden force field that had taken me during those few seconds had been the same as the one in Ganymede. And no one around me had seemed affected before or during the chaos.

I stared at my device long past the last news reel, rolling my charcoal pencil between my palms.

When Will's emergency message came through, I was expecting it.

Chapter Eighteen

MARSGROVE REDUX

I HAD ASKED WILL if he could somehow hack into Marsgrove's mage frequency—a sort of internal cell phone everyone but I seemed to possess—to determine when the man might return to campus. Will, bless him, hadn't asked too many questions and had just said, "I know someone who can do it, I'll take care of it."

Since I didn't have my own frequency established—and frankly, after knowing about this whole hack thing, wasn't sure I wanted one—Will and I relied on old school communication. My bracelet would ping me with incoming messages.

Meet at library as soon as possible. Person of interest on the move.

I gathered the emergency bag I had put together for just such an occurrence and sprinted back to the library as dusk drew its dark curtains across the Sunday night sky.

Will wasted no time setting up a silence enchantment. "He's returning home to check something and then he's going to hunt the *other* full time. The negotiations have collapsed." The full time designation might have amused me in other circumstances, as Marsgrove seemed permanently assigned to hunting Mr. Verisetti.

"Thanks, Will. Seriously, thank you." I squeezed his arm and quickly slung my bag back on. "I may be absent for a day or two. I'll send you a note when I'm back," I said, my words running together as I backed away. "Then I'm going to dedicate two days to being your work slave for all twenty of your projects."

I didn't give him a chance to respond or ask any questions I didn't want to answer. I took off to the nearest campus arch and made three jumps down the mountain until I reached Marsgrove's street. I walked carefully inside. The magic seemed extraordinarily relieved to have me back. It sucked in toward me and gave me a little push toward the stairs. I pushed back, walked to Marsgrove's desk, and returned all of the books and papers I had stolen, arranging them quickly according to the mental snapshot I had taken. There was nothing I could do about the missing money, but hopefully that would go unnoticed.

To the delight of the pressing magic, I ran upstairs, threw my trash bags haphazardly in the closet—stuffing pillows and books inside each, with a shirt or sock peeking out, to make each bag look full.

I messed up the bed, tossed two shirts over the desk chair, grabbed a drink from the fridge—crap, what if he checked the back-end supply, wherever it was, and saw I hadn't eaten anything?

My midsection clenched, but I turned on the television. It was too late for second guessing.

I refilled the paperclip box and stuck the rest into my pockets, just in case. It took me a moment of psyching myself up, before I finally closed the door. The magic re-engaged with a snap, sealing me in. The soothing net settled, totally relieved to be back in place and I let it lead me to the bed where I lounged on my stomach and elbows as I might do at home while watching tv.

Marsgrove arrived an hour later.

I could feel his magic press against the door, questioning. The abject fear that ran through me nearly made me fly off the bed and back into the corner with my hands out, ready to defend myself. I took a deep breath, then another, forcing my inhales and exhales to expand and contract my torso normally.

I could imagine him looking *through* the door, and tried to school my expression into vacant lines. I wanted to crawl under the bed.

I dug my fingernails into the bedspread. Everything was riding on this.

The door clicked open. "Miss Crown?"

One of my fingernails ripped.

"Hmmm?" I said, turning my head slightly, trying to keep my expression as absent as possible.

"You look well."

"I'm watching a new episode." I could barely think, and the words came out mumbled and garbled. "Janie and Tommy are dating behind Freda's back."

I focused on the morphing colors of the tv trying to gather my thoughts. Concentrate. Focus.

Without the magic that usually, readily answered, I focused my thoughts down the edges of a mental pyramid. Calm. Calm.

The fear and panic slowly pushed into the center of the pyramid, desperately bulging the sides of it outward. I allowed some of the soothing magic to trickle in and kept thoughts of calm pushing along the lines, caging them in, allowing the apex of my pyramid to funnel my words and tone.

"Can you believe Tommy?" My voice grew stronger. "Doing that to Freda? And Janie—I thought she was her friend? Don't you think Sonya should say something?"

"Er, yes, surely. I will leave you to your program." Through my tightly bound fear, I could hear his relief. I could also hear his underlying stress. The negotiations—whatever they truly were—had failed and the danger for his side was increasing. "I was just making sure you were well. Everything looks fine."

I sent an emotion I didn't feel down my mental construct and produced the best placid, inane smile of which I was capable. "It's home." I indicated the mess. "Comfy."

I needed to curb any notions that he might have about cleaning the space. Cleaning would undo my deception.

"Good, good. I'm just going to leave this bag of clothes here for you. I must have forgotten to remove it." He put my missing trash bag on the ground. "I'll check on you again soon."

He seemed like such a nice man at the moment. Normal. And yet, here I was caged like a Persian cat. He terrified me.

"Ok." I waved over my head, fear and adrenaline blasting through my construct as I stared unseeingly at the images flickering on the screen. My back was completely to him. He could do anything to me at the moment.

But the door lock reengaged, and after another agonizing thirty minutes Marsgrove vacated the house. I sagged against the window, where I had scrambled to watch him depart. There was nothing so relieving as seeing his back disappear around the street corner.

Marsgrove was overconfident and exhausted. And like any adult seeing what he expected and hoped to see, he had underestimated his opponent. Thank God.

The soothing field pressed harder, as if it realized it needed to establish a firm hold on me as quickly as possible.

I quickly got to work. Unfortunately, the lock's diabolical nature was still the same, and my hands were less than steady. But a few hours and six paperclips later, I was free again.

Before exiting the house, I took stock of the new items on Marsgrove's desk.

My eyes lingered on a report Marsgrove had left. Upon touching it, a news reel hologram bloomed.

A newscaster I had seen on my reader's news feed before, wearing a trench coat and Darby said, "Is it true about Raphael Verisetti?" The man's voice dropped to a whisper. "Is he one of...those?"

A woman in a posh living room sat with her ankles crossed and her posture perfect. She looked like a bird of prey that would launch at any moment. Olivia would like her. "Previously, he had never given any indication of such abilities. The public should calm themselves. Everything is under control. If we discover that that particular mage type exists again, said mage will be dealt with, as we promised the public long ago." Her voice was as icy as the smile on her face.

The scene shifted to a woman in an open doorway. "I went to school with him. He and his crowd were a dark, secretive bunch. Spread out in powerful positions now. Should look to them for questioning. I don't care what the authorities say. They didn't all disown him."

The scene shifted again to a man being interviewed on the street. "Had to be an accomplice at Excelsine or in Lolinet Village. There was an event in both after the Ganymede Circus tragedy. Law enforcement tried to hush it up, but the coincidence makes one wonder. The Department should be allowed to do full sweeps of both."

I took my finger away, shutting off the hologram. I exited the house shakily. Marsgrove had been right to check on me.

Raphael Verisetti *did* have an accomplice at Excelsine. An unwitting one. Me.

Chapter Nineteen

PREPARATIONS

FOR ALL OF MY CRAZED REVELATIONS, the only action I could accept was to move forward. I wouldn't let Raphael Verisetti find me or use me again. It was common, spoken-about knowledge that strict wards had been placed on campus to keep him—and all registered terrorists—out. Since he had been a student at the Academy, his blood was registered, making such wards easy.

At least that is what they said.

As I walked back from another session with Draeger, I covertly watched a group of five students wearing round purple hats hold a meeting in a small stone circle near an arch that lead to the fifth circle.

"I want full sweeps of all the twentieth circle arches. Report back at the end of the day."

Round hats nodded and they set off.

Another small group of three nearby sneered after them. "Useless. They won't find anything new. We should be going through the student registry and looking over new entries. Get Gravesman on it."

"He's already on probation for accessing—"

"Do I look like I care? Get him on it!"

Thank God I wasn't registered.

I chewed a fingernail. I showed up as a student for the cafeteria, though. Would I be on that list?

I needed to get Christian raised as fast as possible, then find a way to get us out of here.

All over, campus fell into a tense, anticipatory atmosphere that I tried to ignore by working harder. But eyes were everywhere, weighing and watching.

By the end of my second week, I had fallen into a daily routine:

* Magic-breaking work with Stevens.
* Chaos fields in sneaked into engineering classes.
* Soul binding and cleansing rituals and research in the library.
* Shielding and identification practice with Draeger.
* Watching the news feed, listening for another Marsgrove alert, and jumping at shadows.
* Working off punishments.

All wasn't terrible, though, as I had fallen into a daily routine of steady meals with Will *and* Mike.

Mike, I'd quickly learned, was Will's roommate. With his easy-going personality and interests, he and Christian would definitely get along when I brought Christian back. Sports came first for Mike, then girls, then food, then weather.

I picked his brain about weather mages and their work as frequently as possible, always liking to hear others speak about their passions and doubly interested because Christian's lightning seemed quite on par with Mike's field.

"If you have the talent, it is the best major on campus. Who else gets revenge by making rain clouds follow people around?"

I snorted and continued fashioning the design for my chaos field, trying to perfect the simulated 3-D space.

"Jealousy is a beautiful thing, Crown. I embrace yours," Mike said with an affable gesture of acceptance.

It provoked an unwilling laugh. Yes, Christian and Mike would be fast friends.

"So, what are you drawing today?" He pointed at my paper.

"Just a practice piece." I flipped my page and diverted the conversation. "Materials class with Stevens is fascinating. I've been making and testing pencils. The better the magic in the pencil, the more effortless the animation—and if you make it yourself, it connects and brings everything together. So the magic in the pencil becomes a direct conduit to my magic and intentions."

Way better than the boatload of concentration and the resulting complete exhaustion that ordinary pencils required.

The paint samples I had tried in the vault—sneaking touches in while Stevens had her back turned—were even more spectacular. Not quite Verisetti-Crown "true" paint, but as soon as I could use paint freely, I had a good feeling about how my rate of progress would increase.

"Watch." I made a list of the weather events Mike had been relating, then prodded the words into dancing as they arranged themselves into the desired order. The h's and n's were kicking their little legs in a Can-Can rhythm as they moved. The m's started dancing too, but because they had three legs, they kept getting out of beat. I considered using the middle leg as a stabilizer so its outer two legs could lift and extend.

His brows rose to brush the brown fringe of his hair. "You make that look easy."

I froze. I did? Had I just done something freaky and feral? My x's started doing jumping jacks on the page, their little arms and legs whipping up and down, faster and faster.

"May I try your pencil?" Mike asked, thankfully not sounding horrified or repulsed.

I handed him my pencil and he drew a dark cloud on the page. Drops of rain sluggishly emerged. He looked at the pencil and smiled, returning it to me. "You make good pencils. And seriously, Crown, though you might find pencil-making interesting, most mages would rather pull off their toenails. You should sell them."

I stared at the pencil. I had been helping Will make sketch templates for his experimental designs, so that he could record his results and tweak his variables in paper simulations. Maybe I could get him to set up a scientific magic booth during the Art Expressionists meetings and we could convert some of our extra items into cash.

I made a note to ask.

Mike and Will were opposite in many ways—Mike had a steady rotation of girlfriends, in a sporty guy, casual way, while Will seemed quite happy dating his research work—but a hum permeated the air when they performed magic together, which indicated a high degree of magic sympathy. It made me wonder about roommates, magic, and Olivia.

Will's lack of a social life—and mine—made it really easy for the two of us to meet. And he was always jazzed about everything he was doing, which was a very Christian trait. Even though their hair color wasn't the same, every once in a while I would catch myself looking at Will's bent head and thinking he was Christian.

Christian didn't like that. He was usually quite vocal about it too.

They were dissimilar in many ways, though. Christian had been a social lion. And it wasn't that Will was socially deficient, he was just wrapped up in his projects. Because I expressed interest in his work, and he in my art, we easily found common ground to chat for hours. This was likely the reason I felt the similarities to my brother.

It made me wonder...maybe I wasn't socially deficient either. Just...otherly focused.

Mike was more like Christian socially and sports-wise, and often made me laugh. Hanging out with the two of them made my heart lighter than it had been since my brother's death.

Will did have some secret life, though. Occasionally, he would get a shifty look on his face, touch his tablet, and say he had to be elsewhere.

When our eating schedules didn't mesh, I braved the cafeteria alone.

I learned from my first experience that I should go to the cafeteria before the rush. Once there, I would snag a free table and pull out my reader. The other seats would fill in eventually. I had met a few nice people that way, though they were fleeting acquaintances in a sea of fifteen thousand.

And I was very careful to stay quiet around or away from mages whose eyes were too quick and too cold in their watching of everyone else. That included Camille Straught and her friends. I avoided their tiered section completely.

But besides spending time with Will and Mike, joining the masses in the cafeteria was worth it for another reason. The food was excellent.

The different serving lines offered various types of ethnic food, something for everyone's taste—even the mage chefs had lines that allowed their magic to combine the raw ingredients on display into unique, personal concoctions. After a particularly disastrous episode in their red line—in which I had envisioned preparing paella and ended with raw squid tentacles dangling from my hair in seafood dreadlocks—I had avoided it. Neither my magic nor my experience in a kitchen was yet up to the task, so I had stuck to the already prepared food lines since.

But to my half-delight, half-disturbance, the ten-eyed folks *read* a bit of one's surface magic to make a single food selection for each student in the brown line—and that answering positively to the "caniopidas" question gave them permission to do so. The food they chose was always disturbingly good and perfectly suited to my palate.

More importantly, though, meals were the times when I watched everyone around me and conducted social reconnaissance.

People seemed to be people, no matter what their magic abilities. However, the ability to shape life around them gave mages a slightly more mature outlook. Sixteen-year-olds spiritedly discussed terrorism and political tactics here. And mages like Dare, who I had discovered was nineteen, guarded the gates with their lives.

I wondered if the twenty-two-year-olds on campus withdrew magical Social Security.

When mages performed interesting magic or discussed thought-provoking topics around me, I took note, and researched the topics later—

how one embedded spells, the history of magic, how magic *actually* worked between mages as a conduit and magic as an energy...a thousand things that I skimmed and flagged for later study.

Since I watched everything and everyone around me, it was impossible not to notice Nephthys, the girl who had healed me in the library. She sat alone three meals in a row on the second tier, head lowered over a reader. People would sit around her, but no one ever seemed to speak to her.

At the third meal, there was an empty chair next to her, so I decided to brave my crappy meeting skills and join her. Surprised, she glanced up. I gave her a determined smile that I hoped was friendly and not strange. Her eyes were kind, but sad, and I wanted to know her better; to make her smile.

"Do you mind if I join you?"

A small, genuine smile grew on her face. "Please do."

The dream-like quality of sand and veils she had exuded in the library, hiding strength of character beneath shy innocence, was still present.

"What are you studying?" I pointed to the images on her reader. People were leaping and twirling on the screen.

"I transferred from the Sakkara Institute this season." She looked a little tense at the admission. "I'm a Terpsichore mage."

Other than Sakkara being the name of an Egyptian city, I didn't know much else.

"I'm embarrassed to admit I don't know what a Terpsichore mage is."

She smiled, her face lighting up. "Really? But you noticed..." She shook her head lightly, but her smile stayed warm and her eyes were happy. The feeling suddenly seemed to transfer to me and seep right into my bones. "Ignore my babbling. It is a fancy way of saying that I dance."

The increased energy made me feel like I was hovering on the edge of the zone—like I'd be able to do anything if I just tipped over and into it. "I paint. And draw odd structures."

She tilted her head. "But you aren't a muse." It was not a question.

"Er, no." I didn't know what a muse meant in the magical sense, but I was far from anyone's reason for success.

"You were always my reason for success."

I hugged Christian mentally.

"Suck out the other one's soul!"

I gave his evil twin a dubious mental pat.

Nephthys glanced at my notebook, the front of which was now covered in moving patterned doodles. "I've always wished skill with a pen or brush."

"I've always wished to be able to belly dance." Guys seemed to like that kind of thing.

She smiled again, a soft smile that lit up her face. Her eyes danced a bit in the light, as if some part of her needed to be in motion even when she was gracefully still. "Perhaps we can teach each other." She looked suddenly unsure. "If you wish."

"I'd love to swap skills. And to hang out."

Her tension released and the air suddenly felt like a warm blanket of my favorite paints collecting on a canvas. "I'd like that too."

Making friends with Nephthys Bau was like making friends with a gentle wind or a comforting stream. Just being near her was soothing. It was never a pacifying kind of soothing, though, more like an energizing one. I didn't forget my goals, they became *brighter*, as if anything were possible.

She joined the three of us for meals when our schedules coincided, and I started getting to the cafeteria even earlier in order to secure a table with more room. It was strange at first that I needed to repeatedly call attention to Nephthys. The eyes of the other people at the table would just...slide right by her.

Considering that Nephthys was beautiful and Mike was always eying pretty things, it was decidedly strange. But I put in serious, daily effort and, as if a veil had lifted suddenly, I was rewarded one lunch period. The boys stared at her for an entire minute until I poked them both with my fork.

Will turned to me with a look of amazement a moment later, then gave me a warm smile, as if I'd done something wonderful. Weird. But I was happy to smile brightly back, feeling the warmth of the moment.

Her soft wit was a good counterpoint to Mike's more raucous vibe, my half-ramblings, and Will's nerdy expositions. Strangely, I always accomplished a lot in the hour after a mealtime with her.

But far more than that was the bright look in her eye. Nephthys would fit in anywhere, so it was strange that she seemed overly thrilled to hang out with us, as if we were extending her an immense favor.

Reaching out to someone else made me feel more self-confident than I had in a long time.

Focus. Concentration. Knowledge. Confidence. They weren't just the cornerstones of magic. They were the cornerstones of my life now. I put them into action in every task I undertook, building my personal pyramid brick by brick.

By the end of my third week at school, I had settled into a modified routine:

* Magic breaking work with Stevens and Draeger.
* After hours recon on the art vault—carefully noting schedules, professors, and the manners in which they each exited the vault.

* Attending any class that was studying anything remotely like a chaos field.
* Watching for Marsgrove.
* Trying not to make eye contact with Alexander Dare, who always seemed to be outside the battle building when I exited.
* Testing ordinary paint drops systematically around campus.
* Serving countless hours of punishing tasks for my offenses and attending two mandatory substance abuse classes.
* Eating meals with Will, Mike, *and* Nephthys.

"Did you find it?" a boy anxiously asked another outside the cafeteria one day.

"I got the list. Shut up about it already!"

"We discovered something at Arch Twenty-Two-Fifteen," a girl said. "We need a better device, though. Ask your cousin."

Campus lockdown was making people seriously edgy by the end of week three. Horrible and strange things were happening in the other magic layers, but other than keeping tabs on Marsgrove and listening for news on Mr. Verisetti, all of my mental resources were needed for other things.

Will and I had set up our art-science booth at the Art Expressionists meetings. Sitting unobtrusively in the back with Will, a hundred different types of artists argued and shared tips during the town hall format, then browsed the booths. I made enough sales to purchase a number of items I needed for soul binding rituals, and thirty small glass containers of regular paint.

Meanwhile, I racked up a half-dozen more Level One Offenses and two Level Twos testing containment fields.

Most of the time, the students who came to mete out punishments were civil, though by now I was pretty sure all of them thought I was a raging druggie. I used the small glass containers of paint for testing and watched each one zip away.

Unfortunately, Peters had responded to three of those calls, and he loathed me. He had made me attend and assist the creation of a new Blarjack pool. Without Magical Moses to magic the resulting mess off, I had trudged across campus and through the dorm covered in clinging green-snot swamp water, mouth firmly closed.

Upon entering our room, however, a chorus of "Nooooo's!" had emitted and the lot of it splatted upon the floor.

Olivia had been coldly displeased. But I was getting pretty good at scrubbing surfaces with magical cleaning products.

One afternoon I saw Olivia stop and sniff some blue flowers near the dormitory. I plucked a few later that night and put them in the common area atop the fridge. The lines at the edges of her eyes had loosened a fraction upon seeing them. I kept the vase full after that.

And I was getting really close with my containment field, I could feel it. Something was missing, but I finally felt I had enough knowledge to go into the art vault and determine what the missing piece was.

"Yes, then you will help me."

Christian's voice was sly again. He fully alternated now between raging against the world and consoling me. Encouraging me to test more and cautioning me to be careful. Telling me to save him and telling me to let him go.

His voice was always clearest in the moments before I fell asleep—which made my nightmares worse. I dreamed of him suffocating somewhere, being held in thorny chains, begging me to help him. And occasionally, his words turned cunning, like now. The warnings in the necromancy books were messing with my brain.

But I could hear his calm, confident voice clearly too, suppressing the other voice that sounded like him, but not.

"You can do it, Ren."

Yes. I just needed to figure out the art vault's wards. Simple observation. Easy. No reason to feel apprehensive.

It wasn't like people died doing this sort of thing.

Chapter Twenty

DEATH AND CONSEQUENCES

THE NEXT MIDNIGHT, I watched the vault door open and began the countdown in my head. Three. Two. One. Wearing my soft moccasins and dressed in black, I slipped from the bushes and moved from the east as the professor exited to the west—as was his routine. As he moved, so did I. I had five seconds. The professor continued straight west, finger pressed under his ear, paying attention to whatever was playing or talking there. The steel door started to slide shut. I sprinted forward and dove inside, the heavy door clipping my ankle.

The door sealed solidly behind me as I rolled into a crouch, and the room lit, registering a presence. I rubbed my ankle and let the throb ebb before carefully standing. No alarms shrieked, but there was no time to waste. I unstrapped my pack and fished out my reader.

Juleston's *Giant Tome of Wardery* popped up in full book form. It was passive device magic, but I spent a tense moment scanning the room, waiting for a siren to engage.

No alarm sounded, so I began. The instructions were simple—weave my intention to make the ward lines visible, then match the colors to the text for identification. I should be able to get around the active magic restriction, as identification or study was considered passive magic.

I placed the book down on the counter, and put on the magic-enhanced goggles I used with Stevens when conducting experiments. Ready. I took a deep breath and constructed my mental inverted pyramid. Intent, focus, knowledge, confidence. Chartreuse paint puddled the mental base. Just a little more depth of color needed...there. I sent it sliding down the lines and to the focal point of the pyramid's tip. Studying was passive. Identification was passive. I kept my intent passive.

A mist of light green slipped from my mental pyramid and wrapped into the air revealing colored lines and glittering points.

My shoulder touched a ward, and the field quivered. The vibrations bounced down my arm, making me shudder. The protection wards were so like Christian's electrical sparks during his Awakening.

I cleared my throat and concentrated on the book, trying to get my mind back on track. Fuchsia for protection and offense. That meant the pink line running around the perimeter of the room was likely a protection ward, since offensive magic would make no sense in an art room.

Forest green meant tranquility *or* trickery. It ran down the center of the ceiling. It was amazing how many things in magic seemed to have an equal and opposing side, depending on the intention of the caster.

There was a light hum in the room now. Not unpleasant, but strange.

I took a mental picture, then sketched out the ward design with regular colored pencils and a First Layer notepad—just in case magical art supplies under my control might trigger active magic. I ran down the list of the different colors again and what they could mean, making notes in the sketch margins. Another book I had in my reader was required for discerning intent. I would triangulate the two books with a third in a reading room directly after this. I needed to do a little poking at the pink ward, though, to see and feel what I was dealing with.

I didn't have the base knowledge to do much else yet. I would though. I'd figure all of it out. I'd figure *everything* out.

The hum became a buzz. I breathed deeply—calm, tranquility, control—then very carefully touched the pink perimeter line. It vibrated, then stilled. It gave me a strange set of impressions, but nothing firm. I would need to use a bit more magic to be sure.

I hesitated. But not being allowed to truly paint and do some real soul testing was making me angry and unhappy. Not having Christian back *now* was frustrating. I needed to know how to make wards that would let me paint and experiment.

Uncontrolled magic leaped out from under the edges of my cuff. Focus and intention, but without the requisite knowledge or confidence, streamed out in jagged lines. "No!" I tried to pull the magic back. But sensory input was streaming through my body at the contact. Overwhelming. Knowledge and intuition. A crystal shard flew off the table and shattered across the floor.

The pink thread of the ward snapped tight and expanded.

Boom.

Something exploded outside the room.

"No, no, no." A siren began blasting, and I automatically covered my ears in response. The action pulled the pink ward toward me.

Oh, *no.*

The pink ward wrapped around my finger, and the siren grew louder, shrieking painfully. I could hear people running toward the room from the jump point outside. *No, no, no.* In my panic I tried to shake the pink ward off. It snapped from my finger in the direction I pointed, and the door to the vault exploded. My hand whipped back, and I obliterated the easels behind me in a shower of wood, paper, paint, and wild magic.

I had to get out of here. My eyes went to my supplies and they flew into my bag. I put my arms out—flinging more pink offensive magic—and my bag zoomed onto my back, the straps fastening over my shoulders.

A tight net bore down on me, trying to squash my magic, an external magic force trying to bind and cut off mine. My panicking magic responded, inverting, and I could feel Marsgrove's shield working with whatever Mr. Verisetti had done to it, thrusting hard against the outside magic, repelling it forcefully.

I tried to pry the pink thread off my hand. I had to escape; I couldn't be found here, but the harder I tried to release it, the more tightly it clung, responding to my panic as it continued streaming more information to me.

And then they were upon me.

My shield tightened, green and black mixing with gold, blasting toward the mages who were spilling into the vault. My magic twined with my shield and pushed against the spells they were unleashing.

Magic was bouncing off me and ricocheting back at them just like it had with Mr. Verisetti. I watched a bolt bounce off of me and blow a ten foot hole through the western wall. I had seen Mr. Verisetti kill. And with Mr. Verisetti's spell mixing with Marsgrove's on me, I didn't think my magic was set to stun. Another bolt flew at me, the trajectory of it forming a diagram in my mind—it would hit the mage standing ten feet and thirty-two degrees in front of me.

Draeger's voice barked an instruction in my head, and I fell to the floor and sunk my hands into the tiles. The tiles disappeared, and I fell sharply through space until I hit dirt. I buried my hands in the earth, thrusting the energy downward, then something exploded within and around me, and I fell into darkness.

~*~

I woke to bright lights and Christian's voice in the back of my head babbling apologies, insanities, battle cries, and regrets.

"Ah, you are awake."

That wasn't Christian's voice. I blinked a few times and the blurred vision of a man turned into one dressed in a crisp white shirt and pants. The men in white had finally come for me.

Chapter Twenty

"You are in a spot of trouble, Miss Crown." The stranger's voice was even and calm, nonthreatening.

I just hoped my padded room wouldn't feel like—

"Do you Jell-O the walls?" I asked, panicked.

The man, whose face was unexpectedly more rugged than his voice, looked at me sharply, then ran a scanner over me. A blue beam slid across my vision.

He muttered something about delusions and sent a tendril of magic into the scanner, then scanned me again.

A doctor? Or worse? Had Marsgrove captured me? Had the Department bogeymen? I tried to grab the scanner, but a clink and jerk made me realize I was handcuffed to the bed rails. Christian's mutterings grew louder, but I couldn't make out the words in my panic. "Listen, I just don't want the hard kind, ok?" I jerked at my restraints again. "I don't like Jell-O force-fields."

Clink, jerk, panic, clink, jerk, panic.

"I don't like Jell-O skin. It's unnatural."

"Settle down, Miss Crown. You're going to hurt yourself, and I can't get a good reading."

"I'm fine. No Jell-O needed, I swear." Clink, jerk.

"What is the date?"

All that Libra Rising and Gemini Falling crap. "It's Ewok Day, for all I know." Clink, jerk, clink, jerk.

There was the hint of a smile on his face. "In what dorm do you reside?"

It was getting harder to breathe and Christian had gone completely silent. Clink, jerk, clink, jerk. "Twenty-five, north point."

"And what was the last class you attended?"

"Second Layer Engineering. Hermitage Building." I really hoped he didn't ask me if I was registered for it.

"Good." He sent another tendril of magic into the scanner. Then he tried to scan me again.

But I couldn't keep still.

"Listen, do you think you could unclip me?" Clink, jerk. I tried breathing through my nose. Clink, jerk. I wasn't sure I could pick the lock in my panic, but even if he gave me a rubber chicken, I'd try.

"Please be still, Miss Crown." I was obviously making it hard for him to get a meter read. "It's procedure to keep students who have performed Level Five Offenses chained, until an enforcement official arrives. I'm sorry."

I had no idea what a Level Five Offense was classified as. Poking at wards? I opened my mouth to ask, but then the sliver of Christian in me promptly shut it. Best to say as little as possible. "Ok?"

He looked at me for a long moment, then sighed. "Not again. Damn pencil pushers." He looked at his tablet. "Your record is only three weeks old, and without an official start date. I'm not even going to ask how long you've really been here, who created your account in the cursed Administration office, or who your orientation guide was."

He reached over and unclipped me, and I could have kissed him. I quickly brought my arms close to my body, hugging them to me.

"Thank you," I whispered.

He waved a hand and I could see black tattooed lines dart out from the edges of his sleeves. Lines also peeked out from beneath his collar at the back of his neck. "Let me get a good reading, and we'll call it even. I'll try to get someone to help you with your account."

Hopefully he would forget that part and just let me go. I held as still as possible and watched his teasing tattoos, which moved, darting forward then pulling back inside his cuffs.

His scanner beeped. "Your head seems fine. No Jell-O detected. But I take it you've had some rather unusual experiences with Wobble Walls in the past?"

I etched the words into my memory banks, unwilling to move my arms and access the bracelet encyclopedia. I would look it up later. I wondered if the translation enchantment rendered it to me as the too cutesy "Wobble Walls" and translated to something completely different for, say, Olivia. She probably heard "Transcendental Particle Freezer."

"A mage once prevented me from running away, before he told me about magic."

The doctor's lips thinned, and he shook his head. "The government programs need an overhaul. How about we fix you up completely, before someone comes?"

"Fix me completely?"

"You had your first recorded death. Congratulations."

I blinked. I couldn't remember anything. Had I seen Christian when I'd been dead? I leaned forward, gripping the guardrails. "How long was I dead?"

"Thirty seconds. Would have been less, but you had some impressive shields up even after death. Medical personnel respond to Level Fives automatically."

Thirty wasted seconds. I had nothing. That at least answered one question. I reluctantly struck temporary death from my mental list.

"Except for a broken toe, you are in shipshape condition. Easy enough to fix, if you want me to do it magically."

I leaned forward, interested to know about magical medicine. "Yes, please. What do I do?"

"Well, I use you as the conduit to fix your bone. You open your magic to me, then I can proceed with the work."

I hesitated. I wasn't sure I wanted to open my magic to anyone.

"It's really you healing your own bone, but with me driving the procedure. It isn't terribly invasive. Think of a whirlpool, and your malady is at the bottom of the vortex. I dive down, fix it, then we switch the polarity to bring me back up and out." He leaned in conspiratorially. "I've never gotten lost, I promise."

He had misunderstood my hesitation, but what he had said was useful to know. "Ok. So I just open my magic to you?" I could do that. I could.

"That's it."

I opened too much, but the doctor seemed to anticipate it, and the feeling of gentle hands gathering in the plastic bag of my magic—before it blew wide in the wind—slid through me. He pulled the figurative bag into a point and aimed it toward my foot, then the tingle of his magic shivered against my own. It was a clinical feeling. A doctor's touch. And he was indeed diving down. I felt heat on the smallest digit of my right foot, then as if someone flipped a switch, the magic swirl reversed.

The doctor raised a brow and smiled at me. "I recommend a few extracurricular meditation courses."

"Yeah, I haven't been too successful with that." There was always too much else that needed to be done with those minutes or hours.

He shook his head.

"Sorry?" I was oddly sad that he was disappointed in me.

He sighed. "No, it's not you. Damn bureaucrats. They are supposed to make sure you get the right training before—"

Peters chose that moment to burst into the room.

No. Why him? He was looking down at his chunky, bright, sunshine yellow tablet. All of the enforcement students carried one, and all the colors were different. That Peters had that color never ceased to amuse me usually.

"Doctor Greyskull?"

Upon hearing his name, my doctor suddenly grew even more awesome.

"I'm almost finished with my examination of Miss Crown, Mr. Peters," Greyskull said.

Peters's head jerked up at the mention of my name, and he glared at me, as if I were the lowest level of criminal filth he had ever seen. "Did you sedate her, Doctor Greyskull?"

"I highly doubt that is necessary, Mr. Peters." There was disapproval in Greyskull's voice.

"She burned down the entire Shangwei Art Complex!"

I winced. Oops.

"And this is her first offense, is it not?"

"It is decidedly not! She has perpetrated a slew of petty crimes. I first observed her breaking regulations in the library! She attacked Mr. Dare!"

Both of Greyskull's eyebrows rose at the last statement. "And she had no idea what she was doing, most likely. I'll bet if you look through her records, you'll find that she is a transfer student they pushed past some of the orientation classes." Greyskull sent me a significant look.

I withheld the urge to salute him.

"Which is neither your fault, nor Miss Crown's," Greyskull said in a neutral tone.

Peters's pursed his lips together. "I am sure procedures were followed."

"Mmmhmm." Greyskull prodded and poked me a few more times, looking in my eyes and examining a finger.

I had the feeling he was just killing time to irritate Peters. I think I was in love.

"See me immediately, if you experience any pain, Miss Crown."

"I will." I stretched my limbs, hoping I wasn't about to be handcuffed again. I sent a surreptitious glance around looking for anything small enough to palm that might be useful as a pick. "Thank you, Doctor. I appreciate everything you've done." I tried to signify that I appreciated more than just the scan and toe fix.

He tilted his head and his eyes crinkled. "Of course."

He turned to Peters. "Good to see you, Mr. Peters. I imagine you are still following procedures to the letter. Good man." Then he gave me another small smile, turned, and stepped from the room.

Peters looked disapprovingly at the open cuffs, but didn't try to reattach them. I put "practice picking cuffs" on my lengthy to-do list, if I made it out of here.

Peters rifled through my bag, which was on the floor. I was relieved my supplies had made it, but watching Peters look through my things made my teeth clench.

He pushed a button on his shiny, yellow tablet. "On this day of Libra, Forty-Two and a third, I Joseph Aldwin Peters, do sign in to swear to the accounting of Miss Florence Crown, who is charged with a Level Five Offense. Furthermore—"

I examined Peters for a second time as he talked to his tablet. He was still upright, uptight, and moderately tall. Clipped hair, pressed shirt. A boy soldier with a badge.

"—and following all laws, I do so swear."

I saw magic lift off the tablet and twine around him. Interestingly, magic was easier for me to see at the moment. I wondered if dying or rebirth intensified the ability temporarily, or if it was the aftereffect of attaching to the wards. The justice magic settled back above the tablet, hovering there.

"How did you get into the vault, Miss Crown?"

The hum of the justice magic warned me against lying. I had done little research on the law officers, as they tended to make quick and unexceptional visits to me, but the tablets used truth spells when activated. The thought of my mind being probed always produced a slimy, itchy feeling under my skin.

How to answer... "Um, a little like this." I stood and dove toward the floor. Yup, that was about right. I let my palms skid outward, though, skin peeling back from the bottoms. Ouch. But the whole thing looked like a giant trip now. "The door nearly shut on my foot."

Peters's mouth looked as if he'd sucked a lemon. "What were you doing near the vault?"

"Oh, um, I was intending to draw." That was true enough. I had been planning to draw a box after checking the wards. And I could play this game. "There is a great spot there. I go there often." All true.

"At midnight?"

"Er, I use art as stress relief." Also true.

"Students are not allowed in the vault without a qualified professor."

"Ok." I was denying nothing. I was going to be in real trouble if he asked pointed questions or got Stevens in here, though.

"Records show that tonight you have committed two Level One Offenses, a Level Three Offense, and a Level *Five* Offense. Do you know what the punishments for those are?"

"Um, no?"

The tablet zapped me. "Ow!"

"Lying?" He raised a brow and made a notation.

I rubbed my arm. "Well, I know punishments for levels one, two, and three, but not for five." I knew how to run, scrub, and battle firesnakes. Point me to one.

Peters smiled. "Well, I expect you will remember your expulsion long into the future, as you twiddle your thumbs in the ordinary world, after being stripped of your magic by the Department."

Oh, no—times infinity. "Are you serious?"

"Yes."

To my amazement, the tablet zapped him. I stared for a moment, then a smile worked its way to my face. "Lying?"

It was probably not a good idea to piss him off, but I couldn't help it.

"When I escape from here, I will end him," Christian said.

"You are in major trouble," Peters said harshly, rubbing his arm.

I nodded, trying to figure out how to work this new angle that had been presented. The enforcement mages had to tell the truth too when they were wrapped in the magic? "Right. What has happened in the past to Level Five offending mages?"

"Level Five offenders have been expelled."

But being expelled wasn't the worst thing that could happen to me, and Peters shouldn't have given himself away, by receiving that prior zap. "And what are three other punishments that have happened to mages who have committed Level Five Offenses?"

If I thought there was ever a possibility that I hadn't angered Peters, it was definitely gone. He gritted his teeth and shouldered my bag. "You can ask the provost."

So I didn't have to answer—my answer just had to be truthful. That was some relief.

A long forced march—by the same type of magic that had prevailed the night of the door prize ticket—to the provost's office found me sitting, cuffed again, in a rather uncomfortable seat, awaiting my fate. There was a toothpick stuck into the area between the seat cushion and back of the chair on the seat next to mine. I quickly grabbed it and threaded it into the hem of my shirt. Gross, but I wasn't going to start being choosy.

"Get out of here. Don't let them tag you completely!" Christian said.

I tried to keep calm. Magic wouldn't let me leave. I could feel it hovering, waiting. Like the ticketing magic, I had to fulfill some sort of contract—likely something tied to the enrollment enchantment Marsgrove had put on me. But I wasn't out of options yet. And if the provost knew about Marsgrove's dictates and was going to do something horrible to me, hopefully he would lock me up first.

Ten minutes later, Peters stormed out, bypassing me without a word or glance.

"Miss Crown, enter."

I rose and walked inside, as calmly as I could. The man behind the desk was a solid, robust man. A jovial business type.

He swirled a finger and the cuffs dropped. Maybe a good thing, maybe bad.

I took a quick look at the name plate on his desk. "Good afternoon, Provost Johnson."

"Let's cut to the chase, Miss Crown." He had a kind, but booming voice. "You have committed a Level Five Offense along with a number of lower level offenses. You are in danger of suspension. Should you commit even one more Level Three Offense, I may be forced to expel you."

Relief swept me that we were still talking about school infractions and punishment, rather than prisons and testing facilities. And I took note of Johnson's wording—*may* be forced.

"I could suspend you now, but Doctor Greyskull submitted a sympathetic note, championing you, and I am partial to the good doctor's character assessment. He said you are a transfer student and don't yet know our ways." His eyes dropped to the papers on his desk, and a disgruntled look briefly passed over his features.

Johnson hadn't been able to find my records and didn't want to admit it. I had a school record because of my prior offenses, but didn't have an academic record, which obviously presented a conundrum.

"Greyskull suggested community service, and I am obliged to grant the request."

I nodded quickly. Maybe I could get out of here before Johnson investigated further. Chasing snakes, planting flowers, and picking up trash? No problem. Maybe I could volunteer to assist Professor Mbozi or a chaos mage and advance my research at the same time.

"Answer two questions truthfully, and I will assign you to community service."

"Ok." Something magical wrapped around me.

"Mr. Peters said you truthfully told him you tripped into the art vault by accident." Oh, yes, yes, yes. I thanked Peters's questioning oversight profusely. "But once you were in there...were you trying to break down the wards in the art vault?"

"Uh..." I paused, trying to figure out the angle of the question.

Johnson's smile turned less pleasant. "Failure to answer will result in your immediate suspension."

"Don't you have law wizards or defense attorneys?"

"Legal mages, and yes. Next time you should think about calling one, before you agree to speaking directly to me. Agreeing to my questions made your trial inquisitorial, instead of adversarial. That means I am now in charge of your fate instead of a jury."

If I had known, I might have been tempted to beg my evil roommate to represent me, since I'd figured out she was vigorously studying law, in between her world takeover plans.

I held my breath, then answered his question. "No, I wasn't."

Nothing attacked me. Johnson looked surprised. "You weren't trying to break down the wards?"

"No," I said much more confidently. I had been there to study them. I chose my next words with care. "I accidentally attached to the perimeter ward and couldn't get it off. I panicked."

All true.

Johnson looked visibly relieved. "So, it was an accident."

"Yes."

"Good. Now, since I have you here and am asking everyone when given the opportunity, the second question you must answer is are you a terrorist?"

My eyes must have bulged, because they felt like they were pulling from my sockets. "No."

"Great!" He made a little checkmark on the paper in front of him. "I will see about getting some of the orientation sessions you missed made available to you via vid screen. And a stint on the squad should save you from becoming a troubled soul."

He said this cheerfully enough that I doubted his sanity—which made me wonder what the "squad" was. "Community service, Miss Crown, will show you what happens to the criminal types on campus. And will imbue you with a sense of duty to right any wrongs. Community service folks always use such creative solutions too. A win-win situation."

He looked thoroughly convinced of his own reasoning. I was still choking over the fact that he had just blithely asked me if I was a *terrorist* while I was under a truth spell.

"Let's put it at...two hundred hours." A second spell settled over me.

Two hundred hours?! But I just nodded, unwilling to test the bounds of the spell I was under.

"Excellent. The spell will motivate you to complete your hours in a timely fashion. I'll put your compliance on your transcript. In fact,"—he cleared his throat—"Let's just start a lovely new transcript, shall we? Give you a fresh start?" He waved his hand and a pile of paper leaped into a crisp folder. "Just press your finger right here."

For a long moment, I looked at the paper he held as Christian yelled wildly in my head. Then I pressed my finger to the page. I could feel a thread prick my finger and the blood seep into the sheets.

I was now fully tagged. Easily found in the system. Christian's hysteria started to ooze into my veins.

"You will need to re-register for classes, but you can do that tomorrow. I'll leave a note in your file. Report to Professor Wellingham and begin your service by Sagittarius Rising under Maiden's Drawers."

I just nodded, because otherwise, I was going to attract the white coats again with mad laughter. I think he had just given me some date in

December. Or a date with a naughty archer. I might need to take Will up on that app for my translation enchantment. And perhaps increase my research on how to get off campus completely.

"Plus, I think you should help put the vault back together, at least the preliminary laying of the lines."

I stared at Johnson, unable to believe my ears. Opportunity simmered my panic for a moment. He was telling me my punishment was to assist the reconstruction and warding of the vault? I would have *burned it down on purpose*, had I known that might happen.

"I know." He held up his hand. "Laying ward lines is grueling grunt work, but you must be punished, Miss Crown."

I nodded. Yes, yes I must.

"Wellingham will have that information too. I hope we meet under more favorable circumstances next time, Miss Crown." He handed me my bag.

"Thank you, yes. Good day, Provost Johnson." I needed to get out of here.

"Good day, Miss Crown."

I exited as quickly as possible. Thankfully, I felt the truth spell pull off and dissipate behind me, leaving only a shiver across my skin in its wake. *Free.*

Yet still trapped. Far more trapped.

Two hundred hours of community service? I could only hope that I would be able to serve that much time and not be arrested or captured beforehand. Two hundred hours of cleaning flower beds and picking up trash was infinitely more painful than ten, but I was going to watch a chaos field being constructed. I headed out to find Professor Wellingham right away. The sooner the better—for everything.

~*~

Professor Wellingham was an associate professor of political science among other things. He was a harried and wan looking man, with wildly spiked hair and an ashen complexion. I hoped like hell that it was the craziness of the political world, and not that of community service, that made him look like a street artist who hadn't slept for three months.

He gave me a handful of papers that contained the information for remaking the vault. I clutched them to me.

He muttered a few sentences that I was pretty sure veiled obscenities, then communicated my service task and unceremoniously handed me another stack of papers.

I blinked, certain that I had heard incorrectly. "I'm going to do what?"

"You are joining the Justice Squad. Or being forced into servitude, I suppose."

"The Justice Squad?"

"A group that addresses all student behavior issues that are Level Four and under, such as students cheating on exams or doing prohibited enchantments. They also do the preliminary questioning for Level Fives."

Like *you*, his look said.

"Wait, you mean I'm going to police the student population?" I was going to be *Peters*?

"Yes." He didn't seem put off by my obvious mortification or panic.

I needed to remain unnoticeable. I was going to be punishing people—who were definitely going to *notice* me. "But...but...I'm a delinquent too!"

Christian's sane voice groaned in my head.

One of Wellingham's brows rose. "And the thought is that you will be rehabilitated by doing service and assigning punishments."

That made some weird sort of nonsense. "You don't believe that, do you?"

"Not in the slightest." He searched through a bag. "But Provost Johnson does, and his opinion is the one that matters in this situation."

Wellingham finally pulled out a chunky tablet like the one Peters had. The intent of his actions seemed to indicate that I would be getting the strangely colored olive and lime tablet.

"This tablet will be your responsibility until the end of spring term. You have until then to complete your two hundred hours. You can accept special assignments that will help you burn more hours, or you can just be part of the daily or weekly on-call roster. The tablet only works on campus unless you receive special permission to use it off campus. The enchantments on the tablets are actually the one thing that is student proofed around here."

He looked at me in a sort of deadened way. "But feel free to try it—attempting to modify the tablet means automatic expulsion. And I don't think I need to tell you what will happen, if you fail to complete your task or lose the tablet?"

"Expulsion?"

"Right-o."

Wellingham desperately needed a Prozac and a girlfriend. And I needed to improve my time management skills, if I was optimistic enough to think I would survive past spring. And...I wanted to survive. I wondered if dying had caused the change in my thinking, or if some other complicated mess had taken place unknowingly inside my head.

"Good, good. I want—I need—you to survive, Ren," Christian said soothingly.

If my math was correct, Justice Squad would require a little over one hour of service every night. One hour, every night, away from my research for Christian.

On the other hand, I was going to watch and help the vault wards be placed. Worth it. This whole debacle was worth the tagging, the punishment, and anything else that happened if just for that. Time was not on my side, though. I took a deep breath as Wellingham handed me a thick book, a stack of papers, and my tablet.

"There are operating instructions in that manual, along with information on various offenses and punishments you can administer."

I couldn't believe I was seriously going to be *punishing* people as my punishment.

"You can activate and deactivate a clip." One popped up on top of the tablet in his hands, making it into a clipboard. "Sticking a paper—any paper—under the clip will meld it into the tablet and the information will become part of the device."

"A magic scanner, got it."

"If you just place a piece of paper on top of the tablet, nothing will happen. It's the clip that activates the enchantment."

I nodded along, thinking of rogue tablets gobbling my homework, and wondering if I could use this one in class.

He outlined the workings of my tablet and the magic therein, in one large info dump that had my eyes glazing over and my butt numb in the chair. I probably should have waited to speak with him until I was more clearheaded. I still couldn't wrap my head around the notion that I had actually died. I hoped that in my present dazed state that I didn't accidentally zap myself into a coma by deactivating the clip incorrectly.

"Once you write the offense in the tablet, magic will shoot out and entwine the parties, sealing the contract, terms, and intentions in magic."

"This information is all in the manual?"

"Yes. Familiarize yourself with the unit, the rules, and procedures, then come by next Wednesday evening at eight to start."

The look on his face indicated that he didn't think there was a chance in hell I would come prepared, but using a number instead of zodiac time gained him points with me.

"The first night you will respond to low level offenses only," he said. "Unless..." He shook his head. "No, you wouldn't be that unlucky. Good luck."

"Thanks." I shuffled from the room with my new tablet and reams of paper overflowing my bag. The ward sheet remained clutched in my hand.

~*~

The next morning I cautiously entered a building cut into the third circle of the mountain that looked an awful lot like Lycian rock-cut tombs embedded with dark windows. Inside, dark patches of brown stained the stones, suggesting hundreds of years of continual bloodshed that hadn't been cleansed. But at some point, the interior of the building had been redesigned to open it up to the light. Floor to ceiling windows were inset into the massive columns of stone—where I imagined manacles had once been hammered—dividing one lab and office space from another. The old mixed with the new. Culture and magic—past and present—entwined and melded.

How wonderful to be able to construct new creations without having to sacrifice older elements due to wear. Not having to sacrifice anything.

"Sacrifice, sacrifice!"

"Don't sacrifice, Ren!"

I skirted around three students and two assistant professors arguing in the main hall. Another student—languid, tall, and very good-looking—leaned against the glass wall with his arms crossed, watching them through a long fringe of hair, as if they were his own personal entertainment.

I saw Professor Stevens in a glass lab farther down and hurried toward her. She looked up and waved me inside, lips pinching as her gaze traveled behind me. I entered her personal, sterile domain to find her stirring a humongous pot. "Stir this carefully, while I sort out those idiots. Do *not* add magic to this, or I will expel you myself."

Crap. I immediately took the rod and started stirring. I had hoped with the number of hourly explosions on campus that she might not notice that the art vault and south complex had been blown to smithereens.

I had hoped I could gently break the news to her concerning my culpability. The whole south quadrant of Old Town was like a constant fireworks display, and Professor Stevens's personal lab here was three circles away from the art vault. It had seemed...a hopeful plan.

Stevens was muttering as she grabbed something from her desk. "Look at him standing there after working them over. Stupidly brilliant and horrible. Bane of my existence." She stalked out of the lab.

I could clearly see the drama through the glass panes. The boy smirked at Stevens. Ballsy. And made a "who me?" gesture, but innocence clearly wasn't his forte. If sexuality could ooze off someone, this guy was constantly perspiring. He was one of those guys who was a little uncomfortable to look at.

My eyes narrowed. Actually, his posture, height, and hair were the same as the firesnake thief's. He said four words and the others sputtered and began arguing again—with each other. He gave a slow smile, his hair hiding it from the others, but not from me in my viewing position. Dangerous.

Chapter Twenty

Stevens cut the others off with a quick hand motion.

The liquid in the pot began to boil fiercely, catching my attention again, as strange bubbles started to rise. My stir rate increased. The mess was a reddish-brown mixture that was beginning to solidify beneath my rod—a Karo Syrup shade nicely associated with old horror flicks. I hoped I wasn't stirring previous assistant professors, while Stevens was looking to add the lot in the hall to the pot.

A bubble formed at the top and pressed up to form into what looked like a fist. I batted it down with my rod and stirred more vigorously. Stevens had managed to keep the concoction flat without...things...poking out. I tried to channel my mother and stirred in a quick, controlled pattern.

That didn't stop a gawping face-like image from pressing at the side of my pattern. I sat hard on my magic to stop it from reacting. I whacked the face with the rod and quickly rotated figure-eight designs around the bowl. Great. I was going to have nightmares tonight.

Stevens strode back in, obviously irritated. I wondered if she was angry about my destructive tendencies, or life in general. I eyed her apprehensively as she took the rod and started stirring in spiraled circles and hard lines.

"You look like a frightened chicken," she said. "I should just let you cluck like one."

"I'm sorry. I ran into a spot of trouble outside the art vault last night trying to do some extra work. It was an accident, I swear."

"Hmmm..." She eyed me without giving anything away. "Did you complete the homework I assigned?"

"Yes." I dug my three perfect charcoal sticks from my bag and handed them to her. I had worked right through the dawn hours to get them like this, even though I had been exhausted and feeling half-again dead. I needed to be on Stevens's good side, especially with the whole vault debacle, and she valued perfection and hard work.

She looked them over, then nodded. "Fine. The vault should be rebuilt by the end of next week. We will work here every day this week and next. Don't do it again."

Professor Stevens wasn't much for asking questions thankfully. She did her thing, I worked my tail off to help her, and that was that.

"I won't. I will stay out of trouble." I couldn't afford the attention I had now, but I also couldn't afford lamentations. Onward, forward, watch your back and do better next time, Ren.

I looked through the windows. The students and assistants were in the other lab space throwing spells. The troublemaker was no longer in the room. I wondered where he had gone. Magic whipped from my cuff and my sight inverted momentarily, befuddling me, but I could clearly see the troublemaker smirking from a position at the side of the room, where moments ago he had been invisible to me. He made a motion with his finger and Karo Syrup floated into a ceramic container, then floated toward his bag.

My vision cleared, and the image of the container disappeared along with the boy. Maybe the shock from dying was affecting me still.

Professor Stevens's back was to the window as she stepped slowly around her pot, stirring constantly. "If you ruin anything in my domain, you won't be worrying about expulsion. I will hunt you down and erase you."

I saluted her before I could stop myself. She wasn't amused. And the motion brought her attention to the other room and her expression became furious.

"Idiots!"

She tossed the stirring rod to me again, then ran over to help them contain whatever was forming into reddish swamp monsters. Blasting the matter seemed to produce a monster from each splatter. My attention swung toward the windows looking outside, and my eyes narrowed on the tall boy walking casually away, a bag slung over one shoulder.

The angle confirmed he was in fact my firesnake thief.

The pot in front of me started to form up, and I had to concentrate once again on what I was doing.

Stevens returned, even less amused.

During our session, I blew up eight pounds of clay, trying to get the right amount of magic to settle with the exact formula I had been tasked with creating. I grew five man-eating clay plants instead.

She *really* wasn't amused.

~*~

Vibrating, I headed off to my first session of vault construction. Professor Mbozi, whose research I'd been stalking, was in charge. I took it as a karmic sign.

By the end of the week, the amount of knowledge I had on encapsulation chaos wards could only be termed dangerous, but I was fanatical in watching, taking notes, and asking questions during the construction. Professor Mbozi was as fantastic at material construction and laying wards as he was at teaching classes and being sarcastic, and I had volunteered to do everything he would let me do.

I would learn everything. As long as I was making progress and going forward, sorrow didn't exist.

Mbozi had actually done a spell on me at one point to determine if I was either cursed or being compelled to be enthusiastic.

Chapter Twenty

But thanks to his work, his awesome class syllabuses, and his somewhat patient teachings on site, I was totally going to enroll in the engineering program now that the provost had activated my class transcript.

After asking my three dozenth question, Mbozi had told me that chaos wards needed to be set up in areas already touched by chaos. Otherwise, chaos needed to be *infused*—a far more dangerous task. Since we were putting the vault right back into its original spot, we just needed to do the material construction and the warding. I felt pretty good about my reconstruction abilities—I now knew what I had been missing before—Debrout's beam, duh.

I started constructing small containment fields based on the vault wards and embedding them in devices, ala Will. I just had to find a private spot on campus touched by chaos magic so I could test.

And there was really only one spot for an obsessed optimist determined to succeed—the three mountain circles of pure, untamed chaos magic where sane mages rarely ventured. A place that accounted for *eighty-five percent* of the cases on campus where mages had not been successfully revived.

Sane mages didn't go there.

I packed up my bag and trotted toward the fog barrier shrouding the tenth circle.

Chapter Twenty-One

THE MIDLANDS

THERE WAS A TREMENDOUS magical backlash occurring all the time at school—magic intrinsically messed with all sorts of physics—and the twisted energy needed to be released, sorted, and defragged, just like it had in Ganymede Circus. A knot shaking itself free—a lumpy section of the layer vibrating until it was flat.

Therefore, the twisted energy was funneled to a place where it could explode, twist, and morph at will, without endlessly endangering students and staff. That somewhere was the Midlands. It was the magical exhaust system, the "flush of the magical toilet." Every magical fume was directed to the Midlands, from the bottom of the mountain up, and from the top down, collecting in the middle in a chaotic, misfiring, compost heap of the magical.

I imagined a wonderful place full of magical whimsy and strange industry.

My first impression was exactly that. Upon passing through the smoke that veiled the Midlands, the territory became a mish-mosh of ecosystems and illusions: swamps, rain forests, deserts, oceans, mountains, and post-Apocalyptic cities. Exotic creatures scampered and soared.

My second impression involved rage-induced slobber and certain death. And whereas the path had been smooth upon entering, as I was sprinting flat out with a humongous roaring troll-beast thundering behind me, the path magically turned rocky and fierce.

I threw myself across the misty border and onto the grass of the ninth circle, landing poorly as I rolled and whacked a warning sign.

I scrambled behind the sign and waited for the troll to burst through the smoke.

Nothing emerged.

Clutching my chest, hoping that my racing heart wouldn't kill me first, I shakily edged around the sign. Obviously, I couldn't just enter the Midlands, throw up a field, and start painting. I laughed a little hysterically and walked warily along the barrier.

I stepped carefully through the barrier four hundred yards to the west of my previous position. An entirely new landscape of dense woodland immediately surrounded me.

Whether the troll was real outside these levels or an illusion that purely existed within didn't matter. Unlike the practice rooms which simulated reality, the Midlands made things real.

Four mages in battle cloaks appeared suddenly a few hundred yards away, their backs to me. They started creeping forward—away from me—spears in their hands. A monster with horns and a forked tail appeared suddenly behind the group, stalking steadily after them. I opened my mouth to yell out a warning, but the mages and monster blinked from existence like a channel that had been suddenly switched.

Monsters, trolls, and unidentifiable beasts appeared and disappeared at will. As I ran, ducked, and dodged different hairy pursuers, I passed a leopard-sized dragon, three large mechanical praying mantises, and a school of piranhas flying through the air before they too vanished.

The one simple line in the research book—that mages were hunted here—was unforgettable in the midst of the melee.

Finding a solid structure to inhabit that had four walls, locked windows, and impenetrable doors went on my checklist as a must.

As if on cue, a crumbling manor collapsed, then the bricks stacked themselves and smoothed into an obelisk.

Ok, finding a building that stayed *solid* was a must.

I looked up. Like the fish, other strange things flew through the skies. But it seemed far safer to be up in the canopy than down on the ground. I took a quick breath and climbed an oak with solid branches. A moment after gaining my position, there was a huge crack and the tree started to fall.

I hung on for dear life as the wind and leaves whipped across my cheeks, and the ground rushed up to meet my face. *Christian, I'm sorry.* I closed my eyes at the last second.

But the tree continued its plunge right into the ground without damage. I kept my grip tight as we whirled in the ensuing darkness. Moments later, the top of the tree lifted, pivoting us into place in an entirely different landscape.

Breathing hard, I clung to my large branch and let the tree take me on a roller coaster ride through the Midlands as it ported and pivoted through a hundred different spots.

* The Midlands *

The landscape shifts were unnerving at first, but they were so frequent that they quickly became normal. And they were...tiled. The tiles weren't the same size—one could be a few inches, another a hundred yards, but each tiled section of earth moved, collapsed, and reformed as a unit as if it was a piece on a game board.

The shifts themselves were not a problem once I became used to them. What I could never count on was what I would shift next to—like a yeti or chupacabra.

Two students died during my first two days of reconnaissance, their companions whisking them to medical. I stayed as far from anyone or anything as I could get, which usually meant perched up a tree. There was a vast ecosystem that lived in the canopies, though. Like firesnakes. And lizards and monkeys who moved like lightning and threw magic.

And some of the trees...had a sweet tooth for mages. Ensuing nightmares of barked tongues and grasping branches caused me to examine trees carefully. Christian's voice was always most upset and insane after a mage-eating tree episode. That feeling of being trapped was bad for both of us.

Guard Rock had emerged from under the bed and tucked himself into my bag after my first eventful day. As if he had read my need, he had been my constant companion in the Midlands ever since. He was quick with his pencil jab and proved to be a good listener, occasionally gesturing to me with a small rock hand.

I had never dodged and dived so much in my life—not even in Draeger's training or running drills with Christian. I had been accosted by no less than fifteen unknown-to-me species of animals and plants.

Since the territory was a hotbed of churning energy and magic activity, the levels sometimes attracted attention from those pursuing adventure. Students traveled in groups, though, since death here was off the Academy's radar. Even some of the gutsier combat mages, who came here to train, did so in pairs, just in case.

Bar one.

My second afternoon was very pleasantly spent huddled in a non-mage-eating tree, watching Alexander Dare battle demented yetis and giant, animated rock beasts—quite unlike my loyal little Guard Rock. Dare wore a black, buckled cloak similar to ones I had seen other combat mages wear, but his...was magnificent. It moved like an extension of his magic, and it was like watching liquid metal. *He* moved like liquid metal. Mercury moving in glass.

It was hard not to watch him. More even than his astoundingly good looks, the way he held himself and moved drew my eye to him—and my

245

pencil to paper.

Mages were either arrogant or desperate to come to the Midlands alone. After a few notable observations, I was pretty sure Dare's arrogance was earned from being a badass in everything he did. Sometimes a fellow mage in a black cloak would accompany him, but it was rare. The combat mages seemed to be tasked with patrolling the Midlands. That made things dicey for me sometimes in trying to stay unnoticed.

Because the landscape of the Midlands shifted so frequently and quickly—and I always shifted with the tree I was in—many times I just caught quick glimpses of Dare. But each time I saw him, I felt the pull. I wanted desperately to ask him about the night Christian died and about his missions with his uncle in the First Layer, but I couldn't afford the connection he would easily make.

I saw no one as frequently as I did Alexander Dare. It was almost like he was hunting me, instead of the thousands of predators surrounding us. By the third day, I had researched and erected a shield that would make me invisible to one specific person. An anti-ex enchantment, hilariously enough. I set it to respond to Dare, but he always seemed to find me anyway. The shield was taxing to maintain and made me collapse in exhaustion at the end of each reconnaissance mission, but visually, at least, it seemed to work.

But there was always something about the tense set of his shoulders that suggested he knew there was someone else nearby.

I was far from unhappy that he was frequently my unwitting companion, though. He had unknowingly saved me countless times due to his proximity and prowess.

Like the flotilla of rabid croc-geese that were waddling around on their webbed feet, sniffing out my tree with their snapping jaws, and propelling their knife-sharp feathers into the base. He moved faster than anyone I had ever seen—twirling, then knocking his staff into the ground. A quake shook the earth and the croc-geese were expelled in four directions, swept away with a multi-directional shift in the landscape. I cataloged his movements to memory so that I could draw and animate them later.

I also collected some *great* intel about how he looked without a cloak or shirt when he was hot and sweaty. *Great* intel.

Ensconced safely in the branches of another tree for the third day, I settled in for another bout of shirtless drooling while buildings formed and disappeared, and I drew and took notes. I wasn't furthering my needed goals fast enough, which made me tense and anxious, but reconnaissance had advantages.

The pleasant feeling of using my magic heavily—working my bones off with Draeger, Stevens, and Mbozi every day, with Will and Nephthys (and sometimes Mike) mentally at night, and being surrounded by chaos magic for much of the rest of the time—made my body happily lethargic. The tiring workouts produced a gratifying physical ache.

But there was an itchiness between my shoulder blades that wouldn't ease, no matter how I tried to shake it out.

I had started to register it as my magic further escaping the cuff, increasing my need to touch the tube of paint. Safely under the nearly completed vault wards, when Mbozi wasn't looking, I had started sneaking in moments of uncapping the tube and sniffing the comfort of the lavender paint.

The itching increased and I scratched the skin near my cuff.

I looked down to see Dare engaged in some very complicated martial arts forms. He obviously wasn't going to be finished anytime soon, so I was stuck. I always tried to keep quiet when he was around. If I alerted him to my presence audibly, I had a feeling that he could easily break through the shield enchantment hiding me from view. But the wind was currently howling through the trees, covering most sounds.

Normally, I would be nervous in the current scenery of dilapidation and devastation—I had firsthand knowledge that zombie-like beings hid out in these types of places in the Midlands—but I always felt safe when Dare was near.

Stupid, really, as he would likely just as soon destroy me due to my Raphael Verisetti connection. But my first encounter with Dare had been too intense to overcome. Seeing him utterly destroy everything that launched an attack here had only strengthened the feeling of protection I associated with him.

My shoulders itched.

I touched my latest ward device and the tube of paint. I could chance one test...I needed to see if it worked, and with the wind, Dare wouldn't be able to hear a thing, engaged as he was.

"Do it, Ren," Christian said.

"Let this go, Ren,"

I flipped out my notebook, balancing in the fork of the tree's branches, and started drawing a 3-D space, using what I had learned from all my previous attempts. I rotated the box in my mind, shading the areas underneath and behind the box's edges with my magic. I shaped it much like I would my cornerstone pyramid, only the focus was a flat holding space. I put forth the intention that it would be able to hold three small acorns.

Pressing the ward device box, a small field activated a foot around me in all directions. I breathed deeply, then carefully twisted the cap off the paint. Its seductive magic hit me instantly, settling the itch. Dare stopped his form dead and his staff came whipping out as he looked around. I froze and Guard Rock immediately pulled his pencil into attack-spear position. Dare crept carefully along the path, his eyes cataloging everything.

My focus was on Dare, but the peripheral feeling of a million eyes suddenly watching me took hold.

His gaze settled on my tree and his eyes started drifting upwards, his shoulders tightening more.

Panic hit me full force as his narrowing eyes focused on my invisible position. His hand started to lift upward and I could see violet magic gathering in his palm. My panic turned wild, and the path tile abruptly changed, throwing my tree into the middle of an urban wasteland, far away from Dare's intense eyes.

Breathing harshly, I clung to my branch. Hopefully I was all the way on the other side of the tenth circle.

Guard Rock relaxed, sitting back down on the branch with his little rock legs hanging over the edge. Zombies liked the urban wastelands too, but Guard Rock had developed a good feel for them. If he was relaxed, I'd trust his senses.

I checked the encapsulation field, which was still up, then shakily tipped the tube. I would never try this again in Dare's vicinity.

The sudden feeling of a million eyes touched me again. There was an abrupt stillness to the already unnaturally still landscape.

I touched the edge of the tube's mouth, then touched the page and focused my mind, intent, and control on what I wanted as the paint absorbed. A box, with depth and dimension. A box that could hold the one pound weight that I visualized in my mind and felt in my palms.

The paint seeped and the edges of the box sharpened. Excitement lit, internally and seemingly from all around me as well. I stuck my now-clean finger on top of the box and willed it to rotate toward me as I pulled my finger down. The box followed my finger. Smiling, I nudged its top aside. The inside was just as I had imagined it. I plucked three acorns from my tree and placed the first on top of the paper. The acorn sank inside, as if a surface of dense liquid had suddenly given way.

A crow let loose a caw in the distance.

I smiled down to see the acorn resting inside the box. It lay flat in a seemingly two-dimensional space, that now contained a three dimensional object.

I dropped in the other two acorns as well. It required a few tries for everything to get sorted, but I could fold the paper and still retrieve the acorns intact and without negligible mass or weight loss. I'd have to test that scientifically later when I set up my lab.

I stepped carefully from the Midlands thirty minutes later and waited for a member of the Justice Squad to come.

No one came.

Smiling fiercely, I made my way to the library to meet Will and Nephthys. I hadn't fallen out of the tree, gotten eaten by a yeti, or received a citation, and I had used paint.

Suck it, Marsgrove.

~*~

I experimented with encapsulation field modifications and tested small drops of paint on projects, but by the time Monday arrived, I still hadn't figured out how to claim a building. My exhaustion was nearly overwhelming, and if I wasn't careful, a yeti was going to claim me as a meaty prize instead. I tightened up my mental pyramid construct to keep my magic alert, but it cost energy resources. Every time I used a drop of paint, I had to fight to retain magical control an hour later, making me work my pyramid cornerstones to their limits.

And campus events seemed to be growing crazier—as if part of the Midlands insanity was following me past the boundaries. A silly thought. They had specific enchantments in place to prevent such things. It had to be that I was just better able to identify the weird stuff popping up on campus everywhere.

Christian's evil voice was growing more demented and his sane voice more wistful and cautious. I was becoming terrified that if I didn't retrieve him quickly, I might lose him completely. I had a thousand soul purification rituals to try. I just needed a moderately safe place to try them.

Opportunity intersected with determination finally on Tuesday morning, the fifth day of my Midlands search.

A building with the letters OKAI emblazoned over the doorway had repeatedly drawn my eye. It looked eerily similar to a building I had drawn for Christian back in the second or third grade. I had gotten angry with him over something stupid while finishing the sketch, and had overlaid a Gothic roof with jagged tiles that threatened to impale anyone who came too near the stoop.

There was an intoxicating thread of magic that came from the building every time it appeared near me—magic that was sympathetic with mine. Magic that stroked and snapped, both embracing and dangerous.

The problem was that the Okai building tended to disappear the instant I walked toward it.

The other pressing concern was that I needed to locate the building in the future, no matter where it popped up. Standard maps didn't work in the Midlands.

I activated my new and improved encapsulation field, then spent an hour making a map dragon and imbuing my own experiences in the Midlands into his consciousness—creating a little beast that wasn't afraid to fly and catalog the Midlands on paper. A concentrated drop of paint later, I carefully removed him from his paper sketch. He flapped his parchment wings and roared out streams of papercut-sharp confetti, then dove downward through the leafy canopy.

I watched the paper I had removed him from and sure enough, as he soared across the Midlands, the lines of the buildings and landscapes started to sketch themselves on the page. I doubted the paper magic would be able to handle the landscape shifts in the Midlands—yet. But cataloging what was actually here at different points in time would definitely help. Tiles tended to attract to their same neighbors over time.

I drew and released three more dragons from the paper and sent them out in different directions. Lines, landmarks, and buildings began forming on the sketch like a possessed Etch-a-Sketch. I made it so I could zoom in or out at will.

A burst of sweat wet my brow as I stared at Okai, which had stayed in my view while I had been sketching and using the paint. I still needed to secure it. *Need* rocked me.

Gold the hue of Mr. Verisetti's spell glowed from under Okai's entrance door, and opportunity presented itself with one thought.

Maybe I could use *myself* to hook the location.

I squeezed a bit of lavender paint onto my forefinger, then channeled my need between the still-expanding map and the real door of Okai. I pressed my painted finger against the door in the map as I concentrated. Both began to glow.

I secured Guard Rock, threw everything back in my bag, shimmied down the tree, and jogged toward the building. It abruptly disappeared, and the landscape changed. My shoulders fell. Christian was screaming again.

My map suddenly glowed, and I felt a tug. I stared for a moment, then followed the tug, keeping my eyes alert for predators and the strange magic swirls that sometimes twisted down the urban streets. I rounded two corners, then three, then the tug abruptly settled, and the Okai building was in front of me again. As if *I* had gone around the block, but it had never moved.

This happened three more times—but each time I was able to approach a little bit closer before it disappeared, as if the building was skittish, but slowly growing accustomed to me.

I took a deep breath as I successfully made it onto the eerie stoop, then touched a painted finger to the real door. The ground shook, and I closed my eyes. At least if I blew up in the Midlands, the chaotic magic would contain the blast.

The shaking abruptly settled and I cracked an eye to find both myself and the building intact. I cautiously opened the door.

Square load-bearing pillars dotted the open single-room space. Dust bunnies littered the area, hopping around.

I carefully stepped onto the parquet floor, thankful it was sturdy, and locked the door behind me. I quickly weaved the spell I had used in the art studio, but this time to check if anything nasty was waiting for me. No trip lines or magic holes presented themselves.

A large staircase at the back of the room lead up to four smaller rooms and a bathroom.

One room contained rows of empty bookshelves. Another contained pedestals and ritual bowls. The third was empty. All three rooms returned neutral results to the spell checking the space.

The fourth room...returned sharp black and white beams. Cracked mirrors surrounded a glossy and undamaged full length Cheval looking glass in the center of the room. I avoided looking in it for no rational reason. Icy chills and visions of fairytales filled me: *Snow White* and *Beauty and the Beast*. No good came of magic mirrors in the sharded worlds of Grimm and beyond.

I closed the door firmly behind me, put shield and alarm wards over it, and decided to set up shop on the ground floor.

There was a weird silence to the building, enhanced by the sweep of wind that flowed over the jagged roof tiles every three or four minutes. The brush of branches, the creak of boards, then silence again.

Creepsville. My new home away from home.

I carefully removed and activated the device I had made just for this moment. Ward lines transformed the space around me into a five-by-seven-by-five enclosure. I would figure out a way to increase the size and permanently attach it to the building later tonight.

I set up my supplies: a large piece of canvas carefully smoothed and affixed to a frame made from wood I had gathered in the Midlands, some paint I had mixed with Stevens, tubes I had purchased from the Art Expressionists meetings, three brushes, six charcoal pencils, some scrap paper. Materials easily stored in my bag for exactly this purpose.

Guard Rock tumbled out of the harness I had made for him, walked over to the front door, and thumped his pencil stick before standing at attention.

Charcoal, brush, and paints in hand, I took a deep breath. "Ok, let's do this thing."

A butterfly—a *real* one—flew free an hour later, soaring to the ceiling then back down to perch on top of Guard Rock. Its wings whispered gently. Guard Rock shook himself and the butterfly took to the air, fluttering up the stairs and away from view.

The exhilaration from my success rocked through me, making me dizzy with adrenaline. I could do anything.

Like free Christian.

"Yes, yes, yes!"

"No, no, no!"

I did a quick sketch, then painted without thought, bursting color onto canvas in some mad Pollock liberation. And the magic burst with and from me.

I could see paint splatters seeping into the floor and around the canvas, but it barely registered, as my creation took form.

The tension in me unwound and stretched, emptying from me for the first time since I'd arrived in the Second Layer. Finally, a place where my magic could fly free without consequence. Magic slipped happily past my cuff.

The features of my brother took shape and he became more and more real on the canvas. I concentrated everything I had on my memories of him and projecting them onto the page.

"Yes, yes, yes!"

"No, no, no!"

I added the last bit of lavender shading, then tentatively reached inside, fingers dipping into the canvas. A thrilled shudder shook me. I touched his wrist, which was cool, but firm and *real*, not paper, and pulled.

Just like the butterfly. Just like the dragons. But real. Come on...

Paint chips fell to the floor.

"Ok." I nodded. "Ok." I grabbed my notebook and tried the soul binding ritual I had been saving up. The backlash knocked me into a pillar. When I finally regained my feet and reached in to the canvas again, dried brown leaves emerged as crumbled paint. And again the second time, and the third. A repeat of my fruitless efforts in my bedroom.

I tried another ritual. Guard Rock started running toward me on his thin rock legs a second before the backlash knocked me clear across the building floor. When I awoke, Guard Rock was pacing on my chest, spear pointed outward. I lifted him, gave him a pat, and dragged myself forward, my head pounding more fiercely than the worst migraine I had ever experienced.

A quick look at the time indicated five hours had passed while I was unconsciousness.

One ritual per day. Right.

But I was running out of time. I narrowed my eyes at the painting and thrust my hand inside.

"Come on, Crown!"

My hand gripped and tugged something free. The lack of resistance sent me falling to the ground.

I stared at the laurel wreath coronet in my hand for a long time. And as I exited the Midlands it burst into flames.

~*~

Bruised, confused, starving for lunch, and determined to do better—while also figuring out a way *not* to ignite my brother when I got him back—I entered Top Circle paying only half-attention to my surroundings.

"*Tricorn!*"

Tricorn?

But, in the magical world, I had figured out quickly that when people yelled things, it meant:

A) you should run;

B) you had to watch for other mages, for as a society they ascribed to the well-used rule that you didn't have to be faster than the bear, you just had to be faster than whoever you had tripped in front of the bear;

C) that you should pay special attention to the exact word being yelled, so you'd know what you were running from.

To fulfill Point A, I started sprinting. B had me quickly sidestepping a particularly sly looking mage with dirty blond hair and errant feet. And, C had me thinking of the American Revolution and men with bayonets and pointy hats charging after people in retaliation for dumping their tea. I could imagine people shouting about reading leaves in the harbor.

A horse with three horns wasn't quite what I had in mind. But when it shot toward me, I quickly changed course and adjusted my mental image.

Tricorn. Got it.

The animal was fast. And it could fly. Well, more a flying gallop, but it definitely was leaving the ground every few strides.

It was faster than I was, and the dirty, blond-haired mage was extending an ankle. I darted to the side before he could trip me—thank-you, football drills—and he swore loudly, then got poked in the rear by a tricorn horn. He leaped forward, leading with his hips, yowling profanities.

"Ha!" I threw over my shoulder. "Creep."

I dashed behind a tree as threads of offensive magic raced toward the tricorn. It sidestepped and ducked as the multiple flashes converged. Then it rolled its head and flung three jets of magic, one from each horn.

I edged around the tree, back pressed to it as people shouted and booms sounded on the other side. My headache had cleared right up with the triple-shot of adrenaline.

A guy ran past me with a sword, charging toward the melee. Seconds later, I watched him flee in the other direction, his rear lit with blue flames.

I needed a weapon. I rummaged through my bag looking for possibilities. Pen, no. I could barely remember how to draw a square at the moment. Though, if I threw some paint on something, maybe a squad member would show up. Notebook, no. Justice tablet? Maybe. But I didn't think the tricorn was going to agree to community service.

Why hadn't I brought my Marsgrove snare sketch?

A loud explosion rocked Top Circle, and a body landed ten feet from me, rag-dolled on the grass. His limbs were entirely too still—like Christian's had been. All I could think of was *ninety-five-percent* and *ten minutes*.

I automatically started for the boy, but loud breathing—huffing—stopped me in my tracks. The tricorn was on the other side of my tree, snorting and breathing heavily. I remained as still as possible, my eyes glued to the unmoving body splayed on the ground.

Not funny. Not at all.

Where were the professors? Or the Justice Squad? Or *whomever?*

Then again, here I was with my justice tablet, a law breaker *and* new purveyor of order. Who in their right mind was running this place and letting people like me dole out punishments?

I could hear a stamp and snort on the other side, and the rampaging tricorn took off again. I ran to the body on the ground and thanked all that was holy that I had read the first one hundred pages in my manual already. First Aid spells used campus magic and came standard on the tablets, due to all the accidents that occurred with magic offenses.

I snapped off a First Aid enchantment by pressing the clearly marked button. I wasn't in the least qualified to do more to help, though. I didn't think the guy would want me leaping ahead of the ten minute death limit, trying to raise him with my purely paper knowledge of how to bring someone immediately back to life or with one of my sketchy rituals. I'd probably make twelve toes grow out of the guy's forehead, even in death.

I kept an eye on the galloping horned beast. It was headed for a door opening in a building directly across from us. The opening door was the only movement in the now-still field.

It seemed a pretty reliable theory at this point that a tricorn's predatory senses relied on movement.

The person opening the door was screwed. Whoever it was had no idea what he or she was about to walk into.

I saw a slick pair of Mary Janes, before my brain clicked to the realization that it was my *roommate* exiting the building.

I lurched in her direction, chasing after the rampaging beast.

"Get back, Olivia!"

She looked up, startled, and froze as one ton of horse flesh lunged toward her.

I threw my tablet forward and magic shot up my arm. I shouted the first thing that popped into my head as the magic raced back through my arm and into the tablet.

"Toad Justice!"

Seriously? Had I just yelled that? *Toad Justice? What the*—

My intentions crystallized with the tablet's magic and flashed out, slowing everything in my view, as if I had hit a frame-by-frame option on a video. Movement to my right immediately caught my attention. I hadn't seen Alexander Dare there, but I saw him now. Whatever the tablet magic was doing allowed me to have just a half a second faster momentum than those around me. He was doing something with his staff. He was going to blast the tricorn before it impaled Olivia, but whatever I had done was going to get there first.

That meant my mojo was going to strike the tricorn, and if it moved the beast, then Dare's mojo was going to hit Olivia. With a surge of adrenaline, I sent a second pulse toward the clear ripple of Dare's spell, and prayed.

Time sped back up and the tricorn turned into a toad and my second pulse hit Dare's beam a split second before it hit Olivia, diverting it, changing it, and causing an architectural gargoyle to fall off the roof of the building and explode on the walk into little stone toad pieces at Olivia's feet.

Dare spun toward me with his lethal staff swirling, obviously expecting another threat. I held my hands and tablet up, cringing, and awaiting the blow.

He spun the staff away and kept it spinning until the energy wound down, and, I suspected, some of his immediate rage.

"What the hell did you think you were doing?"

His non-immediate cold rage seemed in perfect working order.

"Uh..." I looked at the toad hopping in front of Olivia. It had three conspicuous warts on its forehead. "Helping?"

Little wart bubbles of magic popped up and dissipated in the air, as if it was trying to cast. The tricorn toad looked pissed.

People were running toward us. Finally. And I saw Doctor Greyskull bend over the fallen mage, then saw the sudden rise of the mage's chest. Shaking relief seized me. An adult in a polka dot bow tie appeared next to us. He raised a brow, then conjured a cage and scooped the toad inside. "Well, I have to say that is a most...interesting...way of managing a tricorn." He nodded at me. "I'll tell Professor Wellingham what a fine job one of his squad members did."

I didn't correct his assumption that I was on the right side of the Wellingham service camp, but just nodded.

"Mr. Dare, fine job, as always."

Dare lifted his chin in acknowledgment as Bow Tie left. Then he stared hard at me—and not in an *I am in love with you forever* type of way—before turning on his heel.

I sagged in total relief, nerves catching up with the adrenaline. "Whew."

"You saved me."

I startled, having forgotten for a moment that Olivia was standing there. "Er, yeah, sorry about that."

"Sorry? You are sorry you saved me?" she demanded.

"No, no." God, I sucked today. "But it seemed all under control. That Dare guy would have zapped it." I jammed my thumb over my shoulder, as if I wasn't referencing the hot guy on whom I had a stranger crush. I might have to rethink that crush thing, though my brain was refusing to re-catalog him yet.

"He was definitely going to save you," I said. "I had to use another jet of magic to avoid catastrophe." With his blast taking out part of the building, I somehow didn't think he had been intending to turn the tricorn into a toad.

"You used another blast of magic?" Olivia asked in a deadpan manner.

I waved the tablet. "It was this, not me." I hugged it to me. I loved it already.

"Magical items are powered by mages."

"Yes, but believe me," I said. "I suck at magic." Otherwise I would have had Christian back by now.

I thought of the laurel wreath. Soon. Soon I would make it so that I could do anything. So that I would never lose him or anyone else I cared about.

She observed me through narrowed eyes. Then she turned and started back in the direction of our dorm. I hurried to get in step with her. Maybe this would be our turning point, and we could be friends.

"What are you doing?" she demanded.

And...maybe not.

"Er, walking back with you?"

It was amazing how eloquent I could be. Olivia and Dare seemed to be continually impressed by my prowess.

"Why?" she asked.

"I want to?"

Amazingly eloquent.

Christian snickered. I was relieved to hear it.

"Is that a question?" Olivia demanded.

"I suppose it was. You don't seem to want me to walk with you."

She said nothing for a moment, and I almost changed my course in order to leave her alone. She shrugged. "Do what you'd like."

I took that as tacit approval. "Ok. I think I'll walk with you then."

"Fine."

"Great," I said.

"*Fine.*"

I shut up before I could undo my progress. We walked in silence for about a hundred yards, before she spoke again.

"Where did you get that?" She pointed to my tablet, which I hadn't realized I was still clutching.

I tucked it carefully back in my bag. "Professor Wellingham issued it." Maybe she wouldn't know—

"You finally did something bad enough to get community service?" She looked disapproving.

"Er, yes." I rubbed the back of my neck. I suppose she hadn't ignored all those service calls after all.

"What did you do?" She was looking at me coolly, as if I'd murdered twelve mages in a blood sacrifice of epic proportions.

"I sort of blew up one of the art complexes."

She looked as if she would have been more supportive of the bloodshed. "That was you?"

"Er, yeah." I rubbed again.

"And they issued you a justice tablet for your ill deeds?" She shook her head. "When I'm in charge..." she muttered.

"Hey, apart from the brush with accidental death at the hands of a combat mage, the tablet came in really handy. Maybe they should issue one to everyone. Save the hotshots the trouble."

She gave me a distasteful look. "Lots of people have weapons. There is an entire mage force at this school that carries them. Having a weapon means nothing, if you lack the courage or self-preservation to use it."

I felt like maybe she was giving me a compliment in there, but then again, maybe she was calling me an idiot.

"I'm glad you are ok," I said, pretending it was the former.

She stared at me through narrowed eyes, then sniffed. "Thank you, and thank you for your help."

I hoped she meant it, and that she wasn't just following the rule of good manners. But Olivia's manners seemed to be impeccable, cold, and unfeeling, so I couldn't be sure. She would probably thank the gum on her shoe, if it was required by the magical version of Emily Post.

I decided to press my luck. "Why did it take so long for the professors to arrive?"

"Excelsine has a strict student-led policy. The Justice Squad and the combat mages are in charge of our security. The professors are on the advisory council and used as the last resort. They consider it good practice for real life." She looked coolly at me. "Then again, they are putting law breakers in charge of campus security, so perhaps it is time for a change in policy."

I laughed nervously.

"Who assigned you to community service?" she asked.

"The provost."

A tight smile worked over her lips. "I see."

She obviously did, but I didn't. "Why does that matter?"

But she didn't say anything and we finished our trip back in silence.

Ren Crown secret lair = +10
Ren Crown secret crush = -5
Ren Crown roommate situation? I tentatively decided to put it at even.

Chapter Twenty-Two

SERVICE WITH A SMILE

I ARRIVED PROMPTLY at eight Wednesday night for my first bout of community service but with horrible, chartreuse streaks coloring my hair.

Earlier in the day, I had conducted a soul-binding mirror ritual in the empty upper room of the Okai building that had backfired. I had thought for a moment that I had seen something in the mirror shard I had borrowed from the mirror room, but then...well, the mirror had tried to scalp me. I'd accidentally shattered the shard, and a gross, misty green substance had striped me down to my toes.

Soap had washed my skin, but nothing had worked on my hair. That was the last time I was attempting that Bloody Mary and lighter than a feather crap without the benefit of a sleepover.

Christian had alternately lamented my lack of past sleepovers and disturbingly talked over plans to collect nubile young mages as future sacrifices.

I didn't want Will and Nephthys to know what I was doing—I didn't think I could handle their disapproval—but maybe I could get them to try a group ritual that I knew would only hurt the magic caster—me.

I had tried the paint I had mixed with Stevens, and though not as powerful as the lavender, I was getting some good results with depth and shading. The lavender tube was half gone, so I needed to save it until I was sure of the test. Promising preliminary tests with my Stevens'-mixed paint would determine its use.

My magic was running more freely again. I was going to need Draeger to check my limiter once more. Events were getting close, I could feel it.

Standing near the coffeemaker was the good-looking, uniformed guy with smooth, dark skin and closely-cropped hair who had handed down my first offense. He was scrolling across a royal-blue tablet with his finger.

Chapter Twenty-Two

"Hi, I'm Ren Crown," I said, as he looked up.

"Isaiah Gellis." He smiled and barely glanced at my peculiar hair. "You are the student who took down the tricorn, right? Welcome to campus law enforcement." He smiled warmly. "I'll be setting you up. Did Wellingham show you how to use your tablet?"

"Briefly."

"Well, just keep your intentions pure, and you'll be fine. Easy to learn on the job." I pulled the tablet out as he talked. "The amphibian tablet is a great one."

I looked at it. It didn't have any resemblance to a frog other than the strange green colors that happily mirrored my hair at present.

"It turns people into amphibians," he said, holding out his hand. I handed it over, and he magicked something on the screen. "It's one of my favorites."

The tricorn toad suddenly made total sense. "I think...I think the tablet communicated with me." I didn't think I normally would have yelled "Toad Justice!" otherwise.

"Yes, the tablets are made of fantastic magic."

"...I can actually turn *people* into newts with this?"

"Yes, but they'll get better."

We exchanged smiles, and I thanked my luck. Peters would never watch *Monty Python*.

"Be careful, though. Service can be fun—it's all in what you make it—but if your intentions aren't perfect, you'll be the one to turn into the newt."

"So...how do I turn people, and why?" I really hoped I didn't have to go around yelling "Toad Justice!" at everyone.

"You zap them. But only if they resist." My blank stare must have registered with him. "There is a practice mode. Here."

He handed me the tablet and grabbed a pink eraser from a large bin. "Only use the practice mode on these erasers, though. I mean that." He shook his head. "Or else you will turn into the newt instead. You can push the round red button in the corner of the tablet display or funnel your magic through."

Funneling my magic? I thought of the roses growing uncontrollably in the engineering classroom, then replaced the image with frogs, toads, and newts. For now, pushing the button, it was going to be.

"So what is the deal with the tablet colors and size?" Other than Greyskull's, they had all been strangely hued. "Wouldn't something the size of a card be easier to carry around?" Or a cell phone?

"The tracking magic could be used in rings and holograms and magic manipulation, but the karmic magic strains and storage systems require a bulkier container." He shrugged. "A smaller item would require a mage to manipulate universe space, and only one mage type can do that. And that mage type would send people running scared *without* justice magic on their side."

I blinked and opened my mouth, but he waved my question off.

"Don't listen to the whispers. There hasn't been one in three decades. Back to the tablets, beside the necessity of their size, the unmistakable colors of the devices make it plain you are a justice wielder or service provider. Trustworthy."

A ringing noise sounded through the room, and Isaiah checked his tablet. "Lousy timing. Level Four offense. I have to answer." He stood and picked up a messenger bag. "You should only receive ones and two's tonight, unless the rest of us are overloaded. We have a few bad nights every so often. Be a shame should you get one your first night, though. You have your manual handy?"

"Yes. But I stuck it in my tablet," I said nervously.

"Good. That was a smart thing to do." He smiled. He had a very reassuring smile. I felt infinitely better about campus law enforcement already. "I programmed an emergency code for my tablet into yours, in case you run into trouble, but I think you'll do just fine. Refer to your manual, take your time, don't let anybody bully you, and above all, keep your intentions pure. The tablet will take care of the rest. And if you get a call that needs reversal, send it to the Neutralizer Squad."

He started walking backwards toward the door. "Check the manual on how to do that. Just in case I don't see you again tonight, stay here in the break room, so that anyone here can answer your questions, or accompany you, if needed. After a few days you'll get comfortable with the procedure, and it won't be necessary for you to report in here, if you'd rather not. You will be able to answer calls from anywhere, as long as you keep mobile."

I nodded and watched him go. The break room was ominously silent in his absence. Ok, practice time.

I put the eraser on the floor, aimed the tablet at it, took a deep breath, and punched the button.

A bolt of red flew out and connected with the eraser. BAM. A toad croaked in its place. I stared, wide-eyed as it gave another croak, then a small, uncoordinated hop. It adjusted, then gave a steadier hop.

I grabbed another eraser.

I had zapped seven erasers, before I realized my toad population was getting out of control, and I didn't know how to turn them back. The first toad managed to make it out the door and another two wedged themselves under the large refrigerator box, before I figured out that aiming the tablet and double-tapping the red button turned toad four back into an eraser. I zeroed in on toads five, six, and seven in a display of shooting around tables that pumped the same primal urge paintball produced. Christian would love this.

"Definitely," he said.

"Eat them! Eat them, legs and all!"

The refrigerator toads were hunkered down, so I looked for the lone escapee. It had only been about two minutes, but the long corridor was empty and the hallway toad was long gone. Concerning. I had no idea what happened to them if they were left magicked.

I tried to coax the refrigerator toads out with some lettuce, but they refused to budge. I tried zapping one, but it seemed that the more time they spent as toads, the smarter they became. It dodged left on the first zap, then right on the second. Toad two taunted me by doing a cartwheel to escape the last blast.

Two uniformed students entered the room, while my butt was raised to the heavens and my face was pressed to the floor.

My cheek turned hot against the cold tile. The toads smirked at me. Well, I'd kind of feel bad zapping them at this point, so I gave a wave of defeat and hoisted myself off the floor.

The girls snickered and exchanged glances. I wondered if it was the "newbie" type of glance or the "new troublemaker" type.

"I just completed a three day stint on duty, do you know why we are being called in?" one girl asked the other after staring at my hair, then dismissing me completely. I tried not to touch the strands in response. There was nothing I could do about the black magic backlash right now. If I didn't work off the punishment or transfer it to someone else, another worse punishment would simply replace it.

"Level Four somewhere in the Midlands. And we need teams of four to enter."

Seems I had gotten out of there just in time.

"Ugh." The other girl looked down at her bubblegum pink tablet. "Source and aspects are clouded, as usual. I hate going there. They should just pave those levels."

"Right. Some of those creatures don't exist outside of the Fourth Layer. Some of that magic can't be found anywhere but in the Fifth. The research professors would have a cow. Besides, the whole mountain would probably explode. Just in case you are feeling extra slow—that means you would too."

Two more students joined, giving them a group of four, and they left, cursing.

I fiddled with my tablet, less keen on turning more toads until I could figure out what happened to them. I decided to scan the manual instead. The tablet was quite ingenious. And using it was a little like using a First Layer tablet computer. Learning how to maneuver through the screens was quick—especially for someone who lacked basic survival skills and had far too much curiosity. Click, click, click, went my fingers. I only got zapped twice, and luckily they were electric zaps instead of amphibious ones. I figured out how to change my first name from Florence to Ren in the student and administration directory. I considered making my last name Brown to throw off Marsgrove.

More people came through the room. They'd look at me, snicker, then their tablets would issue alerts. Maybe I'd just be the local sideshow here. I could only hope.

My tablet bleeped before I got the full "p" out of hope. Then bleeped again. I took a deep breath, then activated the map spell to track the calls.

Before long I had two Level One calls under my belt—a student misusing a homework spell and another who had melted a magical book. The calls were similar to my own lower level offenses, but I was on the other end, doling out the punishments. Both offenders had looked highly amused while I had hemmed and hawed, trying to discern appropriate punishments.

My third bleep was a whopper on the meter—a Level Three. Technically, Isaiah had said I wasn't supposed to receive those the first night. As I trudged to the sixth floor of Dorm One, two more bleeps registered on my tablet. Judging by the number of calls I had already received, and the number of uniformed students in groups of four running down the sidewalks and through the arches outside, something big was happening. I keenly hoped they didn't destroy my secret lab in the pandemonium.

I checked the two newest calls on the tablet display—one Level Two and one Level One. I continued on my course to the Level Three, since it still registered as the most urgent.

It was suddenly apparent why sometimes a Justice Squad member showed up right after I committed an offense, and at other times it would take twenty minutes.

I stopped in front of room one hundred sixty-nine. "I69" was on the door—the number one having been changed into the letter "I." If the occupant had picked this room himself based on humor value, I was probably going to find some kid on the other side that had tried to turn a toad into a hot date and ended up with a troll.

Sighing, I knocked on the door, tablet in hand. I didn't know what I'd do if there was a troll on the other side. Zap him with my tablet, I guess, and wonder what a troll toad would do. Which made me think of the Troll Bell ritual referenced in one of the necromancy texts. It was supposed to secure a spirit to a bridge of the caster's specification. The bridge, luckily, was metaphorical.

But I still had to find the bells and I had assiduously avoided trolls in the Midlands since my first incident with one.

Maybe a troll toad could lend me some. Far better to try that ritual next than the ones involving goats and guts the *Black Grimoire* advocated. Or the five human sacrifices referenced in the book *Bob Jones Studies the Dead—You Can Too!*

I knocked again.

I could hear someone moving around inside, but I had to knock three more times before the door opened. I was already irritated, but the lazy smile that greeted me upped the level.

"Forgive me for taking so long," drawled the tall boy who Professor Stevens had proclaimed the bane of her existence. "If I had known *new meat* was on the other side, I would have moved more quickly."

His dark hair was too long in the front and the back, and he was extremely good looking in that charmingly sordid and insouciant "I buy the best designer drugs and use them frequently" way that old money kids sometimes had.

I was supposed to read him the riot act on getting a Level Three, but the first thing out of my mouth was, "You stole my firesnake skin."

"That was you?" He looked me over, tall gaze resting on the tablet in my hands, my ugly green hair, then my lack of uniform. "I used it well."

"You stole it."

"Larceny is one of my many faults." His smile didn't reach his surprisingly sharp eyes. "But I am being remiss as a host. Welcome to the club."

I darted my gaze between creepy, hot thief and making sure my exits were clear. "We're in your dorm." I said gently, irritation folding beneath forced calm. I had found that was the best option with people on a high.

He laughed. Even that was dark, sparkling, and edged. False, like black champagne. "Exquisitely new."

I hadn't thought to ask, but I wondered if I should be on the lookout for creature-blooded students. It would just round out my day to have dark and sparkly here be an incubus or vampire or, I don't know, some kind of soul-sucking demon.

"There are demon wards on campus and creature-blooded students attend schools in the Fourth Layer with the rest of the hybrids. I'm surprised you don't know that." He lazily twined a long dark ribbon around his finger, piercing eyes at odds with his seductive smile.

Great. Either he had read my mind, or I had just voiced my thoughts out loud. Odds were good on the Ren scale of tiredness and stupidity today that it was the latter. I expected Christian to make a comment, but he was silent.

I sighed. "Sorry about the demon comment. Listen, I'm here because the meter registered a medium level of bloodshed in this quadrant."

"Yes. That was me." He was still smirking down at me, lids low over his eyes.

"You aren't supposed to be practicing blood magic outside of class."

"That's correct."

"I have to write you up."

"If you must."

I checked my tablet. This job sucked. Not that I was looking to make friends with the guy who stole my first firesnake skin, but what better way to make everyone on campus hate me, while simultaneously showing all and sundry that I didn't know some of the basic magics that other mages threw around likes shallow smiles.

And all while having a really bad hair day.

"Ok, I have the truth spell activated for writing in this thing. That means if you tell me your name is Old MacDonald, and I write it down, it will reach out and zap you. Which, frankly, I don't know if that means you get electrocuted or toadified, so best just to be honest, ok?"

"What if my name is Old MacDonald?"

"Then we go to question number two. Listen, I have a feeling you've done this before, so if—"

"What did you do?"

Surprised, I looked up. "What?"

"What did you do to get community service?"

"How do you know I'm not a volunteer?" I hedged.

"It's obvious, and I know everyone on the squad."

I'll just bet he did. The guy looked and acted like he did something like this every night. And even though I was here to write him what probably amounted to his one hundredth magical ticket, he wasn't getting expelled.

"Do you pay off the officials?"

I wondered if the ticket enchanting magic would be satisfied with monetary payment for individual offenses. I doubted it. That seemed like cheating.

The left side of his mouth tightly lifted. "Dear Daddy makes sure I stay enrolled."

Chapter Twenty-Two

I nodded and fiddled with my tablet. "So...what's your poison here? I'm betting you already have something in mind for punishment." Probably something like writing *I will not relieve five more girls of their virginity then toss them to the curb the next morning* a thousand times. In blood.

"I want to know what you did first."

I folded my hands over the ticket tablet. "I respectfully decline your inquiry."

He looked more interested, and the ribbon shivered in the air for a moment, seemingly of its own volition. "I simply must know how you've joined the club."

Ah. His reference finally clicked, as well as the amused looks on the faces of my first two cases. I had realized I was the only one not in uniform in the break room, and it looked like that was a dead giveaway for repeat offenders.

"I get only members of the volunteer squad or the *select* club, of which you are now assuredly a part." He smirked. "The boring offenders don't go out on matters of true interest. But if you landed me...well, I don't register on the single night service roster. Not even on an exceptional night."

"I have more than one night to serve," I confirmed. I was likely going to run into this guy again during my two hundred hours. In fact, I'd probably run into him two hundred more times. Might as well be polite. "But the tale is quite boring."

"I am sure it isn't. So, either assuage my curiosity out here, or come in and do so over a drink." He smirked again. "It's fresh."

I thought about what the meter had read. "Right. Listen—" I checked the tablet just to make sure that the name I had heard uttered by the blond boy who had bought my firesnake skin and the girls in the library belonged to the guy in front of me. If the offender took too long to answer, the name popped up.

Yup.

"Constantine Leandred, I'm charmed and all, but I have two more bleeps after you."

The tablets were only supposed to register things directly related to the incidents—and only those mages who had been tagged as the offending parties—but still, the idea that these devices could be used for other things...well, it was disturbing. And it furthered the realization that I had basically signed away a decent number of rights—or Marsgrove had signed them away for me—in order to enroll in this school.

"A three bleep night. I'm enthralled. And devastated that you are passing me over so quickly."

He looked anything but devastated. The lovesick girl in the library had wanted to bespell *this guy* to love her back? I nearly snorted. He probably had a list of conquests as long as his designer clad legs. Slick and cool and slippery. The kind of guy in the movies who left a girl in the morning with nothing other the crushed feeling that she had been used hard.

And I wasn't attracted to him. I smiled, pleased with myself. An image of arrogant Alexander Dare without his shirt on flashed through my head.

Right. Perhaps I simply had my stupid crush quota already filled.

"Then you should join the squad, Mr. Leandred. I could let them know you are interested."

He leaned languorously against the jamb, like a panther resting. "Tut, tut, new meat. What did you do? Don't make me strip it out of you."

I tilted my head down toward my tablet, trying to decided what to say. I needed to figure out how to channel Stevens. No one messed with her.

When I looked up Constantine's eyes were narrowed. It gave him a decidedly more dangerous look, his languid posture turning predatory. "You are Stevens's new student." He said it as if it was the crime I had committed. "The other day in her personal lab—that was you. I saw you. How did you get service?"

I saw you, too, being a pain and a thief, I wanted to say.

"I accidentally blew up the lab we had been working in." I admitted, trying to make it sound as dull and non-newsworthy as I could. Stupid truth spells that were attached to the tablet made lying difficult and painful. I remembered Peters getting zapped, and what that had felt like on my end— so I had made sure to read up on it in the manual. You could make fibbing jokes only as long as you made it clear you were kidding. Who thought it was a good idea to send investigators out on criminal jobs and stop them from lying? "There. Now tit for tat, Mr. Tut-tut. What do you want to do about your punishment."

But Constantine's posture and magic now mirrored what his eyes had hinted from the beginning—a sharp and deadly focus threaded through his external insouciance. "You're feral. Newly magicked." The black ribbon jumped in agitation.

And he was decidedly Old Magic. Everything about him screamed wealth, privilege, and youthful waste.

"I can feel how feral you are. Yet Stevens took you on."

"I'm a transfer student." Curses looped in my brain. Feel it? He had to be lying or guessing. I had looked it up and normal mages couldn't just tell someone was new. "Now, pony up your punishment, or I'll choose for you."

A nice stint gathering firesnake skins was just what the doctor was prescribing. And maybe I'd hide behind a tree, at the ready to grab his first one.

"One of the art complexes exploded and an unbelievable rumor said that a chunk of the art vault landed in the Third Layer." His smile pulled wide, but his caramel-colored eyes were dark. "A rumor everyone completely dismisses, of course. As that would be...disturbing."

All of my danger alarms started ringing. Christian was suddenly yelling obscenities in my head along with his alter ego.

"So many rumors," Constantine said, pulling a finger along the edge of the door, eyes never leaving contact with mine. "I wonder how many apply to you?"

"Mmhmm." I feigned nonchalance. "And you are about to pull firesnake duty." The tablet dinged in my hand. Yes! The punishment would be accepted. *I needed to get out of here.*

"I will thoroughly clean the chemistry lab and prep all level one potions three times next week, by my magic I so do vow," he said, voice languid, but with an underlying intensity that had been missing before.

The tablet dinged and the magic wound around us, testing, then seeped back down. The tablet vibrated then lay silent.

I wouldn't get my firesnake retribution, but whatever, I was out of here. Two more calls, then I would go work off some nervous energy with Draeger.

"There hasn't been a newly feral student at the Academy in years."

"That's nice." I checked my pockets, as I backed away.

"And one with artistic aspirations who attracts the notice of someone like Stevens...you've been contacted already, I'm sure."

I looked at him suspiciously—more suspiciously—and stopped patting my pockets. "What?"

Contacted? Like Raphael Verisetti and whatever terrorist organization he worked for? How would this guy know?

Constantine Leandred smiled dangerously, as if I had answered affirmatively. "Watch your back, new meat, I'll be seeing you again." He shut the door.

I gripped the tablet in my hands. *Miss Angelie's School for Girls* was sounding better all the time.

~*~

I knocked on the door of my next call and scrolled the tablet a little more thoroughly this time, castigating myself as I did. Should have done this with Constantine Leandred. I was such an idiot. I needed to be far more paranoid.

I scrolled. Level Two Offense. Enchantment on Unknowing Student. Serial offender. Tracking device implemented and alarmed.

The door opened to a familiar face framed by black bangs and an outfit Erté would have designed.

"You." I narrowed my eyes on the girl from the Student Center. I needed to be far more paranoid, indeed. I looked down at my tablet, then back at her. I noticed the green band glowing on her wrist near her cuff. Alarmed, eh? Now that I had an idea of what was going on in this screwed up system...

"You were doing community service. They decided to make you man the Student Center for *community service?*" I really questioned some of the officials at this school. "And you got a Justice Tablet to do it?"

Delia Peoples smirked. "Hey, the tablet karma worked, didn't it? It read you and said you needed a map and that you needed to work on meditating. I just fulfilled those needs. In my own way." Her smirk grew.

"Great. Thanks a lot, Goat Turd."

She tsked, shaking her head and sending the ends of her black bob flying. "Temper, temper."

I narrowed my eyes, then smiled brightly. Her smile dropped to suspicion. "So, should I look through the list of punishments, before I ask a few pointed questions?"

I looked down, but could feel her shifting in front of me.

"Let's see. Level Two. Old recommended punishments include...oooh, waxing the entire entrance hall with a two-by-two piece of cloth and one toe. Kind of like mapping the hall, and that would give you a wonderfully long time for meditation and reflection. Or...popping camel zits. Wow. Who knew they even had them? I wonder where they are located? But that sounds too mundane for you. Hmmm..."

"I get it." Her voice was tight, with an edge of defeat that pleased me, given the circumstances.

I tapped my finger against the tablet, mind working quickly. "Name?" I didn't look at the tablet.

"Delia Peoples."

"What enchantment did you put into place that made your alarm bracelet ring tonight?" I worded the question very carefully.

Delia's eyes narrowed, then focused on my messed up hair. "That hair of yours looks like you've been doing some naughty things yourself. It was far too much fun playing a game with you, though. They rarely let me play around here." She lifted her wrist, shaking her bracelet.

I nodded pleasantly. "Please answer the question, or I will have to up your Offense Level."

"It was a suggestion enchantment."

Ok, that sounded like it could be really creepy, actually. I narrowed my eyes. "Who was your victim?"

"I—"

"Scratch that question." The magic complied. Reading that manual had been worth every minute of non-toad-turning time. "Who was the recipient of the enchantment that made your alarm bracelet ring tonight?"

Her teeth visually gritted together at the verbal modification. "Anastasia Kaparov."

I nodded, more disturbed. "I'll get someone to take care of the enchantment right away." I sent the designation into the tablet so that it would go on the Neutralizer Squad's list. They would reverse the spell and effects.

"What was the suggestion you attached to the enchantment that made your alarm bracelet ring tonight?" I asked, carefully structuring the words again.

"To take an exam for me."

The tablet didn't zap her. I felt my shoulders relax. Thank God. But I still put it on my list of things to research. I wondered about the strength of the anti-dust protection.

Maybe I could ask Stevens what normal people did to protect themselves. The chemical stuff, at least, was totally within her jurisdiction.

I had to take solace in the fact that the campus had this type of monitoring, though it had been through Delia's bracelet. That meant she had likely slipped some suggestions through before and gotten away with it. It also indicated that she had been reasonably certain that she would slip *this* one through too.

"Was that the only suggestion attached?"

"Yes," she said in such a disgusted manner, that I had a feeling she was not a huge fan of this Anastasia person.

That helped me make my choice. Though I would word it to leave the option up to the victim. "Do you agree—should she ask you—to do all of Anastasia Kaparov's laundry, errands, and cleaning for three days to the best of your abilities?" I had learned from the manual that the magic would make it so. Delia couldn't put reds in with whites, if she knew better.

She was watching me, her eyes narrowed. She didn't answer for a moment, but finally said, "By my magic I so do vow."

I smiled and tapped the tablet. "Great. I now consider us even." The tablet didn't zap me. "Do you now consider us even?"

Her expression shuttered for a moment, but then she got a considering look on her face. "I do." The tablet didn't zap her. "You are an interesting addition to the club."

I nodded. "So I've been told. I'm off to another call. It

was...interesting...meeting you again, Miss Peoples. I hope I can look forward to the next meeting."

She cocked her head. "Perhaps."

Well, good enough for no zap. I saluted and turned.

~*~

Service took up a lot of my time. So I divided my hours into blocks—working with Stevens, attending classes, working with Draeger, attempting to secure Christian's soul in fifteen thousand different ways, figuring out how to hide how magic punished me each time, answering calls, and working out all of the ins and out of this new world. Not in that order.

I guarded my cafeteria time zealously, and always met the others there, even though there were times I nearly fell asleep in my potatoes. And days when I bled through the bandages under my clothes.

I didn't know why I was having such trouble securing and binding my brother's soul. But I was losing a little confidence in my planning and execution abilities because of it. The rituals and enchantments should have worked. At least *some* of them should have worked. I wasn't used to failure.

Each day that Marsgrove didn't return was a gift. I wouldn't be able to get away with my deception twice. I developed some tactical art magic with Draeger—trying out snares and other art creations to formulate practical defensive and offensive uses—and kept my news feed running silently at all times.

Community service kept me on my toes. Not everyone opened their door willingly. Handing down punishments was a quirky business—some of the malcontents tried to be quicker than the tablet magic. I had ended up glued to the wall, thrown through a window, and blinded.

But I always got the perp in the end. Thank you, paintball. And my tablet always felt that an attack on us earned the perp double punishment, so it really sucked to be them.

After a punishment got logged, there was no need to do anything else. Magic was a funny and vicious mediator, I knew firsthand.

The karmic magic did its trick, and if it felt the punishment was satisfied according to the terms set down by the spell's creator, it rested without issue. The problem really was that last part—according to the spell's creator. Many of the repeat offenders had realized how to work the system to their advantage, while still serving their punishments, and the officials seemed happy and absent, using the service students for projects when it was convenient.

I leaned against the jamb of room one hundred sixty-nine in Dorm One. "Another Level Three, Leandred. You want lab duty again?"

Constantine folded into the high-backed leather chair he favored. Today

Chapter Twenty-Two

he looked like a weary medieval baron who had just surveyed his crumbling estates; projecting a jaded disdain with the world. Sometimes he was Loki—wearing a playful façade that wanted to cause mass mischief. Occasionally, he mixed the two. Luckily, he hadn't tried the seducer persona on me since the first few minutes of the initial call.

I'd been terrified to return on the second call, but he had been all languid insouciance—only showing the predatory nature that had been in evidence during the first call when I could see him in my peripheral vision.

I never forgot it, though. The evidence of it always simmered behind his eyes.

But after responding to five calls to him, I was used to his routine.

"If I must, Crown." He repeated the necessary words to bind him to his punishment.

I shook my head and let the magic wrap, then tucked my tablet back in my bag, moving my latest box sketch and reader to the side. The latest ritual text was waiting on my reader and I was eager to read it as soon as I got a free moment.

The absent thought that maybe the Ritual of the Troll Bells would work where the others had failed sifted through the forefront of my mind. As I was securing my bag back on my shoulder, I caught sight of something on one of Constantine's shelves in his huge and richly appointed room. My feet took me forward automatically.

"Are those *troll bells?*" I asked in disbelief.

"No." But he was smirking and playing with the black ribbon he always had nearby.

"Where did you get them?"

He lifted a negligent shoulder. "I can't recall. And they aren't for sale." His eyes moved to my bag. "However...for the right trade..."

I blinked. "I'm pretty sure they won't let me give you Justice Toad."

He looked unimpressed with the name I had given my tablet. "You have something else in there. A drawing. I saw it when you opened your bag."

I looked down to see my most recent box sketch. I hadn't put anything in the box yet. The drawing looked flat and uninteresting—what would prompt him to ask? "You want a sketch of a box?"

He leaned back in his chair, winding the ribbon around his finger and watching me. "How much does the space hold?"

I touched the edge of the paper, fingers feeling the flat threads. "How did you know...?" I shook my head at his knowledge and his raised brow. "It holds two pounds, but no more than eighteen inches in each direction."

His eyes never left mine. "I want it."

"Why?"

"Do you want the bells?"

I did. They were horribly hard to get a hold of, even by catalog—I had been trying to find some for weeks. I lifted the sketch and examined it. I could make another. Why did I feel reluctant to give it to him? Because it contained a drop of precious paint?

One drop of paint for the possibility of bringing Christian back?

I held out the paper.

He looked at it, then back at me. "Will it to me, when our hands are both upon it."

I did as he asked and felt magic zip through my fingertips and travel across the page to his. I let go as he pulled the paper to him. I ticked off a research task in my mind. Ownership transfer. That was why Marsgrove's paper had been reluctant to serve me.

But...Marsgrove's paper had served me. I unticked the mental box, modifying it to ask why I had been able to use the paper without an ownership transfer.

Constantine carefully put a pencil on top of the paper, watched it disappear, then retrieved it. He had obviously either seen Marsgrove's paper or one like it, as he knew exactly how to work it. And since I had modeled my design after it, they worked the same way. He looked decidedly gleeful—as gleeful as Lothario could look—before floating the bells over to me, his eyes barely leaving the paper. "A word of advice, Crown," he said in his satiny voice. "If you make more of these, keep them hidden a little better."

I elatedly checked over the troll bells, nodding absently to him. I went through all of the ingredients and objects I needed in my head. I had everything. I could definitely try this ritual tonight and push back my other Level Three ritual to tomorrow. The rituals were supposed to be spaced out more, but I could handle the aches, pains, and fractured bones that doing them one day apart got me.

I wished I could handle the consequences of doing more than one in a single day, but in addition to gross physical ailments, I lost track of time, passing out for long hours that would be far better spent with research and other smaller trials.

"You have no idea, do you?" The satin of his voice turned gruffer.

I looked up at him, then over to his shelves again, not following the thread of his conversation. The ceramic container that sat innocuously on his shelf was the same one I had seen him with the first day in Stevens's lab.

Constantine, as one of Stevens's primary students, was often in and out of her lab while I was there. I had the sure notion that he was trying to figure out what we were doing. But since we were always making art supplies, there wasn't much to uncover.

I should check into what he was keeping in that container. I had suspicions.

"No idea about what?" I asked.

The predatory look was back for a moment before he smoothed it out. "Keep your sketches like that out of sight." He waved a hand, his ribbon following the motion. "I'm feeling decidedly helpful toward you. But I always collect on helpful advice given." The edge of his mouth lifted.

Predatory.

"Well, I'll just have to disregard it then." I smiled and turned.

The one foot satin ribbon was suddenly six feet long and wrapped around my left wrist, turning me back toward him. He said nothing, but his eyes were piercing, and the satin binding tightened.

Then, abruptly, the smooth ribbon trailed from my arm and shortened back into a twelve inch decoration hanging from his hand.

Nothing further was said. But I purchased a security folder to hide my box sketches in.

~*~

The Ritual of the Troll Bells turned out to be...complicated and painful.

Three hours after beginning it, I limped to Nephthys' room. Since I had started necromancy testing with abandon, I had fried my hair, caused it to fall out, turned it horrible colors, burned different parts of my body, and lost three fingernails.

"Sit right here." She gracefully pointed to her dressing chair.

I perched delicately on the plush brown cushion. I had needed to attach the troll bells to every imaginable part of my body, and the resulting burn marks...fiercely burned.

She produced a bottle of sparkly gel and a stack of light gauze pads. "These will absorb the burns fully in time."

She squeezed the gel onto a pad, then pressed it against my arm. The pad...absorbed...into my arm. The relief from part of the pain made me abruptly sag. The burn scar looked as if it had been healing for a week.

I closed my eyes. "I love magic. Thanks, Neph." Being in Nephthy's presence was an automatic relaxant, in and of itself.

"Of course."

She asked me about classes and projects as she applied the salved pads to the rest of my singed areas. If Neph didn't ask me soon about what I was doing to get this injured, I was going to start wondering about life back at the Sakkara Institute. She'd calmly produced a bottle of nail glue last time I'd come for a patch job. Glue that *made* nails instead of repairing them.

"What about you? How have practices been?" I looked at Neph. "Did you want to redo your choreography tonight? I can tweak the animation in any way you need."

"You need to sleep, Ren," she said soothingly. "The animation is lovely as is."

I mentally squeezed in a block of time in my overly crammed schedule to do it tonight anyway.

There were too many things I needed to do and so little time. I crossed off the bell ritual from my mental list. It had produced a ghostly image of a shrieking bat. The shrieking had sounded a little like evil-Christian in pain, but a bat was not what I was looking for.

I touched the burn marks at my waist as she worked. Bells had been strung, like a loose belt, all the way around. It was just a good thing nothing had been attached to my neck. Even healing at seven times the normal rate, those marks would have been hard to hide.

"No, I feel great. Tonight, I insist. I can tell you have been working on different moves." I looked around her room. There were well-worn paths of magic in the air that spoke of repeated practice.

"You are seeing magic better." She tilted her head, then placed the next gel pad.

"Practice." I grimaced. "Hideous practice." With all of the defensive magic I was using in order to protect myself in some of the rituals, I was getting far better at identification. That, and now that we were back in the vault, Stevens was upping her expectations of my performance, so I had been working extra hard with Draeger in the Battle Building.

I had even unknowingly connected through the building to Alexander Dare's room during one practice session—my magic unconsciously connecting to his—and been squished to a pulp in under thirty seconds while we "sparred." More like while he sparred and I had been tossed about. Lying spreadeagled on the ground afterward was the first time I had heard Draeger snicker.

"I'm coming back tonight and we are working on your choreography animation," I told her, pointing my finger.

She smiled and finished applying the gel pads.

~*~

I was happy to see Isaiah in the Squad's break room that night. He motioned me over. "How is it going?"

I shrugged, then winced, the burned skin at my back pulling beneath the healing salve. "Well?"

"Good to hear. You missed the thousand shrieking bats that appeared in the middle of Top Circle earlier." He shook his head. "Had to call in the combat mages to help. Strange things happening around campus. Things appearing and parts of the mountain being blocked as if chaos magic is running amok."

"Blocked?"

He waved a hand. "Things that worked previously with magic, but now suddenly it is as if their magic or...or *space*...was sucked dry. Arches or spots turned non-magical or altogether ceasing to exist. Some geology mages said there were a few small magic zones inside the mountain that have been petrified recently."

Huh. Strange things were always happening around campus. And magic often influenced magic. Therefore, maybe my ghost bat had simply been a reflection of whatever had happened on Top Circle. Annoying, but it meant that if I tried the ritual again, maybe I would get something else.

I pulled out my mental list and made the appropriate modifications cheerfully, removing the strike-through from the bell ritual. I made a note to procure burn cream in advance of my next experiment, though.

My third service call was a welcome distraction from thinking about the failed ritual.

"Will!" I exclaimed as he opened the door.

He looked surprised, then grinned. "I wondered what you had been sneaking off to do these past few nights. Welcome to the club."

I beamed. And now I understood what Will had been talking about weeks ago with his shady club references. Justice magic made it so that punishments couldn't be discussed with others.

And I had figured out quickly that it was an unstated rule amongst the repeat offenders that club members chose their own punishments. One never knew when another miscreant was going to land service and be in charge of *you*.

I was beyond relieved that I could come clean about having community service with someone I knew. Leftover concerns about friends turning their backs on me had lingered. "Thanks."

He motioned me in. "Come on, you can write the ticket in here. I just got off community service two weeks ago. They assigned me research to work off my offense hours." He closed the door behind me. "Best punishment ever. I was given a tablet for two months to record my research. They cost a firstborn child to purchase otherwise, since they require origin magic. *And* I got to meet you and get an adventure."

He walked over to his desk and poked a slim black device that looked to be mid-creation, and pushed it under his papers while winking at me. "Too bad the tablets are so difficult to duplicate that no one tries."

Obviously, Will had used his time with his justice tablet well.

"I'll show you what I'm doing." He motioned me over.

I walked forward, curious. I had never been in his room before, since we usually met in the main library. Unlike Constantine's luxe pad, Will's room space was much like mine.

Half of the room was filled with sports equipment and posters—Mike's side, obviously. The other half was filled with dangling devices and strange objects. A workbench, instead of a desk, lined Will's side of the room, with a loft bed overhead. The sword from the sketch was hanging horizontally on the wall above the bed. A mark on the floor was smoking.

"This the problem?"

"Yeah. Don't step on it."

I scooted back. "What does it do?"

Will looked around furtively. I mimicked the action. I had thought we were alone. He pulled out a scanner and hit a button, then set it on the workbench. "New project."

"It looks like you have quite the mad scientist setup here."

"Thanks!" He looked at my tablet. "Do you mind activating the pause?"

I stared at him blankly.

"You tell the tablet that you are off the record."

I looked down at my tablet, and did so.

Will glanced at his scanner, then relaxed. "That gives us five free minutes."

"Oh. That's nice to know. I am only on page six hundred and fifty of the manual."

Will laughed. "Yeah, the user manuals are kind of dense. Most people don't bother getting to page thirty."

"So what are you up to?"

"I'm working on portal pads."

"Really?" I wanted to try one, but Marsgrove's restrictions on me would probably make me disappear into a black hole forever.

Will leaned forward and pushed his glasses up, clearly warming to the subject. "The best ones on the market only come with ten programmable destinations. I think I can increase that to fifteen. And my goal is to make them infinite. Your gophers inspired me."

I thought of the trivets sucking the gophers inside, then popping them back out. "Er, if someone's magic goes crazy, couldn't someone get sucked in and never return?"

He waved a hand. "Sure."

I imagined myself stuck inside the pad's rubber-looking threads...on Mars.

"I have the makings of a device to limit that though. It funnels only the correct amount of magic."

Chapter Twenty-Two

My body automatically took me a step forward. I didn't have enough money or nerve to order a magic controller from a catalog yet—and most of the catalog control devices had a distinct infomercial vibe—but I was beginning to grow desperate as more of my magic kept sneaking out and I kept having to redo my pyramid structure to control it. For some of the more hardcore rituals, I really needed something to funnel the *exact* amount of magic through the first time.

Will looked down at my feet and nervously motioned me to the side. "Until the spot stops smoking, stay at least twelve inches away."

I decided to take a seat in a chair to the right—after checking it over thoroughly to make sure there weren't any disappearing elements on the surface. "So, this funnel device...does it work on everything magic-related?"

"It should." He cocked his head. "Are you having control issues?"

"Er..." I suddenly felt like I was about to admit to incontinence. "Most of the time I get a grip on it, but when I want to be precise—" Like when I was working on anything Christian related "—I want to be *precise.*"

Will nodded. "I'm sure you'll work the problem out. Everyone eventually does. You want to try the device?"

His easy acceptance helped me relax immeasurably. "Most definitely."

"Ok." He fished around a drawer and pulled out a googly, tentacled thing. "It's a little...obvious right now. I haven't been concentrating on it. Hmmm...maybe I should do that." He started fiddling with something. I recognized that look. It mirrored mine on many occasions.

"Yo, Will?"

He blinked up at me. "Yeah?"

"Er, how about I just try the funneler out as it is and see what happens? And you can concentrate on your portal technology."

"But I can now think of ten ways to make the funneler better. Especially if I fit it to you. Do you like headbands?" He looked at my wrist. "No, a bracelet would be better. I could use separate threads in the leather band. And I could fit it around—"

"Will?"

"—the magic in your veins. The junction of the ulna and radius make a good channel to separate two magic streams and then bring them back together—"

Huh, that was interesting, and my mind started traveling down that path.

"Grab the sword! Suck out his soul!"

Christian's crazy voice snapped me back, and I noticed the heat gathering in my tablet. "Will?"

"—under the wrist guard. Because a ring might separate the magic incorrectly through the separating channels, so—"

"Will!"

"Yes?"

My tablet had started burning my fingers, and it was radiating through all my other burns in some twisted sympathetic magic. "How about we take care of your punishment first, then talk more?"

"Oh, right. Tablet starting to warm?"

"Yes."

"Here." He put two tongue depressors together and wrapped what looked like Saran wrap around them, zapped a bit of magic into the junction, then handed it to me.

I stared at the contraption he had made, then looked at him blankly.

"Sword, soul, suck!"

"Right, put that on top."

I did so and the heat released from the tablet and from my other burns—a pleasant by-product of the sympathy. The junction of the sticks went red for a moment, then cooled.

"You should have"—he paused and cocked his head—"ten more minutes, I think. We best keep it at eight, though."

"Wellingham said I'd be expelled if I tried to change the enchantments." I looked at Will's door in dread, waiting for Peters to bust through.

"Oh! No, this doesn't change anything, it just...reroutes the focus for a bit."

"Ok." I wondered if I could use something like that for death. A death release? I settled more comfortably into the chair, happy that I was pain and expulsion-free for a moment.

"So, how have you been doing with service?" he asked.

"It's not terrible. A little embarrassing. And I've had...moments."

"Some of the members of the club are notorious pranksters."

"Yes." I thought of being stuck to the hallway ceiling. That had been less than fun. And when I'd ended up thrown out into the bushes that one time—it had taken hours to pull the prickers out of my hair. "Since the pranksters have been turning into toads, though, the pranks have trickled to a stop." Isaiah had shown me a handy enchantment that activated the tablet's magic automatically if someone was "attacking" me while on duty.

"The amphibian tablet is a great one. I got stuck with the flower tablet last time." He grimaced. "Couldn't get the rose smell out of my clothes for the first two weeks. And if I left it running too long, violets would bloom underneath. One still grows from a crack in the wood of my desk every few days."

I hid my grin behind a cough. If the violet colored tablet created flowers, I hoped that meant Peters was perpetually producing canaries. "So, how are you testing the pads?"

"I've only been working with the scientific and magical constructs. I'm still deciding what to send through first. I'd really like to send a golem of some sort."

"You have blob matter?" Blob matter was similar to human matter and featured highly in the references to a number of darker necromancy spells on creating golems. I hadn't found a good book detailing the matter yet, though, as it was a taboo subject.

"Not yet. Making golems is restricted—the ability to make new creatures scares the pants off the politicians. Has ever since the War of the Hybrids." He frowned. "I don't want to send a live mouse or gopher through the pad, until I have credible data. And a mechanical mouse just isn't the same."

I had given thought to using paint on a sculpture instead of canvas, so I was semi-familiar with at least the periphery of the topics he was discussing.

"Maybe I can help you get some."

He smiled. "That would be great, but I'll probably delay that until spring, when I get permission to travel to the Fourth Layer. Hopefully the customs embargo will be lifted by then—there is a faerie infestation hex; the faeries are revolting against the system."

I blinked. I had seen pictures of the Fourth Layer in the library, and it was a darkly fantastic place filled with every sort of fairytale enchantment and childhood nightmare—a little like the Midlands, but spread over the entire Earth with distinct societies instead of random events. Vampires and werewolves were real there—human/animal hybrids that were created long ago. "What about catalog orders?"

He shook his head. "Blob material is not allowed through the mail system. It has a highly dark magic classification and there are tracers to prevent its transmission. Though"—he looked around, then at his scanner again—"one can procure many things through club channels."

Certainty was growing in my mind. "Do you have a picture of it?"

He shook his head. "It's dark and reddish. You ever see *The Blob*?"

I nodded.

"Like that. That's where it got its street name."

"Professor Stevens's group might have made something like that in the lab," I said carefully.

Will raised both brows. "Stevens? She'd be more likely to send me through the portal to test it myself than to make blob matter for a student. Though, she'd definitely be capable of creating it and be permitted to use it for research purposes."

I'd have to make a quick trip to the library after service.

"Hey!" he suddenly said. "Maybe I could use one of your paper gophers.

280

Have you gotten the kinks worked out?"

I shook my head. "No, but we can try making them again next study period."

"Great. I'll try those in the interim. Club channels will procure blob matter sooner or later, if I can't find it otherwise. Speaking of which, we should get on task."

He pointed at the enforcement tablet and I removed the sticks. I could feel the tablet come to life.

Will looked directly at the tablet. "I am working on a school project doing deep research that involuntarily triggers alarms. The magic I am working on is not officially prohibited, it just tweaks the system."

The magic from the tablet swirled, then settled. I lifted my eyebrows at Will's explanation, and he continued speaking.

"I will try and keep this research from triggering alarms in the future. In order to repent for this offense, though, I swear to clean the transportation research facilities for two days. By my magic I so do vow."

I looked at Will sharply and tried to empty my mind, as the tablet magic wound around and did its thing. I didn't want to jeopardize Will's punishment with my thoughts on the matter.

The magic settled and Will nodded to the clock on his wall. Later. He would tell me later. I rose from the chair, and he cheerfully stepped around the charred spot on his floor. "See you later, Ren!"

"Bye, Will."

Cleaning the research facilities, eh? I'd just bet. Oh, they'd be clean when he was done, but it just reinforced the notion of how "punishments" were used to further magic offenders' goals.

No wonder all of the Academy floors were squeaky clean.

~*~

"I am a seeking mage! Like the ancient diviners. Do not speak to me like that!" a girl screamed shrilly.

"You haven't found anything yet," was the snide response.

"I will."

"If she can't find him, that means the mage is powerful," another girl pointed out. "Possibly...rare even."

The group exchanged looks.

"We should grab the appropriate equipment then," one said grimly.

I kept my head down.

I had a thousand other things to do, but Will wanted blob matter, and I had a chance to get him some.

I buried my head in the index of my fifteenth library tome, then randomly flipped through. Because of the restrictions on time spent in the

Chapter Twenty-Two

reading rooms, I tried to be selective about the texts I chose before entering the room. I always used the full time, though. I couldn't seem to help myself.

Even after finding the information I required, I would keep sifting through chapters, threading ever deeper into practices and studies of magic—the pulsing veins of it seemingly just out of my view. It simmered there on the edges. I felt that if I dug deeply enough, I would find the answers to everything.

This was the real danger with the reading rooms, especially to someone like me who could become forever lost. I fingered the large data disk that would save my research. It was a risk to save information on the blacker subjects I searched for, but I needed to make sure I didn't miss anything or incorrectly copy data. I'd erase the disk later.

Texts on black magic housed on the lower floors contained theoretical information, allowing students to do research projects, but nothing practical. Frustratingly, black magic texts in the Second Layer were highly regulated and watched. There was no legal way for me to obtain texts that would give me step-by-step instructions. I had to obtain my information the hard way.

I selected three cards full of competing theories and entered a room.

The grid flew up to greet me, lines formed, words flashed, and soon I was diving through threads and intersections.

"All three agree that blob matter has a shelf life of thirty-nine days, in three thirteen day stages, beginning with the day it is used for the first time. See intersecting point five hundred and thirty-two for information on preservation. Should the matter be preserved correctly without use, then a mage should be able to maintain the matter in a stable state for six months. If at the end—"

I rotated the grid with my hands and searched for seedling points in the data. I tagged a few nuggets of light to return to—places where pictorial intersections occurred, places where the magic sometimes didn't know what to do with the information. A dozen ways to make magic recognize pictures invaded my mind, and, as usual, I had to suppress the divergent paths my brain wanted to take. One project at a time, Ren.

The tiny, hard nuggets in the grid...those were the speculative intersections. Places where the text and magic was parsed and re-encoded to show lists of things that the authors didn't explain.

I had come across my first one during a thorough search of three beginner's texts. I would have dismissed it as dust in the air, but I was used to looking for small things and creating them myself. For finding or inputting that one tiny poppy in a painting that pulled all of the rest of the scene together.

I sifted my hand through the tiny data point.

"It is illegal in all regulated layers to create or use blob matter. An infraction is subject to—"

I pushed it to the side and touched another. I had heard all of the dire warnings a hundred times in these texts. They popped up at me in big, blaring magic letters and booming voices.

A second reading room realization had come after speaking with Neph. It was my magic that influenced the reading room. The experience of a room was unique to the mage controlling it. I was seeking out this type of information, so nuggets of that type would "float" to the surface, so to speak. Another student's magic might not think to look for such things, but their magic might find something I missed.

I guessed it was like reading or viewing anything. People absorbed, interpreted, and used data differently. Even as an introvert and someone who worked well alone, such a perspective made working with interesting people exciting and dynamic.

I plucked a red nugget, spreading it open, then yawned into my upper arm. Doing these searches always exhausted me. But it was worth it. The end of my yawn turned into a silly grin. The nugget contained a list for creating a golem from blob matter based on corroborated sprinklings throughout all three texts. It also contained a dozen dire warnings: death, destruction, and taxes, should a mage attempt creation without a permit. There were no directions given, but all texts agreed *on* the ingredients. I flung the chart toward my well-used storage device with a smile.

Two far smaller nuggets, each with a corona of black, were nestled at the back. My smile grew. I folded the grid around and to the sides, bringing the nuggets toward me.

A list for creating a doppelganger.

A list for creating a new being.

Some of the tension in my shoulders released. Here too, only a list of ingredients was given, and not the amounts or directions, but it was a beginning. Because of the dark magic associated, the cost of making these enchantments would be high—far greater than burns, bruising, or the loss of my hair. I could worry over that later.

I gently pushed the lists to the device and watched as the information sucked inside.

I smiled and deactivated the cards, as the first warning bell sounded to indicate my time was up. I yawned again around my smile. Perfect.

I stumbled out of the room and collapsed into a chair. I was going to have to do some plotting. I would get some blob matter for Will, and keep a tiny bit for when I was ready for Christian.

Chapter Twenty-Two

It was all moot until I secured Christian's soul, but my paint had animated a *rock*—a rock that thought itself my guard. Like some mad sculptor or Geppetto and Pinocchio, all of this was worth further study. Clay and metal sculptures and life-sized dolls—making a new being from dirt, if I had to. I would start making molds right away while resting between rituals. *Something* would work.

I could only imagine if the roles were reversed...Christian, my seat-of-the-pants twin, would rush in with his charisma and ingenuity blazing on all cylinders, succeeding by a thin margin and laughing all the while, as he planned moment to moment. I, however, was the boring planner twin. Perhaps in this instance it was a point in my favor.

I would never be raised in time, if the situation were reversed.

Smiling, I yawned and made my way toward Dorm One while plotting a new strategy.

Professor Stevens was particular and exacting. She didn't make the kind of mistakes most people might. But as Will had said...club channels. I'd bet anything that blob matter was what Constantine Leandred had stolen from the lab that day.

Chapter Twenty-Three

OF BLOBS AND MISTAKES

THE TERRIBLE, HORRIBLE, BEAUTIFUL MAN still had it sitting right on his shelf. In plain view. It looked like a perfectly normal ceramic container—one that would normally not demand a second glance.

I pointed at it. "Ok, Leandred, what's it going to take for you to divide your blob matter with me? And what the hell are you drinking?"

One perfect eyebrow went up. "A perfectly shaken martini."

"You're eighteen."

"I will be nineteen in four weeks. Remember to buy me something. And I have the ability to both pour and consume liquid."

"Whatever. The blob matter?" I hoped we didn't share a birthday, if even a year apart.

"What blob matter? You must be mistaken." He took a sip, then nonchalantly dangled the glass over the arm of the chair, one long leg was slung over the other arm. His ever-present black ribbon hung loosely from a free finger.

I pointed again. "It's right th—" My finger jabbed toward a picture of a horse. One that hadn't been there a moment ago. Freaky illusion magic. I crossed my arms. "I know it's there. I saw you take it that day, and I just saw the container."

"Blackmail?" He hummed into his glass.

I frowned at him. "I'm not going to blackmail you, but do you need all of it? If not, I want to buy some."

He observed me over the rim of his glass, then languidly poked at the olive. "I'd blackmail you."

"No you wouldn't. Come on, what do you want for it?"

His lips curved in amusement. "I can't decide if you are foolish or brilliant. A bit of both, I think."

Chapter Twenty-Three

"Great. Blob matter?"

He gave an exaggerated sigh. "Fine. You can have one liter. But I want another box. A better one. And I want to design it."

His warning about hiding my box sketches rang in my head as his eyes held mine. I was getting that matter for Will and Christian, though. "We'll design it together. Deal?"

He watched me for a long moment, caramel eyes giving away nothing. Then he tossed down the rest of his drink and waved me away. "Tomorrow night, bring an appropriate vessel in which to contain it. I'm not chasing down blob separations."

~*~

I showed up promptly, ceramic vessel in hand.

"First thing's first." He smirked, then touched the skin on my arm. I felt a flicker of magic test me, then retreat.

He led me into one of two rooms that was always closed during squad visits, and again the magic flickered over me, verifying permission to enter. To my amazement, the room contained a fully equipped chemistry lab and large worktable.

The differences between my dorm and Constantine's were considerable. Constantine's five room suite was more like a luxury condo than a dormitory. I had no desire to enter the open door to the bedroom, but I wondered what was behind the other closed door. His mysterious roommate's secret lab?

Designing a box with Constantine was...interesting, to say the least. We bickered across the table for nearly two hours, but I finally started to construct three dimensional edges around the flat box in which I had originally placed *him*. He was actually brilliant when he was serious, just like Stevens had muttered. But his sincerity was short lived, as if he always remembered some part he needed to play. He preferred flashy magic and verbally shredding those around him, all while holding a martini glass and doing obscene things to the olive with his tongue.

Two different girls had stopped by to visit him while we'd been designing. He had fielded them in the living room, away from me, but I could hear them clearly enough. He hadn't been...kind...to them, though both girls had continued to sound hopeful as they'd left. Which made me seriously want to go out and shake them.

I drew the storage box to his specifications, then spent an additional two hours embedding protection wards inside it based on the ones I had set up in my secret lair. While in my zone, I didn't notice too much about what Constantine was doing, but he wasn't an amateur rule-breaker and remained quiet and stayed out of my way. In fact, a few times when he thought I wasn't paying attention, I had seen him working on another project, hair falling into his face as he worked out equations and formulas, black ribbon trailing across his papers.

Near the end, I had to excuse myself to make a quick trip to the Midlands to activate the sketch with a dab of paint. It worked perfectly. If I had thought he was gleeful before, the expression on Constantine's face when he tested the new storage sketch was downright smug. He immediately embedded a few protections. Anyone else trying to use or steal that paper was going to be sorry—and quite possibly disemboweled. I hoped he was never assigned to the service squad and in charge of anyone's punishment.

Finished with his project, I cheerfully walked back to the Midlands with Will's blob matter carefully tucked in a ceramic container in my bag. I looked around to make sure no one was watching, then stepped over the high northern border. Immediately, the tug toward Okai bloomed in my chest. I followed the feel of it, dodging three croc-geese, a shade bat, four zombies, and two crumbling buildings. The more I came to the Midlands, the stronger the pull to Okai became and the quicker the building appeared to me, glowing softly, as if it too was eager to work.

It appeared in front of me during the next Midlands shift. I smiled and entered, patting Guard Rock affectionately as I closed the door.

My lab was rocking now. I had put together a collection of workbenches and cabinets that I had appropriated from other buildings in the Midlands—a hazardous proposition as I'd nearly been eaten, absorbed, and swallowed by a number of unsavory things while dragging furniture around.

Guard Rock had poked at the tube a week ago and absorbed another drop of lavender paint while I'd been thinking about cleaning, and he now kept the place neat and tidy. He had no head, but he had nicely formed opposable thumbs and a fine precision grip. He had subsequently moved all of the broken glass upstairs into a storage box I had labeled "shards," but there was still a layer of dust about two feet in diameter surrounding the Cheval looking glass. Even he wouldn't approach it.

I had collected apparatuses of every kind, and was storing them as neatly as I could. I could really use some magical pegboard.

I yawned, then shook myself. I couldn't afford inactivity. There was a reason I had become a mage after Christian died, I *felt* it, and it was to bring him back.

I separated the bulk of the blob matter into a second storage container that I would give to Will.

But the smaller portion...

I picked up Will's regulator—which I had already tested—then withdrew a magic neutralizer I had procured from Chen Lifen, one of the friendlier members of the malcontents' club who had done a stint on the Neutralizer Squad. The neutralizer would allow me to do a test, and then when I was done, I could use the apparatus to return whatever I was testing back to its original state. That way I wouldn't waste precious materials, or produce a batch of hazardous ones.

The neutralizer would allow me to use the good old-fashioned scientific method on the blob matter. Change one thing, neutralize it, change another thing, neutralize that. A saving grace, as I didn't have a plethora of matter at my disposal. The original state of the blob was reddish-brown.

I made a note two hours later that I would need to regulate blob's desire to eat human flesh. Maybe it was just a symptom of the blob matter being a one-foot-tall burgundy humanoid at present—not quite a golem—but Mom would be none too chuffed if Christian ate our neighbors.

Perhaps I could get rid of his penchant for onions as a by-product of my testing? We could band together against our parents and strike them permanently from the menu.

I swallowed hard, then cleared my throat and swallowed again, trying to get the block out. I shakily wrote onions in the margin. I'd work on it, then tease him mercilessly.

~*~

"I am entering the Shift Festival," Will announced at dinner. The ecstatic joy from thirty minutes prior—when I had given him the blob matter—was still present in his voice.

I stirred my *caniopidas* soup. Tasty, but hot. "What's a Shift Festival?"

Nephthys cleared her throat. I looked up to see two of the other people at our table looking at me strangely, mouths agape.

"What do you mean, what's a Shift Festival?" one of them said.

"No, Ren said *Lift* Festival, which is what I heard you say too, Will," Neph said.

The skin on the back of my neck turned hot and pinpricks of discomfort crawled. Will already knew, and Neph had figured out *how* new I was rather quickly, though we had never discussed it.

Unfortunately, I had invited a couple of people I had seen wandering around to sit with us, then briefly forgotten not to ask magic world-related questions.

Will smiled brightly. Too brightly. "I...I have been working on a lift. Elevator charm. I think we need to tweak our translation enchantments again, though. *Shift* Festival. You know, the period between the fourth and fifth full moons every year when there are continual Layer shifts."

"Should have done something to eliminate them completely by now."

Mike looked grumpy as he set down his tray to join us. "Weather mages get all our big exams during that time because of the repetitive and horrific disturbances. The professors tortured us last year."

Will looked at Mike earnestly, as usual. "The yearly events keep us on our toes. Highly civilized societies need such things. The Nile floods in Egypt in the First Layer, the grasses explode in Taratanga in the Third, the Shumei rains fall in the Fourth...here, in the Second, we can count on the Layer shudders and shifts for scientific and magical advancement."

"So what are you going to do as a project, Will?" I asked.

Mike groaned.

Will leaned forward, brimming with excitement. "Well, the Layer magic is trying to work out the magic knots and kinks from all sorts of activity, but especially from those caused by traveling. We travel far more in the Second Layer than in any other. It is a daily activity to travel somewhere. Pinching, prodding, waving..." He tapped a finger. "Which is why part of my portal pad design limits the amount of impact on the Layer by *skimming*."

"Please." Mike put his forehead on the table, narrowly missing his mashed potatoes. "No more talk of skimming, I beg you." Mike looked up at me, eyes pleading. "He got a permit to test in our room inside of a small travel field. Now everything in our room has been skimmed. I lost a pair of shorts the other day when the pad flew over the top and sucked them into the abyss. Then the pad burst into ash." He stuck a finger up toward the ceiling. "Mike Bessfort's shorts—a flat pickle somewhere in the layer sandwich. Forever stuck."

"Maybe they will come flying out and whack you smack between your eyes, in the middle of the most important meeting of your life," I said. "Then you can exclaim—'my pickle, my pickle has returned to me!'"

"Hilarious, Crown."

"Or maybe your shorts are toxic," Nephthys said.

Will started snickering.

"Wow, the lot of you are simply a riot today." Mike pointed his fork around the table. "Will is going to end up as one of those extreme eco-mages, mark my words. Living in a hut without magic."

Mike's expression was deadpan, but I could see the sparkle in his eyes.

Will rolled his eyes, and directed his attention to me. "Lots of people don't want to get rid of the shifts, they just want to use the magic better—like Ganymede Circus used to do, funneling the shift magic through the dome and center statue, then pushing it into the shops. Mages use shift magic for everything from irrigation surges to capturing it for chaos events. Which provides fantastic research possibilities also. Last year I worked on a smoothing function that would unkink a small section of the Second Layer, then power a generator for a year."

The other two people looked impressed. "Nice, Tasky," one said.

Mike looked at us, expression deadpan again. "Ask him about the results."

"Er, how did it go, Will?" I asked.

Will had turned bright red. "The generator worked. It's, uh, still working."

"Wow." I was impressed. I wondered if I could use that type of energy alteration to power some rituals. Maybe I could use the power from another town like Ganymede? Unless Ganymede had used their shifts to power their daily reconstruction and other towns did the same. Huh. What about—

"And?" Mike's voice was coaxing.

Will started rubbing the back of his neck. "It wasn't so bad."

There were a few moments of silence, with Will looking agonized, before Mike turned to us. "He stripped the entire delegation of judges of their clothes, smoothing out every wrinkle for fifty feet by simply making any matter that contained a single tiny wrinkle disappear into his generator." Mike couldn't stop his smile from forming, though it was obvious he was trying to be the comic straight man. "Some lovely, lovely mages on the science and arts council. Gorgeous assets in that department. I never miss one of his presentations now."

~*~

I waved to a familiar face as I took the last set of stairs back down from Top Circle. If there was one thing to say about community service, it was that it provided a serious avenue for meeting people.

That had really helped me in other aspects of my campus life. I began keeping an eye out for anyone in the cafeteria who looked out of place or for the loners from the "club" and would invite them to join us. Such choices proved to make our motley table a pretty lively and interesting place to be. Will had started grinning foolishly before he even set his tray down. He had sported a downright sloppily drunk smile after the table-wide debate and antics concerning Foam Magic.

I desperately wanted Christian to experience this new world with me.

I stopped, panic gathering in my gut. I hadn't thought about Christian at all during dinner.

A figure covered in red appeared ten feet away.

"Demon!" Someone yelled.

"The terrorists must be here!" a girl shrieked.

I was forgetting my brother. Losing focus. Chatting like I was normal.

Worried about friends and fitting in.

Forgetting about my brother. For even a *moment*. I was a horrible person.

Nausea overcame me and I bent over.

"Demon! Everyone run!"

But I couldn't run. Couldn't move.

"It's powering up a killing blast!"

Emotion built within me, confusing and horrible. I just wanted things to be right. For everything to be ok. Magic blasted out from around my cuff. I heard an outraged roar, a terrifying boom, then all was silent.

~*~

I spent the next two days away from everyone and their crazy talk about demons, working with Draeger and Stevens and drowning in blob tests and rituals. Christian's voice would alternately urge me to move on with my life, then demand that I help him live.

I showed up in the cafeteria on the third day with bloodshot eyes. Everyone gave a soft greeting as I set my tray down.

I...I couldn't be afraid to live.

Chapter Twenty-Four

LIVING AND HELPING

EARLY ON, I had realized that if Olivia ate in the cafeteria, it was in a nook somewhere unknown to me. Because frankly, I had looked for her as a familiar face in a crowd of strangers and would have very likely attempted to sit with her in those early days, despite her obvious frostiness toward me.

But...what if Olivia ate in our room all the time? She had a fridge and a microwave. No one visited our room for her except to discuss class work. And through a semi-deduction of her shorthand, I had occasionally seen her check names off of her "minions" list.

None of those visitors were friends.

After the brush with the tricorn, she had thawed a little toward me. She didn't snap at me directly or give me frigid glares. The looks were more southern Arctic in intensity now.

In the grand scheme of her hatred of the world, I thought maybe I rated on her scale as "I hate you slightly less than most of the other people in this Layer."

In my new, tentative optimism, I thought, maybe if I made a few overtures, we could achieve a more harmonious relationship. If not as direct allies, then occasional conversational partners.

I made my move on a Wednesday morning. I had noticed that she was a habitual breakfast eater and had just run out of Bran Flakes, or whatever her dry looking stuff was.

"Um, so, do you want to go to the cafeteria to get something to eat?"

She didn't answer.

"It's time for breakfast," I tried again. " And, well, we have to eat, right?"

Her lips pinched together. I was about to let it go, when she closed her book with a thump. "Fine."

"Great!" I was entirely too excited sounding. "Wednesday is pancake-extravaganza. And they have tubs of melted butter and powdered..." Right. Bran Flakes. "And the cereal is always well-stocked."

She pulled on her sweater and gave me a flat look.

I kept up a steady stream of chatter on the way over, trying to repress any stray guilt-ridden thoughts about how I should be thinking of my research instead of chatting. Her eyes stayed narrowed on the building that housed the cafeteria. As if at some point it had done her a grave injustice.

We had come at the right time. We had the place pretty much to ourselves. People came in and out much faster at breakfast than with the other meals, and were generally either groggy or ultra-focused.

I didn't see any of the people I normally sat with in our usual second tier section of the cafeteria. Nephthys wasn't a huge pancake eater. Will and Mike were on opposite ends of my wake up scale—with Will rising earlier and Mike far later.

"So...I'm going to get pancakes," I said.

Olivia gave me an arctic look in response.

"I'll meet you once I get my tray. But if you find a table, I'll find you."

She nodded stiffly, and we went our separate ways.

I loaded up my pancakes with chocolate chips and powdered sugar, then drenched them in hot melted butter.

I was surprised to find Olivia at the end of my line holding her tray stiffly.

"Great! Let's find a seat," I said.

She followed me to a small empty table, and we sat on opposite sides. She gave my plate a disgusted look, but I just smiled.

"Pancake extravaganza day is not a day on which one should ever feel bad," I said, then swallowed and nodded to myself. Christian had loved pancakes. Celebrating pancakes was not an activity that necessitated guilt.

Finding joy in life was good. I repeated that sentiment to myself twice, forcing myself to believe it. If I couldn't find joy in life, then why was I trying to bring Christian back to a joyless world?

We dug in—me to my decadent, luscious pancakes, and she to her cardboard flakes.

Ok, so Olivia didn't dig in so much as take a ladylike taste after her spoon skimmed the opposite side of her bowl. And I wasn't totally without manners—or nerves—so I cut my pieces into small bites.

"So, do you have a focus, Olivia?" I could have tweaked my translation charm with Will's help to make "focus" into "major," but I liked the way focus sounded. The translation charms worked both ways, with the person speaking in a way best designed to be understood by the listener.

293

Chapter Twenty-Four

"I'm studying law."

"That is great." It confirmed what I had seen around her desk. Law was a very...mature focus. I had no plan yet as to what I was going to study as a focus. That I was studying necromancy at the moment was not for public exposure. I was pretty sure I was on the hook for some sort of art focus. "Law is great."

Olivia's eyes narrowed. What had I said? Did she take my nervous ramblings for insincerity?

Joyful world or not, I still sucked at communicating with my roommate. But law—I wished I'd had her to advise me before I'd been sentenced to a billion days policing the student populace.

"I think that is a great career," I stressed. "Are you going to declare?"

Disdain. "I declared the second day I was here."

I gripped my fork and took another bite. I knew I was an oddity who asked weird questions. Being reminded of it sucked, though.

Feral. God, I hated that term. It made me feel like some rabies-infested raccoon. Will had said three years studying in the magical world would wipe the title of feral from my record.

"The second day? The first day was full?"

Olivia's face grew cooler. "I have had no *issues* knowing what I wanted to do."

The implication was clear.

"Well, I have no end of issues. What's one more?" I tried to keep my tone light, but I just felt exhausted all of a sudden. I sighed. "Listen, I honestly admire that you have your career chosen and know your path."

Olivia said nothing, so I ate my pancakes in silence. The world was a joyful place. I tried repeating it twice more.

~*~

It shocked the hell out of me, when Olivia joined me for a late dinner the following night. We arrived fifteen minutes before closing time and quickly picked out our food.

Our conversation was...about the same. And there was more than a little of the sense that I had dragged her with me. But I had had a good day with Professor Stevens, I had learned how to manipulate space vectors in my secret lair without blowing anything up, and my blob was aging into a very fair imitation of a four-year-old. I could tweak that up thirteen years within a few days. I was riding a nice burst of confidence—my magic happily humming under my skin and riding through my veins.

So I chattered and Olivia relaxed a tiny bit—I hoped—and I considered the whole day a step in the right direction.

The workers had started to magically close down some of the kiosks and lines—flipping chairs and freezing machines.

I considered my roommate as she forked the last bits of her salad. "Would you like some ice cream? I know it's not a smart food, but it's a nice treat. And they keep the machines running until the last student leaves."

Her fork paused as she lifted it to her lips. "Perhaps," she said, with a touch of uncertainty—the first I had ever observed in her. "If one of the flavors is good."

Success! No one disliked ice cream. Though someone who was allergic to ice cream might not like it because it made them sick. And if someone—

"What are you frowning about?" she demanded.

"Just thinking about ice cream." I pushed back from the table before I could do something else embarrassing. "I'll return with information about the flavors."

I was checking the labels on the machines where you didn't magically have to mix the ice cream yourself—Banana Swirl again—yes!—and Strawberry—also, yes!—when Delia Peoples bounced up next to me.

"So, it took me three weeks to narrow it down to twelve candidates. But there is something about you." She looked at me, then nodded. "You're newly feral."

I forced some laughter, my excitement dropping completely. I had no idea what to expect from this girl or her knowledge of what I was—other than something bad. Something told me that she only found the information interesting in what she could spin with it.

"So how did you Awaken?" she asked.

"Like a troll finding himself under the wrong bridge," I muttered. I might have to stop getting ice cream. This was my second such encounter. Who knew the machines were fraught with such peril?

Thankfully she was only half paying attention. Her eyes were scanning the dwindling crowd, and she was throwing a little wave to someone else every few seconds. She was one of those people who was always on the lookout for someone more interesting.

I cleared my throat. "I'm new because I transferred from Four Corners Academy."

"Hmmm." She cocked her head at me, obviously doubting that claim. "Well, where are you living?"

"I'm in Dorm Twenty-Five."

"Oh, you got stuck with Olivia Price?" The girl seemed to rally back on this piece of information and chortled. "I wondered, when I saw you sitting with her. You poor thing. We went to primary together. Her last roommate here magicided. Ran screaming from this school and that cold, bitter fish.

Chapter Twenty-Four

Living ordinary now."

Putting aside the notion of "magicide" for a moment, I was pretty sure I should be actively and personally offended by at least some of the insinuations there, especially with her derogatory tone about the ordinary world.

"She is a complete troll," she continued, only half looking at me again. "I heard even the law professors can't stand her. You should request a transfer immediately. She's had five roommates in five seasons. Five! I hear some of the Dorm Twenty-Five crowd take bets when she gets a new one."

It was a blink of color out of the corner of my eye. A sense that I had relied upon as the pass receiver from a prankster brother. That extra bit of intuition that told me that something in my peripheral vision deserved my attention.

I looked to the people standing near us at the other machines. They were talking and laughing amongst themselves. Or filling cones and cups. No, that wasn't it. I wondered if it was my intuition—my magic—telling me my ice cream machine was about to explode. Stranger things had happened around me. It was actually kind of relieving that I now had something to blame the strangeness of my life on.

But I was getting sidetracked. I let my eyes wander farther and saw the tip of a Mary Jane sticking out from the far edge of the row of ice cream machines. I kept my eyes focused above that shoe, while Delia Peoples continued her catty recitation, and was rewarded with the end of Olivia's nose, then the rest of her face as she peered around. As her eyes met mine.

She stared at me in cool, uncaring disdain. The way that she had since I'd met her—her sole expression. Totally without one care that she was being gossiped about or that I was hearing it.

I wondered if that was what she was actually thinking. Was that how she felt?

My magic, still happily thrumming after a good day's work, took that moment to kick in full-force and I struggled for a moment with visions of the entire cafeteria blowing up in a glittering display of glass, pork chops, and Banana Swirl. I wrangled with my magic for a moment, my gaze still on Olivia.

The magic pointed, swirling around and latching onto my focus. My intent. It was like casting out a net, letting it settle and then pulling it in, hand over hand. I had no clue what I was doing, but I did it anyway, half-hoping that I wouldn't blow the place to bits.

I wondered if this was a side-effect of my soul rituals, with me now tasting a bit of her soul. Unnerving. But my brain, my heart, and my magic told me that I was doing something right. And I knew better than to mess with that feeling.

So I drew the net toward me. Some sort of essence—eau-de-Olivia. And I inhaled. Sadness. Anger. Loneliness. Dark intentions. Hope. Black certainty. The hope was a tiny flame, a mere wisp of light, and all of the darker emotions suddenly grabbed it and pinched, leaving only snuffed smoke.

Olivia whirled around and disappeared from my sight.

That cool, haughty, unaffected girl was a fraud.

My God. The old echo of my own loneliness and sadness gripped me. I felt the edge of the loneliness and sorrow I had experienced after Christian's death, especially in my darker moments, coming from Olivia. But I had always had my Mom and Dad to lean upon, even when they hadn't believed me about Christian's death, and even when I felt they couldn't understand the relationship I had had with my brother, my twin.

They had lost their son and that was something they shared together, without me. But regardless, we still had each other. It was something special. I realized in that moment just how special. I felt the urge to run up to my room and send a note to my parents telling them how much I loved them.

But Olivia felt...completely alone. Brittle and angry under that cold façade.

"What amount should I place on you?" Delia said, obviously still talking about the bets of a dorm full of people who, even though unaware, were making someone feel even lonelier.

The thread of my roommate, and whatever I had done to gather it, withered and released. Leaving me with only the memory of the feeling. Of the realization, for that moment, of the ache hidden by someone so seemingly cold.

"Eat shit," I told Delia, and shoved my empty ice cream bowl into her hands, not bothering to catch her reaction, as I hurried to follow the path of my roommate.

I wouldn't let that loneliness continue. Determination gripped me. The desire to be occasional allies was gone. I would be Olivia's friend, and she would be mine.

~*~

I found Olivia bent over her giant tome when I entered the room. Even over that large book her back was ramrod straight.

"You didn't get dessert," I said as I closed the door.

"I was not hungry anymore," she said in her precise, clipped voice.

"I'm never hungry when I eat dessert," I joked. "I brought some cookies to share." I set a few down on her desk, wrapped in a napkin.

She didn't say anything for a moment. "Thank you."

"You left abruptly."

"I saw no need to engage in further conversation." She opened another book.

"You didn't wait for me."

"Why should I have? You were speaking with someone with whom I had no wish to engage."

Delia had said they'd attended primary together. "You two have history?"

"No."

I wasn't sure I believed that statement, though it was delivered without ire, but my magical mojo wasn't helping me out this time, so I could only rely on what made sense.

"She said unkind things. I hope you don't think I believed them."

"Why not? The things she said were true."

"Ok. So what happened to your other roommates?" Better to just get it out in the open.

"Why? Worried that you might catch the disease?" She started darkly underlining something in her book with magic.

But now that I was listening for it, I could catch the subtle darkness in her voice. The complexity of tone that indicated high confidence battling a thread of insecurity.

I needed to stop thinking thoughts to myself though and voice them out loud with this girl. I was not very good at expressing myself, but determination was going to *make* me good. "No, I think it is better that we get everything out in the open." There. That was a good start.

"So you can feed the rumor mill?"

Ren Crown = -1. Olivia Price = 0.

"No, because I want to be your friend."

Olivia gave a short laugh. "Why? You don't know anything about me."

I thought about saying "I sucked out your essence, so I know you a little bit," but then thought maybe I should keep *some* things close to my chest—like the things that could cause someone highly skilled in magic to freak out and obliterate me.

"That is part of wanting to be friends. We talk and get to know each other. You know, make friends with each other."

Wow, lame.

"That sounds stupid."

I had to hold onto the memory of her loneliness for a moment. "Yes. That is the first thing you will learn about me. I can be quite infantile at times."

Olivia looked less dark at that. I readdressed the mental tally. Ren Crown = 0. Olivia Price = 0. SAT practice = +1.

"It is a fault you can correct with practice," Olivia said. "I have a primer on proper manners."

Loneliness, loneliness, remember the loneliness. "That sounds great."

I congratulated myself on changing her expression. Only I wasn't sure that suspicion was better than disdain at the moment.

"Sooooo," I said, searching for something to bridge the gap. Or at least to lay down a first plank. Previous roommates were obviously off limits. So I dredged up what I knew of her, which was minute. "I'd actually love to know about the magical legal system. Is there a good book? Or...would you like to help me?"

"You don't want to do the work yourself."

I am working to be friends with you right now...

"I don't mind hard work. Though I would rather everything be easy—who wouldn't? But it would be nice to have someone to question and talk to. Discussion, you know? Discussing ideas? Books can't do that." I stared at her giant book and thought of the reading rooms. "Or, can they? I can't believe they let me in to this school. I am so screwed."

She examined me for a long time. "You do study a decent amount."

Decent? I was studying all the time. What was her measurement here?

"Fine. Ask," she said.

"Er...ok." The pressure... "What kind of legal recourse do mages have when people insult them?"

Telling a delinquent gossipmonger, who was probably ready to tell everyone that I was feral, to eat shit had probably not been so smart.

"Are you serious? You want to know how to sue someone who insults you?"

Actually I wanted to know if I was going to be sued, but like usual my thoughts ran faster and tumbled, fractured, from my mouth. "Sue? So that type of thing is like the normal, er, ordinary world?"

She squinted, then turned and sifted through books on her desk. "Feral mages are never given enough information. Which is only a good idea if the system is going to actually use them for their power."

"Er, feral?"

She gave me an unimpressed look.

My shoulders dropped. "Am I wearing a sign?"

She shrugged. "People are generally unobservant and stupid, but there has been talk about feral students and rare mage types on campus, so people are looking. And frankly, it wasn't difficult to figure out in your case." Her eyes pointedly took in my desk and me.

Chapter Twenty-Four

"Great."

"Here. This is a book for ordinary-born mages. To help them catch up." She pinned me with a dark stare. "Fold a corner or scuff an edge and die."

I carefully took the book. "Thank you," I said softly. "I really appreciate this."

"It used to be that you'd find a lot of the Old Magic users related distantly, but once the Magic designations opened up, things freed immensely. Now, it is a growing group. Which is good, no matter what the Provenanciers state, or else we would likely be finished off by magical narwhals at some point. Simple logic, there. For the last ten years there has been a system in place so one can be considered Old Magic."

"Really?" I leaned forward.

I never knew when something I overheard or participated in would lead me to a jump in logic toward resurrecting Christian. The magical world was too new. I knew *so* little. And I had realized that while what I could learn in books would help me immensely, without the right injection of magic, nothing worked the same.

Being pubescently-challenged sucked. If I had become a mage earlier, I could have saved Christian.

"Yes, but you have to go through a number of tests, then be on probation for fifteen years before you are even considered for a status change. Unless you marry an Old Magic user, of course."

The way she said that indicated its likelihood. Though Will's cousin had married a feral.

I shook my head. I wasn't going to marry some Old Magic user just to become one. I would be happy just to be normal, and I could earn that with a few years under my belt.

"And there are a couple of other tricks too." She gave a tight smile. "But most people don't look closely enough or study the right books in order to discover the loopholes."

I looked at all of her books and thought of the never-ending reading she had done since I had arrived. "Have you ever tried cases here?"

"What do you mean?"

"Student cases."

"Students try their own cases."

"But they don't have to. Provost Johnson said that a student could seek legal representation. What if students sought you?"

"You are suggesting I deal with student riffraff?"

I shrugged. "I think the riffraff would hire you in an instant." I would. I could see that I needed to appeal to her own motivation though. "It would give you practical experience. You could actually list on your resume that you tried"—I waved a hand—"two dozen cases, or whatever."

Her eyes immediately narrowed, but the look was inward, considering. She turned abruptly and began rummaging through her neat stacks and compartments.

She pulled out several pamphlets. "Yes. Work experience is valuable. And I could practice crushing the authority figures in my way."

"Er, yes, exactly."

~*~

I kept drawing Olivia further into my sordid little world. She consulted on five cases in three days and defended three more. At first, club members had been very uncertain about her qualifications and intent, but so far she had won every single case, and more members were discussing the merits of representation.

Olivia seemed very pleased. I had seen her note on a paper, that once she was in power, corralling the malcontents into rebellious activities that she herself spawned "merited serious consideration." And then she had muttered something about how if she kept them occupied in side projects that "seemed" to be rebellious, but actually benefited her, that she could control everything.

Olivia's thinking was sometimes a little warped and scary. Always nose deep in a book and plotting out a way to trap everyone inside the pages.

"You know, you should take those to the reading rooms." I pointed at the books spread in front of her. "They have equipment to scan a book onto a card. It takes about fifteen seconds to convert a book."

She probably knew that, but I had noticed that a lot of people didn't use the library for anything other than as a meeting place. They relied on the knowledge they had already obtained. I, on the other hand, had started with nothing and yearned to know everything. I hadn't grown up with fairy tales that converted into actual knowledge or watched my parents manipulate their environments magically. Magic was taken for granted by many magical users.

She looked at me, and I couldn't read her expression.

"You probably know that already," I said. "I just think the rooms are great."

She looked like she was weighing a deep decision, and also weighing me. "I've only tried them once," she finally admitted, reluctantly.

"Really? They are great. I had a heck of a time with them at first, though."

"I had to be pulled out." Her admission was accompanied by a "tell and die" glare. But I was too ecstatic that she had shared something with me.

"Me too! I would probably still be in there if Alexander Dare hadn't pulled me out."

"You were pulled out of a reading room by Axer Dare?"

"Yes. Peters, the Justice Squad guy who has come by here a few times to sanction me, was pretty displeased about the whole thing. Nettled him something fierce."

"I don't know whether to observe you more closely or run from you." She made a note on a paper. I think I had just been upgraded from minion to berserker.

"Why don't you come with me to the library?" I offered. "I'll show you how to use the rooms. I've been practicing. I may pick up a part time job there."

One thing that had become obvious was that Olivia didn't ask for help on anything, ever. If she had been pulled out the first time, I was unsurprised she hadn't returned to the rooms.

Since she didn't have anyone else that could be remotely called a friend, Olivia relied on her own knowledge and that of her books to color her world. I was trying to make her comfortable enough with me to ask me questions, but in the meantime, I tried to anticipate any question she might have and provide it in conversation.

"You have been busy since you arrived," she said, eyes sharp. "You rarely sleep."

I was hoping she hadn't noticed. "Well, I'm dreadfully behind in this whole magic thing."

She ran one finger along the spine of her book, then she carefully put the book in her bag along with the other two and rose to her feet.

"Ok, let's go."

I blinked, but rallied and grabbed my bag too. When Olivia decided on something, she wanted to do it *now*. But it was all worth it, when I saw a true smile on her face after she exited a reading room on her own for the first time.

It was also a bonus that she had opened a text in the room that had "Properties of Blob Matter—How to determine and prosecute its use" as its chapter heading.

I happily made a five-foot blob-man that night who promptly tried to eat me.

Chapter Twenty-Five

AMBROSIA FOR ME, AMBROSIA ON YOU

DELIA PEOPLES CORNERED ME in the cafeteria—at the stinking ice cream machines again. She smirked at me from underneath her black bangs.

"Hi," I said, waiting for her to tell me that I was on some feral hit list or something.

"You're the one who blew up the art studio?"

I let out an internal sigh. "Yes, that was me."

"Good. Got me out of two weeks of classes there."

I blinked.

"There is a party over in Dorm Twelve tonight. You should come. You can even bring Brittle Britches."

"Olivia is very nice." Okay, perhaps nice was the wrong word. But Olivia was only being disdainful every other day now. I had great hopes for the future.

"Mmmhmmm." I noted that Delia wasn't looking around this time. Her attention was focused totally on me. "You are interesting—more than just being newly feral, something which makes you a person of interest on its own."

"I told you, I transferred from Four Corners. And you are making my heart beat wildly in excitement." Maybe there was just something about telling someone to dine in a toilet that made it easier to converse later.

She smirked. "Good. See you tonight?"

"*Go,*" Christian's voice said. I shushed him and considered it myself. Did I want to go? I cocked my head. "Maybe. How do I know you aren't just setting me up for some kind of weird revenge?"

She handed me a card, which my fingers automatically accepted. "You don't, but I'm not. The club is useful, but not my kind of people socially.

But I can mold you into something decent. We are going to be friends. See you tonight."

And I blinked, finding myself on the other side of the coin. I looked at the card, which contained her name in a sprawling script. I could feel the tingle of the magic imbued in the card. Connecting to the magic in the card would allow me to connect to Delia's frequency once I established my own.

Of course, Olivia had flat out told me I'd be stupid to establish a frequency until I could fully control my constantly burgeoning magic. But I knew what frequencies were. Most of the students had them. Walking around, I always saw them touching their ears to activate answering, or touching their chins to activate speaking. Or a dozen other motions that did other social networking things.

It was how groups automatically found one another in the cafeteria, as opposed to the notebook texting I used with Will and Neph, or my manual tactic of bumbling around and collecting people.

It was a big deal that she had given me this. You didn't just allow anyone to know your frequency. Though, perhaps as a highly social butterfly and a devious delinquent, it was life for Delia.

~*~

After extensive blob testing—getting so far as creating a blob caveman complete with loincloth and bat—and only suffering a third degree backlash burn on my side and a headache from where cave blob had whacked me—I dressed for the party, energized. I had successfully gotten the blob matter through the first thirteen day period, and had five more days remaining on my second thirteen day period.

Since the two large soul locating and cleansing rituals I had spaced out for the next three days looked very promising, I might be able to spring Christian by the end of the week and not have to worry about getting the blob matter into the tricky final thirteen day period.

Olivia flat out refused the invitation to go to the party, and Will had declined as well. He was close to a breakthrough on his portal pad technology and was putting in extra hours in order to capitalize on the remaining days he had left with his second stage blob matter. Since he was doing proof-of-concept testing, he was using a golf-ball-sized and shaped portion of matter, without doing any of the maddening human-characteristic testing I was doing. But when he was ready, I would have everything he needed for a human golem.

Once again, not listening to the label of "nearly impossible" had been the right thing to do. Those books which labeled golem design as such— pffft. Mental raspberries blown at all of them. And at the authors trying to corral us into dreary little anti-innovation boxes.

Neph and I had taken Will cake slices the previous night when he had missed dinner for the third night in a row. He was single-handedly trying to keep the Third Circle pizza place in business. I wondered if boys had a third leg somewhere to contain pizza slices.

Nephthys said she would go with me, but she would have to meet me there, as she had a dance class. I needed a break from my craziness, so I pushed across the grass alone. It would be far easier to just stay in my room or go to Okai, but I couldn't test further on the blob until the neutralizer magic did its job on the matter, which would take all night. And I had done a failed soul locating ritual that morning.

And for all of the excuses I could think up, the simplest part was that the Christian-like part of me was whispering, *go*.

The door was propped open and people were entering and exiting freely. I tucked in behind a group as they entered. Dorm Twelve was arranged in a manner more consistent with an expensive frat house rather than the severe dormitory space of ours or the posh exclusivity of Constantine's. I glanced around at the nineteenth century architecture.

As with everywhere on campus, people were dressed in all manners. Some were wearing scarves around their necks and bodies, or hats arrayed with what looked like spiral parking ramps that lifted into the air. Others looked as if they had been painted into their dresses—I wasn't sure you could get a dress like that on without using magic... Some had loose, caftans, or First Layer business suits. An eclectic bunch. It made me feel less out of place.

You could often tell people's majors or interests by how they were dressed. I wondered how a feral art mage was supposed to dress. Dripping Dali pants, whacked out Picasso sleeves, and googly-eyed hypnotic belts?

And an origin mage? Maybe just a strapped-on bomb vest, complete with a finger trigger.

I had seen people of every ethnicity around campus—I had even seen a few people change ethnicity or gender in the cafeteria via short term enchantments—but at least half of the students at any one time were European—or whatever posed for Europe here.

Which meant that Excelsine was most likely a humongous, layered version of Glastonbury Tor rather than Babylon. Either would fit ancient site parameters. My fingers hovered over my encyclopedia bracelet, ready to ask, when my eyes caught on a half-circle of deep chairs occupied by a mixed group of guys and girls who shared an expensive vibe.

As if a view of him was mandatory, Alexander Dare was sitting in the middle of the half-circle. A guy was trying to gain Dare's attention, while Dare absently twirled a little ball of magic around his fingers like a small yo-

yo with a magic tracer flare for a string. He nodded, obviously bored.

The fingers of his other hand tapped the arm of the chair in an offbeat rhythm. The movement seemed strange, until I realized he was the only one in the group without a drink.

Stop staring. The last thing I wanted to do was make eye contact.

I tore my eyes away and saw two miscreants from the club on the other side of the room. I could head over there. One of them was Magical Moses, who was seriously strange and sometimes a complete viper, but at least he was a known quantity.

Speaking of vipers...Constantine Leandred was lounging in a chaise chair in the corner. Two girls were perched on the arms, leaning over him, and one was almost in his lap, leaning forward in her chair between his spread thighs.

The corner they were occupying was unnaturally darkened, but I could still see plenty well. He turned his eyes to the girl nearly draping him on his left. He said something and her entire body gave a shiver, her eyes closing as she leaned closer.

Seriously? But no one said anything to them about the serious "get a room" moment. And he turned to the girl on his right and repeated the action. I needed to look away. But something was keeping my eyes focused. Tendrils of magic. I just bet that sly bastard practiced some kind of freaky sex magic. In fact, I'd bet—

"There you are."

I jumped and turned to see Delia on my right, her brows rising at my blush. I hoped she hadn't seen where I had been looking.

"You came," she said matter-of-factly, looking me over, no doubt cataloging my outfit and passing judgment. She was dressed in a sharp white top stretched across the tops of her shoulders and what had to be designer jeans—though the weave of denim here was just slightly different from what I was used to. A research topic far, far down my list.

"I came." I had a feeling I was going to regret it too.

"Great. Let me introduce you around."

Seven introductions later reinforced my distinct lack of talent in remembering names during introductions. I was too consumed with assimilating sensory data on each person to remember the two words that labeled them. I wondered if there was a spell for it. I added it to my research list. But I had categorized everyone with an interim name—"girl who likes far too much blue," "boy with scuffed shoes that sport anime characters," "girl who motions overly with her hands," etc.

"Anime Boy" was an art student, and we began talking about Art Expressionists meetings. I was just happy that Marsgrove had forgotten to limit my ability to attend clubs. I was unable to enter art classes or the art stores on campus, unfortunately.

Unless Stevens was present. It was a theory that I had tested one day when she'd needed a canvas and I had tagged along. No alarm had issued when I'd walked through with her.

Later, I had gone back and the alarms had shrieked.

I wondered sometimes if Stevens knew.

Delia thrust a glass into my hand. "Here. You are doing well, so I'm going to sample the rest of the selection."

I sniffed the drink. It smelled like fruit. "What is it?"

"Ambrosia."

I sniffed it again, trying to deduce if it was truly the nectar of the gods, and took a drink. It was fantastic. I blinked. "It's really good."

She rolled her eyes. "Of course it is. Drink slowly and don't move from this spot. I'll be back in a bit." She disappeared into the crowd.

"Anime Boy" continued to be a good conversational partner and a few others joined us. I mused along with the rest about the blown up art complex and what could have happened. No one seemed too torn up about it. I almost said something in admittance, my tongue feeling oddly loose, but a voice that sounded distinctly Christian-like kept the admission back just in time.

Weight descended in my hand and I blinked as someone with a pitcher filled my glass, then moved on to the next person. That explained how the level of my liquid was staying high. At some point "Anime Boy" and "Sunglasses Girl" took me to the other side of the room to examine some prints on the wall.

I felt like maybe I should stay in my spot, but couldn't recall why and my magic felt great, so I nodded and followed along.

From there, we drifted into another room. Then "Anime Boy" and "Sunglasses Girl" were gone and "Snake Earrings" and "Yellow Eyes" were in their place. I blinked but kept talking about—what were we talking about?—oh, yes, aviary migration over the Western Plains.

I nodded along. "Very beautiful. I can picture it." I wish I knew what the Western Plains were or what three-footed westrals were, but I stuck in my own mental versions of Montana and weird bald eagles and kept nodding.

The snakes were doing a charmed dance, swaying back and forth hypnotically under the girl's ears. "But that doesn't explain all of the weird things on campus." She shook her head, making the snakes lurch as if striking.

"There are always weird things on campus." Campus had never been my idea of normal, though I was seriously starting to shift my view on what was normal.

"Not like this," she said mysteriously. "It's the beginning of the end."

"Yellow Eyes" gave both of us a significant look. "You know what it is," he said.

I nodded mysteriously back.

Such conversations continued everywhere I traveled, groups morphing and shifting without me really processing it. At meals we usually stuck to scholarly topics, much to Mike's dismay. But here at the party everyone seemed far more concerned with the social. I hadn't realized there was so much politicking going on around me.

I'd have to sign up for a political science class. I tried to remember how to sign up for something. The thought flitted away, just like all the others in my head during the past few group changes.

The edges of the magic running along the walls swirled around, settled, then swirled again. Wow. I felt a little like I was in a psychedelic 3-D painting. I could hear Jerry Garcia singing in the background.

I wasn't sure I felt so well, suddenly. I decided to sit. I was really close to the comfy chairs I had seen when I had first entered, so I weaved my way to the nearest one. There was something in me that said I shouldn't sit in one, but I couldn't remember why not. The floor went uneven, and I tried to compensate. Who had raised the floor there? I didn't compensate well enough, and I stumbled the last step toward the comfy chair closest to me, and my hand with the drink flung forward.

"Son of a—"

I caught the edge of bright ultramarine blue eyes in a homicidal gaze two inches from my own as my hands gripped the chair's arms to stay upright, putting me directly over the person sitting in the chair. Whoops. I looked down to the large wet stain spreading on his white shirt, my cup resting in the crack between his body and the edge of the wet cushion.

Someone reached over and tried to pat him down. Another pair of hands joined in. He blocked both attempts.

I could see people turning toward us and people leaning toward him, but my focus was narrowing in on the stain, and all of the other things tunneled out of view. I pulled myself upright and poked my finger through the air toward his shirt and the remaining white turned the rose pink of the stain. Whoops. I tried again, but my finger motion was lazy, and he was squirming instead of letting me fix things, so his pants turned pink. Interestingly, they were a far darker shade than his shirt. I could probably learn something from that, if I could just figure out what I had done.

I concentrated harder on what I had done, but the thought slipped away and at the same time my well of magic increased. I could feel it. Taste it on my tongue. It tasted like ambrosia and excitement.

I drew my finger in an arc as my dratted target moved again, flinging himself to the side and over the edge of the next chair. He somehow landed on his feet and kept moving. My finger made an arc of color across three legs. I wondered if there was a three-legged person at the party—were they like a westral?—then let the thought flit away as I increased my finger speed to nab my target.

Irritation bled into my thoughts as my pink prey wouldn't stay still. I had the sudden notion that pink wasn't the right color. Of course! The color of the arc turned blue, and I raised my aim and lined two midriffs in ultramarine.

All of a sudden, someone grabbed my wrist and blue splotched someone's crotch.

"I think you've reached the limit on his *vaunted* patience," a deep, satiny voice said. It sounded smug and amused.

I found myself abruptly turned and marched toward the stairs. All around me people were shooting colored arcs, fast and furious. Three different colored blasts came my way, but disappeared just before they hit.

As I climbed the stairs, I looked back down onto the chaos. Alexander Dare's shirt was white again and he was standing untouched in the midst of the current chaos, sending me a very black gaze.

My brain decided I had zero preservation instincts and that Dare looked hot when he was furious too.

I realized that Constantine was the person leading me upstairs. "Don't you have women to whisper to?"

He smirked. "Maybe I am going to whisper to you."

I considered this for a moment as the pictures on the walls formed into whispering couples then changed again into scenes of what happened as a result of those whispers. Huh. I paused for a moment and stared at a particularly engaged couple, one of whom morphed to resemble my previously pink target downstairs, and another into the guy next to me.

"Do I even want to know what you are seeing?"

"Nope." I put my hand to my head. Cognizance and ambrosia mixed unpleasantly. "Pardon me for a moment." I slipped into the bathroom I could clearly see on the right. I locked the door, then leaned back heavily against it, closing my eyes. Meditation. Deep breaths. Drops of water, paint spreading, petals on a rose, a feather in a wind.

Hopefully Constantine would wander back to the party. I had no idea why he had helped me. Couldn't be for anything good.

The dark look in ultramarine blue eyes downstairs flashed in front of me.

The room started spinning, and I started shaking. Too much like the uncontrolled feeling of Dust.

I pushed away from the door, as I felt the magic well up in me, then shoot out. The trash can blew up, and its contents rained down upon me. Shaking, I put my forehead against my forearm and leaned both on the tiled wall. The edge of the ambrosia was gone, but I now felt horrible in a different way. My head still resting on my arm, I looked down at the mess on the floor. I closed my eyes. I was going to have to clean that up, but not yet.

I couldn't believe I had just spilled my drink all over Alexander Dare. Then turned him pink. Repeatedly turned him pink. Then started the magical equivalent of a food fight. Wait. Of course, I could believe it. I wiped absently at my striped tan-and-coffee skirt that now sported an abstract splotch of bright rose. I should have worn jeans. I should have put that drink down immediately. I should have stayed home. In the non-magical world home.

I could feel Mr. Verisetti's anti-dust moving inside of me, touching the remnants of ambrosia still in my system. Anxiety made my heart beat faster.

Voices and footsteps registered, coming down the hall and drawing closer to the bathroom.

"I want off campus. It's driving me insane. There's no way the strange campus happenings aren't related to some terrorist sympathizer or crazy, feral, rare type. They should just quarantine anyone new or odd—or anyone who was seen in that general area of the mountain—so that the rest of us can go about our lawful business."

"My Dad works in the Department. He said to keep an eye out. He has high clearance—he can lock rare types up without a trial. Or anyone on the Watch list. Names are easy enough to add in the system."

"Excellent. We were talking about forming a group. Going over the Ganymede arch site and information. Always fancied being part of a good detective story and witch hunt."

"Yes. *Yes.* We will find out what is going on, then get in good with the Department, collecting a major line item for our resumes and entrance requirements."

The anti-dust and ambrosia were combining together with something else—something like tiny spatters of paint that had seeped inside of me.

The outline of a gargoyle formed on a bathroom tile to the right of me. My breath was coming too quickly and the gargoyle—drawn as if by my hand—started to move.

"And we get to take down one of the radicals. Filthy terrorists. You know it is all connected."

"Right. Start by looking for anyone you didn't see here last year. Or anyone alone or doing anything odd."

I wiped at the gargoyle, trying to erase him with my fingers, but the motion just moved him to the next tile. He gave me a withering look.

"Trail them. Collect information. Submit their names."

The gargoyle's ears flattened and his wings spread.

"Then corner and tie. I have a little trick to keep the campus patrols from picking up on a Level Three for ten minutes. Ten minutes is all we'll need to do some questioning and...a bit more." I could hear the smile in the unfamiliar voice.

The gargoyle's mouth opened and peeled around him, unzipping to form a snapping harpy, the lines sharpening with intent. My magic turning from protection to offense.

Oh, no.

The harpy crouched, ready to lunge out. I plastered my hands over the top and tried to peel a dozen roses in my mind. They were all black and prickly. Everything around my hands turned to black-and-white checkerboard through my vision.

A wing tip, sharp and deadly, emerged around the side of my hand, folding over my pinkie. I pressed harder and the claw sliced my skin as the creature tried to get a better grip. The claw was real and I could feel the leather of the wing.

Nothing that I had seen so far of this crazy world suggested that creatures who launched themselves out of bath tiles were normal.

"Oh, I have quite a list of things that can be done to different types of rares."

The checkerboard pattern grew sharper and a second wingtip curled around my other pinkie. I could feel a torso emerging, pushing against my fingers. The magics combining inside of me were rapturous and terrifying.

Christian was screaming again.

"What I wouldn't give to have one of the more powerful rares under my control, even if for ten minutes. Can you imagine the possibilities of such a pet?"

The beak of the harpy pressed against my palm and I could hear her dark chuckle.

Please...please...

"And what the Department would pay for one of them?"

The harpy was halfway out.

Please...please...

A wave of something incredibly powerful—a heavy, dreamy wave—

washed through the air. Then another wave crashed, then a third. I shuddered under the onslaught. The magic felt like...heat and satin against my skin. My muscles loosened, my lids drooped, the harpy stopped pushing. Lethargy combined with the intense desire to press closer to something.

"Mmmm...hunting..." The most militant voice on the other side of the door said—his tone suddenly languorous. "Yes. We should gather downstairs first. To discuss hunting and capture tactics...together."

There was the unmistakable, astonishing sound of bodies and lips pressing together in the hall. Transforming the vocalizations instantly from battle-ready stimulation to another form entirely.

"Oh, yes," two of the other voices agreed in tandem. The group moved in an odd pattern down the hall, as if they were groping each other while stumbling.

Someone had sent some sort of sexual magic through the dorm. I didn't care who or why, I was simply thankful.

I shuddered as I shook off the effect in the same way I had shaken off the edge of the ambrosia. I could feel Mr. Verisetti's anti-dust settling again, waiting.

I lifted my hands. The gargoyle-turned-harpy was gone, but filmy remnants of the checkerboard pattern remained. Waiting too, just like the anti-dust.

Five minutes later, when I finally got my vision back to normal, I plucked a tissue and herded the bathroom trash into a pile. The remnants of the trash can, unfortunately, were part of that pile. This meant I couldn't push a button to magically flush the waste. A cleaning spell could send the rubbish to the Midlands's processing factory, where all the trash went, but I would likely blow up the dorm at this point.

I rummaged under the sink and found a thin cardboard box of soap that was just large enough for my purposes. I removed the two bars inside, stuffed the trash in, then scrubbed my hands. I'd send a new trash basket—and some soap—anonymously tomorrow.

The harpy slices on the sides of my pinkies glistened. I was the one they were after.

I needed to get out of here before I unleashed hell on someone, or before that group came back to find and lynch me.

Turning the knob, I quickly stepped out. Halfway down the hall, a shape parted from the dark shadows of the corridor. I clutched the cardboard box as I stopped abruptly, magic swirling.

"Feeling better?" Constantine asked, stepping fully into the light.

My shoulders loosened. "Not really, no."

"Pity." His body held the languorous edge that it always did—like a great cat sunbathing, but one who could pounce at any second. His eyes were ever sharp.

How had he disappeared into the shadows like that?

Constantine smiled, then raised a brow at the cardboard box in my arms.

I shook my head. "Don't ask."

"Don't taunt me with such a statement, Crown." He motioned toward another set of stairs farther down the hall. I was happy to see they led away from the main area downstairs.

"Thanks."

"Not a problem." One edge of his mouth lifted into a smirk. "First time with ambrosia?"

"Yes. And last, I do believe."

His eyes were darkly amused, reflecting his smile as he walked next to me down the stairs. "That's what everyone says."

"Well, I tend to keep my promises."

I sighed in relief, as we reached the main floor and a doorway to freedom. I couldn't restrain a peek into the main room, though. People were coiled together as if they had developed sudden rabbit genes.

I also realized something else, as I saw the groups that had molded together in lust. That eclectic mix I had reveled in at the beginning of the party was a myth. When I had first entered, people had been arriving, moving around, getting drinks, and finding their spots. So it had seemed like everyone was interspersed. But the party goers had settled into distinct factions. The groups dressed like each other were all cloistered together.

I looked down at my clothing, which was just dissimilar enough to be noticeable.

The members of each group intertwining made it all the more noticeable.

Except for Alexander Dare, who had his arms crossed, leaning against a wall, glaring toward the other staircase. I quickly pulled my head back.

Yup, time to leave. Perhaps leave campus entirely, even if it meant banging my head against an arch until something broke.

"You could try it the next time under my supervision. Come around any time." Constantine's eyes were heavily-lidded.

"Right." No way. "Anyway, thanks for helping me."

His smile grew to something a little more real, though it was still edged. "Anyone who throws a drink on Mr. Perfect, then turns him pink, deserves a free helping hand. And it was my pleasure, though these activities won't last long even with the previously established inhibition field in place. It would be *more* my pleasure if you joined in."

Chapter Twenty-Five

"Right. Listen." I put a hand to my forehead, trying to press my headache into submission by force and will alone. "I appreciate the empty flattery and all. It's good for a girl's empty ego. But I'm just as happy to try and be normal friends with you."

I couldn't read him for a moment as he stood frozen. Then he was in motion again, smirking. "I'll keep that in mind. Have a good night, Ren Crown."

"You too, Constantine Leandred."

He whistled as he sauntered back into the party. I wondered if his honey bunnies had been busy in his absence. If so, he wasn't the type to have trouble finding others.

His reference to a "free" helping hand caught up to my slowed thought process. Even with my head pounding and my energy zapped, the origin of the sexual spell was clear.

And free, of course, was figurative. Most people in this world expected something in return.

Like Mr. Verisetti's exchange for the anti-dust and the paint. The students would begin hunting me harder if they knew I still owed some nebulous debt there. The anti-dust was undoubtedly what had allowed me to shake off the lust spell and ambrosia when I'd put my mind to it. Worth the exchange? I wasn't feeling optimistic.

Which, speaking of...how was ambrosia not a substance abuse charge? I rummaged through my bag for Justice Toad, and checked the screen that kept track of my offense hours, adding or subtracting them each time I earned or paid one off. Nothing had been added.

Paint = offense. Ambrosia = nothing. So unfair.

I sent a quick journal note to Neph that I was no longer attending the party, and caught her just before she left her dance class. My headache and shakiness immediately disappeared. We went to Will's for late night pizza instead. An altogether better way to wind down the night.

And far safer.

I needed to get Christian raised and then be completely normal as quickly as possible.

314

Chapter Twenty-Six

NEVER NORMAL

AFTER SIX GRUELING HOURS of creating twelve different types of sculptures and dolls that might house Christian during preliminary soul-binding rituals, I trudged back across the cloudy border between the tenth and ninth circles.

I cleared the Midlands border and slogged toward the Battle Building and the arch that was on the other side of it. It was long past lunchtime and I was starving.

There was a group of ten people in front of the arch, talking. They all looked strangely exhausted, and quite determined.

"That was the worst one yet. I didn't realize they could have so many horns."

"Just giving Straught here a little practice before the combat demonstration this evening."

"I'm not entered. Demonstrations are beneath me," Camille Straught said. "I'm *not* for display."

Another girl sighed. "And no Dare or Greene, Lox or Ramirez either. I guess I'll put all my money on Nathanson."

"The winter competition is the first week after break. That's when the big guns will be competing." A girl I recognized from my first cafeteria table disaster nudged Camille. "Like our girl here. Daggers."

I slowed my steps, interested.

"You are going to need those skills," one of the others said. "This morning only proved that."

"I just think the lot of you are barking up the wrong tree. It *has* been messier than usual," a boy admitted. "But that doesn't mean a feral or rare is responsible. Nor a terrorist. These outbreaks occur in waves."

My steps stuttered.

Chapter Twenty-Six

"Plus the professors you have approached have scoffed at the suggestion," he finished.

Someone snorted. "They are interested in their funds and research, teaching and recognition, not the actual populace of the school."

"That isn't true," someone said. "Professor Trout—"

"Most, then. And the administrators are only concerned with the bottom line. As long as the reputation of the school doesn't diminish, and the funds are streaming in, they don't care. And we benefit from that. Usually."

Despite the alarming nature of the conversation, I had found most of the stated sentiment to be true. The hands-off nature of the staff, and magical gifts of enterprising students, combined to create the atmosphere of campus—competitive, invigorating, and dangerous. If one graduated from the prestigious Academy, to the community it meant you could take care of yourself.

"Well, they will care when the school is destroyed."

"Revolution," someone whispered.

"Collapse of magic," someone else said. "Just like those half-formed horned beasts we just battled."

There was almost never a line at an arch. And the group was clustered in front, rather then actually trying to get through. The magic under my cuff moved restlessly, as if it too thought that getting in the midst of the group would be entirely the wrong move.

I made eye contact with one of the boys at the side of the group. Then with another boy who was watching me as well. Both boys I had seen frequently over the past two days...now that I thought on it. Watching me.

Ringing alarms exploded in my brain and kicked in some much needed adrenaline to my slowed system.

"Get out of there, Ren," Christian said.

"That's her? You have to be sure," someone whispered, though with my senses suddenly so sharply attuned, I could hear it clearly.

"A bunch of us from Lolinet have been investigating and we *are* sure," one of the two boys who had been watching me said.

"We are next here, if we don't deal with the perpetrator now. It was *our* arch that was destroyed," said the other.

"Get out of there, Ren!" Christian yelled.

"Fine. We'll know soon enough. Do you have it?" murmured the pretty girl from that first cafeteria table.

They were going to use some device, to keep their attack on me from registering. Just like they had said at the party. I connected to my shields. I would go down fighting.

"There you are, dearest."

I turned sharply to see Delia sauntering toward me from the west, a wicker basket hanging from her arm.

"I thought for sure that you remembered the place where we met for Henry's sixteenth birthday party."

My focused mind immediately entered her track. "Memory loss. Sorry." I accepted her loose embrace.

Delia leaned back, shaking her head. "All of these strange events happening. Henry was diagnosed with proximity madness yesterday. I bet you caught something. Let's get you to the clinic. They cleared up Henry in a quick minute."

The other students muttered harshly to each other and slowly dispersed, though Camille Straught's eyes lingered upon me, as did those of the two boys.

Delia hooked her elbow with mine and pointed us toward the dorms. I mechanically followed her lead, bypassing the arch and walking across the wide field and toward the stairs that would take us to the eighth circle.

"What are you doing here?" I murmured to Delia as we drew far enough away from the lingering members of the hunting party.

"I was looking for you." Delia handed me the basket, keeping one arm hooked with mine. "To make up for leaving you alone at the party."

"How did you find me?"

"You still have my card in your pocket."

I blinked. I had put on the same jeans, it was true. I hadn't realized I was carrying a tracking device. I had to restrain the urge to pluck it out and toss it in panic.

"Why?" I asked as we walked, figuring she would understand the real question. Or questions really. Why had she helped me? Why had she lied? What did she want?

She cocked her head. "You are interesting, and I am excellent at emotion magic. You have a weirdly strong loyalty vibe. Abnormal. I want it. We are going to be friends."

I looked at the basket in my hand.

She laughed. "The apples are not poisoned. Listen, a bunch of us are going to the combat demonstration. Do you want to join?"

In another life, yes. Combat mages were revered on campus, and the demonstrations, games, and competitions were the sporting events to go to. However... "I don't think it's a good idea."

She looked at my outfit. "You do need to change, but that's not the worst I've seen."

I looked down at my jeans and long-sleeved t-shirt.

"Come on. We'll sit smack in the front and talk about dear Henry and how you, too, were cured. Totally back to normal, nothing newly feral about you."

"No, I can't risk going to the demonstration." I couldn't risk being trapped.

"I'll just have to spread the tendrils of subterfuge myself then. I'm excellent at it," she said without a hint of modesty.

Delia had just helped me out in a big way, but still...

She squeezed my arm, the edges of her mouth lifting in the sharp humor she always seemed to display. "Stop thinking. *We* are going to be friends."

~*~

Delia joined us at lunch every other day from then on, and Delia and Mike got on like crack partners on...crack. That they had never found each other before was almost sad. And Mike had taken to teasing her in a disturbingly flirty way.

Delia, true to her word, spread all sorts of stories, and the two boys who had been watching me had started to watch others again as well.

The list of people who knew some of my secrets was growing, though. I wasn't sure whether Mike knew, but Neph, Will, Olivia, and Delia were well aware I was newly feral. I was pretty sure Stevens had known it from the first. And, unnervingly, Constantine too.

He reminded me a little of Mr. Verisetti. Enough to be on my guard. Though I sensed that Mr. Verisetti had come from nothing and clawed his way to dark false insouciance, whereas Constantine had very obviously been born to extreme wealth with the type of careless blitheness that only came from bitterness.

I came back from a squad visit to him, annoyed. There had been a girl outside his door when I had arrived, and she had been sobbing, "He doesn't love me!"

Constantine had been unrepentant when I'd asked him about it.

"She's boring," he'd said. He couldn't even come up with her name.

"So how did it go?" Olivia asked as I entered and flopped on my bed.

"Lousy. Two small toads and one giant one."

"Someone turned into a giant toad?"

"No, I have a friend who sometimes qualifies." I wasn't completely sure Constantine *had* friends, to be truthful. But I couldn't very well say he was a repeat offender who blurred the line to fellow conspirator. The justice magic prevented such a thing.

Olivia frowned. "Who?"

I leaned back against my pillows and looked at my framed sketch before focusing on her again. "His name is Constantine."

Olivia straightened—and that was a hard feat considering her back was straighter than anyone's I had ever seen. "What did he do?"

I shook my head, hazarding a guess from her reaction that she knew him. There was an anti-gossip enchantment in the tablet's magic, not that that stopped determined teenagers and twenty-somethings from figuring things out—as Olivia obviously had from his name, and the fact that I had returned from call. But the enchantment helped at least make things shadier and unconfirmed.

"No, I mean, what did he do to you."

"Oh. Nothing." In fact, Constantine seemed to look upon me as some sort of strange pet he wasn't sure yet if he was going to keep or kill. "He just isn't very nice to people in general."

She looked relieved. "Oh, good. He's bad news."

Like all those crying girls hadn't given that away. "Old magic?"

"The oldest." She shook her head, mouth tight. "He should have been expelled first season here, but it will never happen."

"I kind of got that impression. You know him outside of school?"

"My mother and his father are fierce allies and fiercer enemies." She shrugged, as if that weren't a little creepy. "But he and I have little to do with each other."

That didn't surprise me. Olivia was upright and uptight. Ok, well, there were all those notes about taking over the world and finding minions, but so far she hadn't stepped a toe out of line and was a repressed and staid lady of privilege, working hard to exceed every expectation. Constantine was a rich boy with far too much money, time, and probably magic, on his hands—seeking to undermine every expectation.

And he had made enough references for me to guess that his father was his least favorite person in life.

"Are all the old families connected?"

"No."

"What about the Dares?"

Thankfully, Olivia never seemed to find anything I asked strange. I was a little like a weird pet for her too, I think.

"They don't deign to enter politics. They barely leave their island fortress. They just buy and fund what they are interested in. A more high set and close-knit family would be hard to find. And the Dares are only ever interested in *anything* for the good of their family." She gave me an unreadable look—she was great at those—then pulled a tome off her shelf. "This has a comprehensive listing of the old families, their alliances, and affiliations."

"Debrett's for magic users?"

Chapter Twenty-Six

"Yes."

I should have been less surprised that Olivia would know the reference. "How do you know what Debrett's is?" I only did because of a project I had done on the British Royal Family.

"I know the lineage of everyone of consequence in every layer."

She didn't look as if she was kidding. And Olivia *didn't* kid. "Oh."

She went back to work, but I really wanted to talk for some reason. "What are you doing?"

She gave me a look that said I was edging close to a zap. "Practicing lines for my debate class."

I blinked. "How do you practice lines for a debate?"

Her expression said I was *four words* away from a zap.

"I can help," I said quickly. "Do you want to debate me?" I could really use the practice rallying from verbal stupidity.

"I don't think that will work." But there was a hesitation in her words, and I jumped on it.

"I would really like to help."

I could feel the need inside Olivia. I caught glimpses of her covered emotions every now and again. Like my magic had tagged her and was keen to notice and point out changes when they occurred.

"Very well."

"Great!"

Two hours later my eyes crossed as Olivia verbally crushed me again.

"I'm not sure I am helping you," I said, feeling like I had been run over by my own brain—and lost.

"You have a unique style of argument. Half of it is measured and thoughtful, and the other half jumps all over the place—random and emotional." She pursed her lips. "And you are very naïve. Arguing with you makes good practice for dealing with less logical beings."

Great. "Great! Happy to help."

We set a time for her to crush me every other night. I was wiped half the time, but the contentment radiating from Olivia at the end of each session made it worth the loss of my dignity. And I was learning valuable information about mage culture that I wouldn't have otherwise—social customs and ethics about this world that would have slipped me by.

~*~

At three weeks remaining until deadline—in the literal sense of the word—my pace increased from feverish to frenzied. I was painting and experimenting in Okai, attending classes and doing homework, doing projects for Stevens, helping Olivia with her debates, helping Will with his Layer project, helping Neph learn how to draw while I learned how to

320

dance, helping Delia and Mike with a weird weather project that had sounded unbearably interesting, helping Constantine make a vortex inside an ottoman—something that was assuredly illegal, but also unbearably interesting—and staring at Alexander Dare when he wasn't looking.

My first red milestone—which I had scheduled for thirteen weeks' post-mortem—was approaching at breakneck speed, and I had only managed to make my blob matter into a four foot zombie before running out of fingernails and ear lobes.

Thank goodness for Nephthys, who had managed to magic everything back on me so far. Community service kept me extremely busy too, as a yeti, a troll, and a Level Six green dragon had popped onto campus in the last two weeks. We had experienced an earthquake, a tornado, and three layer shifts, all of which I had been told in passing were not normal.

But I was too busy to worry about normal.

I accidentally forked my hand at lunch one day.

Mike stared at me frankly. "You look terrible."

"Gee, thanks."

Delia raised a brow. "You do look terrible."

"I haven't been sleeping much. I'll catch up this weekend." There was no way that would be true, though. I had a full schedule planned for Saturday and Sunday.

"Ren, Ren, Ren. Sleep is for rejuvenation. The life force of all good mages."

Olivia stabbed at a leaf in her salad. It was her version of a verbal sneer. I'd had to coax her to lunch today, and with Delia here, I had a feeling Olivia was regretting it.

"Will and Olivia barely sleep." I felt it necessary to point out.

"As I said, the life force of all *good* mages," Delia said.

Mike snickered, then jumped up, swearing.

Will innocently took another bite of his sandwich.

"Where's Nephthys?" Mike asked, rubbing his side as he sat back down.

"Practice." I tried not to fork myself again as I attempted another stab at a tortellini.

"That's too bad. She'd help you."

"You can transfer sleep to someone else?" I asked, interested.

Mike looked at me as if I were an idiot. "She's a Muse."

I stared at him. "Oh." That explained...a lot...and nothing at the same time. "She helps people feel restful? I do always feel great after being near her."

Mike and Delia were looking at me like I was a moron. Olivia gave a large sigh.

Will smiled, and didn't hide the fondness in his eyes, which made me return his smile. "You didn't know?"

"I think I still don't. But you should probably explain it to me tomorrow." I put my head down on my arms feeling slightly better, as I always did when I thought of my friends.

"Dream of good things," Christian's voice soothed.

I took a tiny nap, hearing them arguing over me in my dreams, Delia demanding that someone tell me something and Will telling her to shut up.

Olivia nudged me awake and I looked up to see that we were the only two left. I contemplated my lack of sleep and whether I truly needed more as we left the cafeteria. The bright sunlight hurt. But I was fine. Just a few more weeks, then I could catch up.

Olivia stiffened next to me. I followed her gaze to a girl approaching us on the grass.

"Well, it if isn't little Miss Perfect Defender." The girl sneered at Olivia.

It was really strange. The tablet was in my hand, and I was zapping the girl before I even realized it.

I promptly turned into a toad. I tried to swear, but only a croak emerged.

Olivia heaved another great sigh and stepped over me, shielding me. I could barely hear anything with my toad hearing, but I got the gist from Olivia's suddenly giant body movements that she was arguing vehemently on my behalf.

Or perhaps she was agreeing with the other girl, as to how stupid I was, but whichever it was, she was doing it vehemently. I was very proud.

The girl turned, nose in the air, and stomped off.

I turned my toad nose toward my roommate again. She looked at me, then at the tablet. She was considering what to do, I could see it on her face even from the great distance now between us. I gave a croak. She squatted down and nudged the tablet with her finger, then nudged me. I tried to look affronted, but all I managed was another croak and a sideways hop-slide. Being a toad made one entirely uncoordinated.

Olivia's brows furrowed. "Karmically based?"

I nodded my toad head. God, I was going to get it from Wellingham. Would he expel me for this? I gave a mournful croak.

Olivia sighed. "I can't believe to what levels I have sunk." She touched the tablet with one finger and touched my toad head with another.

"Ren promises to clean the entrance hall of Dorm Twenty-Five." She looked at me darkly. "Don't you Ren?"

I fervently nodded my little toad head beneath her finger. The magic swirled out of the tablet and around Olivia and into me.

Olivia gracefully rose and stepped back, as I transformed back into a girl.

"Ugh." I frantically wiped my mouth. "Being a toad is awful."

"Well, you shouldn't have done that." Although, Olivia didn't look as irritated as I would have expected. The other girl was obviously not on her favorite person list.

"Yes, yes. But thanks. How did you know what to do?" I brushed my hands against my legs. I still felt vaguely toadish.

"Many things are karmically based in Old Magic households. One learns how to use the spells."

"Well, thanks. The spell bound you to it too, didn't it?"

"Yes. But you will complete the task." Or I will end you, was left unsaid. "Next time, hop on and make your own deal."

I considered the tablet. "Hey, that's a great idea."

If I was caught alone...as long as I was willing to pay the price... I gave a dark laugh and rubbed my hands together.

Olivia didn't seem to have any trouble interpreting the gesture. "Do it, and I won't take your case, if you get in trouble."

"Olivia!" I put my hand to my heart. "Why would you say such a thing?"

She rolled her eyes and started walking back to the dorm. I hurried to follow.

"But what if I'm outnumbered?"

"In defense of yourself, the tablet likely won't penalize you."

"Psshhh. Like it knows." Of course, I well knew that the freaky thing did know.

She gave me an "I-can't-believe-I-put-up-with-you" look. "Did you intend to defend yourself?"

"Er...defend your honor?"

She shook her head.

"Defend my good name for being your roommate?"

"Ren."

"Defend my future children's good names?"

"Your future toadlets or tadpoles, you mean?"

I stopped, my mouth hanging open. "Did you just make a joke?"

"No. And you look ridiculous. Close your mouth and come along."

I hurried to catch up, smiling. "I think you did." I poked her. "You made a joke. Good job, Olivia."

"I will make a nice simmer hex under your toes too, if you poke me again."

"Just let me bask in the wonder for a few more moments." I tilted my head back toward the sun. "Oh, yeah. Yeah. Yeah, awesome."

She rolled her eyes, but her expression wasn't as tight as usual as we ascended the stairs.

"*She's kind of hot when she loosens up,*" Christian mused.

"*Out, outitty, out, out! I need that soul to suck,*" his insane voice said.

I decided I didn't need sleep at all that night.

~*~

I hobbled painfully all the way to Nephthys's room the following day, after a few harried hours of botched experiments. She opened the door, took one look at me, and waved me inside.

Neph didn't say anything, as she patched me up. Again. Like everything about her from her waterfall of hair to her soft brown eyes, her magic was soothing as it dipped and delved and prodded the magic in my body to focus on regrowing my toe.

"You are really good at this." And that was fortunate for me, because I couldn't go to Dr. Greyskull. He would totally add two plus two and figure out what I was doing.

My black magic experiments kept demanding more from me.

"My mother is a healer and midwife. I've been helping her with this type of thing for a long time. And it is easy with you."

I blinked at that. "Does she want you to be a healer too?"

"She is concerned that I will make little money in the arts. Dancing can be a poor field."

"Yeah. My mom is a chemist. It is pretty obvious she wants me to be an architect rather than a painter."

Nephthys waved her hand in a graceful arc over my foot, her magic pulling delicately on mine, and the toe stub began to push out slowly. "What do you want?"

"I don't know," I said quietly. I wanted to raise Christian. I wanted to survive mostly intact. I wanted to be normal. "I really like engineering. Architecture is a good field for me, truly, but it feels a little like giving in to parental pressure."

She made a little noise, between a sigh and a laugh. "Don't let someone else dictate your life path—by pressuring you or causing you to rebel. It is your choice how you react."

"Thanks, Confucius." There was a light pinch on my forming toe. "Hey, hey, hey, sorry, sorry!"

The pressure instantly stopped and she continued the gentle ministrations.

"So, where is your roommate?" I had never met her and Nephthys never said anything about her.

"She has a boyfriend. When we first arrived, we had to sleep here every night for four weeks in order to set the balancing magic. Now that that has passed, she rarely spends time here."

"Doesn't that mess up the balancing magic?"

"No. As long as she sleeps here once a week, the magic renews."

That reminded me of something I had been wanting to know. "Do you know how roommates get chosen?"

She nodded. "There is a lottery ball that identifies sympathetic magics between mages. It is available any time for students who want to use it. During the first season, roommates are chosen very specifically based on magic sympathy from the magic that goes into the system. For transfers, it is more based on available slots. It was the same at Sakkara."

She sounded sad suddenly. I wondered if she felt the loss of her roommate from her original school. I felt a trickle of magic slide through my cuff toward her.

She smiled at me, then gracefully extended her fingers again and pulled my toe stub a bit longer. "If you feel discord in your magic when you first meet your roommate, you can request a change. A settling feeling, like a shield net, indicates at least an adequate level of sympathy."

Oh. Maybe that was why Olivia hadn't killed me that first day or kicked me out. Based on that first meeting, we were in sympathy.

"Olivia and I are sympathetic then. But she didn't speak to me for weeks." I'd really had to pull it out of her, being friends.

Neph shook her head. "Your magic can be sympathetic with enemies and incompatible with friends. All it means is that performing magic together is easier and stronger. The dorm rooms and sympathies facilitate a more restful rejuvenation for each mage. That is why we have to live here on campus until our magic is fully matured—to keep everything balanced. I'm sure you've noticed how prone to accident mages can be."

To her credit she didn't point at my toe, which was actually starting to look like one. Toenail and all.

"Like how the cafeteria works?"

She nodded. "The magic balancing enchantment siphons off too-high energy and soothes too-low energy, tumbling over us as we eat. A small magical recharge shared and balanced over thousands. They like that explanation rather than the one where they are able to keep track of and calm us for a period of the day."

I blinked.

"There." She touched my toe and gave me a penetrating look. "Are you planning on losing any more digits?"

"No?"

I was really hoping I wouldn't lose a finger next. I needed those to paint.

Chapter Twenty-Six

I was just happy things like this could be regenerated. At least so far.

I looked down, wiggling my toe. Milestone red was tomorrow. The serious rituals were about to begin. I had a gnawing feeling I wasn't going to be able to regrow the backlash from those.

But it would be too late to raise Christian even using black magic if I didn't gain some progress soon.

I straightened my shoulders and gave her a bright smile. "Thanks."

Neph didn't say anything for a moment, then looked at me with an inscrutable expression. "Will told me that you talked about me being a muse."

"Yes, though I still am not quite sure what that means. You inspire people?"

"That is part of it." She tilted her head. "Muses are generally encouraged to join troupes. To inspire on a mass level. It's a symbiotic relationship that helps the muses too."

She carefully arranged a few veils—veils were draped over most of the surfaces on her side of the room. "Once we reach maturity, around sixteen or so, we gain access to our inspirational powers, and they can be great. But they come with cost. Anyone who knew you before, will still be able to look upon you. But if you are cast out of your group after sixteen..." She looked down. "It is very hard to be seen. Muses are like wraiths, silently helping those we come across, but not as people in our own right. Muses are very clan-oriented for this reason."

I looked at the vying expressions on her face. "You left Sakkara."

"I was no longer welcome at Sakkara," she corrected. I waited, letting her decide whether to say more. "I have unfortunate family ties that impacted my enrollment and friendships there, and even here within the Muse community."

That seemed decidedly unfair. "So, being...cast out?...it makes it hard to make friends?"

"Very. The community here had to take me—I'm too valuable—but accepting me isn't the same as embracing me." She didn't look at me for a moment. "But you noticed me."

"Well, you did say something to me that night in the library. You helped me." I was the taker in this relationship. That thought made me anxious. "I'm not forcing you be friends with me, am I?"

"No. It doesn't work like that. I'm not a Jinn." She smiled. "And back to your comment, a muse exists almost on the subconscious level. I say things to a lot of people, but they don't actively notice."

I knew what it was like not to be noticed, or to be noticed...poorly. "It took some effort to see you," I said, apologetically.

She smiled. "Of course it did, but you made the effort. That is what counts."

"Can't people take, I don't know, Muse Appearance Pills?"

She laughed, and even that was soft and flowing. "Our energy automatically makes people want to look past us, to absorb our energy as their own. Compounding that, it is considered better to have access to many muses. Once you embrace one and force others to see her or him, other muses can't influence you."

I blinked. "Ok."

She looked a little uncertain. "It would have been lovely just being friends with you, but once you made the others see me...I'm your only muse now. You can...revoke seeing me, in order to regain mass access."

"What? No way."

She gave a bodily sigh, so obvious was her relief.

"Unless it means you are tethered to me? Are you sure I'm not making you be friends with me?"

"No. It doesn't work that way. I can still influence whomever I want. That is why it is more of a burden on you. On the other hand, you made friends with *me*, not because you wanted to gain energy. That gives you...benefits."

I shrugged. "I have to tell you, I'm not sure I'm muse-able. I still suck at dancing," I said frankly.

She laughed again, and this time it was a much deeper sound. "That's not quite how it works either. Dancing is how I power my energy and release it. It doesn't make anyone else into a dancer, unless that is their passion already."

"Well, I should probably work on making that my passion instead. Dancing is way better for social cred than drawing."

She touched my wrist and I felt a soothing tendril of magic. "No, you have so much potential. Your magic is like a blinding light sometimes that I cannot focus upon."

I blinked. I could feel her magic spread. I felt like I was on the right path. I wanted to draw, to paint, to create. Ideas and plans flew through my mind, connecting and threading. "Wow. You really are a muse. I feel like Da Vinci."

She laughed. "Better not. You might need more muses, if so."

"Sounds sordid."

She laughed harder.

The eyes of the watchful students on campus might draw more closely to me. But standing out enough to make friends...was worth it.

"I want you to be happy like this. I want you to stop trying to free me, Ren,"

Chapter Twenty-Six

Christian said.

"*Pain!*" the other voice cried.

Milestone red was tomorrow.

Chapter Twenty-Seven

REALITY IN DEATH

I HAD PROCURED a twice-blessed teaspoon through Will, goblin blood through another club connection, magical pomegranate seeds from Delia, and *two* whale-squished rats through Chen Lifen. Constantine had even infused my mirror shard with a suggestion enchantment and taken legal punishment for it in exchange for a third paper box—one that had taken me three more hours to design with him, bickering together while I drew.

They needed to seriously rethink community service. It put all the pranksters, malcontents, and crazies in thick contact with each other.

And Constantine...I was starting to wonder what he had begun constructing in his lab room. The vortex in his ottoman was one thing, but the whirlpool in the bottle of liquid that looked like magical Drano was weird. At some point he must have decided I was trustworthy, because the last ten times I had visited he had been pretty lax in letting me see his experiments and functioning workspace. His chemistry workshop always contained foaming potions, rotating drawers, and swirling bottles when I was there.

Daddy obviously paid well.

But who the devil was his roommate? I could see a second bed with a pillow and expensive-looking bedspread through the open bedroom door, but no identifying pictures or items existed in the living room. There was nothing personal to indicate a second person lived there at all. There was the other connected door, though, that I had never seen opened.

I was getting much better at distinguishing wards, but the door contained so many magic threads entwined together that it looked like a big, dark blur had been overlaid.

Either his roommate was horribly suspicious of Constantine, or

329

Chapter Twenty-Seven

Constantine kept him chained up in there. Both explanations were possible.

Constantine looked seriously elated—and elation was a disturbing expression on him—when I finished the storage paper for his chemical materials.

The design of the paper forced my mind onto other paths, as I'd needed to put wards inside the box space to prevent the chemicals from interacting with each other. And later that night, after leaving him, I had figured out how to magically suppress the judicial detection field from seeing the contents inside one of the storage box drafts by creating a hypercube.

It had taken an additional drop of paint to facilitate the added dimension, but it was worth it. Why hadn't I thought of a tesseract before? Could I do a penteract? I flipped through Mbozi's syllabuses and papers looking for research aid possibilities.

Upon returning to my room, Justice Toad informed me that I had five more hours of community service as punishment—added to my tally—but the paint jar suspended inside the hypercube wasn't taken...until ten minutes later when it had ejected from the sketch and spilled all over my floor.

It had zipped off to the Midlands at that point and Justice Toad had racked me up another five hours.

The suppression field only lasted for a limited amount of time—though I had great hopes for future field trials and tweaks. But for delinquents, ten minutes meant the difference between enrollment and expulsion.

And I still only had a limited amount of time to work off my community service. The added hours each time I was caught were a big deal. But in order to make useful products that I could trade on the club circuit, I needed to test them outside the Midlands in areas where I could be caught by the Justice Squad.

However, if I couldn't get my offenses under control, I was going to be doing community service every hour of every day soon.

Constantine always had the best illegal stuff, though, and he would want one of those detection suppression boxes for sure, which would give me a significant exchange value.

Two hours later, after a festival of blood, seeds, rats, stones, mist, three rituals, two herbal sacrifices, and an enlargement enchantment on the golem—because, hey that four foot zombie was just not going to cut it for my six foot two brother—I was pretty sure something in my right wrist was permanently broken. There was a deadened space there now that my magic wouldn't touch.

Christian babbled apologies over and over in my head, his words barely making sense.

I swallowed the thread of despair and loss. I had other rituals to try. I drew with my left hand. It would be fine.

I trudged out of the Midlands and back across top campus. It was going to be rough using a broken wrist for the hour of community service I had scheduled tonight, but I would have to make do. Pain was a product of my mind that I could suppress with enough will. My end goal was worth it.

A narwhal appeared in the air ten feet away, looked confused for a moment, then flopped bodily onto the grass.

"Narwhal!" Someone yelled, and people scattered.

The narwhal looked completely nonplussed, and blew out a stream of magic water from its tusk and rose into the air, surrounded in a field of magic water. I looked at it and covered a yawn with the inside of my good elbow. With a little over six weeks under my magical belt, I had started to wonder why people yelled so often. Weird things happened everywhere here for no apparent reason at least three times a day. Sometimes that number bumped to twelve. I would think people—*mages*—would grow used to it.

Without urgency, I retrieved my justice tablet with my good hand. I had branched out from toads, and was now getting the other amphibians—frogs, newts, salamanders, wormy things, and mudpuppies. I briefly contemplated what a salamander with a long pole protruding from its forehead would look like.

Zap.

The narwhal turned into a tadpole just as it was about to impale someone. A tadpole. Huh. I tucked Justice Toad back into my bag, unscrewed my bottle of water using my armpit and good hand, and scooped the tadpole inside. The tusked tadpole looked pretty irritated, floating there. I could release it down in the river after service. Fresh and saltwater currents ran side-by-side there, so the narwhal would survive in one of the currents as it made its way to icy waters.

Or perhaps flew away in a magic water bubble.

I shrugged, screwed the cap back on using my armpit and good hand, then stuck the bottle of water in the back pocket of my bag.

Cold water. Hmmm... If I used a cold water base, could I keep the blob matter going for a *fourth* period of thirteen days? Or was I going to need to freeze my golem? If he wasn't Christian-ready, what did I want to freeze him as? If I got to that point without meeting my end goal, should I make him as Christian-y as possible, and hope for the best? I chewed my nails and mulled the issue all the way to the service break room.

My schedule called for another ritual tomorrow. I had given in to my panic a few days back and tried to use the lavender paint on the blob, but as I drew closer, my hand had vibrated fiercely and been forcibly pushed away.

It had unnerved me enough to wait for one of my soul rituals to work.

One working ritual. Just one, was all I wanted and needed. Why was I so useless?

I had nicely simulated flesh and features with the blob, but I would need to do some side projects animating statues and dolls, just in case of failure so close to my endpoint.

And still, while the paint made things animate according to my will, producing the *real* Christian—versus a version my intentions would produce—was still a key philosophical issue I struggled with. I needed a soul ritual to work. I had even drawn up a soul version of a dream-catcher inside of a storage space, hoping that it might call Christian to it eventually.

Tomorrow. I would have to patch myself up enough tonight to hope that I would be punished on the right side of my body again. I was hoping that some of the swell reduction pads, like the ones Neph had, were in the squad's supply closet. I could worry about consequences later.

I was awkwardly pawing through the pad container with one hand when two squad members entered.

"Have you figured out the overflow magic?"

"No."

Ding.

Ding, ding.

Ding, ding, ding, ding.

"Not again." Large sigh. "Level Four. Illegal vortex portal. Expelling offense, right there. Should be a Level Five, shouldn't it? Can't get a good read on where for some reason."

I froze, left fingers stuck in gauze. Illegal vortex portal? And magical misdirection? I had given Constantine a rock from the Midlands earlier, enchanted to misdirect serious activity for ten minutes' time. At the ambrosia party, the student who had wanted to hunt me had given me the idea. The Midlands hid magic, and through trial and error I had found that the nullifying magic would carry over for a ten minute time period on campus, if used within twenty-four hours from when the item left the Midlands.

I ducked out of the room and raced to Dorm One, holding my broken wrist painfully against my chest. Constantine had an enchantment to downgrade the offense level on illegal magic performed in his room. In fact, he had hinted that it downgraded *more* than one level. That meant he was doing something seriously Level Five. I wondered if there was a Level Six that no one spoke about.

He opened the door as soon as I reached it. He somehow always knew now when I was approaching. Proximity ward or something. I didn't care at the moment.

"Whatever did you do to your wrist, darling?"

I pushed inside and closed the door firmly with my good elbow. "A portal, seriously? You idiot. I don't even want to know what you are really doing."

Actually, I did want to know. Maybe it would get me off campus?

Later. "They will be here in seven minutes to arrest you." I reached into my pocket with my good hand and pulled out my newest storage paper. "I modified the design again. Put everything you can fit in here, then bury it outside. It holds crazy crap inside a field for two hours. You *have* to get everything out of this paper before the two hours are up."

I didn't have time to read him the consequences. During testing, he had seen early drafts blow me across the room and destroy everything inside. And Constantine was always quick on the uptake. After our many drafting hours spent together, I was sure he would quickly figure out how to work a tesseract that came from my mind.

He regarded me, all heavy eyes and dark insouciance and didn't reach for the paper. "Are you protecting me, Ren?"

"Yes."

Constantine had kept my status as a new feral secret, along with whatever other suspicions he had about me. For his own aims, most assuredly, but the repulsion I had initially felt for him had simmered weeks ago into simple distaste with his personal life. We worked well together. I enjoyed working with brilliant people, and our magic was very sympathetic, making joint projects easy. I wanted him to stick around.

"And we haven't even slept together yet." He gave a slow smile. "I'm getting better every day."

I turned.

His hand caught my arm. "Wait." His smile dropped like the false mask it was.

I looked at him expectantly, though I wasn't expecting much. Constantine had armor as thick as Olivia's, except his was disguised as a slippery, shallow façade. And I didn't think highly enough of myself to think I would be able to pierce it. His other hand dropped and slowly pried the paper from my left fingers. I willed the paper to share ownership between us before letting go completely.

"Why?" he asked, voice low.

I didn't really know exactly what he was asking of me, nor what the answer to that question was. "Because you are not so bad."

He examined the paper. "No, I'm worse, darling. And this...this is a gorgeous piece of work."

Chapter Twenty-Seven

I ignored the latter part of his statement. "You are egocentric and narcissistic and treat people in a shoddy manner." I had seen girls run crying from his room on four separate occasions. I had also seen the same women trying to get back in his good graces days later. Made me want to shake them a bit. He'd never stop his games when he was so rewarded. "But you are a good business partner, and a stimulating intellectual, and I don't wish to lose you."

He gave a short laugh, then smiled again, leaned toward me, and grabbed my broken wrist. "I'll use you too."

If I had been less numb, I would have been writhing on the floor in pain. "If I let you, maybe." I leaned toward him as his magic touched my wrist. "But I'm rather stubborn."

His magic wound through me, somehow fixing the wrist I had been sure was a total loss. I could see bruising steadily spreading across his strong forearm, leeching the black magic from me. It was the reason I never went to Neph before I worked off the height of the consequences. Saying something to Constantine about the bruising, though, would make him sneer. Very likely he was doing this in order to keep us even in his mind. For someone who used people ruthlessly in the social sphere, he hated business debts.

We were so close that I could see the speckles of gold in his brown eyes as he looked steadily into mine. For all that I might think of him as my friend—to Mr. Verisetti's friends versus allies lament—Constantine didn't have friends.

One side of his mouth lifted immediately. I had long wondered if he had an ability to sift through surface thoughts.

I turned and began walking away, his hand slipping from mine. "Thanks for the wrist." I put the bottled narwhal-tadpole down on the side table. "Offer the officers this guy, if you want, since I'm sure they will believe you like deadly pets. But don't let them kill it, and don't get caught."

His bark of true laughter echoed behind me as I opened the door. It made me smile.

"You're a weird bird, Crown," he called.

I gave a wave of acknowledgment over my shoulder without turning back, gripped my working fingers gratefully, and descended the stairs. Constantine Leandred was on his own now. But then, I thought he was probably used to that state of affairs.

~*~

I got through service without further trouble, and the next morning tried the second red experiment...

...which left me with only one lung. Freakishly unpleasant and

334

horrifying. I had needed to use a drop of special paint on my own chest to grow a new one, along with using the focusing magic I had been practicing while watching Neph regrow my body parts. I had been very careful with the tube Mr. Verisetti had given me, but I had used enough drops now that it was getting low. I really hadn't wanted to waste a precious drop on me.

I couldn't stop rubbing my chest at lunch at the memory of the lung-less sensation, so I doodled a sweeper sitting on top of a mage, whose arms and legs were raised in the air, torso squashed flat.

"I told Ren she should sell her pencils," Mike said. "And now she is making a killing."

Neph nodded. "It was a good idea."

"But, anyone can just make one." I made the sweeper rise, then sit again, the mage's breath exhaling in an "oomph." I could eke out sound, if I put massive effort into it.

Neph laughed softly. "It takes time and skill to learn a craft. Most people don't have time to learn even a one thousandth of the possibilities open to them. Specializing grows a civilization. Even the First Layer folks buy what they need instead of making everything from scratch. You invest your time in what interests you, knowing you can buy anything else from others."

Mike pointed his fork. "Interests are fine and all, but more importantly, do what makes you *money*. Those pencils are better than the generic ones at the bookstore. People will buy or trade for them as long as you keep selling them."

"There have to be art students who make far superior ones," I argued.

"Maybe." Mike shrugged. "But if so, they aren't selling or trading them on the open market here. And sometimes a mage just gets a freaky skill at something. I can make it hail in a two inch space at any velocity I desire. Can I make it snow without also causing a deluge of rain? Noooo. Stupid snow. Stupid rain." He forked a piece of steak. "But I can outdo any fifth year with precision hail. Then again, I *am* unbelievably awesome."

~*~

Five days later I had performed seven more rituals—forcing double days twice—and had even had a moment of panic and used my precious lavender paint on the golem, trying to force it alive. The golem had brightened, its flesh and hair looking absolutely true, but with flesh-tone eyes completely empty of soul. I had received nothing else other than looking like I had gotten in a fight with a sweeper, and lost. My bruises were nursing bruises and I had a lovely black eye. I was also missing a toe that was showing signs of not growing back.

Things were...not going well. And my lack of sleep was making it worse.

But I was still eating in the cafeteria. I was still working with my friends. Helping them with anything I could. I always volunteered to do research, to debate, to sketch a diagram, to go on missions, or just to work quietly with someone in the library. Sometimes I worked with Will on the fourth floor, where the black-and-white book always watched from far above. And slipping off to the Midlands was actually very easy, because everyone assumed I was with someone else.

It didn't give me much time to sleep, though.

Tucked into the northwest corner of the main library—with a wall at my back courtesy of a front facing stack rack behind, I rubbed my chest. I had lost a rib earlier in an utterly failed biblical magic experiment.

I had known from the start that I was never getting that rib back, but the rending of it had left me breathless on the floor.

And the ritual hadn't worked.

But Guard Rock had toddled over, chipped off a piece of his rock, and stuck it against my chest. Astonishingly, my rib had grown back.

I had immediately used a precious drop of paint to make a Guard Friend for him. When I left, they had been sitting guard together, rock against rock side, arms and legs pressed against each other. Even utterly exhausted, and shaky, the sight made me happy.

I was going to have to figure out why the rib experiment hadn't worked—nothing had happened, besides *me* losing a rib—but I'd figure that out later. I wanted to think of something happy instead. Like the pair of loyal Guard Rocks.

Beings that protected and saved.

I withdrew a sheet of paper with one hand and sketched out a square jaw. No. Too square and overly puggish. I softened the lines just a hair. Not toward anything remotely approaching soft, not for Alexander Dare. But definitely not bulldoggy.

He was strong and assured, arrogant even, but not pugnacious.

I propped my chin on my hand and chewed on the end of my pencil cap, staring out at the spectacular view over and down the mountainside.

Students began filling in the seats to the right of me. I propped my cheek on my right hand easily enough, my elbow holding the paper, as I sketched with my left—sketching out the night Christian had died and the way I remembered it. I let my hair fall in a wavy curtain to the right, not wanting anyone to see what I was doing. I was decently adept at the maneuver, long practice with my brother letting me test out necessary angles.

I had sketched this scene before. Animated it. Tried to see if something twigged my memory and showed something I had forgotten. What I might have done.

But today, with bone-weary exhaustion riding me, instead of one figure saving the other, staff in hand, my doodles started...*doodling.* Or was that noodling? I slapped my left hand down automatically and dragged the sketch into the space of my arms, heat blooming and spreading down my neck and up from my palms.

"Excuse me?" a deep, lovely voice said.

I jumped, startled, and lifted my fingers slightly to peer down at the page. But my Dare doodle was...doodling...too enthusiastically to have said anything like that. There were other noises being emitted instead. Frankly, I wasn't sure of my ability to recover from the sight and sounds.

"What the devil are you looking at?" the voice asked me.

I jerked the paper to me, crumpling it under my palm a bit. The voice had not come from the paper, it had come from my right. From a person leaning over me. No. No. I *couldn't* have.

I hunched over the paper—and I could hear the blasted figures contorting around the bends under my fingers, swearing, then finding their places again. My mind separated between the image of the contortionist positioning that must be happening on the page and the real problem next to me.

Head still tilted down, I peered to my right, through a curled break in my curtain of hair. Alexander Dare, square jaw and all—though not *too* square—stood in all his glory at my side. My moist palm grew damper and I peered down to see the two figures on my page glistening and frolicking together in the sudden downpour. The water making their skin gleam...and...and they began...and...oh...dear...god...

The speaking voice grew more annoyed. "Ren Crown?"

"Yes." I cleared my own throat, trying to liberate the squeak. I did my level best to crumple the paper against my chest while still keeping it on the table. I couldn't risk taking my fingers away. I turned to him, hunched. "Can I help you?"

"You can hurry up and come with me. We have five minutes left to do this."

My mouth dropped, but he was striding away, so I grabbed everything and stuffed the sketch in my bag, hurrying after him. I couldn't let him get away. But...five minutes to do what?

Too much light suddenly flooded my vision, but I couldn't get my eyes to narrow. I probably looked like a gobsmacked owl fluttering behind him.

Oh my God, I had created and produced a full-fledged Alexander Dare out of my sketch. One who wanted to...doodle. I cast eyes around the halls. Surely, someone would notice at any moment what I had done.

I checked him out from behind. I had done a really nice job actually. My magic had filled in everything.

"For magic's sake, hurry up," he growled over his shoulder.

I glared at his back. Next time I was going to concentrate on creating one who was slightly friendlier. My eyes went to the edges of the sketch crumpled in my bag. That one sure was friendly. How had he not translated?

Wait. My exhausted, slow thoughts froze as I looked at the crumpled page. That Dare was still in the sketch.

I took a few quick steps, reached out without thought, and pinched the Dare in front of me on the back of a muscled arm.

He whirled and I looked at my death for a moment. Then I wondered what showed on my face, because the thundercloud expression on his flattened. "What?"

"Are you real?"

"*What?*"

I looked at the edges of his body, trying to relax my mind and magic and see if any color existed there. Agitated as I was—along with a keen mixture of mortification and horror—it took an agonizing two seconds to see, but faint aura lines of ultramarine blue and warm mocha mixed and swirled into my vision.

Well, that made it official. I was screwed. None of my projects had been able to produce magic on their own.

"Is there something wrong with you?" he demanded.

"Yes," I said frankly and wiped a hand over my brow. This sucked. I tried to gather my scattered wits. Luckily for my body I was already perspiring and flustered, so it didn't have to do too much work to keep those responses going. "Um, where are we going? What is going on?"

He looked down at a black device in his hand that I had taken little notice of in my flustered state, and his expression was anything but happy. "There is a Level Five and all hands are requested. You weren't answering your tablet, and I was sent after you, since I was passing this way." His voice indicated his thoughts on such a task.

Crap. My tablet was in one of the silencing pockets Will and I had created together last week, which protected me from Justice Toad's karmic rage when I was being delinquent. I fished the tablet out of the pocket, where it was shrilly ringing.

Dare's eyes narrowed and stayed focused on the pocket for a long second, before returning to me.

"Oops," I said weakly.

He turned and began striding again. I hurried to keep up.

We arrived at the training station, and Dare immediately walked to a boy standing at the perimeter. The boy looked barely sixteen, but there was enough of a facial similarity to indicate some sort of familial association between them. The boy was sitting upright and looking far less stoic than Dare. Combat mages were everywhere—I could even see Camille Straught looking beautiful in her uniform. They stood alongside every justice squad mage I had ever encountered.

Isaiah raised a brow at me, and I mouthed a "sorry" back. He held up his hands to the room. "Here is the situation. We have a Level Five somewhere."

People started muttering at that. I checked my tablet, so tired I was barely able to read it. They didn't know where? But...Level Fives were prompt response. That meant someone was probably dead and without help.

I channeled a kick of adrenaline.

Isaiah held up his hand again. "Let's not get excited. As many of you have been discussing, magic on campus has been pushed out of alignment." People started muttering louder to each other, and Isaiah held his hand higher. "Not irreparably, not yet. We can still fix it. We think there is an illegal focus somewhere on campus giving off chaos vibes. It is possible that this focus is what has been pulling things through the campus wards and killing off magic spots in others."

Hands went up all over the room.

Isaiah pointed to one. "Yes?"

"What about the rumors that the feral students are causing it?"

Isaiah's expression grew forbidding. "Now is not the time to start with political theatrics. It is extremely unlikely that one mage's magic could have vortexed. This is a deliberate enchantment style, which indicates an object or a group of similar objects emitting random pulses."

Whew.

"But—"

Isaiah cut the person off. "Ok, that's it. Who has a question that isn't feral or rare-related?"

No hands remained in the air.

"Then listen up. This is still Level Five *right this moment.* We have to find out who or what is responsible and locate anyone injured. There might be someone out there pushing their ten minutes."

My heart increased its speed. No one had irreparably died since I'd been on campus. I had gotten complacent to the fact that magic fixed most things.

"We will start our search through the Midlands first because of all these factors," Isaiah said.

Dare didn't really *move*, but all eyes focused suddenly on him. He was looking around at the combat mages. "Three bits, then you check in. No questions."

The combat mages nodded slowly.

Isaiah looked at us. "Justice Squad, your team assignments are already in your tablets. Remember that there are no maps for the Midlands. Each justice group will rely on combat mages to get through. Two combat mages to a group of three of us. Form teams between the two groups and no arguing. Everyone have their emergency buttons?" Everyone nodded, and many people exchanged nervous glances.

I didn't share their fear or explicit self-preservation. Though I came upon new elements and dangers every time I entered the Midlands, there was something I embraced in the chaos—that something lost might be returned.

Plus, I had my "Marsgrove snare" paper on me, if things turned rough. I had trapped two yetis in it a few days back and it had held them for two hours before barfing them back out covered in pulp.

"Form up and let's go."

I stood and looked at my assignment and grimaced. Peters. But also Isaiah, thank God. Peters gave me a dark scowl, but immediately turned on his heel and approached Alexander Dare. Double great.

Dare raised a brow at whatever Peters said, but he nodded to Isaiah and walked over. His gaze fell upon me and his lips pinched. Still sexy. I was hopeless.

The younger boy he had been speaking to followed him. "Nicholas Dare," he said. He had the look of a boy who was not yet totally comfortable in his own skin but had had arrogance bred into him. The rest of us murmured our names in response.

"Any cousin of Mr. Dare's is welcome on our expedition," Peters said obsequiously. I rolled my eyes. Of course, Dare glanced at me right then, and his expression darkened.

I sighed internally. I really needed to get rid of this crush, but for some reason his dark responses only made it grow. As if firmly planting it in the "*never* happen" category just made it more appealing to dwell upon.

I returned his dark gaze. Crushes rocked *because* they were fantastical. The *real* Alexander Dare could bite me.

We got to the Midlands quickly and began scouting. Our tablets and the combat mage devices functioned as magic tracers, but the Midlands gave a lot of false warnings and readings.

I wiped a hand along my brow. I could feel Okai calling me. The urge to paint was overwhelming—the less sleep I got, the more the urge drove me. I aimed my tablet at the ground with shaking fingers, trying to get a read.

Dare was very focused. He was talking quietly to his cousin and pointing at things around them, the epitome of equilibrium and control. I thought of the rock beasts that I had seen him battling here.

A two-foot-tall rock beast popped up in the middle of the street. Isaiah, Peters, and Nicholas scattered to the sides, weapons out. I just blinked at it and stood in my spot. The rock beast—shaped like a pro wrestler in small rock form—looked completely stunned as it looked around. Two feet tall was kind of small, though. Guard Rock, though far smaller, could take him. And it would be no challenge for Dare.

Suddenly it grew to the size of a twenty-year old tree. Peters dove for cover, Isaiah smartly took a step back, and Dare stepped in front of his cousin, staff out and spinning. I wondered if Dare could handle a rock tree. The thought worried me.

The rock beast decreased to a foot tall.

Everyone stared at it. Even the rock beast stared, eyes large as it looked down at its rock hands and feet.

Nicholas was trying to get around Dare, who was holding his left hand out, staff still spinning in his right, the ends producing sparks as it readied for a blow.

"This isn't normal," Dare said. "Stay back."

A tutu appeared around the rock beast's waist. It hesitantly poked at the puffed pink tulle.

"Nothing is normal in the Midlands, Ax," Nicholas argued. I wondered if only Dare's family called him that.

The rock beast suddenly held an ax in each rock hand.

"No. Though chaotic, everything here has a purpose and its own magic." Dare's very confident deep voice made people want to trust his words. "This is outside of a natural purpose."

I was a little stunned by that pronouncement. It was true, though, the magic here was chaotic, but not the type of chaos that made pink tutus appear on rock beasts. Hardly dignified.

The tutu disappeared along with the axes and a little business suit appeared instead.

I wiped the back of my shaking hand over my sweating forehead again. Surely...surely I wasn't seeing this. I was so tired and hungry. I knew I should have painted instead of doing that ritual, but time was slipping away.

Roller skates appeared on the rock beast's feet, and one of his feet promptly slipped out from under him and he landed on his back, causing a little rock quake.

Chapter Twenty-Seven

"What the..." There were other murmurs of dubious wonder.

"Kill it," Peters said, moving forward.

Dare's staff moved between Peters and the monster. His eyes were narrowed on the creature. "No."

"No?" Peters seemed to forget whom he was talking to. "It is abnormal."

"It is a victim, like everything else on campus that has been acted upon." He looked around carefully. "We should be looking elsewhere in this clearing. To what is controlling it."

I looked around me too, thinking of Mr. Verisetti. I didn't know the extent of his traveling abilities, but I knew they were unnatural.

Gold flashed at the edge of my vision, and for a moment I could have sworn I saw my golem in the trees. I blinked, but only greenery remained.

Of course it wasn't my golem. I had made sure to secure him to Okai, along with the other vessels. I didn't think that anyone would appreciate my mad, half-sentient creations running around.

Gold flashed again and my skin prickled the way it had when Mr. Verisetti had put hooks into me.

I cleared my throat. "Do you think...do you think we are looking for a mage?"

Dare looked at me, and I could see the magic he was controlling rolling around him like waves of clear water. I had never been able to see that before. "I don't know."

I nodded. "Ok." I took a breath and concentrated on the gold spell I could clearly see on the back of my right hand, surrounding me. Just like my tie to Okai, that gold was clearly a tie to Raphael Verisetti. I let my consciousness float along the threads, tugging them, and let my feet take me where they would.

I could see the rock beast trying to scurry back on his feet, roller skates defeating him. An unhealthy green mist surrounded him, slipping around him in slithering tendrils.

I tried to shake away the vision and concentrate on the gold, but there were new colors everywhere, surrounding everything. And there was something ahead of me. Something in the grass.

Three more steps, and I made eye contact with the savage person hiding in the shrubbery. I jerked in surprise, the gold threads attached to me jerking as well, and the very feral looking and familiar person surrounded by a mist of unhealthy green magic instantly vanished from the reflection of the glass shard. I had run across random shards and objects in the Midlands before, but never one that had made the blood drain from my cheeks as if a vampire had decided to make me his final meal.

My exhaustion cleared as immediate self-preservation instincts zapped through me.

I looked at my hands and let my magic loose. The same green trails of color rose from my skin. My gaze traveled to my left wrist, and with my sudden second sight I could see the pitted remains of my control cuff, almost eaten through by two dozen tiny speckles of lavender paint.

The paint, I thought numbly. It was the paint. All this time, the paint was what had been eating the cuff. Making it easier for me to do magic, yet harder for me to control. I was nearly an uncuffed mage in a society that was terrified of such a happening.

Perhaps for good reason. I looked at the image of my face in the shard. My features were surrounded by unhealthy green.

It wasn't an object causing the trouble on campus. It truly was a mage and her magic. Not Mr. Verisetti. Me.

I pushed away from the shrubbery, from the mirror shard nestled in the grass at the base of the tree. A mirror which clearly indicated the vestige of perpetration.

They had all been right. It was a feral who was causing all the problems. The sickly green magic on the rock monster was the same as the magic pouring from me.

And finally all of the puzzle pieces fell into place, as if dumped there by a cement truck pouring too fast. Creation magic. In order to truly create out of nothing, I had to pull the matter or magic from *somewhere*. Physics. Messed-up, magical physics, but physics all the same.

I had killed parts of the mountain. Parts of magic. Like the Origin mages who had pulled nearly all of the magic from the First Layer in order to create the others.

Oh, *shit*.

My magic had accidentally pulled things in from other layers in order to compensate for elements of my rituals. I had destroyed things in order to create spaces for something else. My map dragons continued to catalog the Midlands—I would see them every once in a while. Temporary constructs were pulled and released, the layer shifts shaking them free. Creating a new being entirely was something far different.

And the magical backlashes hadn't been contained in the Midlands like I had planned. I was either leaving the environs *too quickly*, carrying my backlashes out of the Midlands and on to campus proper, or my chaos field wasn't strong or large enough. And I purely and simply had not designated spaces to borrow magic from. Spaces that could take a bit of a drain.

I looked down at my wrist. The cuff that Marsgrove had given me was supposed to be unbreakable. It was supposed to control my magic, but my magic had been slipping through the cracks since my visit to Ganymede. My wonderful, insidious paint had been licking away my safety net, and I hadn't even known it. I had been working my tail off, working my magic to the limit each day, and that one small fact—that I had been sapping dry any and all excessive magic—had probably saved the mountain from exploding due to horrible, feral Ren Crown and her freaky magic.

It seemed clear now. My control slips had increased and I had needed to work my tail off to try and gain better control. Magic had been getting easier and easier—magic and energy responding to me instantly, my intentions clearly met each and every time—the storage spaces, my classwork, the *pencils*. I had even been making great paint. Not up to the lavender standard, but I had made a storage vault painting the other day solely using the newly homemade paint I had crafted with Stevens.

I had thought I was learning and growing more competent. Over-confidence in my intellectual abilities had blinded me, and I had focused on my lack of social skill as my primary weakness.

In fact, the only thing that was surprising, was that I hadn't gotten Christian back through all of this. Magic should be begging *me* to grant him back.

Instead, I had endangered everyone around me.

Even the one who had granted *me* life. I looked automatically to Dare. He was looking at me strangely. I wondered if he could see the swirling green—and if he had noticed it on the rock monster. He looked to the grass where I had just been and moved forward.

He would see the mirror shard. And somehow, somehow I knew he would *know*.

A drop of paint dripped in my mind. *Christian.*

The four others in the clearing suddenly touched the sides of their necks, beneath their ears. Peters's face drained completely of color.

Isaiah quickly set his frequency to speaker so everyone was getting the same feed.

"All medical mages report in. Twenty-three casualties at Top Circle— nine minutes and fifty seconds remaining. Forty mages in critical care as well. A smoked giant...bone...thing...appeared and is currently razing the literature buildings. Estimated time to Dormitory Circle is less than fifteen minutes. Evacuation signal sounded, casualties mounting, toll growing too high for proper tending."

Dare was already sprinting. Change rippled over him, a black cloak overlaid his outfit like scales flipping out, then flattening, one after another, all the way down. The bottom of the cloak snapped in the wind as he sprinted through a port on the edge of the Midlands border, then disappeared.

His cousin was hot on his heels. Isaiah was running too. Peters was frozen in a strange state of immobilization, but as combat mages burst through our area, running to port to Top Circle too, Peters rallied.

"Get up to Top Circle to provide support and help. All hands." Isaiah's voice yelled through the speaker-set frequency of a mage running past me. Everyone else ported to Top Circle. I ran to the dorms.

I was nearly hyperventilating as student-generated holograms sprung up all around me as people shared news feeds. I saw Medical tending the scores of wounded students at Top Circle. Keep it together, Ren.

Bone, smoke, enlargement charm.

Bats during the bell ritual. The tricorn after I had set up shop. The demon that I barely remembered. The narwhal. Countless other incidents.

Some of them had been black magic backlashes and soul-binding ritual repercussions. All facilitated by my eaten-away control cuff. And the storage papers. Where had I pulled the space from? How was I creating the space in those papers? Why hadn't I thought that the space had to be coming from *somewhere*. In my single-mindedness, I had simply never thought about *where*. I had been too mono-focused on *everything*.

Ever since Christian had sparked electricity between his fingers, my world had been turned upside down and everything had been crazy. I just wanted him *back*.

And instead...I had created a bone giant. From my rib experiment, there was no doubt about that. With a shaky hand, I entered my room. I was responsible for this catastrophe. And I had the only solution.

Things couldn't possibly get worse.

Olivia surveyed me in that narrow-eyed, cool way that she had. "We need to talk," she said as soon as I had shut the door.

Neph and Will burst through the door behind me, knocking me to the side. "Ren, we need to talk to you. Thank God we found you first."

Neph slammed the door closed, leaning heavily against it as if she had just run a long distance. They seemed to realize Olivia was in the room at the same time. Will stood awkwardly in the middle of the space, breathing more heavily than normal. "Er...that is, we need to speak to you."

I thought Olivia might spin around in her seat and ignore them, but her narrow-eyed gaze turned to them, to me, then back to them. "I think we might possibly have the same thing to say."

Will and Neph looked nervous. "Oh. Just something homework related for us."

Screams and roars shook the building.

Olivia wore a very jaded look as she surveyed them without response.

Chapter Twenty-Seven

"It is a *dire* homework issue," Will appended.

A long, strangled scream made me grab my hair in both fists.

"Well, I wouldn't want my roommate to get a bad grade," Olivia said. "It would reflect badly on me."

"Yes, exactly. If you could just come with us, Ren, we can get this straightened—"

"I was just thinking I had a proper roommate for once." Olivia shrugged. "But if you think you can talk her out of raising the dead and into fixing this problem without getting expelled or imprisoned, feel free."

She turned around in her chair. I could tell that the other two were staring stupidly at the back of her head along with me, but I couldn't get past the pit in my stomach. The abject fear.

"How...how did you know?"

She just turned and stared at me.

I swallowed and looked at the others. "And you two?"

Will and Neph exchanged a glance. "The eyes of the bone giant are like those black-and-white patterned designs you draw."

My heart thumped loudly in my chest.

"And we started talking about your...wounds." They both looked uncomfortable at the admission that they had been comparing notes. "And put things together."

"Ok." I took a deep breath. "Ok."

"Who are you trying to raise?" Olivia asked without emotion.

"My brother. My twin." I couldn't seem to raise my voice from a whisper. "He died three and a half months ago during his Awakening."

"You've been experimenting the whole time you've been here," Will said softly. "Trying to beat the four month mark."

I couldn't look at him. I didn't want to feel that I had betrayed him by not taking his warnings to heart all those weeks ago, but I had *needed* to ignore those warnings.

"Yes. Since nearly the minute in the First Layer when I realized I could do magic, I started planning. Before I even asked you about necromancy. Before I even knew there was a time line."

I could see glances exchanged. A giant tearing sound reverberated through the building.

Neph won the silent exchange and turned to me. "Studying the souls of the dead in a passive, non-invasive way is not a problem, Ren. Trying to raise the dead? There are reasons it is forbidden."

"The dead don't listen well." Olivia's expression was perfectly smooth. "It is better to have sentient beings that can follow explicit orders, yet still make moment-to-moment decisions. Very wearing to try and control all of them at the same time."

We all stared at her. She haughtily stared back. "What? It's why war czars are always ordering their scientists to make golems, even though the scientists continually fail and die horrifically in the process."

Neph took a deep breath. "Right. Back to raising the dead. Ren, it's invasive. Souls find rest in a very short period of time. You rip them away if you try to bring them back later."

I felt the tears trickle down. I never wanted to hurt Christian. But those books were full of lies. "He calls to me."

Neph immediately moved toward me and gripped my hands. "My Father died three years ago. I felt the same way. It's normal, I promise. They teach the consequences to us early because it *is* such a normal reaction. I can help you create keepsakes. Capture memories. They aren't the same. I know that too. But it will help. Ok?"

She was telling me that I needed to let him go.

"He calls for me to help," I whispered. "He's not at rest." And I didn't know how to let him go. To rip apart that part of me that he held and always would.

"Magic and emotion do funny things to us sometimes." I could feel her magic trying to soothe me. "Let me help you later. But we have to fix this now."

I nodded without speaking, then wiped the back of my hand over my face. "Yes, of course. I need to fix it. I know I do. I do." The bone giant roared in the background.

I verbalized the thoughts running through my head, trying to make sense of the situation. "It is a two-pronged problem. The immediate one." The roaring repeated. "And the growing repercussion. Every time I did an experiment, something happened outside of it. Something smaller. This is none of those. I didn't use black-and-white drawing patterns in any part of the rib experiment—I used them in an earlier one. The magic is collecting." I knew I was babbling almost incoherently to them, but I didn't have time for explanation.

I grabbed the storage paper containing my research. I turned it over and concentrated. My magic came out shrill and uneven to match my emotion, but the books and papers and tokens poured onto my bed. I pointed at the three of them, my friends. "I need you to stay here and figure out why. Because the collection problem has to be neutralized separately—or else each individual attempt would have done so—I don't have time for more explanation. This is all of my research. The journal is detailed. I have to go get rid of that thing."

I grabbed the beautiful, perfect charcoal pencil Stevens had given me, and shoved the tip in the hole of the haunting lavender paint tube. "Whatever you do, *do not* touch the paint tube," I yelled as I ran to the door, lavender sparkles swirling along the surface of the pencil. "Give it to Stevens, if I don't make it back."

"Ren!" Will and Neph both shouted.

Olivia stepped behind me, blocking them, as I slipped through the door. I had known Olivia would understand. She saw the big picture—she was a general, a queen. I was merely an errant knight off to do my duty. A general didn't waste all of her pieces on the frontal assault.

~*~

I didn't have far to run. The rampaging smoked bone giant was approaching Dorm Twenty-Five, leaving a path of devastation behind him.

It was like a piece of war art come to life. The visual and sensory details displayed in fine detail. Combat mages running forth even as their comrades fell, crushed at their feet. Flung like ragdolls to the side. Students were running in every direction, ripped clothing on usually impeccably dressed mages acting as tattered flags flying in the wind.

Combat mages were sprawled to all sides of the beast's path, broken. Only five minutes had passed since Isaiah had broadcast his feed. Five minutes for this type of complete ruination to occur.

Five more minutes until some of these mages wouldn't be able to be revived.

"What is it?" someone yelled.

I rubbed my ribs and swallowed. The beast whipped around and I caught sight of its face as it swatted another mage to the side and roared.

"Christian?" I whispered.

"I've never seen such a thing. Argh!" Another mage went down, her dark hair snapping against the dirt.

This, then, is what my experiments and magic had produced. My feet were firmly stuck to the ground, and I was unable to do anything but watch as the beast's patterned eyes swirled and its large bones turned to smoke, spells cast by defending mages passing clear through. It returned to a solid state and swung. Another mage down.

Christian? My lips formed the word without sound.

It roared and its intended target ducked. Another two mages went down, but two others slid on their knees beneath a strike. I blinked and looked more closely at the group. A contingent of five combat mages was working together as a unit within the melee, and they were clearly getting the most accomplished.

Alexander Dare and Camille Straught were two of the five. The other three were guys I had seen often around Dare.

Their cloaks whirled and sliced, black scales rippling down to points as the edges lengthened, then rippling up to reform.

Camille whacked off a piece of a thigh bone with a red-edged sword. Dare had traded in his staff for a sword as well—this one deep black. He severed an elbow with his thrust and the knobby chunk of bone rolled off. The beast turned to smoke, rippled, then reappeared, completely intact.

"Third form!"

Camille and one of the other guys thrust their sword blades through the swirling black-and-white eyes. When they pulled them out, the blades were gone.

"Son of a—" Camille Straught looked gorgeous and *pissed.* She did a magic-enhanced backflip to avoid the bone arm headed her way, and landed on one knee, hand upon the ground. Her fingers gripped a blade of grass, and she pulled a green sword from the ground.

One of the other guys knocked off a piece of the giant too, but the bone smoked, then repaired. "It's no use, it doesn't—"

"It doesn't matter," Dare shouted back sharply. "Just keep it occupied."

I looked around me at the rescuers dragging the wounded to two of the campus portal arches, and understood his plan.

"We've been keeping it occupied. It is almost to the dorms!" one of the guys yelled.

"Pay attention!" Dare shouted.

Bone whacked flesh and the guy who had yelled went flying, then lay still.

The faces of the remaining four grew darker, but none of them ran to their compatriot. They stayed on task, fighting. Dare's cloak swirled out, amputating an entire giant leg as his sword severed an arm. The bone giant touched the fragments, rippled, and stood completely reformed.

I saw someone in a white coat dart in, grab the fallen combat mage, and make for the arch.

The bone beast saw the motions too, and was enraged by the loss of its prize. It surged forward, howling, but Dare leaped between the retreating mages and the beast and drove it back in a flurry of swirling lights and flashing sword. The bone beast stumbled back, but hefted a large rock—a piece of some building that had once stood here—and threw it at the retreating medical mage carrying the fallen soldier through the portico. The arch shattered, emitting a concussing blast of magic in all directions.

But the two mages had made it through.

The beast raised its face to the sky and bellowed—a great wail that sent icy chills through me. It was moaning the loss of its dead.

I grabbed my throat in response, as if the howl was emerging from my own gut.

The beast started heavily walking forward, forcing Dare away from his position, and stomping toward Dormitory Circle where students were fleeing. It would find its dead there. Surround itself with them. I could feel its thought.

Oh. God.

Christian.

The magic around the beast slowed and solidified to my eyes. Ugly green mixed with tarnished gold. But the eyes were covered in neither green nor gold. They were black-and-white swirls with a haunting lavender film over the top. Like the paint that was splotched all over my cuff; the paint now in my pencil.

It roared again and tried to charge. Dare did something to stop it, but it struggled against the bonds and broke an arm free. I could see how this was going to end. The monster's path was going to take it crashing right through Dorm Twenty-Five. Through...our dorm room which had a window facing down the hillside. Olivia, Will, and Neph, if they were still inside, would never see it until it was destroying the building around them.

I reached down numbly and picked up the fallen elbow bone Dare had severed, letting it burn the skin of my palm, watching intensely as the green and gold mixed. *Christian...* No, not Christian. That wasn't my brother. Even the golem which I had finally made into a reasonable facsimile wasn't my brother. The sculptures and dolls weren't, and neither was this.

But what if...

No.

I pushed the emotion down and drew a precise series of splintered black-and-white spikes across the surface with the enhanced pencil. I tucked the bone against my body, uncaring of the seeping burn, and picked up the smaller sliver of thigh bone Camille had chopped. I repeated the design, channeling my thoughts, my pencil focused.

I could see Alexander Dare, alone now, standing between my monster and the dorms. The last three combat mages were splayed on the ground around him, their bodies still but the edges of their cloaks jerking up and down like the last gasps of flopping, dying fish. Camille's blonde hair was spread out around her, the perfect, fallen heroine.

Dare threw a concussive wave of magic at the monster that blasted it into a thousand pieces and took out two buildings that had survived the initial carnage. But like it was made of boned blob matter, the monster's pieces rolled back together, quickly reforming the whole. A one-headed Hydra that continued to reform.

He threw another powerful wave of magic at it and his sword turned back into a staff and I saw him do a maneuver I had witnessed in the Midlands. Twirling twice, he struck the ground with the end of the staff and one knee. Blue lightning spread from the strike, shooting along the ground toward his foe. The earth didn't shake, it fully shifted, and the monster exploded into particles as fine as sand, spraying in every direction.

Destroyed. My pencil paused and grief filled me as I watched the destruction. My hand dropped.

The energy around Dare dimmed completely, as if his shields were no longer powered. He was watching the explosion, still kneeling, and his mouth was pulled tight. He was watching the explosion with...resignation. My hand lifted and I quickly finished the strokes.

The mist of sand swirled, spiraling out and around in loose beige curls then gradually pulling back in a slow motion rewind. The sucking sound of my inhaled breath was a thousand times magnified. The regenerated monster bellowed a horrific battle cry and thundered toward Dare in rage, lifting its mighty arm to whack the last obstacle, who was now unshielded. Ugly green tendrils whipped around it, spiked and deadly.

Mages whose injuries were too severe didn't survive magical death.

Everything in me focused on the boy rising from his bent knee, holding his staff for one last strike. The boy who had saved me. The boy who had given me, an ordinary girl, his precious First Layer container magic. The boy who had given that girl one last cherished moment with her twin.

The patterned drapes in my mind swirled and ported me straight through the Academy magic to the exact space where Alexander Dare stood. The energy pushed him back two steps. I held out the two bone splinters, as he stared at me in complete disbelief, his staff raised to deflect the blow that would not now hit him.

"Throw them into his eyes."

I felt Dare's hand touch mine, then something exploded at the back of my head—*Christian, I'm so sorry*—and the world went dark.

Chapter Twenty-Eight

MOVING FORWARD

THE WORLD opened to white.

"Welcome back again, Miss Crown."

"Why are you calling me miss, Christian?" I muttered.

"Hmmm...are you feeling like Jell-O?"

What? I turned my head to see Dr. Greyskull passing his scanner over me.

I shut my eyes. "I'm alive?"

"Barely. Mr. Dare carried you to me promptly, but...your damage was high. It was close."

"What about..." I had to clear my throat twice. "Everyone else?"

Greyskull was silent for a moment. "We got to everyone in time. A student sent an emergency call to the Department, bypassing all protocol. They sent fifteen full medical teams. It was just enough." He shook his head. "I'm happy everyone was saved. But they will do a full investigation now, and that is never pretty."

I briefly wondered who might have a bat phone to the Department. But I was glad. Glad that everyone was alive. That I hadn't killed anyone.

I'd hand myself over to the Department for that.

"Talk says your quick thinking enabled Mr. Dare to defeat the beast."

"My thinking was the farthest thing from quick." I had to be the slowest person on this mountain.

"Well, I'll bet you get a thousand hours shaved off of service for this."

"I don't want my hours shaved," I said hollowly. I needed to serve for the rest of my academic existence.

"That is good work ethic. But they likely will do it anyway for your part in enabling the beast to be destroyed."

So Dare had killed it. It hadn't really been my brother. It had been a failed experiment. A creation by a poorer Victor Frankenstein. The unraveled emotions the beast had displayed had been a reflection of my own anger and grief.

I desperately wanted to convince myself that I hadn't created something alive, even if completely by accident, only to allow it to be slaughtered. Or that I hadn't formed a true piece of Christian, then handed over the necessary tools of his destruction—*knowing*. I curled onto my side.

"Miss Crown?"

Christian was silent. Not in my head. Gone.

"I think I'm in shock, doctor. If Skeletor comes, it's ok to let him have me, ok?"

"Miss Crown? Miss Crown!"

~*~

I trudged slowly back to Dormitory Circle in the dark, walking through the path of destruction in penance. It was eerily quiet on campus. Greyskull said the traveling ban had been lifted in the wake of the attack and many mages had ported home in order to relax and recuperate with family over the weekend.

It was also eerily silent in my head.

Stupidly, I felt more rested than I had in weeks. Probably fourteen weeks, to be exact. Greyskull had done something to fix me. He had thought the magic drain and exhaustion were due to a combination of fighting the beast and my resulting wounds, so he had fixed both.

More stupidly, an insidious voice inside of me was wondering what spell he had used to restore me and fix my need for sleep.

I had mentally castigated Marsgrove for being overconfident and exhausted, but I hadn't paid attention to my own state of health and judgment. Desperation was an emotion incapable of producing self-awareness until after the damage was done, I decided. But after, it was great at showing what an idiot a person was. Joy.

I walked into my room, unsure of what to expect.

Will, Neph, and Olivia looked up as one.

I couldn't look at their faces. They knew. They knew that I was a monster. Of course they did. And they could piece together the rest, if they hadn't already. The creation paint, the data disks I had never erased, the margin notes in my papers. Nothing was explicitly written, but it was all there—all the random tidbits of information. The processes and experiments. The successes and failures. The concepts and connections that had formed. The sum of which indicated the type of dangerous mage I might be.

I had placed a dozen different cloaking spells on my research box. I had taken every one of them off when I'd dumped the contents out.

"The Department was called," I said softly. The ruse was over. I put my now-painted pencil down carefully. "They'll come for me eventually. You should disavow me now."

I took my courage in hand and met their eyes.

Neph's eyes were steady. "You are my friend," she said simply.

Will looked surprised, as if he hadn't realized that such a declaration was necessary. "Mine too. Of course mine too."

Olivia's gaze was even. "I will keep this secret."

Emotion so profound rushed through me that I sagged against my desk. Maybe they didn't know everything then, but they weren't turning their backs on me yet.

"Er." Will rubbed the back of his neck. "So, let's figure out how to remedy this. We've been going through your notes. Discussing theories. I just got to your notes on Ganymede Circus and the Midlands and have a thought. Ren, my Layer project last year—"

I straightened, pushing the suffocating cocktail of emotion to the side to deal with—and make amends for—later, and let crisp logic connect Will's words to others running through my head.

Twisted magic.

"Of course. And with a third—"

"—and a foam block—"

"—mixed with evening enchantments—"

"—and a granite base—"

"—and Mbozi's four person containment spell."

"—I think it will work."

We smiled brightly at each other, and I felt a bit of hyper energy weave around my bones. Though sometimes our magic threads felt oddly similar, Will and I were neutrally aligned magic-wise—neither sympathetic nor antipathetic. But our *minds* were frequently directly in line.

"What are you two discussing without us?" Olivia demanded.

"You get used to it," Nephthys said sympathetically to Olivia.

"I know a mass containment spell we can utilize, and Will did a Layer project last year on smoothing the wrinkles that gather to promote shifts. He was able to smooth the space around him for fifty feet."

Olivia looked at him. "My Mother was on the judging committee for that project."

Will looked horrified. "I'm sorry."

Olivia's facial expression didn't change, but there was something very strangely satisfied to it. "It was the highlight of my Spring."

"Well, there were obvious kinks," Will said, cheeks red. I hoped he wasn't picturing Olivia's mom naked. "And I stopped working on the technology as an alpha project when I saw that it was a dead end for at least a few years—until the press died down."

"That means he only works on it every third weekend," I said. Will didn't give up on much.

Will continued to blush. "Well, yes."

"You should continue it," Olivia said. "The Department took your results and they are working on modifications."

Will stared blankly at her. "What?"

"You didn't think they flunked the project and buried it, did you?"

"Yes."

"You should never show the Department your best game, William. They steal everything that has merit." She smiled coldly. "My Mother is a high ranking official there."

I suddenly couldn't breathe. Olivia knew...no, it would be ok. And if it wasn't, I deserved whatever punishment was demanded.

I needed to make provisions for the people in my life, though—the people around me. So they wouldn't be taken down with me. I let a portion of my mind work on the details as I listened to Olivia.

"She absolutely loathes you. If you didn't know." Olivia's nails clicked against her desk, her voice unconcerned. "No one vaporizes Helen Price's clothes and lives to tell the tale. She will try to hire you and make your life hell. She is an excellent game maker and spinner. You have merit and she hates you, there is nothing she likes more than that combination."

Olivia's cold smile after that statement prompted a subject change.

I quickly spread out Mbozi's class notes and outlined the four person containment spell, then we decided to move to Will's room in Dorm Twenty to go over his project. Mike had been called home immediately by his overprotective magical parents, so we wouldn't be disturbed.

Upon entering, my eyes went to the sword on Will's wall and something in the back of my head vibrated. *Christian?* I sent the inquiry out more than a little desperately. But no response was returned. Just a faint buzz of...something. Something I couldn't place.

After a few hours, we had a decent plan in place that worked to all our strengths. Will's ingenuity, Nephthys's grace and balance, Olivia's iron will, and my...craziness. Being feral..and possibly *other*...actually figured beautifully into the resolution. Of course, being feral with freaky abilities had also contributed to the problem. So it was really just a matter of using my abilities to fix the problem I'd caused.

"I should go alone." My shoulders were tight. "Tonight. I don't want any of you hurt, and it doesn't matter what happens to me."

Olivia gave me a frosty look. "I will think you stupid if you continue that train of thought. *We* are going tomorrow night. Not tonight. It is foolish to go when all the medical support is exhausted and unable to help, should we require care. You can sleep on your guilt tonight, if you feel like being masochistic." She shrugged. "Though I see no reason you should feel guilt. There were some good, sound tests recorded in your notebook. And useless, weak mages shouldn't be here if they can't cut it defensively. Whether you cull the herd or others do, is unimportant."

Nephthys's face was blank. Smoothly blank. Will was trying to keep his face blank too, but wasn't succeeding as well.

"Er, Ren," he said. "I agree that tomorrow makes far more sense. You aren't going to conduct any necromancy experiments or binding spells tonight. Since those are what cause the problems, we should have a period of rest, and it is better to get this right the first time."

The last was too true. "Ok."

"And we are all going. Together. So don't make me tie you to a chair."

~*~

Campus looked worse in the morning. The bright rising sunlight showed the damage to the buildings, trees, and the mountainside itself—some structures had been totally demolished while large chunks were missing from others. Dark brown stains marked the grass and path.

The cheerful morning bird songs seemed deliberately offensive.

Students in outrageously green outfits were speaking in low tones about how to regrow and regenerate the flora by the end of the weekend. Students in crisp white shirts and khakis were looking at blueprints and plat maps.

But the disturbing mages were the older men and women in black who held devices over the areas, taking readings and making notes. I avoided all contact with them, choosing to use an accessible arch that took me in the opposite direction I needed to travel—down a level instead of up—but it took me all the way to the other side of the mountain, away from the crime scene.

I walked up from there to join the emergency strategic meeting of battle and justice mages. When I walked in, a few people were already clumped together discussing strategies.

"We must find the problem's origin and deal with it swiftly," Camille Straught said. My lips pulled into a tight line unwillingly. "You are adamant, Isaiah, that it is a magical focus, but I, for one, am not so sure."

"I know that well, Camille, and you should present your findings to the squads, as should everyone who has a report. But without proof, being an alarmist is not going to solve our situation."

He turned to the rest of the room, which was now far fuller, people having filtered in around me.

"Ok, folks. You've probably seen the Department's CSI division on campus already," Isaiah said. "And the high officials will be coming for a campus audit in two weeks, after finals and the break for winter solstice."

Which basically meant I had two weeks of freedom remaining in my life.

"You will all be expected to report and receive assignments the night before winter term begins. We will be tasked with interviewing the student population."

Mutterings grew in volume. Isaiah held up a hand.

"I know. Everyone wants the problem fixed before the Department takes over. So let's show the Department that we are on top of things."

"It's a matter of campus and academic pride!" A boy said.

"The reputation of the Academy is at stake," a girl said.

I didn't care much about that aspect. I was more worried about the death, destruction, and enslavement part.

However, even though the mages around me were speaking of pride and reputation, the underlying worry was for their way of life. For their layer of the world and all the people inhabiting it. For what was happening outside of the campus bubble, was reflected inside of it with this trouble. But worry for the world...was just beginning to touch me. I had come into this world fighting for my brother, and any other struggle had been far out of focus.

"Let's do a quick recap, then break into groups."

I inched over to the kitchenette and made a manual cup of tea as people outlined the last seven and a half weeks' worth of campus events along with eye-witnessed holograms. Knowledge of a few of the events was new to me, but I recognized my stamp on each of them.

Mages getting pummeled, running for their lives, having their spells explode.

Captain Destructo. I swallowed heavily, wishing it were Christian uttering the dig inside my head instead of my brain trying to recreate the sound of his voice.

I carefully carried my mug to a corner seat in back, hoping to blend in with the wallpaper there. Since I had been the definitive outsider on the Justice Squad since day one, it was possible that I could disappear in the room full of people. I was the only community service offender serving currently, and because of my earlier offenses, many on the real squad still thought I was a hopeless junkie. Isaiah was the only one I'd call a friend and he was assuredly going to be supervising.

I didn't know, and had never worked with the combat mages before yesterday, but I was pretty sure being on Camille Straught's work team would not be a good thing for me.

Besides, I was going to fix this whole mess with the friends I had allowed to be embroiled. Whatever was decided here wasn't going to impact our success unless the squads got in our way.

People started to break into groups. I bent my head down and blew cool air on my hot tea, focusing my thoughts and magic on making people's eyes slide past me.

Alexander Dare appeared suddenly in front of me. Startled, my magic exploded, and I threw my tea in his face. The air shimmered between us, and I looked at the tea leaves dripping from where his cheek would be, if not for the thin, nearly clear shield he had quickly erected. His base shields were fully pulsing again. I wondered why I could still see them.

I also wondered if he had started creating that thin top shield because of his prior experiences with me. The shield dropped, releasing the leaves and liquid to the floor. One sweep of his hand and the mess was gone.

I looked at the clean floor in envy. Far more useful than using magical cleaning products. I didn't have a tenth of the knowledge and control required to do what he had so effortlessly done.

"What the hell discipline do you study?" he demanded.

"Art," I squeaked.

"Why are you here?" He swept a hand to indicate the meeting room which was now completely composed of groups of four to six mages, barring the two of us. People started looking our way, curious.

"I like turning people into toads?"

He put both hands on my table, leaning into my space, and I felt embarrassing, conflicting urges to both lean closer and push farther away.

"This job is not a joke." His deep, smooth voice was intense.

"I...I know," I said quietly.

I didn't know much about him socially—a crush didn't dictate that I needed to—but I was intimately familiar with one of his core values. He was someone who helped others, no matter the cost. A warrior who protected those in need. His helping me that night so long ago—someone without magic, on the brink of death, easily left as a casualty—by using a stash of magic that he might have needed to protect himself from terrorist predators scouting the First Layer, said everything about his desire and willingness to protect.

His actions yesterday had only confirmed those thoughts.

He studied me for long moments, both of us staring at each other in silence. "Why do you feel familiar?" It was a demanding statement rather than an absent question.

Heat traveled through me. "Um, because I keep trying to ruin your wardrobe?"

His eyes were hard and searching. I felt stripped apart. "You have power. I can feel it. It was obvious yesterday. It has been every—" He clamped his lips together. "You can help us," he said finally, voice low.

"I'm trying," I said quietly. "I am giving it my full attention, I promise you." My mess, my job to clean up. "I just think better on my own. I'll join up with whatever is decided."

"What were those rocks made of?"

I needed to be very, very careful. This was the boy who had saved me, yes. But also the one who had family who hunted people like me. I was surrounded by people who would be horrified—terrified of me—if they knew what I suspected to be true.

"They were pieces of the beast your team struck off."

"There was something on them."

I had no idea what had happened after I'd died. But I was pretty sure it must have happened quickly. Less than ten minutes, to be sure, since I was still breathing. And I was betting more in the neighborhood of ten seconds. "Dirt?"

"A pattern."

"A pattern of dirt? Or cracks that formed after the bone fragments separated from the body? To reform, the monster didn't seem to need the chip fragments until you blasted it."

In fact, with some Monday morning quarterbacking and time to think, he would likely have destroyed the monster on his own with one more of those strikes. He had been breaking the particles down.

Without his shields, though, he might not have survived the last strike to do so. And that he might not survive had been my sole thought.

I shrugged, trying to look casual. "Maybe the magic in the bone fragments morphed or cracked upon separation. The eyes were different and didn't possess the same magic screen. I took a guess and picked the pieces up."

"You draw that kind of patterned thing. I've seen it on your notebooks."

Everything in me went into red alert mode—sirens screaming, and little people jumping down poles and ladders to man battle stations.

I nodded, sweat gathering in my hairline. "They are just repetitive doodles." Did he notice things about everyone? Or was I in the "security threat, keep an eye on her" category?

His hands were still on my tabletop, his eyes far too close as they dissected me. "Second question—how did you get in front of me and push me back? There is no port spot there."

"There were people porting mages out all over the place."

"They were *carrying* them to port spots. Traveling magic is restricted on the mountain for security reasons. No one can do what you did."

I put my hand to my forehead and leaned back. I tried to remember how to breathe. "Listen, I don't know, ok." It was true. "The wards must have been down. Magic pushed me to you. You were able to kill the creature. I'm a little tired."

Christian, I'm sorry. So, so sorry. It's my fault, all of it, even if the decision was the correct one.

Alexander Dare's *Last Judgment* eyes surveyed me, likely reading my black soul, then he nodded shortly and pushed away from the table. "Fine. But you're with us."

He returned to his five person group, who were going over plans and looking at schematics.

Camille Straught was watching me, arms crossed, considering. Great. But at least she had been dead too and hadn't seen me being freakish.

Dare looked back at me, his expression clearly telling me to hop to it. I dragged myself to their group, which thankfully, *thankfully*, drew Peters, then everyone else in the room, to form a larger group around them.

Because of the formation of one large group—and the people who were eager to offer suggestions and prove themselves to the core battle mages, offering suggestion upon suggestion with barely a breath between—I was able to slowly edge my way back to the perimeter. I discovered exactly when and where everyone was going to search, then escaped—citing overwhelming magical death exhaustion to Isaiah.

But I could feel more than one pair of eyes follow me out.

~*~

Constantine was on the path walking toward us as our merry band of four headed for our mission to the Midlands. His footsteps slowed. He took in our motley little group one by one, then tilted his head at me. "Interesting."

He proceeded to ignore the others and stepped forward, holding out a hand. I had no idea what he was doing, but I held out mine as well. His long fingers slipped over mine, leaving a folded sheet of paper and a small rock in my palm.

"Have a productive afternoon, Crown."

I nodded and slipped the items into my pocket as he sauntered off. The paper was the last storage box I had given him, obviously. But the rock? I turned to see the other three staring at me in various ways. Will looked astonished. Neph looked faintly amused. Olivia looked irritated.

"I question your taste, Ren." She resumed walking.

I surreptitiously stuck my hand into the paper box in my pocket and removed the slip of paper. It simply said, "Fortress."

I would bet anything that this word combined with the rock would downgrade the offense level we were about to perform—a boon we desperately needed. A Level Three was pretty standard for the Midlands. A Level Four called for double squad attention and might attract some of the Department spooks still floating around the upper levels.

I was going to have to buy Constantine some quality olives.

~*~

It didn't take long to find Okai. It was practically singing its call to me.

I had to talk Guard Rock and his companion down from attacking the others, surprisingly. The rocks finally, grudgingly, moved to the side, but Guard Rock kept his stick at the ready. Oddly, he kept it pointed specifically at Will.

But that wasn't the truly alarming thing. The golem was gone. My statues and dolls were gone. I checked to see if everything else was in its place, but my empty vessels were also gone. If they hadn't been empty, I would have said they had up and walked away.

I looked at Guard Rock, who quickly pantomimed that they really *had* walked out the door and he and Guard Friend had been unable to hold them in.

Fractured thoughts about war czars and golem armies marched around in my brain.

Meanwhile, Olivia, Neph, and Will looked around my workspace, then as one turned back to me.

"Yes?" I asked nervously, freaked out. Could they see that I had lost a legion of empty dolls and vessels?

Will frowned. "Let me get this straight. You work here?"

"Yes?"

"You've had a secret lair for weeks without telling me?!"

Neph elbowed him. "It wouldn't have qualified as a secret lair then. Besides, it's in the *Midlands.*"

"You have a secret lair without me." He crossed his arms grumpily.

Olivia's tapping foot registered.

I stepped forward. "Let me just grab a shard, then we can go." I needed to get them out of here and figure out what had happened to my creations. Nothing was going right.

~*~

It took us four hours to form the correct ritual circle half-inside and half-outside of the Midlands border—on an area of the ninth and tenth circles that was densely populated with trees instead of humans. As soon as we positioned ourselves correctly, everything clicked. Our magic wrapped harmoniously together over Will's device and the virtual drawing I had made of the upper half of the mountain. Nephthys chanted words of purification, then Olivia guided the tendrils unerringly through the swirling chaos magic and through the sword I had created for Will.

Our team worked well together. Will and I had neutral magic sympathy, but the sword, being made of my magic, was a bridge. Neph had already "mused" me, and Olivia and I were highly sympathetic. Our four person ritual to clean up my magic was diamond hard in its strength.

Will pointed the blade toward the mirror shard, which absorbed the energy as we untwisted and settled the magic around us, sending the chaos swirling into the glass. The plan was to repeat the cleanse tomorrow, then to leave the shard on the edge of the Midlands to be found.

Since Isaiah had already presented the idea that the problem was likely a focal object, and the group had centered the discussion upon it, the shard was exactly what the squads were looking to find. Between now and tomorrow, the four of us would permanently clean up the problem and provide the focus for them to find, all in one item.

I was wiped out when we finally headed for the dorms. Olivia and I split off from Neph and Will, who called out that they would see us in the morning. Now that they all knew, I could figure out how to key Will into Okai so we could share a secret lab. The thought of his reaction to such a thing brought a smile to my face.

Olivia entered our room first, and I took the time to close and turn the lock on the door.

"You think anyone will notice that the Midlands are quiet tonight?" I asked. "I give it an hour to stay that way once everything returns to normal on campus."

Olivia didn't respond. I turned to look at her, but she was frozen in place.

"Hey? Are you ok? Don't tell me that we forgot a bunny soothing enchantment or something. I don't think I could handle rabid rabbits running around."

But she didn't move. I moved forward and touched her. "Olivia?"

"She'll be fine in a bit."

I jerked around and magic flashed everywhere.

Raphael Verisetti was lounging against our window's frame, spinning an enchantment. It was a very Dare type of thing to do, manipulating a ball of magic.

"What are you doing here?" My voice sounded far away, cold and distant.

"But you called me here, Butterfly." He motioned around the room. "Invited me in."

"I never invited you in."

"You tugged upon my thread and asked it to find me, to make me known to your eyes. An invitation."

I stared straight ahead. In the Midlands, right before the smoked bone beast had appeared, I had tugged upon the thread and done just what he had said, thinking that by doing so it might show him hiding in the bushes. Obviously the tug had done something far different than what I had intended. Yet another thing I had done without knowledge. Another bad thing.

Olivia moved, just a fraction. Mr. Verisetti looked at her in interest. "Quite an interesting roommate for you, Butterfly." He motioned with his finger and her body slowly pivoted with the motion. Olivia's eyes were dark on his. She looked surprisingly alert, and supremely pissed. "She's aware. Very interesting indeed."

I stepped in the path of his gaze. "Leave her alone."

He smiled. "For now. Let's make it so that she can't hear us, though, shall we?" He waved his hand.

I threw up a shield between them a second too late. "Leave her *alone*."

"Ah, Butterfly. I want to thank you for a front row seat to the chaos you've sown." He motioned to the window, and I knew he was referencing the devastation caused by the monster, though we couldn't see it from our side of the dorm. "I couldn't have done it better myself. Nor could I have gotten one of our scholarly sympathizers here to do as wonderful a job with the madness as you have done in your ignorance and determination. Beautiful."

He had gotten here, on campus, in my room, and not a single alarm had been raised. Traveling restrictions, *sure*. I thought of Marsgrove and his words those many weeks ago. "What did you get from the sketch, Mr. Verisetti?" My voice was strangely cold.

"So formal. Call me Raphael, Butterfly."

"What did you get from *my sketch*? And where are my vessels?" The second question emitted from my lips before I registered the words in my mind. "You took them," I whispered.

He smiled. It was a gorgeous smile. And in that moment, I knew that he somehow had. "But now is not the time for that. They are entirely the wrong questions for you to be asking. A chess master plots and plays other pieces, waiting for the perfect moment to deliver a checkmate."

"What is your checkmate?"

"That is a good question, Butterfly. It might be providing you with the knowledge that you haven't delved deeply enough into the extent of your abilities and what they actually mean."

His smile grew, which meant something must have shown on my face. "Or maybe you have. Excellent. But a check you might like better is, why haven't you enjoyed my gift to you?"

"What?"

"The gift I left in the world of your sketch. Your greatest desire, above even your own life's force, was to have your brother back with you. I could taste it." He pulled a finger along his lower lip. "You almost vocalized it in your Awakening—and your magic would have granted it. It took all my effort to hold you back."

The cold hand of certainty gripped my heart. "I hate you."

"No, no, you don't. You are simply overly emotional. I couldn't let you have your heart's desire instead of my prize, it would have ruined my plans. But I am not a horrible man. Didn't you wonder why none of your experiments worked?" He motioned toward my research box, which he had obviously rifled through. "Quite ingenious, some of them were too, as are your vessels. Though, the experiments would have taken a massive toll on you, had they worked, instead of the piddly temporary loss of body parts you experienced. And some of your experiments *would* have worked."

I could feel a tear slip down my cheek. "You...I hate you."

"No, Butterfly, no." He was suddenly in front of me, and I wished I could gather the magic to stab him. He scooped the tear with his thumb and brought it to his lips. "Didn't you wonder? How could you resurrect someone who was already resurrected?"

"No." My voice was choked and low.

He smiled his beautiful smile as he stepped back. "Examine your world, Butterfly. My gift to you."

"Why didn't you just tell me before?"

"Where would the fun have been in that? You did so much better on your own. And you made me such a beautiful start to my army. Besides, I'm telling you now, am I not? A sketched trap needing only its external vessel. Completely karma free. At least, it is for you. Don't forget my generosity."

"I won't. You may consider this all a game, and playing me as a wild piece to manipulate, but it made me stronger. Your machinations have made me stronger. And someday, I will come for you."

I didn't care that I was threatening him while he still held the upper hand.

"Oh, Butterfly, yes. I look forward to it. We are linked now, you and I. A chain that cannot be escaped. Our journey together is just beginning."

I could feel the truth of his words. The echo of his statement weeks ago that I was now forever involved. "I will break that link."

"Never. There are so few people around to surprise and intrigue me."

He smiled. "In fact, I have something to reward such bewitching gall. For such a lovely, dark treasure who is beginning to bloom."

He held out a sample tube of paint, then placed it in my hand, wrapping my fingers around it. "I can't wait to see what you do with this—such a destructive color. When you are ready to negotiate again, do let me know. There is so much more to come for us. Until next we meet, Butterfly."

And then he disappeared in a black-and-white patterned mass, sucking him from my existence. The feel of the fading patterns told me that he was truly gone. Likely to another layer, even though Will had said that type of traveling was impossible.

Impossible for a normal mage. For a normal mage who didn't have access to a rare mage's magic.

I closed my eyes tightly together. Devastated, tempted, then devastated again. Over and over. Did I really want to risk devastation once more?

I strode toward my sketch and snatched it from the wall, staring at it, searching its depths.

Sound and movement made me look up. Olivia was striding to her desk. She picked up a pen and scribbled something on a note, tacked it to her wall, then scribbled something on another.

"Are you ok?" I hugged the sketch to me.

"Yes," she said shortly. It looked like she was making a list. "That will never happen to me again. Why, may I ask, was Raphael Verisetti in our room?"

Her voice was clinical, though I could hear the grim certainty underlying her tone. Olivia would make sure whatever he had done to her really *wouldn't* happen again.

"Um..." Keeping the sketch firmly against my chest, I checked under the cap of the sample tube in my hand—the garish orange mixture made from betrayal, the last of the three colors I had created so many weeks ago. But merely a sample, which meant, like Mr. Verisetti—no, I would not call him that like some terrorized youth—like *Raphael* had said, there were more tubes of my Awakening paint in his possession. I put the sample down and fished out my nearly-depleted tube of lavender paint instead of answering her.

"Ren?" she demanded, turning to me.

"I'm sorry. I swear I didn't invite him intentionally. If he fell off a cliff and into a pit of eternal hellfire, I'd be ok with that. I'll figure out how to ward the room against him, I swear."

"Do you know who he is?" she demanded.

I peeked up, rubbing the end of the tube between my free fingers. "A terrorist mobster?"

Chapter Twenty-Eight

Olivia's gave me *the look*. "A terrorist mobster?"

"He's not?"

She pulled her list to her lap and wrote something else down. "It really *was* you all along. It's a good thing you have me as a roommate. Anyone else in my position would have handed you over to the Department five minutes ago. Did you destroy the Lolinet Arch after the Ganymede Circus Arch blew?"

My shoulders drooped. "I'm a feral, unsafe mage, a dreadful necromancer, and an unwitting terrorist." I looked at the sketch. "Well, actually, I might be a pretty decent necromancer, all things considered. He did say my tests would have worked."

"*You*—" She pointed at me sharply "—will tell me everything you know about Verisetti and *how* you know him, then we will get you out of this stupidity. Have you learned nothing in our political debates? If he buys a pack of *gum* from you, it will get you on the Watch list. He is a man too dangerous to know in this world."

"You're not kidding." I looked at the empty sketch in my hands. *My Awakening magic could have brought Christian back.* "It really sucks knowing him."

"*How* do you know him?" Her magically-controlled pen flew over her paper as she mentally scribbled everything down.

"He was my art teacher."

The pen stopped abruptly. "I think I misunderstood you."

"That happens a lot." When her face took on *the look*, I sighed. "He was the art teacher at my high school when I Awakened."

There was something in her eyes then—a spark—like she had just slotted a puzzle piece into place. "Waiting for you," she said, almost softly, completely unlike herself.

"Yes. Unfortunately."

"Of course he was," she said grimly. "It is what I would do in his place." She looked at the picture in my hands, then at me. "What are you going to do with that?"

"You heard?"

"I can read lips just fine."

I wondered what she had read. We had been moving about the room, so she couldn't have pieced together the entire conversation.

I also wondered what she had figured out a moment ago as well. I had a feeling she guessed just what kind of rare mage type I might actually be.

It didn't matter, unless she was going to fry me where I sat. Nothing mattered at the moment save one thing.

"I'm going to bring Christian back," I whispered. "Are you going to stop me?"

"No." She looked at the note-filled board above her desk for a moment. "I've never had someone I would want to raise from the dead. I envy you this insanity," she said in a low voice.

My heart clenched. "Well, if you want, I'll share my brother with you. He can be annoying"—I stared at the sketch and readied myself—"but he's still mine."

Olivia said nothing.

My fingers traced the glass above the circular portals in the drapes. All this time I had been on the correct mental track, but the physical track had been right in front of me.

My magic broke the glass. I wiped the pieces carefully away, my heart stuttering in my chest. I opened the lavender tube and touched my painted thumb to the page. "Christian?" I whispered. "Are you there?"

I could feel a large presence shifting behind the drapes. Could see the slight billow of the fabric at the bottom.

I swallowed and wet my lips, then touched the stitches on the drapes and pulled each one apart.

The root of a tree slid around and pulled the right drape to the side. Another long root shifted the left drape. The roots were just as I remembered.

A tree figure stepped through, like a large dryad in an older myth. *Christian.*

"You were the sapling in the girl's hands," I whispered, touching the bark of his cheek. "She planted you when Will entered the sketch."

"Yes." Bark moved roughly across my palm as his mouth moved.

I gripped the edge of the sketch with my other hand, happy the paper was still in the glass-less frame, or else it would be irreparably bent. "It wasn't a lie." My hand was inside the sketch, touching his rough cheek, and I realized it was raining in the sketch world, fat drops of tears falling into the paper.

A branch reached around my hand, and he touched my hand over his cheek, his eyes closed. "I thought you would never answer the call." His voice was the same. *Christian.* The sound bounced around inside of me, lighting places that had been dark for months. Then his words registered.

"You've been calling me from in there." I held in a sob with effort. "All this time. You've been waiting."

"It's ok, Ren," he whispered, patting me. "It's ok. You were listening. You always listened. Even when I didn't know what to say. Even when I couldn't speak."

"Why didn't you come through the drapes?" It was agonizing. The sketch had lived next to my pillow ever since I'd been here. He had been trapped in there all that time, while I had been out here. Separated, yet always together.

"Your magic sealed the drapes when you pulled Will out."

"I...have you been aware of everything that has happened since?"

"No. Bursts of things that I can sometimes stitch together, and that sometimes fracture apart. It is easier when you are sitting close. Easier to tap into your consciousness when you concentrate hard. When you dream. I'm so sorry." He reached his hand toward me, rippling the sketch face. "Such terrible nightmares."

"I have been so alone without you."

His branched fingers stilled, then stroked the space in front of him. I felt it on my cheek. "But you found something to love. The magic inside of you. And people to love."

"I...yes. But nothing can replace you."

"Of course not." He smiled in the cocky manner I was used to, breaking his seriousness. A sudden harsh light came to his eyes. "And you could suck out their souls for me."

His hand covered his eyes and he bowed forward, like I did sometimes when I was trying not to faint. His eyes were haunted when they lifted back to mine. I could *see* the struggle inside.

"Christian?" I kept my voice from going high and desperate through will alone.

"Ren." He took a few harsh breaths. "Use your magic when you think of me? It's so alive inside of you."

I grabbed his arm, the bark coarse beneath my fingers. "I can't wait for you to experience it *with* me. Think of the magic we can create together." It was a wild, wonderful thought that spurred a dozen images and feelings of magnificence and contentment.

"Keep your friends close. I like them. I trust them with you. I..."

I could see that he stopped his alter ego just in time from saying something more. "Stop being so serious," I said lightly. We would get through this. "You are supposed to be telling me that you are going to give me the equivalent of a magical swirly or something."

He smiled, a cracked smile. "I wish."

I straightened. "Well, enough of this chatter. Let's get you out." I picked up the tube.

"No."

I stared at him. "What? What do you mean, no?"

"I don't have a body, Ren."

I looked at his treed state. "Will—"

"Had a body when he entered the sketch."

I opened my mouth, and he quickly shook his head.

"No, you don't understand, Ren." He released my hand and backed away. "If you tried to remove me like this it would be worse than the bone beast you dreamed of all last night. I would..." He shook his head, as if to rid himself of the thoughts.

"Then I just need to make you a new body." I straightened up. Raphael had said that an external vessel was required. "I can do that. The golem, sculptures, and dolls are gone, but I can make more." I'd give Constantine anything he asked for at the moment, and I wouldn't rest until the vessel was complete. Now that I knew Christian was *here*...

"Just like the old myths, yeah?" I gave him a reassuring smile. "I can work you up a body in no time now that I have your soul. I bet I can even transfer you around. Place you in a temporary vessel now, a more permanent one later. You'd be ok with a sweet robot body for a while, right? You could be like Robocop."

"No. No." He shook his head, as if denying something inside himself. "I'm cursed to a half-life, Ren."

"We will make it a full life once more." I nodded firmly. "I know I can get you out of there."

"You can, yes." His bark smile was brittle. "But can you?"

"What's with the riddles? Yes." I put my hand on his branched wrist and tugged. Nothing happened. I tugged again. "Just give me a day or two. I'll figure it out. Safely." I quickly tacked on the last.

"I *know* how to get out," he said darkly.

I blinked. "Oh. Great. Let's do it."

"I need a fully human body."

I slashed sculpture dolls and blob matter off my list. "Ok. I can get your—"

"Not the one that has been buried for three months."

There were morgues. There was further research. Now that I knew where his soul was, my trials would *work*. "I can be trusted to pick you out a good one."

"There already is one available."

I blinked again. "Ok. Where?"

"In Dorm Twenty."

"Ok. Will lives there, I'll bet he can..."

Christian watched me make the connection, his eyes flat.

"Will...Will was the ritual sacrifice." My voice was barely audible. "The vessel."

"The first person to touch this paper after it was activated by you would get sucked in to provide the host body. After I melded with and overtook him, you would be able to pull me out. That you got him out alive and intact was nothing short of extraordinary."

The words strung together in my mind. Agony burned through my veins. I closed my eyes against the knowledge, but everything Raphael had hinted to me in Ganymede...and here...said that the words were accurate. "Are you sure I can't be used as the sacrifice instead?" My voice was barely audible, my throat needing to force itself to work.

"Never! And it won't work, so don't try it. I did not choose this path—any of it—but I was made...aware...afterward of what was required."

The grasping root tentacles attacking Will. The paint infused rock guards pointing their spears. Christian's evil voice always wanting to suck out his soul. "I missed you. I miss you, Christian."

I hoped Raphael Verisetti rotted in hell.

"I miss you too. Please, Ren."

"No."

"Please."

"Give me three days."

"No. Feel it." He grasped my hand and pulled my arm further into the sketch, wrapping my fingers around the side of his neck. "Feel it."

I could feel the pain and turmoil, the...half needing to be whole. Bit by bit clasping more and more of the darkness to it as it strained to be whole again.

"It's going faster now—again—with the touch of the paint. There are no three days."

The pain made me double over. The paint I had used in the sketch before going to Ganymede... Christian had screamed all night and grown far worse after that. With the amount of paint I had just pushed inside...

I closed my eyes.

Could I have done months ago what I now needed to do? I wasn't sure that I could have. I opened my eyes, and he held my gaze for long moments. It was raining in the sketch again. Fresh, fat, grief-ridden drops.

"Do it, Ren."

"I can't."

"Do not leave me in this half-life."

"I'm so sorry," I whispered, barely able to choke out the words.

"There are no apologies, Ren." I could feel the emotions running through him. The firm undying love for me, the twisted darkness of the other, the corruption that had filled his missing half, left wounded and open for too long.

"I love you, Christian."

"I love you, too, Ren. Don't leave me in here another day."

I shook my head.

He touched my hand to his cheek. "Yes, and you've already made the choice. You *know* what is right. Don't ever feel bad. You are so strong. You never accepted that I leaned on you, just as you leaned on me. You thought because I was the extrovert, I carried you. But you were always my strength."

"But I could—"

"No."

—put his spirit into a vessel. Some sort of thing or animal or—

"Let go, Ren."

—or hand mirror or lamp. Like a genie. I had a hundred different spells I could try. A hundred objects to use.

Anything.

"Let me go, Ren." His voice was gentle. Soothing. Not like the troublemaker or genius he had been. This was the voice in my head that had wanted out at the beginning, but then slowly changed into my constant support, gaining wisdom every day while the splitting voice had become more insane. I could see him holding the darkness back, the evil other shoved in the back of his eyes, clawing, trying to get out.

"I will see you soon," I whispered.

"Not soon. But when we meet again, it will be like no time has passed."

"Yes."

"Like no time has passed at all," he said gently.

I couldn't see through the film. I blinked to clear my eyes and slowly picked up the lavender-enhanced pencil and touched it to my brother's trunk. He fell to his knees, bark cracking, branches breaking. I concentrated everything I had in making the sketch a happy place, a wondrous world. One in which *every* breath taken within it was a happy, joyous one.

Christian fell sideways, bark breaking off in pieces all around him, life-sustaining darkness falling away. Flowers bloomed beneath him, spreading everywhere. The winning moment of the game. The feel of a perfect second extended forever.

He smiled. A glorious, lovely smile.

And I sobbed.

Chapter Twenty-Nine

A NEW BEGINNING

WHEN I FINALLY LOOKED UP, I realized Olivia had witnessed the whole thing.

She said nothing, just tipped her head to the side and levitated a box of tissues to my bed.

"Thank you," I said softly.

She arranged her pens on her desk, lining them up just so.

"*Thank you*," I said more firmly. "You supported me with Christian. You helped quiet the backlash along with Neph and Will. Please, let me know what I can do in return. If there is anything I can do to show my gratitude."

She hadn't shown disgust of me yet, nor fear, but I would repay my debts by turning myself in, if she asked it of me.

Olivia didn't say anything for a few long moments, then she walked over and placed a key on my desk. "Room with me next term." It was said quietly and stiffly, awaiting rejection.

I automatically rose and touched her arm. She froze.

"I would love to," I said quietly. "Without exchange."

She nodded stiffly. "Good. Come with me."

I blinked, but scooped the key into the small pocket of my jeans and followed her to her desk. "Sure. Lunch?"

"You have food on the brain far too frequently," she said, and gathered up a few rather thin, but diabolically barbed rods from her desk and inserted them strategically in pockets in her clothing. Huh. So that was what all those slim, tailored pockets were for. I had thought them an odd fashion for magical businesswomen.

"When it's good, yup." I watched her put a few marbles into the smallest pockets. The marbles were the kind Mr. Verisetti had carried in Ganymede Circus. "Er, may I ask where we are going?"

* A New Beginning *

I had said that I would do anything. And maybe helping her take over the world would be a diversion to take my mind away from the devastating loss that was still drowning it.

She tucked an invisible strand of untamed hair into her perfect up-do. "We are going to clean up a bit of business."

Maybe those barbed rods trapped dirt really, really well. Or maybe we were going to do some mining. Gather up some gold nuggets or some such.

I trailed her down the hall, then froze at the top of the stairs as Will's Marsgrove alert system went off, drumming against my skin in triple time.

Olivia turned to me. "What are you doing? Come on. I want to get this done."

I forced my body to move again and stepped after her. It would be too late to port to Marsgrove's anyway. Everything was coming to roost.

Olivia. I had just promised to room with her, but I was soon going to be carted off to a cell somewhere. I could at least do this for her, whatever it was.

Four arches later and we entered the Administration Building. Olivia immediately headed for the long ramp that spiraled upward along the rectangular edges of the walls of the gorgeous modern atrium. The giant compass surrounded by five concentric silver rings was still hanging in the middle of the atrium, each ring rotating in asynchronous, nonuniform directions around the ones inside it. The inmost circle still lay mostly flat, provoked only by a ripple here and there when the ring around it bumped or bulged against it. The second ring repeatedly bumped the ring outside of it as well—the middle ring, which looked to be at turns violent and utterly lethargic. The fourth ring was dark and whirling—its shadows and darkness suggesting a mysterious void. The fifth ring was a riot of instability.

The layers.

The sudden comprehensive thought jarred me. The rings represented the five layers of the world. It was entirely within the scope of the magical that they were presenting real time fluctuations.

I let Olivia lead me up the ramp as I watched them expand, whirl, ripple, and contract.

The office we entered was white and brown, mixing modern and traditional elements.

The man behind the desk who turned around...was Marsgrove.

Magic crackled.

The door slammed shut and locked. My shields snapped together. I didn't run. Instinct screamed at me not to turn my back on Marsgrove. Three escape routes took shape in my mind, the building layout shifting into a mental construct as I populated it with all of the people, obstacles,

373

and assets I had seen on our way up.

I could see Marsgrove's magic pulsing, his core shields nearly mirror images of mine.

"I wondered if you two had previously met." A queen pushing her pawns around, Olivia took a seat. "I see that you have."

The snare I had made for Marsgrove was in our room. Options flipped through my mind like my Grandma Florence's old rolodex, and I pulled out or discarded each card.

"Ren, sit." Olivia folded her hands together. "Time to iron things out."

Betrayal stirred, but I took in Olivia's expression and felt the lines of the key in my pocket. I nodded slowly and sat beside her, my actions indicating my trust. The look on her face was fierce. I had a feeling if Olivia was the hugging type, I would be in the middle of an embrace.

"A door won't hold her," Marsgrove said.

"No." The fierce expression was still in place. "Friendship will." Olivia cocked her head at Marsgrove. "Such a strange thing. I think I could like it." She nodded.

Marsgrove was far from slow, and he could add two and two together quickly. His expression was dark as he watched me. "So this is where you've been. You took my papers and finagled a way inside."

"You knew I wasn't at the house?" I asked tightly. He was an enemy, and I needed to gather as much information as I could, while I could.

The lines around his eyes clenched. "The house didn't feel right, but I had no time to investigate and all the spells were in place. Even my papers were. But the pile of stash money I remembered leaving on the desk wasn't a figment of my imagination after all."

"You wouldn't have even known if I'd died." Bitterness flowed unchecked.

"There was a first-aid enchantment on the room," he said stiffly. "It would have immediately patched you up, if you'd harmed yourself. And if you'd done something truly foolish, it would have put you in stasis until I arrived. Death would have alerted me immediately."

Like some kind of pet alert that vacationing mages set up for their cats. My hands formed fists. "You imprisoned me illegally."

His eyes narrowed. "You have no idea what I could do to you legally."

Olivia folded her hands together. "Technically, you can do nothing legally at the moment, Cousin."

Cousin? I closed my eyes and chastised the memory of my almost eight-weeks-ago-self. That was the reason he had had those documents on her—finding a roommate for her had been a personal task, not an administrative one.

Olivia continued on. "No tests have been done on her, and you are currently persona-non-grata with the Department. As Ren's lawyer, my client will say nothing more about her personal affairs."

I closed my mouth on what I had been about to say.

"Of course, illegally, there is much you can do, Cousin." Olivia looked at him steadily. "But you won't."

"I was trying to find you a roommate, Olivia, and she took advantage of that. She used you." The look in his eyes wasn't one of outrage, though, it was one of calculation—the two of them sizing each other up.

"I am well aware of it. I knew it from the first moment she showed up, when she was trying to pick the lock to the door."

Oops.

Marsgrove's face took on a startled look of comprehension as his gaze turned to me. "That was how you...? But that is a *triple grade magic lock*," he hissed.

I pressed my lips together and stared at him.

Marsgrove really disliked me, and it showed clearly in his expression. "Olivia, surely you can see—"

"That she has the strongest magical sympathy to mine of anyone I've ever encountered. Yes."

Marsgrove's eyes darkened. "Enemies can have perfect sympathy," he said, bitterness underlying every word.

She lifted a shoulder. "And you think such a thought would sway me?"

I could answer that. Olivia was nothing, if not coldly practical. After talking to Neph, I had done a little research. Sympathetic magic made mages stronger because it made recovery times faster. Ambitious mages would room with their satanic counterpart, if it meant they would achieve more.

Awareness that Olivia had known I was a fraud right from the start, and that only the strong magical sympathy bond had made her overlook it, should have been unnerving. But I had gotten to know Olivia—by soul-sucking magic at first, then chip by chip over the last weeks—and I also knew that she wouldn't be dining with me or speaking with me at all if it was just that. We would simply continue coexisting in the same space. Her actions right now were about more than just sympathetic magic. And that thought kept me quietly in my seat.

I wouldn't ever be deluded into thinking that our sympathy wasn't important to her. It was an aspect like any other compatible or incompatible trait in our relationship.

"She's dangerous. I'll bet everything that has happened on campus is because of her." I could see Marsgrove already piecing it together. "I should

Chapter Twenty-Nine

have returned immediately. Before losing the trail of..."

"Of whom, Dean Marsgrove?" I asked as lightly as I could.

He bared his teeth. "You well know whom."

I could feel him checking his spells on me. I had gotten far more sensitive to anything magical touching me after every soul ritual and with each death. He watched me steadily and darkly, as I did him, as he checked each one. An old western stare-down.

I let one particular thought run free in the front of my mind. *Try another paint spell, I dare you.*

It was a bit of a conceit that I dared him to do anything. That I thought I could get rid of anything he tried by going to the Midlands.

He drummed a militant finger against his marble desk. "Olivia—"

"No, Cousin. She is my roommate now."

"Olivia, you don't know—"

"Don't I?"

"Your mother—"

"Is busy with her projects."

"I cannot allow—"

"I know all about Genesis Omega."

Marsgrove's mouth pulled tight. "You are blackmailing me?"

Olivia shrugged. "It is the family business."

"If anything happens with her—" a sharp finger pointed to me "—you will lose everything."

"Risk and reward, Cousin."

"She is dangerous."

Olivia gave a sharp smile. "So am I. You will do nothing for a term of three months' time and you will swear it now."

"You will not be able to control her."

"Swear it. You know the words I want."

"I will not approach or spell or imprison, nor assist any other in those aims, for a term of three month's time starting today."

"Excellent. I will not reveal my knowledge of Genesis Omega to anyone other than you for three months' time starting today."

I could see the magic wrap them both.

"You are making a mistake, Olivia. A grave one. The Department will take her the moment they see her."

She smiled at him—her legal smile. "We will let you return to your work now, Cousin."

Marsgrove's dark eyes followed us out the door.

~*~

Our four person ritual worked, and the shard was found by Camille, ironically. Joy was had around campus. Joy enough even to cover the lurking fear of the world at large and the turning political tides.

I sat in my room pondering the nature of sorrow and joy and that letting go carried both in unequal measures.

The Department was still coming to campus, but our academic reputation was intact and the strange magical knots had been unwound. Marsgrove left me alone, though I frequently saw him around campus, watching me.

Olivia smirked a bit every time the subject of Marsgrove or the Department came up and told me that we would discuss many things after finals. I hoped that a clue to whatever Genesis Omega was might slip past her restriction then too.

The real prize given by the last two weeks of school, though, was that Olivia was smiling every other day now—real smiles that unexpectedly popped up. Just seeing one gave me a fierce moment of joy.

When I coaxed her to lunch three times in a row during final's week with Nephthys, Will, Mike, and Delia—well, I won't say it was perfect, as Olivia and Delia were...opposites...but they seemed to enjoy disliking each other. And Olivia started eating in the cafeteria without coaxing.

And that was when we became a full-fledged table.

~*~

Olivia and I stood with our bags in hand in the Administration Building, waiting to port to the First Layer for the December holidays. I had been beyond surprised when she had accepted my invitation to come home with me for break. She had had no plans to go home, so I'd just assumed she would turn me down and remain on campus in our room studying. Instead, she was patiently waiting beside me, with a sanctioned defensive magic container tucked in her pocket and a sheaf of discussion topics and tactics for us.

Constantine smirked at me from a few lines over and I could see him rubbing the smooth rock I had given him for his birthday that could contain all of his martini supplies indefinitely. The rocks I had infused to kill the beast had given me the idea, and I was determined to make storage jewelry next with the test results.

I darkly amused myself contemplating the possibilities of hiding myself in an earring.

My covered wrist itched, and Dare walked by in all his beautiful glory. He gave me an unreadable look.

Christian's sketch, now completely overtaken by a mound of beautiful wildflowers, was carefully tucked in the bag against my side. I hadn't told Will or Neph about the sketch and Raphael's visit. In this instance, I thought it better to protect Will. The sketch couldn't be used against him anymore. I had willed it to be so as I'd touched a drop of paint to the page. The paint had spread into gently curling grasses surrounding the burial site.

Raphael's words taunted me, and I had no idea what I was going to do about the debt that I owed him from our encounter in Ganymede Circus. I had no idea what I would do about my golem—with its simulated human flesh and the characteristics I had bred into it—being in his possession. No less the dolls. I had no idea what I was going to do about the world at large creeping toward war—a war that would be in part due to whatever my magic had created during my Awakening and afterward. I had no idea what I was going to do long-term about Marsgrove, who had sent a note saying he was going to check in at my parents' house in a few days.

I had no idea how or if I was going to explain everything to my parents.

At the moment, I just listened to the pulse of my heart. My heart was stuttering, but it was beating. Awakening once more. I would see Christian again. Someday. And it would be like no time had passed.

And in the meantime, I would live. With hope.

I nodded to Olivia, and we stepped through the port.

About the Author

Anne Zoelle is the pseudonym of a USA Today Bestselling author. Anne is currently working on the next book in the Ren Crown series.

Find Anne online at http://www.annezoelle.com.

If you'd like to contact Anne directly, you can reach her at anne.zoelle@gmail.com.

Books in the Series

The second book in the series, **The Protection of Ren Crown**, is now available in ebook and paperback! An excerpt can be found online at http://www.annezoelle.com.

Made in the USA
San Bernardino, CA
22 October 2014